Back Bay

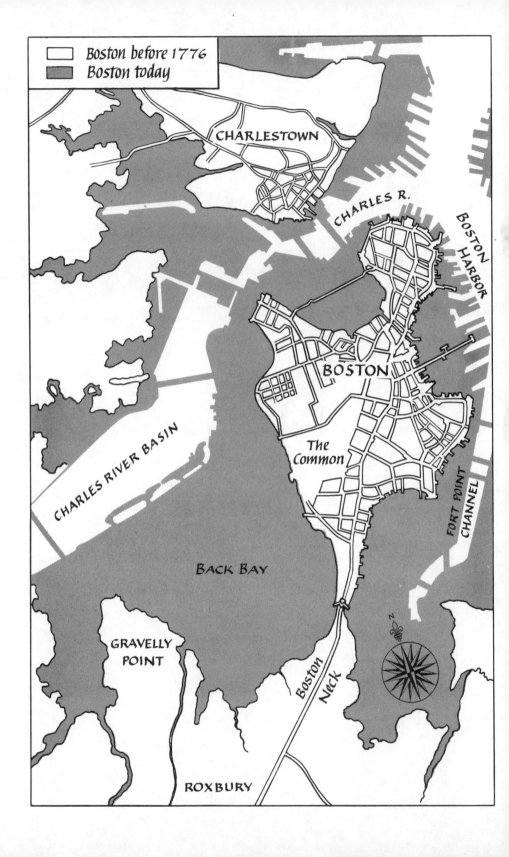

Boston before 1776
Boston today

CHARLESTOWN

CHARLES R.

BOSTON HARBOR

BOSTON

The Common

CHARLES RIVER BASIN

FORT POINT CHANNEL

BACK BAY

GRAVELLY POINT

Boston Neck

ROXBURY

Back Bay

William Martin

CROWN PUBLISHERS, INC.   NEW YORK

For Chrissie

Library of Congress Cataloging in Publication Data

Martin, William, 1950–
Back Bay.

I. Title.
PZ3.M36625Bac   [PS3563.A7297]   813'.5'   79-15706
ISBN 0-517-53602-1

10   9   8   7   6   5   4

Back Bay

HORACE TAYLOR PRATT (1750 – 1825) ── m., 1775

Horace Taylor Pratt II (1776 – 1808)
m., 1799, Franconia Hampshire (1780 – 1824)

Horace Taylor Pratt III
(1800 – 1814)

Artemus Pratt (1808 – 1882)
m., 1834, Cynthia Babcock (1810 – 188⋯

Sarah Pratt
(1836 – 1905)
m., 1865,
James Hannaford
(1835 – 1900)

Artemus Pratt II
(1839 – 1899)
m., 1868,
Lydia Hancock
(1842 – 1911)

Jason Pratt II M.D.
(1841 – 1911)
m., 1872,
Jessica Dilworth
(1851 – 1908)

Olivia Pratt
(1843 – 1920)
m., 1870, James Spenc⋯
(1845 – 1910)
(moved to California, 187⋯

Charles Hannaford
(1866-1938)
m., 1904,
Theodosia Warren
(1880-1940)

Artemus Pratt III
(1872 – 1955)
m., 1894,
Clarissa Henry
(1877 – 1949)

George Pratt
(1875 – 1912)
m., 1896, Evangeline Lowe
(1876 – 1912)
(both drowned, TITANIC)

James Pratt
(1878 – 1943)
m., 1902, Barbara Clar⋯
(1880 – 1920)
(no children)

Henry Hannaford
(1910 – 1976)
m., 1941,
Sondra Blake
(1922-1950)

Artemus Pratt IV
(1903 – 1972)
m., 1925,
Denise Goodby
(1905 – 1974)

Taylor Pratt
(1906-1964)
m., 1925,
Harriet Langley
(1907 – 1960)

Philip Pratt
(1895 – 1917)
(killed on
Western front)

George Pratt II
(1896 – 1912)
(drowned,
TITANIC)

Jeffrey Pra⋯
(1897 – 191⋯
(drowned⋯
TITANIC⋯

Lawrence
Hannaford
(1945 -)

Philip Pratt II
(1931 -) m., 1959,
Candace Emerson
(1934 -)
(divorced, 1973)

Calvin Pratt
(1926 -)
m., 1950,
Elizabeth Lee
(1927 -)

Andrea Pratt
(1933 – 1973)
m., 1956, James Heath
(1931 – 1973)
(no children)

Jeffrey Carringto⋯
(1925 – 1952)
m., 1949,
Avril Dunster
(1926 -)

Philip Pratt II
(1963 -)

Joseph Pratt
(1965 -)

John Pratt
(1953 -)

Taylor Pratt II
(1955 -)

Christopher Carringto⋯
(1950 -)

Alicia Howell (1755 - 1805)

Jason Pratt (1784 - 1830) m., 1807, Sarah Lowell (1786 - 1843)

Abigail Pratt (1790 - 1874) m., 1811, James Elwood Bentley (1790 - 1811) (no children)

Elihu Pratt (1811 - 1870) m., 1836, Charlotte Paine (1808 - 1868)

Ephraim Pratt (1814 - 1815)

Philip Pratt (1823 - 1851, ca.) m., (?) 1850, Samantha Cawley (? - 1856)
(?)

Henry Pratt (1844 - 1910) m., 1872, Eloise Whittier (1848 - 1900) (no children)

Francis Pratt (1841 - 1862) (killed at Fair Oaks)

Henrietta Pratt (1844 - 1846)

Philip Cawley (1850 - ?)
(?)

Jason Pratt III (1877 - 1914) m., 1897, Elizabeth Hill (1880 - 1939)

James Spencer II (1872 - 1935) m., 1899, Mary Glynn (1874 - 1928)

Cynthia Spencer (1874 - 1945) m., 1900, Charles McCord (1875 - 1900) (no children)

Jason Spencer (1876 - ?) (untraced)

therine Pratt (1900 -) m., 1925, nry Carrington 1900 - 1965)

William Pratt (1897 - 1965) m., 1933, Lauren Stevens (1907 - 1974) (moved to Hawaii, 1946)

Joseph Spencer, S.J. (1903 - 1941)

Charles Spencer (1902 - 1953) m., 1924, Nancy Kosick (1904 - ?) (divorced, 1932)

abelle Carrington (1931 -) , 1961, Edgar Howe (1929 - 1974) (no children)

William Pratt II (1929 -) m., 1955, Mary Anoki (1933 -)

Mary Spencer (1925 - 1976) m., 1950, Charles Korbel (1920 - 1958)

James Spencer III (1926 - 1944) (killed at Normandy)

angeline Carrington (1953 -)

Frederick Pratt (1959 -)

Susan Pratt (1961 -)

Sally Korbel (1952 -)

CHAPTER I   *October 1789*

Horace Taylor Pratt pulled a silver snuffbox from his waistcoat pocket and placed it on the table in front of him. He hated snuffboxes. They were small, delicate, and nearly impossible for a man with one arm to open. Whenever he fumbled for snuff, Pratt cursed the two-armed world that conspired against him, but when he wanted a clear head, he had to have snuff. This evening, he wanted wits as sharp as a glasscutter.

He slid the box open, took a pinch of black powder, and brought it to his nose.

"Father!" The young voice cracked, and Pratt turned to his son, a handsome boy of thirteen. "You're not going to sneeze in the presence of his majesty, are you, Father?"

Pratt looked around, his fingers poised theatrically just below his left nostril. "Majesty? I see no king, Horace."

Two hundred of Boston's most prominent citizens sat with the Pratts at a great, three-sided banquet table in Faneuil Hall. The gentlemen were dressed in their finest satins, brocades, broadcloths, and silks. The table was covered in Irish linen and laden with fruits and cheeses. Candles glowed against October's early dusk. John Hancock's personal stock of port filled crystal stemware. The guest of honor, seated between John Adams and Governor Hancock, was America's most royal figure.

"I mean His Presidency." Young Horace looked toward the middle of the table, where a hulking man with powdered hair chewed on a piece of cheddar while Hancock and Adams conversed around him. "You can't take snuff in front of George Washington."

Pratt leaned close to his son and whispered, "He looks rather bored sitting between those two Massachusetts magpies. I daresay he'd love a dash of snuff himself right now."

Pratt inhaled the tobacco and took another pinch in his right nostril. He closed his eyes. He felt the tingle spread through his sinuses. His mouth opened, his back stiffened, and he reached for his handkerchief. Before he could cover his face, the sneeze burst out of him, and Washington jumped as though startled by a British musket. Pratt sneezed again, more violently. Conversation stopped all about the room. John Adams shot an angry glance at Pratt. Young Horace slumped in his chair and counted the stitches on the hem of the tablecloth. Pratt sneezed once more, a final, satisfied bark. Then he blew his nose and looked around. Every eye was on him.

When Horace Taylor Pratt wanted attention, no discreet clearing of the throat or subtle shuffling of the feet would do. He glanced toward the center of the table. Washington was still staring in his direction, and John Adams's bald head was blushing crimson, the color of Washington's satin frock.

Pratt stood quickly. "Before John Adams, in the high dudgeon for which he is famous, chides me for taking a bit of snuff, let me propose a toast." He lifted his glass. "To the health of our Federal Republic and its new President."

"Here, here," grunted Mather Byles, the old Tory minister seated next to Pratt.

John Hancock raised his glass. John Adams lifted his crankily. And the gentlemen of Boston toasted the President.

Then Washington stood slowly and raised his glass to Pratt. "To you, Mr. . . ."

"Pratt. Horace Taylor Pratt."

"To you, Mr. Pratt, and to all your peers in Boston. We certainly hope that your snuff comes from fine Virginia tobacco." Washington smiled, and everyone else laughed politely.

Pratt had introduced himself to the President. When he spoke out later, Washington would know him. He finished his wine and sat down as conversation began again in the banquet hall.

"I must offer Mr. Washington some of my English snuff after the ceremony," whispered Pratt to his son.

"English snuff?"

Mather Byles leaned into the conversation. "Your father may have bad manners, Horace, but he has excellent taste in snuff."

"The English know how to make it," explained Pratt, "along with most other things."

"You have such admiration for British craftsmanship," said Byles, "I sometimes wonder that you weren't a Tory."

"Reverend, fourteen years ago, the British Crown stood between me and a fortune. Had men like me remained loyal, the British would still be here, and I'd still be poor."

"You'd still have your left arm."

"A small price to pay." Pratt smiled, but he showed no pleasure. His deep-set eyes and prominent nose gave him the look of a predator, a man who never rested. Although he was only thirty-nine, his gaunt frame had already begun to bow and his hair showed considerably more gray than black.

Byles looked at the empty sleeve. "You never know when you might need two arms, Horace."

"My son is my left arm, Reverend, stronger and more reliable than my own limb." Pratt wrapped his right arm around the boy's shoulders.

Byles looked at young Horace. "Does the boy enjoy being one of his father's extremities?"

Horace didn't notice the sarcasm. "I'm a Pratt, Reverend. One day, I'll take my place at the head of Pratt Shipping and Mercantile. It is in my best interest to help my father in whatever way I can."

"The warmest of filial sentiments," said Byles.

The sound of silver tapping gently on a crystal wineglass interrupted the conversation. John Hancock was ringing for quiet.

"Watch closely," whispered Pratt to his son. "Your lesson for today is about to begin."

"Mr. President and gentlemen," began Hancock, "you will forgive me for not standing, but the gout keeps me in my chair."

"Three days ago, Hancock was strutting around like one of the Royal Welsh Fusiliers," whispered Byles. "He has no gout."

"The silly ass is play-acting," said Pratt. "When the presidential entourage arrived, Hancock wouldn't visit Washington until Washington visited him. Some foolishness about the governor being sovereign in the state and the President merely his guest. Washington would have none of it and browbeat Hancock into paying the first call. To save his pampered face, Hancock announced that he was indisposed because of the gout. He had his feet wrapped in bandages, ordered three men to carry him to carriage, and then from his carriage into the President's lodgings, where he visited Washington like some Catholic martyr."

"And the charade continues," said Byles.

"Aye. He wouldn't visit Washington's living quarters, but now he's about to kiss Washington's hindquarters."

Hancock was reaching one of the flourishes in his speech. "It is being said, Your Excellency, that men from Massachusetts and men from Virginia led the Revolution, and together we will lead a new nation into the nineteenth century. Let it be so. From the South will come abundant food and raw materials. From the shores of New England will venture forth the bravest merchant fleet the world has ever seen. And the commerce of the nation will thrive."

The businessmen in the hall, most of them certain that Hancock was referring to the brave fleets in which they had interest, applauded his vision. Hancock accepted the ovation as a tribute to his eloquence, nodded his thanks like a gracious monarch, and allowed the applause to last a reasonable length of time before tapping his wineglass again. "Gentlemen, thank you. Your generosity is too great."

"It most certainly is," squawked Pratt, and once again everyone was looking in his direction.

"Excuse me, Mr. Pratt?" Hancock did not like to be interrupted.

"I was agreeing with you, sir. Please go on."

Hancock glared at Pratt, whose gaze never wavered, then he continued. "You were last here, Mr. President, in 1776. "When you drove the British from Boston on that day in March, you also drove from our midst Tories and British sympathizers who preferred rule by a monarch to government by their peers." Hancock sounded to Pratt as though he were trying to rouse the populace against a Royalist uprising. "Those who fled left behind homes and property which the state confiscated and sold to pay for its war effort."

"Most commendably, I might add," said Washington.

"Thank you, sir. However, we retained a store of Tory gold and silver, some of it in plate, some of it in unworked form. For several years, we were at odds over its best use."

"I agree with that as well," announced Pratt, but Hancock ignored him.

"Now, Your Excellency, as a gift from the people of Boston to the

4

new government, as a sign of goodwill from the businessmen of Boston to the new President, this precious metal has taken form sublime. To present it, I introduce a great patriot, a master craftsman, and your fellow Freemason, Paul Revere."

Although Pratt couldn't stand him, Paul Revere was among the most respected men in Boston, and his peers greeted him warmly. He wore a brown broadcloth frock, tan breeches, and waistcoat. At fifty-four, he looked as solid, prosperous, and handsome as his own best work. He bowed to the President, then gestured to a servant, who wheeled a cart into the middle of the room.

"Welcome back to Boston, Mr. President."

"It's a pleasure I've long awaited, Mr. Revere."

"It's our pleasure, as well, sir." Revere rarely spoke in public and spent no further time on introductions. "Now, Mr. President, it is my honor to present to you and the American people a gift which it has been my greatest honor to create." Revere nodded to the servant, who removed the velvet cover from the cart. "The Golden Eagle Tea Set."

For a moment, there was silence. Even Horace Taylor Pratt was dazzled. The tea set seemed to vibrate in the candlelight as though it had been touched by St. Elmo's fire. The men of Boston were transfixed.

Revere had created thirty-one pieces of flawless silver in the Federal style: a majestic coffee urn with an ivory handle, a paneled teapot, creamer, sugar urn, wastebowl, tea tongs, serving tray, and twenty-four spoons. Expanses of shimmering silver, graceful lines, and delicate engravings offset the central decoration, America's coat of arms. On each upright piece, a small golden eagle, talons clutching arrows and olive branch, eyes ablaze with pride, spread its wings against a background of silver.

Finally, someone whispered, "Bravo!" and the applause burst forth.

"The inscription"—Revere began to speak over the ovation—"the inscription on the urn reads 'To President G. Washington, on the Occasion of His Visit to Boston, October 29, 1789. In Commemoration of His Victorious Siege of Boston, Ended March 17, 1776.' We hope that this tea set will remain in the President's House for generations to come as a reminder of our esteem for George Washington."

Washington stood and bowed deeply. "I accept this work of art with the deepest humility and gratitude. I am honored."

Adams rose and began a toast: "To our President and to Paul Revere . . ."

A single fist pounded into the table like a sledgehammer. Horace Taylor Pratt leaped to his feet, shrieking, "Seek the high ground, Mr. President! The enemy has surrounded you!"

"That man is out of order!" barked Adams.

"I will have my say!" Pratt slammed his fist on the table again.

"Be careful, Pratt. That's how you lost the other arm," cracked Byles.

Pratt ignored the nervous laughter that skittered across the room. "The hypocrites are praising your name, they're fawning at your feet, and they'll have their hand out to you in the morning!"

"Are you referring to the gentlemen of Boston, sir?" asked Washington.

"I'm referring to the men in this room, and damn few of them are gentlemen!"

Hancock jumped up like a dockhand in a tavern brawl. "Least of all yourself, Pratt!"

"A miraculous cure, Mr. Hancock?" Washington's voice dripped bile.

Hancock remembered his bandaged feet and sat quickly. "Such words are hard to bear, Mr. President."

"The truth always is, sir," yelled Pratt. "You have no gout, and that tea set is no memorial to Mr. Washington."

"This is an outrage!" boomed Henry Knox, Secretary of War.

Pratt's hand shot toward the tea set. "That is an outrage!"

"If Mr. Pratt sees no gentlemen in the room, perhaps by example he could show us the look of one!" cried Revere.

At the sound of the silversmith's voice, Pratt seemed to grow several inches in every direction. "You dare ask me to act like a gentleman? You see this, sir?" He began to wave his stump in the air. It was one of his favorite tricks. "I once had an arm, a hand, and fingers just like yours, but I lost them and a brother at Bunker Hill. You escaped the Revolution with nothing but a few saddle sores, yet you have the gall to ask me to act like a gentleman! When I am confronted by hypocrisy and stupidity, I do not act like a gentleman!"

"We have had enough of this rubbage!" announced Adams. He called for the guards, and three soldiers appeared at the back of the hall. Adams pointed to Pratt. "Remove this man at once."

"There is no need to remove anyone," said Washington.

"Mr. President, this man is speaking slander on everyone in this room," charged Adams.

"He is speaking an opinion, sir. He has the right to be heard."

Before Adams could respond, Washington turned to Pratt. "Without undue display or unfair interruption, say your piece."

Pratt smiled and bowed. Just as he had hoped, he had Washington's support, and he had everyone else angry. "Thousands of pounds have been spent on that tea set, sir. Public money that might have been used to ease the burden of heavy taxes on men like me, or to help the farmers who rebelled with Colonel Shays, or to erect new buildings at Harvard College."

Hancock slammed his hand down on the table. "Mr. President, I must interrupt—"

"We will hear the man out," said Washington firmly.

Pratt was enjoying himself now. He glanced at young Horace, whose eyes shifted nervously from his father to the President. Pratt winked, and the boy looked again at the hem of the tablecloth. Pratt would explain it all later.

"Look around you, Mr. President," he continued. "You see nothing but Yankee businessmen and merchants, tight-fisted citizens who give nothing away without expecting something in return."

"And in return for the tea set?" asked Washington.

Pratt took a deep breath. He was about to tap the anger of every man in the room. "They expect favors from the new government."

"Why, that's absurd!" announced Hancock, as he gestured for more port.

Now, Pratt ignored the Governor. "New England is the seat of American shipbuilding. The men of Boston hope their gift will put them in favor when it comes time to build warships for the new navy."

"Mr. President," protested Revere, "I donated my time with no ulterior motives whatsoever."

"Certainly not," shouted Pratt. "Your motive is clear. If the government smiles upon you, Revere and Son will make the spikes and sheathings and cast the cannon for the new frigates!"

Andrew Cabot, shipper and Revolutionary privateer, rose in anger. "Mr. President, this man makes a mockery of these proceedings."

Pratt laughed at Cabot. "The new government may consider imposing tariffs and duties on men like you and me, unless we appeal to its head with silver tea sets."

Two more stood to decry him, and Pratt could see the indignation rising like a spring tide.

"I am an architect," announced Charles Bulfinch. "Am I seeking personal gain by showing my esteem for our President?"

"New York City will not be our capital forever, sir. Perhaps the President will give you the chance to deface a new city with your monstrosities."

Elias Haskett Derby, another shipper and one of Pratt's chief competitors, spoke out. "Mr. President, I beg hearing. Horace Taylor Pratt is not representative of the merchants of Boston."

Others shouted their support of Derby, but Washington would not intervene. After two weeks on his inaugural tour, after two days of parades and tribute in Boston, he was finding this little controversy most amusing. He looked toward Pratt.

"I buy goods. I ship goods. I make money. Just like Mr. Derby," said Pratt. "But I curry favor with no man."

"Least of all the men in this room," cracked John Adams.

"Least of all the Vice-President." Pratt leveled his gaze on Adams and felt the anger overflow all around him.

"Dammit, Pratt!" Samuel Adams took the floor. He was the elder cousin of the Vice-President, the elder statesman of Massachusetts. "You're a disgrace. A damnable disgrace, and I demand an apology right now." He looked at Washington. "President's banquet or not, no man worth his salt ought to sit here and take this!"

"Here, here!" Andrew Cabot turned to Samuel Adams and began to applaud. The President's banquet erupted in ovation for Adams, in cries for Pratt's apology. Men pounded the table and stomped their feet like Colonials confronting the British tax collector. John Adams studied the floor and waited for the noise to end, while Hancock rang so hard on his wineglass that it shattered in his lap. Through it all, Washington stood, arms folded and face impassive, as though he expected every banquet in his honor to end with such display.

In an attitude of supreme disdain, Pratt fixed his eyes on the brass chandelier above his head and put his hand on his son's shoulder. The boy did not understand his father's anger, but he felt the pride and defiance in his father's grip. Instinctively, he stood.

The outcry reached its crescendo and quickly abated. Silence expanded to fill Faneuil Hall.

John Adams placed hand on hip and stood like a shopkeeper waiting for payment past due. "Your apology, sir."

Pratt bowed to the Vice-President and then to Washington. "I apologize for nothing."

Washington smiled. "With such temperament among the citizenry, small wonder that the Revolution started in Boston."

"I await the President's decision," responded Pratt.

"Mr. Pratt," said the President after some time, "the gentlemen in this hall, yourself included, are patriots. They would not seek favor through a silver tea set, and you insult us by suggesting that we would bestow favors for any reason. This tea set may be an extravagance, but as Mr. Adams and Mr. Hamilton have counseled, we must retain the trappings of royalty in order to establish our sovereignty in the eyes of Europe. I shall take this tea set to the President's Residence, and I shall leave it when my term ends."

The gentlemen of Boston applauded as delicately as maidens at a spinet recital.

"Your wish, sir." Pratt and his son bowed graciously.

"I thank you, Mr. Pratt, for speaking your mind." Washington smiled at both of them as they headed out of the hall.

In the doorway, Pratt pivoted back to the crowd. "Gentlemen, may I have your attention for just a few moments more. This afternoon, the *Gay Head*, a Pratt schooner, entered the harbor after thirty-six months at sea. She carried silks, spices, tea, and China porcelain . . ." He paused to savor the expressions that were already forming on the faces of his competitors. ". . . from Canton! At this very moment, two more Pratt ships are passing somewhere in the South Atlantic, one bound for the Orient, the other laden with China's riches and stretching canvas for Boston. I've won, gentlemen. I'm the first Boston merchant to establish permanent trading relations with China. Tomorrow morning, I begin the sale of the goods on the *Gay Head*. Bring cash."

Pratt rarely noticed the weather, but tonight the brisk air, laced with the smell of salt, exhilarated him. He had done all that he had intended at the President's banquet. He looked at his son, who was beginning to shiver. He threw his cape over the boy's shoulders and embraced him roughly. "I was proud of the way you stood beside your father."

"Thank you." Young Horace looked down at the sidewalk.

Pratt lifted the boy's chin. "Let other men count cobblestones. We carry our heads high, especially when we visit one of our ships. Would you like to see the *Gay Head?*"

"Yes, sir," answered the boy without enthusiasm.

"Then come along. I'm sure your mother would love a bolt of Chinese silk, and Captain Trask tells me there are gifts on board for both my sons. Playthings for Jason, an ingenious device called an abacus for you, to help you with your sums."

He started toward Long Wharf, but his son didn't move.

"Why did you do it?" demanded the boy.

Pratt smiled. "It was an excellent performance, wasn't it?"

"Performance?" The boy was shocked. "You didn't mean all that you said?"

"Oh, I meant it. That tea set is a waste of good money, and most of those bastards are hypocrites of the first water. The only reason they gave that thing to Washington was to make him feel like a king."

"And you insulted him for accepting it." Horace's tone carried equal measures of accusation and disappointment.

Pratt began to lead the boy toward the waterfront. "I had the fortitude to speak my mind. Washington will remember me long after he has forgotten the two hundred other men in that banquet hall. I made them all look like fools."

"But you made enemies of all of them. That can't be to your advantage."

Pratt stopped and looked into his son's eyes. "They were enemies to begin with, Horace. Every man is an enemy. You must always keep your enemies off balance. Never let them know what you'll do next. Surprise them. When they think you're leaving with your tail between your legs, turn around and tell them about the *Gay Head*. When they think you're content, lash out at anything, just so they won't know what's in your head. And when they think you're quiet, have yourself a damn good sneezing fit."

The boy was beginning to understand.

"But always remember, Horace, whether you deal with president or dockhand, that every man shits, and every man is vulnerable when his breeches fall to his knees. Always keep them shitting over what you're about to do, and you'll always have the advantage."

Young Horace smiled. By the time they reached the *Gay Head*, their laughter was echoing up and down the wharf.

CHAPTER II

At precisely one o'clock on a June afternoon, Peter Fallon turned his Volvo off the main road a few miles outside Marblehead and entered a world which had existed for almost a hundred and forty years. A row of elms shielded the estate from the road, and the lawn rolled to the edge of the cliff, where a house rose out of the fog like a great white clipper. A hundred feet below, the ocean crashed against the granite coast.

The house was called Searidge. Horace Taylor Pratt's grandson had built it as a summer home in 1843, and Pratt descendants had been living there ever since.

Fallon drove slowly across the grounds. He wanted to absorb everything about the house before he drew too close and it overwhelmed him. Searidge stood three stories high, and a fresh coat of white paint made it seem even larger. Pilasters outlined the building in Neoclassical grace. Porticoes, pillars, and circular dormers effected a combination of majesty and simplicity that was a New England ideal.

Searidge had grown over the years. Two new wings, a solarium, and a tennis court had been added. But the house still seemed alive to the past. At the front step, two brass hitching posts awaited the master's carriage. On either side of the walk, Chinese lions reclined in stone, monuments to the China trade that had brought them there. On the roof, a balustrade protected the widow's walk, the platform where women once waited for their men to return from the sea. Empire builders and adventurers had lived at Searidge. Peter Fallon could feel their presence, and he envied them the exploits he would spend his life studying.

He had come to Searidge to examine the papers of Horace Taylor Pratt, one of the central figures in his dissertation and the founder of a corporation that was still a major issue on the New York Stock Exchange. He had been trying for months to contact Katherine Pratt Carrington, the seventy-six-year-old descendant in whose home the papers were stored, but his phone calls and letters had been ignored. He had also written to the home office of Pratt Industries and requested permission to view the Pratt papers. He had received a polite rejection from Philip Pratt's personal secretary.

When he was beginning to think that he would have to choose another New England shipper to fit into his study, "The Socio-Political Effects of the War of 1812 on the City of Boston," he received a note from Katherine Pratt Carrington. It was brief and direct. Mrs. Carrington said she saw no reason to deny a Harvard man access to the papers of an illustrious alumnus. She specified an exact time and date. She told him how long he could stay and what papers he could study. And she said that if he were not punctual, he need not visit.

Fallon had not found the note unusual. He assumed that Katherine Pratt Carrington was another Yankee dowager, which meant she was born to money she never spent from ancestors she never forgot. She was probably slender, wore little makeup, and dressed in clothes that might be expensive but were always sensible. She had informed opinions about everything. And she rarely allowed anyone to enter her world before careful inspection. Fallon had passed, and he was happy to see the Pratt papers under any circumstances. The more he knew about Pratt, the more quickly he could finish his dissertation.

The door opened before Fallon took his finger from the bell.

"Yes?" The maid peered out.

Fallon sensed her suspicion. He understood it. He had black hair, heavy brows, and the sort of rawboned Irish face that seems to be frowning when it isn't smiling. He knew that before he spoke, he usually made an unsettling first impression. He straightened his tie and politely introduced himself.

"I'm sorry. Mrs. Carrington is not feeling well, and she can't have visitors." The words sounded rehearsed, and the door slammed in Fallon's face.

He rang the bell again. The door opened, and the maid filled the doorway.

"Mrs. Carrington specified one P.M. You must be mistaken," he said.

"Mrs. Carrington does not visit with strangers. Please leave, or I shall call the police." She spoke with an English accent that disguised her midwestern origins. She tried to slam the door once more, but something stopped her. Fallon saw the end of a cane protruding from behind the door.

"With whom are you talking, Bette?" The voice was an old woman's.

"Mrs. Carrington, please take your cane out of the door."

She was seventy-six years old, with white hair, a grandmother's face, and a cameo on her blouse. Fallon wondered why she seemed so much younger. He decided it was her posture. She stood like a woman half her age. The cane was obviously an ornament.

"The young man from Harvard."

Fallon tugged at his tie again and smiled.

"Open the door, Bette."

"Mrs. Carrington . . ."

"I said open the door!" Her voice turned shrill, and she punctuated her command by driving her cane into the floor.

"I have my orders," said the maid.

"You have my orders!" Mrs. Carrington pulled the door open. "Come in, young man."

Fallon didn't know what he was stepping into, but he didn't hesitate. Mrs. Carrington closed the door behind him, then turned to the maid.

"You may go about your business, Mrs. Harrison."

"I shall contact Mr. Harrison immediately." The maid turned and disappeared down the narrow hallway that led to the kitchen.

Mrs. Carrington laughed, a self-satisfied grunt. "She can't get in touch with him. He drove my daughter into Boston to the theatre, and then, I presume, headed for some local pub. I usually go with her, but I decided to stay so that you could see the old boy's papers."

She spoke of Pratt with such familiarity that Fallon had to remind himself Pratt had been dead for over a hundred and fifty years.

Katherine Pratt Carrington took Fallon by the arm and led him into the sitting room. Part of the original house, it had enormous windows and twelve-foot ceilings, but the Queen Anne furniture, the fire, and the sound of classical music made it seem inviting.

"I hope you like Mozart, Mr. Fallon. I'm tackling one of his few concerti for single piano this week." She nodded toward the baby grand beneath the window. "And right now, I'm letting Artur Rubinstein give me a few pointers."

Fallon saw the Philco radio-phonograph in the corner. The case was mahogany. The record was spinning at seventy-eight rpms.

"You don't see record players like that too often," he said.

"Forty years old," she announced proudly. "We heard the news of Pearl Harbor right out of that speaker. My husband and I were sitting here reading the Sunday *Times*. The children were outside playing. When the bulletin ended, Henry looked me in the eye and said, 'Now, by George, we'll find out if this country has any character left after nine years of Roosevelt.' Then he telephoned the War Department and tried to get his old commission back."

She sat in the chair by the fireplace. A book of music was open on the arm of the chair. "I've been following along with Artur," she said, placing the book aside. "My daughter keeps telling me I should get a stereo machine, but some of the best performances I own are on old seventy-eights, and I don't see any reason why I should get rid of my faithful Philco just to fit contemporary trends."

The classic attitude for the Yankee lady, thought Fallon. "Do you play often?"

"It's one of the few joys left for an old widow of seventy-six." She spoke without the self-pity Fallon would have expected, and he liked her for it.

He noticed on the mantel above her head a photograph. The hairstyles and clothes dated it in the mid-1930s. It showed a family— husband and wife, son and daughter—in the stern of a sailboat. The boy was about eight years old, and he held the tiller as though he'd been born to it. His father watched him with pride. His sister, about five, nestled in her mother's arms and gazed admiringly at the men. The mother, Katherine Pratt Carrington, looked straight at the camera. She had been a beautiful woman.

"Now, Mr. Fallon, please sit down and tell me all about your work."

He perched on the edge of the sofa and glanced unconsciously at his watch.

14

"Don't worry. You'll have plenty of time in the attic," she said. "But first, spend a few minutes with an old lady. I see very few new faces anymore. Perhaps if Pratt Industries stock hadn't started to fall, my daughter and my nephews might not keep me so tightly circumscribed."

"I don't understand the connection."

"I have a few theories, but I shan't trouble you with them." She rang a small bell, and the maid appeared in the doorway. "Bring us tea and cookies, dear." Mrs. Carrington spoke with the perfect mixture of condescension and annoyance. The maid turned away, and Mrs. Carrington lowered her voice. "At least I can handle her." As though there were others more difficult.

Fallon wondered if her battle with senility had begun. In the next half hour, she dispelled such thoughts. She talked almost obsessively, as though she had spoken with no one in months, but her conversation was bright and witty. She talked about the Pratts, the War of 1812, the China trade, and she seemed especially interested in Fallon's work. He realized that she had allowed him into the house because she was lonely.

"After you've gotten your doctorate at Harvard, what will you do?"

"I'm considering offers from two university history departments." He didn't tell her he wasn't going to accept either position.

"I admire you, young man. It takes a great deal of courage to be a scholar, but it is the scholar who tells us about ourselves."

Fallon hated being called a scholar. He smelled dry rot whenever he heard the word. He smiled and tugged at his tie again.

She sensed his discomfort and changed the subject. "I also admire your neckwear. Its pattern is the Eliot family coat-of-arms, is it not?"

"When I was an undergraduate, I lived in Eliot House."

"So did my son. He graduated magna cum laude in government, class of '49."

"Does he work for Pratt Industries?"

"No. My son had a wonderful future, but his life was cut short when he was twenty-six." Her eyes drifted toward the picture on the mantelpiece. Then she stood abruptly. She was not the sort to dwell on memories, happy or otherwise. "Let's go upstairs and see what Horace Taylor Pratt can tell us about Boston in 1814."

She led Fallon up the stairs. On the first landing, Horace Taylor Pratt, painted by John Singleton Copley, stared into the entrance hall. The eyes were dark, the face long and ghostly pale. In front of Pratt, a map of China was spread on a table, and in his hand he gripped a walking stick as though it were a club with which to beat Canton into submission. He seemed to be frowning, but Fallon sensed that it was his natural expression.

"The patriarch himself," said Mrs. Carrington. "He certainly looks like a sullen old bird, doesn't he?"

As they walked past the bedrooms on the second floor, Fallon glimpsed mahogany and oak, four-posters and wardrobes, and nothing less than fifty years old. At the end of the hallway, he saw an exquisite Chinese chest of lacquered wood and mother-of-pearl inlay. Above the box was the portrait of another Pratt, painted in the mid-nineteenth century.

"That's Artemus Pratt I, my great-grandfather," explained Mrs. Carrington. "He built Searidge and secured the fortune."

Fallon was beginning to feel as though he were touring a very small, exclusive museum.

At the top of the stairs on the third floor, a Governor Winthrop desk covered the entrance to the attic. Fallon moved the desk aside, Mrs. Carrington opened the wall panel, and they climbed eight more steps. The attic smelled of mothballs and dust, and it overflowed with clothes, furniture, books, mementoes from World's Fairs and Harvard football games, and garment bags containing uniforms from most of America's wars. A saber of Civil War vintage hung from one of the rafters, and scattered through the piles of junk were metal boxes and filing cabinets filled, Fallon imagined, with the family papers. On one box, a label read "Artemus Pratt's correspondence," and another, "The Diaries of Abigail Pratt Bentley."

Fallon heard a small motor begin to hum somewhere in the room.

"The dehumidifier," explained Mrs. Carrington. "It helps to protect things up here. I have occasionally considered donating all this to the Harvard libraries. I'm told that the Pratt papers and portrait would make an excellent tax write-off, but I prefer to keep them here, at least until I die. Moreover, the rest of my family is very protective of our past." She laughed. "As though people long dead can rise up and smite us if we don't watch over their privacy."

"Have other historians examined these papers?" Fallon was hoping he was the first.

"There have been a few over the years. Samuel Eliot Morison examined a good deal of the Pratt material for his *Maritime History of Massachusetts.*"

"That was published in the twenties."

"Good Lord, has it been that long? Searidge was still a summer house in the twenties. Henry and I moved up here permanently in 1934. The Depression was making the city such an unsavory place

16

for raising children."

"Was Morison the last one?"

Mrs. Carrington thought for a moment. "We've certainly been bothered often enough. You know, news reporters looking to fill Sunday supplements, snoops of all sorts. But only people with serious intent have seen these papers, and no one outside the family in the last thirty years."

"I'm honored." Fallon was not above flattery.

"Now, then, you may look only at the papers of Horace Taylor Pratt—his logs, his letters, his ledgers.

"I think you'll find them all in excellent condition." She opened a great steamer trunk in the middle of the room and took out several metal boxes, each of them labeled and indexed. "My grandson Christopher has been cataloguing everything we have. It's a hobby of his."

Fallon opened one of the boxes. Inside, he found piles of correspondence, much of it crumbling to dust, and a package of desiccant keeping the dust dry.

"It is now two-fifteen," said Mrs. Carrington. "Mr. Harrison and my daughter will be returning at five-fifteen. I want you gone well before then. And remember, you may examine only what I have set out before you."

Mrs. Carrington went downstairs. Fallon dragged the boxes over to a dormer, where the light was better, and he sat down. He no longer enjoyed the routine research his work required, but when he read old letters, Fallon felt a sort of prurient excitement, as though he were eavesdropping on a private conversation. With a Mozart piano concerto, played by Katherine Pratt Carrington, floating up the stairs and the fog pressing against the window, he began.

For the next two hours, he immersed himself in the letters of Horace Taylor Pratt, which had been collected from his correspondents after his death and preserved for his descendants. In most of his letters, Pratt discussed business and little else. The movement of goods, the speed of his ships, the activities of his competitors and his government were his primary concerns. But one packet of letters contained something more.

From 1802 to 1807, Pratt's older son, Horace, had been in China as the chief foreign officer for Pratt Shipping and Mercantile. Letters of father and son had been filed together, and they revealed men of strikingly similar dimension. The Pratts discussed business, but they also wrote regularly of their hopes for their family and the future of the company.

"Young Horace III is now eight years old," wrote Horace II from

Canton in 1807, "and we are building him a bright future indeed. I see limitless potential for Pratt Shipping and Mercantile, both here in China and around the globe. Every penny we make is helping us to grow stronger and making our future secure. From what you told me in your last letter, however, it seems that President Jefferson may present problems. An embargo on European trade would certainly be a severe blow to us all. I'm sure most American shippers would rather trade with everyone and take their chances with the British and French than rot in port until Napoleon is defeated. We must hope this President keeps his head. In any event, I feel that it is time for me to return to Boston. I have done and learned all that I can here. I know that I can now be of service to you at home, especially if we must contend with an embargo."

Six months later, Pratt received his son's letter and answered it immediately. "I agree, Horace, that it is time for you to return to my right hand. You have been too long away from us, but you have done us proud. I am sending Anson Dabney, a trusted Boston assistant, out to replace you. If you are not already at sea and running for Boston, take the next ship. But bring no goods. The bastard Jefferson has closed American ports to all foreign trade. He thinks he can make the British and French leave us alone by hiding from them both like a frightened schoolboy. I say we take sides with England—they rule the seas, after all—and fight against France, if we must. 'Twould be better than cowering in our boots.

"As for Horace III, I cannot wait to see him. I hope that you have been raising him the way I raised you—to fear nothing but the Lord, to believe in himself and his family, and to prepare himself for the mantle of leadership that he will inherit from you, just as you will inherit it from me.

"On your return voyage, instruct him to study the activities of the shipmaster (probably Chapman, if you return on the *Pemberton),* who tries to anticipate the changes in the wind and set his canvas accordingly. It's a good way to live one's life and keep a full league ahead of the competition."

Peter Fallon was fascinated. He took notes as quickly as he read. Statistics in a cargo muster might illuminate the nature of Pratt's trade, but in this letter he was revealing the motivations behind it.

"Impress upon your son that he will be engaged in a holy war, that by extending the arm of New England business to the heathen places on this earth, he is spreading the Word of the Lord. He must be forever vigilant, forever seeking new ways to use the gifts that the Lord has helped us to wrest from the sea."

Pratt had been raised in the Calvinist tradition that encouraged the merchant and viewed commerce as the most noble profession. Fallon wondered how many nineteenth-century fortunes were built on God's will before Social Darwinism offered a more scientific justification for the pursuit of wealth. But he knew that with Calvin behind them, the Pratts had contributed mightily to the economic growth of New England.

At four o'clock, Fallon heard an automobile pull up in the driveway below. Through the window, he watched a young woman with blond hair climb out of a sports car and run into the house. She was too young to be Mrs. Carrington's daughter, and the fog was now too thick for Fallon to notice her beauty. He returned to his work.

The final letter in the China envelope came from Captain Richard Chapman of the *Pemberton*, a Pratt ship. It was dated April 23, 1808.

"Mr. Pratt, I have sent this letter ahead on a faster ship because I believe it better that you know now the fate of your son. Moreover, I could not bear to tell you myself, and this letter provides me a coward's escape. The *Pemberton* is now put in at Rio Gallégos, on the Argentine coast, for repairs. The foretop and a good deal of rigging were carried away in a heavy blow off Cape Horn. We were running—nay, flying—before the wind on our easterly passage when a heavy squall struck from the north. Such winds are rare in these latitudes, and we were caught without adequate preparation."

Peter Fallon read very slowly. He imagined Pratt's terror growing with every word.

"I commanded my men aloft to reef mains'ls and tops'ls. As they were ascending, we were taken broadside by a wave that suddenly towered over us. We lost three seamen and, I regret to say, your son Horace, who had come on deck to observe the operation. In such heavy seas, we had no hope of finding him, though we did swing into the wind and make search. It was then my terrible duty to go below decks and inform his wife and son that Horace Pratt II was lost.

"I know, sir, that no words of consolation shall ease your pain upon reading this letter, so none shall be given."

After his son's death, Horace Pratt wrote to no one for months. Fallon surmised that he was in mourning. When he began to correspond again, Pratt dictated his letters, as though he no longer had anything personal to say. His tone again became terse and businesslike, and now, it masked his pain. Only occasionally did he reveal his bitterness in an outburst against the policies of Jefferson and his successor, James Madison.

As Fallon neared the end of the correspondence, he realized he had only an hour left before Mrs. Carrington's daughter would come home. He decided to turn from the letters to the ledger books, cargo musters, and logs. Through them, he hoped to trace the changes in the nature and quantity of Pratt trade—the beginnings in 1780, the China success in 1789, the recession of 1808 caused by Jefferson's embargo, and the grim years from 1812 to 1815.

The record for the third quarter of 1814 filled only five pages in its ledger. Four Pratt ships sailed from Boston and one returned. The others, Fallon assumed, were taken by the British. It was Pratt's worst quarter. Fallon flipped through the crumbling pages. He didn't think anybody had looked beyond page five in a hundred and fifty years, because the pages were blank. But toward the end of the book, Fallon noticed an envelope jammed between the end-leaves.

It almost fell apart in his hands as he read the address.

By Presidential Courier

To Horace Taylor Pratt
Pratt Shipping and Mercantile
3 Merchants Row, Boston

Fallon turned the envelope over. President Madison's signature was written across the flap, and the outline of the American eagle was still visible in the wax seal. The words "The President's Mansion" were embossed on the letterhead, and it was dated August 24, 1814, the day the British burned the Capitol and the White House. Fallon noticed that one edge of the paper was blackened as though it had been burned, as well.

To HTP,

The British are taking the city. Our chance is here. The Eagle will arrive at the mouth of the Easterly Channell, Gravelly Point, on the night tide ten to fifteen days hence. Make arrangements.

DL

Fallon read the note again. He had learned to categorize his research in three groups: the discovery which proved a theory and produced immediate satisfaction; the finding which fit with others to form a pattern he could analyze; the total surprise, which turned his theories inside out and caused him to stop right where he was. This note fell into the last category. He didn't know what "DL" or "the Eagle" meant, and he didn't know where Gravelly Point was, but he realized that he had stumbled onto something very unusual. Somebody in the White House had been acting as a Pratt agent, and whatever they were doing, it didn't sound like official business, despite the President's signature.

He studied the note for a time. Then, impulsively, he stuffed it into his pocket and began to sift for other references to "DL" and "the Eagle."

"Excuse me, sir." The voice was very soft, but it startled Fallon only slightly less than the sight of the speaker.

Geoffrey Harrison stood six feet five and weighed well over two hundred pounds. He slicked his hair flat, and his round face seemed to engulf his features. From Fallon's position on the floor, he looked like an enormous China doll.

"I must ask you to leave immediately." He spoke politely with an English accent that was authentic." The family does not appreciate intrusions."

With DL's note in his sportcoat pocket and Harrison behind him, Fallon left the attic and went downstairs. He stopped briefly outside Mrs. Carrington's sitting room. He did not go in. Mrs. Carrington sat at the piano bench while a middle-aged woman berated her for allowing strange visitors into the house.

"Damn, Isabelle," Mrs. Carrington interrupted. "I'm sick of secrecy. He's a young Harvard student with good intentions."

"Mother, it is not good policy to allow people to go poking through our papers. Especially now."

"I don't understand any of this, Aunt Isabelle," said the young woman from the sports car. "Grandmother's been running this house for forty-five years. She doesn't need you to be telling her how to run it now."

"Thank you, dear," said Mrs. Carrington.

"Please, sir." Harrison's voice nudged Fallon gently in the small of the back. The door was closed behind him.

As he walked toward his car, Fallon heard angry voices and slamming doors. The young woman burst out of the house and hurried past him. She was tall and slender and loped along like a jogger.

"I'm sorry if I caused any trouble," he said.

She didn't look at him. She jumped into her car and started the engine.

He approached the car. "I said, I'm sorry."

Still, she didn't look at him.

"I haven't been treated like this since I asked Eleanor Emerson for a date in my freshman year," said Fallon.

She smiled at him, but she wasn't happy. "I'm sure you're a nice guy, but I'm in no mood to talk right now. You've caused my grandmother a great deal of annoyance."

"That's not what you were saying in there."

She glared at him. "I'm trying to be nice to you. Don't spoil it."

"Sorry, but I'm a little confused."

"So am I. Every time I . . ." She paused. She didn't confide in strangers and didn't want to seem too friendly. "You're some kind of professional student, aren't you?"

It was Fallon's turn to be annoyed. Even a scholar was better than a professional student. "I'm a historian."

"Well, whatever you are, my brother may be able to help you. He's been all through the papers in the attic, and he knows everything about the family history. You can contact him by calling the law office of Pratt, Pratt, and Carrington."

"Thank you. What's his name?"

"Christopher Carrington."

"What's yours?"

"Is that important?"

Fallon smiled. "You really are like Eleanor Emerson." Her short blond hair and rather prominent jaw reminded him of a number of girls he'd known, most of them from Wellesley College.

"Evangeline." She threw the car in gear and drove off.

It was getting chilly. Fallon turned up his collar and looked once more at the house. Harrison was watching him from the sitting-room window. He smiled and waved. It had been a very strange visit.

Philip Pratt, president and chairman of the board of Pratt Industries, sipped his gin and tonic and watched a pair of young breasts glide past. He loved California. He had considered opening a West Coast office many times, but beyond a large and unprofitable chunk of American Center Films stock, the purchase engineered by Pratt himself, the corporation had little business in California. So Pratt contented himself with an occasional trip to Hollywood, where he visited the lot, lunched with young actresses, read scripts, and lounged by the pool of the Beverly Hills Hotel.

This trip, however, he was traveling under an alias.

The girl was about twenty, and she had been strolling around the pool for half an hour. Pratt was forty-four with prematurely gray hair, but in swim trunks he looked thirty. He could no longer resist. As the girl walked by, he smiled.

"Mr. Pratt, I suggest you save your energy." Bennett Soames, Pratt's personal secretary, sat beside him and sipped club soda. He was wearing a blue pinstripe suit and a wide-brimmed straw hat to keep the sun off his face.

"You underestimate me, Mr. Soames."

"Remember that you have an appointment in half an hour." Soames sounded like a schoolmaster.

Pratt smiled and called for another gin and tonic. He rarely disagreed with his personal secretary and never made a move before consulting him. Bennett Soames believed in order and efficiency. Pratt knew that without Soames to keep his schedules, smooth his way, and remind him of his priorities, his world would collapse.

A porter brought a white telephone to Pratt's side. "Call for you, sir."

Pratt took the receiver. "Weatherman here."

"Mr. Weatherman? This is Sally Korbel. I'm in the lobby." Her voice was warm, seductive.

"I'll be there in a moment." He hung up. "She's here."

"May I make a suggestion?" asked Soames.

"By all means."

Soames was rankled by the condescension in Pratt's voice, but he let it pass, as always. "Business first."

"Would you like to come along to supervise?"

Soames said nothing. He did not allow himself to show anger. Although he was not perspiring, he removed his rimless glasses and wiped his face.

"That's good. It's a one-man job, anyway." Pratt clapped Soames on the shoulder and left him in the sun.

Pratt's room overlooked the pool and was filled with sunlight that reflected off the water. He stood by the window so that Sally Korbel would be forced to look into the glare. He studied her silently and liked what he saw. She was tall and full-breasted, with brown hair cut very short and a deep tan. If her face had a flaw, it was the stingy mouth, which seemed out of proportion with the rest of her features.

"I like to get business out of the way first, Mr. Weatherman."

"An excellent philosophy."

"You know my price?"

Pratt took four hundred-dollar bills from his wallet and held them out. She hesitated.

"I'm a big tipper," he said. "I want this to be a pleasant afternoon."

She took the money and stuffed it into her purse. "For four hundred, I can guarantee it."

"Excellent." Pratt took off his trunks.

"Very nice," she purred. She knew how to please her clients. Her wraparound skirt fell away easily, then she unsnapped her halter top. She was wearing nothing else. She took a few steps toward Pratt and placed her hands on her hips.

"Before I go any further, is there anything special you'd like?" She sounded to Pratt as though she really liked him. She was a professional.

"A poem," he said.

Her voice grew cold. "What kind of poem?"

"Actually, just a few lines."

She spoke evenly but firmly. "If you want me to read nursery rhymes and play Mother Goose, take your four hundred back and find another girl."

He approached her and put his arms around her. "I want nothing of the sort. Let's forget I said it."

She relaxed.

An hour later, Pratt ran his finger down her spine and into the cleft between her buttocks. She shivered and moved her body toward him.

"Now about that poetry," he said.

She rolled over and sat up. "I'll do it if it's not too freaky. You're a nice guy and all, but I don't like freaky scenes."

"My dear, I rarely pay for the services you render and did not request you for professional reasons. Although"—Pratt prided himself on his charm—"it was a pleasure doing business with you. I asked for you specifically because I collect poems, and I think you may have one that I'm interested in."

"Well, I'm not interested." She jumped out of bed and began to dress. "If you want poems, go to a library."

Pratt slipped into a pair of beige slacks and a striped St. Laurent shirt. "I'll explain on the way."

"To where?"

"Your place."

"We're not going to my place."

Pratt opened his wallet and took out a wad of bills. "There are ten one-hundred-dollar bills in my hand," he said. "They're yours. You pay no taxes on them, nor does your madam take a commission. All you need to do is take me to your house and help me find what I'm looking for."

The money softened her. "Before we go anywhere, you tell me what we're looking for."

"Have you ever heard of John Milton?"

She thought for a moment. "Wasn't he with the Morris Agency?"

Pratt smiled. He was hoping she'd be ignorant, but this was extraordinary. "He's a poet. About eighty years ago, an old woman up in Monterey embroidered a series of samplers with quotes from his poems. I've collected several of them. I need one more to complete the set. It's a gift for my wife." Pratt wasn't married. "She collects samplers."

"What makes you think I have this thing?"

"Well, if my research is correct, the old lady was your great-grandmother."

Sally Korbel recalled that her mother had given her two boxes of family junk just before she died. Sally had never looked through them. "I think I know what you're looking for," she lied. "But I want payment in advance, and no refunds if it's not there."

Pratt offered her five hundred. She took it.

The stucco apartment building spread like pink mold across the Santa Monica neighborhood. "Twenty units, one-two bedrooms, no vacancy." Pratt read the sign with great interest. California real estate was an excellent investment.

Sally Korbel's apartment was three rooms with white walls, green carpeting, and a view of someone else's bedroom windows.

"A high-priced professional like you should be living in Malibu," said Pratt.

"I pay three-fifty for this place, and that's cheap if you want to live three blocks from the beach."

She slid back the ceiling panel above her bed and took down two boxes. Pratt tried to seem relaxed as they dug through photographs, news clippings, and envelopes stuffed with old letters. In the bottom of the second box, they found it. The frame was scratched and the glass was caked with dust, but a quotation from Milton was woven into the cloth in brown and red threads.

Pratt read it to himself. "So he with difficulty and labour hard / Mov'd on . . . / Sin and Death amain / Following his track, such was the will of Heav'n, / Pav'd after him a broad and beat'n way / Over the dark Abyss, whose boiling Gulf / Tamely endur'd a Bridge of wondrous length / From Hell continu'd reaching th'utmost

Orb / Of this frail World; by which the Spirits perverse / With easy intercourse pass to and fro / To tempt or punish mortals, except whom / God and good Angels guard by special grace."

"Exquisite," whispered Pratt.

"That's it?" Sally Korbel was amazed. "No shit?"

"None whatsoever."

She grabbed the sampler. "You'd better come up with fifteen hundred if you want it, mister. If you can pay a thousand for this, you can pay two."

Pratt had been expecting that. He haggled with her and eventually paid another thousand dollars for the sampler. He didn't tell her that he would have paid fifty if she'd held out for it.

"I hope your wife likes it, Mr. Weatherman."

"Nothing could make her happier."

Mr. Soames was waiting when Pratt returned to the suite.

"Book the next flight, Bennett."

"You were successful?"

Pratt flipped the sampler to Soames, who read the lines and smiled.

Sally Korbel felt great. In three hours, she had made nearly two thousand dollars and spread her legs just once. She poured a vodka on the rocks and studied her appointment book. She had three more tricks, regulars, before eleven. Wednesday was her busy day. She wanted to cancel them and spend the rest of the night with her girlfriend Maria. But good call girls never turn down the regulars who tip well. She showered and went back to work.

That night, she cleared three hundred dollars. At eleven o'clock, she returned to her apartment with a bottle of champagne under her arm and an ounce of cocaine in her purse. She hoped that Maria would be awake when she called. She let herself into the apartment and fumbled for the light switch. She never found it.

The door slammed behind her and something slammed her against the wall. She dropped the champagne, but the bottle didn't break. She smelled perfume and wondered what kind of freak wore Shalimar when he robbed a working girl. Then a silk stocking closed around her neck, and she knew it was one of her own. She sprinkled them with perfume every week.

She tried to scream, but the sound was caught. She reached for the letter opener. Too far. She elbowed the body in the ribs. She tried to kick free. The silk was drawn tight around her throat. She heard something pop. The champagne blew its cork across the room.

Thirty thousand feet over Nevada, Philip Pratt sipped Scotch and read *Business Week* as American Flight 5 streaked to Boston.

It was closing time in the Sixpence, a basement bar with low ceilings, cramped tables, and countless violations of the fire code. The Sixpence was a favorite spot with Harvard people, and Fallon had been drinking there since his freshman year.

He sat at the end of the bar while Hank Miller, owner and bartender, served the last call. He opened DL's letter and placed it in front of him. He had been thinking about it all night. It was puzzling, cryptic, completely unlike Pratt's usual correspondence. He wanted to investigate the letter, and he wanted to learn something more about the contemporary Pratts, who seemed so secretive. After a few sips of beer, he told himself that he had no right to invade other peoples' privacy and the letter probably meant nothing. Its references—DL, the Eagle, Gravelly Point—might even be explained in his high-school text. Moreover, he imagined that Pratt would have been more careful about burning the letter, had it contained anything incriminating.

Fallon folded the letter, put it in his pocket, and finished his beer. For a while, he stared into the bottom of the glass and tried not to think. Then he took out the letter and opened it again.

"You been lookin' at that thing all night, Peter. What the hell is it?" asked Miller.

"A puzzle."

"You want another beer?"

Fallon nodded and began to study the letter. It was a distraction he didn't need. He was trying to finish his dissertation by the end of September. Then, armed with a Harvard B.A. and a Ph.D. in history, he would hit the streets. He had applied for teaching positions at sixty-five university history departments. There were twelve openings, and he had received two offers: one from an agricultural school in Minnesota, the other from a Fundamentalist college that boasted of its basketball team and banned alcohol, dancing, and unmarried sex for anyone connected with the institution. And no one had offered him tenure. After three years in history, he was telling himself that he should have gone to law school.

He decided he needed a bender, a full-scale drunk to clear his head and keep him writing until the dissertation was done. He folded the note and put it in his pocket. He resolved that he would not look at it again.

"Hey, Hank, bring me a Jameson's first, then the beer."

"You sure?" asked the bartender.

Fallon nodded.

"I guess it must be early June, then." Miller poured the Irish whiskey. "You know how I can tell?"

"How?" Fallon downed the shot.

"You order a boilermaker the first week of every other month. I can set my watch to it. These things'll kill you."

"Occasionally I need some lubrication." Fallon gulped the beer and left. After six beers and a shot, he was beginning to feel numb. He would know he'd had enough when he stopped thinking about the Pratts, "the Eagle," and "DL."

CHAPTER III   *August 1814*

Dexter Lovell found the First Lady in the northeast bedroom. Although the door was open, he knocked softly.

"Come in, Dexter." Dolley Madison stood by an open window and studied the horizon through a spyglass.

"The dinner is ready, ma'am, and I've set out iced ale and Madeira, should you want a dram to ward off the heat." He was a rangy figure with high cheekbones and gray hair that he tied, in the Revolutionary style, at the collar. Although he wore a white livery and knee breeches, he looked more like a seaman than a servant, and he spoke with a Cockney accent.

"I'll await the President, Dexter. We may be stifling, but it's a good deal hotter wherever he is at the moment."

The sound of artillery fire rolled across Washington like distant thunder. Mrs. Madison shuddered and turned again to the window. In four days, thought Lovell, she had grown old. A large woman in her mid-forties, she wore a shapeless cotton dress that emphasized her bulk, and the lines in her face had deepened with worry.

"We're losing, aren't we, ma'am?"

She handed him the glass. "See for yourself."

Six miles away, in a hamlet called Bladensburg, two thousand British regulars were routing an American force three times their size. From the windows of the President's Mansion, Lovell saw the smoke and dust that hung above the battle like heat haze, and he heard the faint sounds of rifle fire carried on the breeze.

On the other side of Washington, across the mud and swamps and impassable thickets that separated the President's Mansion from the rest of the city, he saw the American Militia straggling back from Bladensburg. Their return had incited a panic. The citizens of Washington had packed what they could carry onto wagons and carts, and they were pouring by the hundreds up Pennsylvania Avenue, past the Mansion, and off into the safety of the Virginia countryside.

"They look like the Jews fleeing Egypt," said Lovell.

"The Jews wanted to leave."

A rider galloped up the drive. It was Jim Smith, President Madison's freedman, waving wildly and hollering to Mrs. Madison.

"Men bringing good news don't ride like that, ma'am," said Lovell.

"We've lost! The President says clear out! Clear out!" Smith bellowed.

"I'll have that Madeira now, Dexter, then I think we should start packing." Dolley Madison left Lovell by the window and went downstairs.

Lovell stared at the caravan streaming past and at the turbulent sky above Bladensburg. His moment had arrived.

He took an envelope from Mrs. Madison's desk. It carried the words "By Presidential Courier" on the front and Madison's signature on the flap. The President had signed several envelopes and left them with his wife, so that she might communicate efficiently while he was with the troops.

Lovell addressed the letter to Horace Taylor Pratt, his old friend in Boston.

To HTP,

The British are taking the city. Our chance is here. The Eagle will arrive at the mouth of the Easterly Channell, Gravelly Point, on the night tide, ten to fifteen days hence. Make arrangements.

He signed his initials in flowing script and folded the letter, sealing it with a drop of hot wax and the President's stamp.

Downstairs, Dolley Madison was directing the evacuation. Her sister and brother-in-law loaded a wagon with china, silverware, and books. Mrs. Madison and Charles Carrol, a family friend, stripped the Oval Room of its red velvet draperies. Jacob Barker and Robert de Peyster, businessmen from New York, loaded the President's papers. In the dining room, Jean Sioussa, the President's door-keeper, and household gardener Tom Magraw struggled to remove the Gilbert Stuart portrait of Washington, which was screwed to the wall and would not come loose.

Descending the staircase, Lovell spied John Peel, one of the President's couriers, leaving in the confusion. Lovell followed him into the sunshine. "Mrs. Madison told me to give this to you. See that it gets to Baltimore as quick as possible."

Peel noted the President's signature on the envelope and stuffed it into his pouch. By coach, the trip to Boston took eleven days. Through the network of military couriers set up during the war, a letter might reach Boston in four. John Peel mounted and galloped off through the traffic pouring up Pennsylvania Avenue. From Baltimore, another courier would take the dispatch to a military outpost in Wilmington, Delaware, then on to Philadelphia and up the chain to Boston.

Lovell returned to the foyer and saw Jean Sioussa rushing toward the dining room with an ax. Known as French John, Sioussa was a stocky man with a cheerful disposition and a bald head that made him look like a monk. He was in charge of the President's household staff, and he stopped when he noticed Lovell.

"Have you loaded the plate?" he asked in a thick French accent.

"Not yet."

"Then hurry up. Mrs. Madison will not leave until everything we can carry is on the road, and I want her out of here in twenty minutes."

"We need that ax, French John!" Dolley Madison shouted from the dining room, and Sioussa hurried off to her aid.

Lovell grabbed Thomas Jefferson Grew, a Jamaican freedman who worked on the grounds. He gave Grew the keys to the cabinet in the small dining room and instructed him to begin packing the silver and gold plate.

"You leavin' dis job all to me?" asked Grew, aware of the responsibility the white man was giving him.

"I'll be along to 'elp you in a minute."

Grew smiled. "Ain't no white man gonna give Jeff Grew the keys to the gold and say 'Do it yourself.' No, sir. Well, Dexter Lovell, you be along in a minute. I be here."

Lovell wanted to crack the nigger across the face. Grew was the most arrogant freedman he had ever met, but there was no time now to teach him his place. "Get your arse to work, or we'll leave you 'ere for the British."

Grew continued to smile. "I like the British, Dexter Lovell. Talk too much about 'em, I be wantin' to stay."

Lovell turned and headed for the dining room, where French John was swinging the ax at the frame around Washington's portrait. Mrs. Madison quivered with every blow.

"Hurry up, John," said Magraw, who could smell the British a few miles away.

"Take as much time as you need," said Dolley Madison. "I'm too old to be raped, and the British are too civilized to set a woman on fire."

"I'm not too sure about that, madame," said Sioussa.

Lovell tried to approach the group very quietly. The Golden Eagle Tea Set was displayed on a cart beneath Washington's portrait, and it had been rolled aside to give Sioussa room to work. Lovell hoped to remove it without attracting attention.

"Dexter," cried Dolley Madison before he was halfway across the room. "We mustn't forget Paul Revere in our haste to save Gilbert Stuart." She grabbed the cart and pushed it toward him. "Take good care of this."

"Mrs. Madison!" screamed French John, "We've done it!"

Dolley Madison turned again to the painting. "Treat it like a child."

Still in its wooden stretcher, the canvas slid free from the frame as Lovell wheeled the tea set out of the room. He put it on the dumbwaiter in the hallway and sent it downstairs. The kitchen was deserted. A pot of stew bubbled on the stove and coffee was brewing for the President's return, but all the servants were loading wagons or fleeing to Virginia. Lovell rolled the cart into a broom closet and locked it with the master key.

Then, he pulled two heavy strongboxes from the storage room. Inside one box, two thicknesses of oak and another of copper protected the velvet compartments which would hold the tea set. The other box had no lining, but was of similar size and shape. Lovell filled the unlined box with pewter utensils and the few silver pieces he found in the kitchen. He locked the box and dragged it toward the dumbwaiter.

"Dexter." Thomas Jefferson Grew's deep voice startled Lovell, and he nearly dropped the box. "Gimme dat thing, Dexter. You be too old. Be lettin' dat damn thing fall on your foot." Grew was six feet tall and solid muscle. Lovell was fifty-six and glad for the help.

"Dis be dat fancy tea set?"

"Aye."

Grew noticed the second box lying by the broom closet. "What's in dat box?"

"Nothing," snapped Lovell. "We won't be needin' it."

Grew could feel Lovell bristling. "You mean you carry dat heavy damn thing in here for nothin'? Not too smart, Dexter Lovell. Not too smart."

"I said we won't be needin' it. Now move."

The black studied Lovell for a moment, smiled cannily, and threw the strongbox onto the dumbwaiter.

Lovell made certain that Mrs. Madison saw the strongbox loaded onto a wagon. He hoped that later, she might think the Golden Eagle had left the mansion with her caravan and been lost en route, or that the wrong box was accidentally loaded and the tea set left behind for the British. If the ruse cast suspicion away from him for a few hours, Lovell would be satisfied. After that, he would never be seen in Washington again.

In the hour between Jim Smith's arrival and Mrs. Madison's departure, a dozen soldiers stopped at the mansion to offer their help before joining the flight. And each one brought news of the battle. The British were entering the city. They were still an hour from Washington. The President had ridden off without escort and galloped straight into the arms of the enemy. He and his entourage were hastening home and could be expected at any moment. Dolley Madison wanted to wait for her husband, but reports of the battle were so unreliable that she had little choice but to believe the worst. At four in the afternoon, she left with her carriage and two wagons full of belongings.

A handful of men remained to secure the mansion and await the President. French John, Barker, and de Peyster loaded another wagon with valuables. Jeff Grew and Magraw guarded the front door from the looters already beginning to gather. Dexter Lovell said he would go down to the kitchen to bring up more food and drink for the soldiers who would be riding with the President.

In the kitchen, he quickly packed the tea set. Then he heaved it onto his shoulder and headed for the stable. He tried to stay close to the south side of the mansion, out of view of the windows on the main floor. At the corner of the building, he thought he noticed someone peering down at him from the East Room. He waited until the figure was gone, then he hurried across the lawn.

In the stable, he buried the strongbox under a pile of hay. For a moment, he knelt in front of it like a pilgrim praying before his journey. With the help of Horace Taylor Pratt and the Golden Eagle, Dexter Lovell was going to be rich. He would never again pour wine for backwater diplomats or clean the boot scrapers in front of the President's Mansion. But for the first time in his life, he was frightened by the journey ahead. He had always been a wanderer, but he was getting old.

Many times in the past few years, he had thanked the forces that threw him and Jean Sioussa together on a French cargo ship in 1800. Lovell, forty-two, was working his way home. Sioussa was leaving France forever. In New York, they jumped ship, and for two months, Lovell educated the Frenchman in the ways of American life. Lovell drifted north to Boston, Sioussa south to Washington and the service of the Madisons. When Lovell's restlessness brought him to the Federal city nine years later, French John offered him a position on the President's household staff. For five years, Lovell kept in a warm room in the basement of the mansion, ate his meals in the President's kitchen, and received payment of ten dollars a month. He told himself that he was secure and happy.

But after Madison's second inauguration, he became melancholy, depressed. He began to feel that his life was ending. At night, he lay awake, thinking of his youth—the early voyages as a cabin boy on an English merchantman; Beatrice Scott, the girl whose beauty inspired him to jump ship in Boston when he was seventeen; the events that brought him to Bunker Hill and placed him on the line between Horace and Ephraim Pratt. The Pratts saved Lovell's life that day, and Lovell never forgot it. He married the girl, went to work for Pratt, and lived in Boston for fourteen years.

When his wife died in childbirth, Lovell took to the sea again. He sailed on a Pratt ship to China, a sixteen-month voyage, but when he returned to Boston, the memories of her lingered. He left the merchant fleet and shipped from Nantucket on a whaler. He lost himself and his memories in the excitement of the hunt and didn't set foot on the American mainland again until he and French John arrived in New York. He wandered to Boston, back to sea, and finally to Washington, where he had remained and begun to grow old.

Then, just after the British clamped their blockade onto the New England coast, his old friend Pratt wrote to him of the price the Golden Eagle Tea set would bring on the European market. They had been plotting ever since.

Now, as Dexter Lovell knelt in front of the strongbox, he realized that the Golden Eagle meant more than money. It offered him one more voyage of adventure, one final encounter with his youth. He would protect the Golden Eagle Tea Set with his life. For the next two weeks, it would be his life.

He turned to leave and saw the figure of Jeff Grew silhouetted in the doorway. Lovell froze.

"I been watchin' you a long time, Dexter Lovell, and I got one thing to say." The black smiled.

"Then say it," barked Lovell, regaining his composure.

"You got a partner."

Dexter Lovell and Thomas Jefferson Grew, linked together by the strongbox they carried between them, left the President's Mansion two hours later and headed toward the Potomac.

They had remained with French John until Madison and his ragged escort had eaten, rested, and continued on to Virginia. Lovell did not want French John to become suspicious at his early departure, and he wanted to wait until dark before sprinting for the river. But when it came time to go, Lovell lingered, knowing he would never see his old friend Sioussa again. Finally, Grew reminded Lovell that the British were drawing close.

"Mais, oui," said French John. "I will put out the cat, lock up, and be off to join the President. I will see you in a few hours."

Lovell had betrayed a friend, but he had no time now for guilt. He wanted to be far down the Potomac when the British torches lit up the sky. As he and Grew scrambled across the meadow which rolled south from the mansion, Lovell felt an excitement he hadn't known since his days on the whaler. Even his hatred for Jeff Grew could not diminish it. But the river was a quarter mile away, the strongbox was heavy, and the ground grew soft and swamplike as they ran. Lovell's excitement turned to agony. His lungs burned. He wanted to stop and rest, but he couldn't. He drove himself to keep up with Grew.

When they reached the bank, they were ankle-deep in mud and soaked with perspiration. Lovell collapsed in exhaustion, and mosquitoes the size of humming birds descended on both of them.

"You must have damn strong sweat," said Jeff Grew, catching his breath. "Most 'skeeters I ever know bite the black man first. Blacker the berry, sweeter the juice. But dem bugs all over you."

Lovell sat up and slapped angrily.

Grew began to laugh. "You know, Dexter Lovell, it's a damn good thing I find you stealin' dat tea set when I do. Otherwise, you never make it across dis here lawn."

Lovell knew the black was right. The strongbox was too heavy for one man, and the tea set was too delicate to be tossed in a sack. He needed Grew's muscle, and later, he might need the machete that Grew had slipped into his belt when they left the mansion. Lovell extended his hand and forced a smile. "I guess I 'ave to take you along, after all."

Jeff Grew heard the white man in Lovell's voice. He didn't like it. In Jamaica, he had cut cane, raised orchids, and earned his freedom by rescuing his master's family from a burning house. In America, he was another nigger. Slave and freedman were treated alike, and it made no difference that the freedman tended the flowers in the President's garden. But Thomas Jefferson Grew was a nigger to be reckoned with. One day soon, he would spit on Dexter Lovell and every white man who ever treated him like a slave.

"I told you back dere, Dexter, you got a partner." Grew's voice was firm. "I let you be boss, 'cause you be smart enough to steal dat tea set in the first place. I figure you know what you doin'. But without me, you never get dis far. I stickin' to you, Dexter, and I gettin' half when dis strongbox gets where we takin' it." Only then did Grew shake Lovell's hand.

They packed the strongbox into a rowboat moored at the bank and headed downstream. Grew pulled at the oars. Lovell took two cumbersome dueling pistols from his shoulder sack, loaded them, and set new flints in each hammer.

"You plannin' to shoot someone?" asked Grew.

"Maybe you." Lovell was only half-joking.

"And maybe some morning, you wake up with my machete in your skull." The black smiled.

The current moved swiftly through the humid Virginia night, and they reached the dock above Greenleaf's Point within half an hour. Greenleaf's Point commanded the junction of the Potomac River with its eastern branch. The city of Washington spread across the triangle of land between the two streams. The American Army had built a shore battery and an arsenal at the fork, and a small community of hotels, saloons, and bawdy houses had sprung up nearby.

Although the main Washington dock was on the east branch, near the Navy Yard, many fishermen and ferry captains kept their vessels near Greenleaf's Point. Lovell had investigated the seamanship, reliability, and character of each one. He jammed both pistols into his belt and left Grew with the strongbox.

"Be 'ere when I get back."

"I ain't goin' noplace, Dexter. We be partners. Besides, somebody see a black man runnin' around with a big strongbox, dey shoot him dead."

Duncan's Blind Pig was the largest tavern on the waterfront. The rest of the dock was deserted, but the Blind Pig shone like a campfire on a stormy night. The sounds of raucous laughter and music, made louder by the surrounding silence, rolled out the door to greet Lovell.

Before going inside, he peered through one of the windows. There were four people in the saloon—Duncan, the wooden-legged barkeep, and three scurvy-looking sailors. One of the sailors, dead drunk, was dancing with Duncan while another played the hornpipe and the third swilled ale straight from the tap.

Lovell entered quietly and stood in the doorway. He was nervous. He gripped his belt tightly so that no one would see his hands shaking, and he waited for the music to stop. Four drunken faces turned to inspect him.

"Come in, mister," said Duncan, whose wooden leg was well proportioned to the rest of his lank body. "Come in and drink your fill. I'll not leave a drop for the bloody British."

"I'm lookin' for Captain Cletis Smith," said Lovell firmly. "I was told I could find him down 'ere." Lovell knew that Smith was an honest man with a vessel large enough for an ocean voyage.

"You been told right, mister," said the barkeep. "He lives on his boat, but he took to the river early this mornin', sayin' he'd give no damn Redcoat the chance to burn the *Rappahannock*. That's his boat."

"Aye," said the man with the hornpipe. "Most captains on the river hauled keel up into Maryland this morning. Them that didn't are off gettin' their fair share of the city's loot before the British do. And then, there's us." The man stood, a scrawny figure with no front teeth and a scar all the way around his neck. "Captain Jack Dawson and Sons. That's Henry drinkin' the beer, and Jeff's the dancer."

Lovell nodded to the two sons, who gazed at him sullenly.

"We own the *Reckless*, that cargo sloop settin' out there, and we're always happy to be of service to a gentleman, even one so muddy as yourself, sir."

Lovell did not look quite as imposing as he'd have liked. His stockings and breeches were covered in mud, and his blouse was soaked through with sweat.

Dawson offered his hand. "Now tell me what three fine sailors can be doin' for you."

Before extending his right hand, Lovell slipped his left around one of the pistols. He knew Dawson to be one of the most scurrilous men on the river. "I need passage down the Potomac . . . tonight."

"Tonight? You're crazy, mister." Jack Dawson and his sons began to laugh.

"Perhaps. But I'm willin' to pay 'andsomely." Lovell was a seaman, but he had never sailed a river at night. With the British Navy anchored ten miles downstream, he wanted an experienced captain to steer him through the sandbars and currents along the bank of the Potomac.

"How handsomely?"

Lovell took a twenty-dollar gold piece from the pouch on his hip and gave it to Dawson.

The captain bit into the coin and nodded his approval. "It's real gold, but I wouldn't sail past a British squadron for ten of these." He dropped the gold piece into his pocket.

"Get me where I'm going, and I'll give you fifty. One thousand dollars. More money than you make in a year."

Dawson's face lit up. "Mister, for a thousand dollars I'd sail up the Thames and shit on London Bridge. Now you just give me the rest and we'll be on our way."

Lovell noticed Duncan reaching behind the bar. He drew both pistols. "'Ands up!"

The barkeep leaped back and threw his hands into the air.

"There's no need to be so jumpy, mate," said Dawson. "We be friendly."

"I don't need friends. I need passage. I'll pay you two 'undred when we cast off, three 'undred at Chesapeake Bay, and the rest when we drop anchor."

"And where might that be?"

"I'll tell you in the mornin'."

Dawson turned to his sons. "The limey gent drives a hard bargain, boys. Are you game for a little adventure?"

"I ain't movin' from the tap till I seen a gold piece," said Henry.

Lovell flipped gold pieces to each of the Dawson boys, who grabbed them like hungry men snatching food.

"It's real gold, Pa," said Henry, weighing the coin in his hand.

"Then I'd say we have a contract." Dawson grinned. His face looked like a skull without crossbones.

Dexter Lovell wasn't turning his back on this cutthroat or his sons for the rest of the night.

Toward one in the morning, as she rode the current close to the lee shore, the *Reckless* rounded into view of H.M.S. *Seahorse*, the forty-gun frigate which led the British squadron. With lanterns extinguished and sails furled, the *Reckless* slipped past, although Jack Dawson nearly tore out the bottom of the boat on a submerged tree.

"Like stealin' breakfast mush from an old maid." Dawson laughed softly, and the journey continued downstream.

In the bow of the thirty-foot sloop, Dexter Lovell sat on his strongbox. He kept his back against a bulwark, both pistols in his lap, and Jeff Grew beside him. All night, he watched the Dawson boys warily, expecting an attack at each bend of the river. All night, the Dawson boys eyed the box, wondering what the man and his slave guarded so diligently, waiting for their father to make his move.

But Jack Dawson concentrated on piloting the *Reckless*. He was accustomed to running in the dark, and he kept in the shadow of the shoreline all night. The British watch never saw him. At three o'clock, he passed the *Euryalus*, the last ship in the squadron. "I think we can relax now," he said.

Dexter Lovell became more vigilant.

Around four, Jeff Grew began to doze.

Lovell nudged him. "'Ave you ever killed a man?"

Grew barely opened his eyes, but his smile told Lovell he was awake. "Easier'n choppin' sugar cane."

"Good."

The sun was half-risen, like a bloodstain on the morning mist, when the *Reckless* reached the mouth of the Potomac.

"Well, mister," announced Dawson cheerfully, "you're in Chesapeake Bay. Henry, let's open some canvas and get this gent where he's goin.'"

Henry leaped into the rigging. Captain Jack and Jeff walked toward the bow.

"I'll be takin' that three hundred now, sir, and I'll be findin' out where we're headed." Dawson casually placed his hand on his pistol. Without warning Lovell stood and fired a ball the size of a marble into Jack Dawson's skull. Like a giant cat swatting birds, Jeff Grew slashed his machete into the rigging. Henry Dawson opened from his balls to his throat. Blood and intestines slopped onto the deck, and Jeff Dawson froze in horror. Lovell leveled the second pistol and fired. It was over in an instant.

Dexter Lovell felt no remorse as he watched the bodies float on the morning tide. They were scum planning to steal his treasure. He did not wonder that they had risked their lives and their ship to bring him past the British Navy. They were simply trying to dull his senses by proving their honesty. But his senses were sharp and getting sharper.

"I never kill three men so fast in all my life," said Jeff Grew.

"We couldn't trust them, Jeff. We had to kill them."

"You can't trust no one, Dexter Lovell."

The black is right, thought Lovell, no one. He smiled and patted Grew on the back. "Now I'll teach you 'ow to be a sailor."

"Where we sailin' to?"

"Boston."

August, 1814. Two hundred and fifty ships, their masts and yardarms stripped, their boards shrinking in the sun, rode at anchor in Boston Harbor. Goods rotted in warehouses. Sailors and dockhands sat in the gloom of waterfront taverns and waited for the war to end. Grass grew through the planking on the wharves. Seagulls circled like buzzards above the fleet. And four miles offshore, the British Navy patrolled the coast, waiting to pounce on anything that made for the open sea.

Every Boston business related to shipping, and that meant every business, suffered through a depression. Ropewalks made no rigging. Sailmakers made no sails. The counting houses needed no help because there was nothing to count. In the offices of Pratt Shipping and Mercantile, on the corner of State Street and Merchants Row, only four men held jobs where fifteen were working in 1811.

Horace Taylor Pratt closed the ledger for the third quarter of 1814 and cursed softly. Not one Pratt ship had cleared for a foreign harbor in months, and since the British had closed their blockade to New England coast trade, his vessels had made no money at all. He ran his hand through his thinning hair and gazed out at the harbor. He was sixty-four years old, his eldest son was dead, and he feared that his empire was beginning to crumble.

"I never thought I'd see a day when Boston Harbor looked like a graveyard," he said softly. "It's a tragedy."

"There's little we can do, Father. The port is closed. 'Our ships in one motion,/once whitened the ocean;/they sailed and returned with a cargo;/Now doomed to decay, they have fallen a prey/to Madison, worms, and Embargo.'" Jason Pratt sat on the edge of his father's desk and recited a popular lyric.

Pratt slammed his hand on the desk. "Our world shrinks with every sunrise, we face the loss of our two newest ships because we lack the cash to meet their payments, and all you can do is recite poetry."

"I'm sorry, sir." Jason was thirty years old, but in his father's presence, he seemed frozen at fifteen. He had his mother's features, a large frame, and a flabby body that he dressed in the latest fashion. He did not look like a Pratt.

"'Madison, worms, and Embargo,' indeed," Pratt hauled himself out of his chair and began to pace about his office. "Those goddam Virginia Presidents. Washington, Jefferson, Madison, they're all the same, with their foolish wars and expansionist dreams. Who needs Canada? Who cares that a few English deserters were taken off American ships and sent back to the Royal Navy, where they belong?"

"The English were impressing American seamen, father," said Jason softly.

"None of mine. Pratt ships hove to for the British hundreds of times without incident. This whole war was cooked up by Southerners and Westerners out to feather their own nests at the expense of the New Englanders who got the damn country started in the first place." His voice rose sharply and his complexion flushed deep red.

"Father, remember your apoplexy."

"Damn my apoplexy. We fought a revolution so that American ships could sail the world without interference from any government, foreign or domestic. Now, a Pratt ship can't sail five miles beyond Boston Light without fearing a broadside."

Jason Pratt knew his father well enough to listen politely whenever a tirade began.

"I intend to support Senator Pickering's resolution for secession. If our government is so blind to our needs that they're willing to declare a war we can't possibly win, with an enemy who doesn't want to fight in the first place, I say we break off and make our own peace."

"An excellent idea," Jason agreed, simply to quiet his father's anger.

The old man paced back and forth, studying the pattern in his oriental carpet and stopping at every turn to inspect the model of the *Gay Head* displayed on the mantel. "That was a ship," he muttered. "Fastest damn schooner I ever saw. She once made the China run in ten months. Now we're facing ruin." Pratt turned to the window and gazed out at the empty harbor.

Jason approached him. "I think it's time we looked away from the sea, Father. The future is in textiles."

"Textiles?" Pratt grunted.

"Yes, sir. Francis Cabot Lowell has completed a mill in Waltham, and several shippers have invested in it. It's an intelligent way to use our capital." Jason hesitated. He could never tell if his father was listening to him. The firmness in his voice diminished. "They believe that within a few years, textile manufacturing will be one of the major industries in America. Perhaps if we free some of the capital that we have invested in—"

"Perhaps nothing." Abigail Pratt Bentley stood imperiously in the doorway, her yellow dress attracting all the light in the dark office. She had her father's prominent nose and firm jaw, but femininity softened her features and made her seem less resolute than she was.

"You have no right to eavesdrop on private conversations," said Jason.

"I hear my daughter." Pratt smiled but did not turn from the window.

"Good afternoon, Father." She approached him and kissed him on the cheek.

He enjoyed the attention but always protested. "Find yourself a young man to kiss. I'm too old."

"You're the only man in my life, Father."

"More's the pity," cracked Jason. "Twenty-four-year-old widows should worry about spinsterhood and leave business to the men."

"To you?" she said evenly.

"We're discussing something of vital importance," said Jason. "I would appreciate it if you left us in peace."

"You're being most disagreeable today, Jason," said Pratt. "This textile business has certainly fueled the fire in that fat belly of yours. Who approached whom about this venture?"

"Francis Cabot Lowell talked with me after services last Sunday. I rode with him yesterday to the Waltham mill."

"Doesn't it seem strange to you that someone so closely related to our competitors would ask you to join him in what promises to be a very lucrative investment? And stranger still that Lowell's own relatives on the Cabot side have not invested a nickel?" His sarcasm had the intended effect.

Jason began to speak, then fell silent.

"You wish to free capital," said Abigail softly. "What capital? Seventy percent of our money is tied up in the harbor. Four Indiamen, eight schooners, and half the property on the waterfront. To sell any of that in this economy, you sell at a loss."

"Quite so," said Pratt.

Ordinarily, Jason did not persist. "We could sell the tobacco lands in Connecticut, our interest in the New Hampshire granite quarries, or the foundry in Vermont."

Pratt did not even look at his son. "Your brother learned well, but I sometimes wonder if I've taught you anything. You do not sell land or business that is earning an excellent profit in order to invest in an industry that, in the past, has shown only the most marginal returns. I see no reason for Mr. Lowell to have any more success than any of his predecessors."

The conversation was over. Pratt dismissed his son with the wave of his hand.

"We will talk again, Father." Jason's eyes shifted to Abigail. "When we can speak without interruption."

"My mind is set," said Pratt.

"Your mind can be changed, but you cannot change the future, once it becomes the present." Jason stalked out of the office.

"Our brother is sounding rather bold today," said Abigail.

"Bold, but stupid."

"I agree with your decision, Father. We must try to hold on until the war is over."

"That's all we can do."

She put her hand on his arm. "Would you care to have lunch with me?"

Abigail worried about her father. Since the imposition of the British blockade, she had been visiting him each day at his office. Early in the war, the British had left the New England ports open in the hope of encouraging secession, and Pratt's trade had flourished. He also had made large profits in the Peninsula trade, supplying wheat to the British troops fighting Napoleon in Spain. Now, the pressures of the blockade weighed heavily on him. He looked forward to his daughter's visits and the distraction she brought. But today, she couldn't brighten his mood.

"I'm not hungry."

"A glass of port might relax you."

"Secession would relax me more. I have a great deal to do, Abigail, so please leave me in peace."

"Very well, Father."

"I'll be home for supper."

For a time, she stood beside him in silence as he gazed out his window at the ships rotting in the harbor. Then, she slipped out.

A younger Horace Pratt might have jumped into textiles. He had been the first to send ships to the Pacific Northwest, where his agents had traded trinkets for otter pelts with American Indians, then otter pelts in Canton for the riches of China. Now, short-term solutions seemed safer than visionary schemes. Horace Taylor Pratt II, heir to Pratt Shipping and Mercantile, was dead, the victim of Jefferson's Embargo Act. Jason Pratt was a dabbler and daydreamer with none of his brother's perseverance. And Abigail Pratt Bentley was a woman. Only the prudent management of existing resources would keep the company solvent until Horace III grew to replace his father in the Pratt hierarchy.

Pratt smiled whenever he thought of the boy. He liked his other grandchildren well enough and thought that Jason's son Artemus might have a bright future, but young Horace was special. At fifteen, he was the image of his father, with the same lean frame and incisive intellect, with the same bright promise for the future of Pratt Shipping and Mercantile.

Pratt turned expectantly when he heard someone at the door. Young Horace had promised to visit.

It was Mr. Howe, Pratt's secretary. "Excuse me, sir. There's a military courier here, says he has a dispatch that must be delivered to you personally."

Pratt was puzzled. "Send him in."

Preceded by the clanking of spurs, the rider entered Pratt's office and saluted. "From the President, sir."

Pratt recognized Dexter Lovell's hand. Clumsily, he ripped the letter open and read it. He wanted to laugh out loud. He was venturing nothing in partnership with a man who was risking his life. If they were successful, he would split twenty thousand dollars, enough to keep the company intact for six more months. In one stroke, he was avenging himself on the Virginia President who started the war and on the Yankee merchants whose gift to the government brought nothing in return but embargoes and blockades. Although he read no verse but Milton, Pratt relished his poetic justice. The Golden Eagle Tea Set was returning to Boston.

44

"I have other dispatches to be delivering in Boston, sir," said the courier. "If you'll excuse me, I'm in a great hurry."

Pratt flipped him a silver dollar. "Be about your business, lad."

"Thank you, sir."

Young Horace III arrived as the courier was leaving.

"Come in and close the door," said Pratt cheerfully.

Dressed only in knee breeches and cotton shirt, Horace was still a boy, although his hands and feet had already grown into manhood. "Hello, Grandfather."

"Can you keep secrets?" asked Pratt.

"Yes, sir."

"Then read this."

Pratt gave the boy Dexter Lovell's note.

"What does it mean?"

"That we are going to make a great deal of money with very little effort. It's the sort of investment I like."

Pratt gave the boy pen and paper and told him to sit at the desk. Lacking a left arm, Pratt found handwriting difficult and dictated most of his correspondence. "Address it to Lord Henry Hannaford, 157 Leicester Street, London. 'Dear Henry,' . . . Did you date it?"

"Yes, sir."

"Bright boy."

Horace had never seen his grandfather so enthusiastic.

"'Dear Henry, The Bird is aloft. Contact the buyer and make him bleed gold.'" Pratt signed his initials and sealed the letter.

Since American correspondence could not travel directly to England, a rider would carry Pratt's letter to Halifax, and from there it would be mailed to London. It was the established channel.

Pratt tossed Lovell's note into the Franklin stove and blew on the coals, which glowed red and began to burn.

"Must you destroy that?" asked the boy.

"Yes."

"I'd like to keep the signature, Grandfather."

"Incriminating evidence, Horace. We can't have it around."

The boy was accustomed to his grandfather's indulgence. "Please, sir?"

"No." said Pratt firmly. "Now come along. I must send this dispatch. Then, we'll have lunch."

The boy noticed that the flames in the stove were dying quickly. "Yes, Grandfather."

When they returned from lunch, Pratt stopped briefly in the outer office to confer with one of his bookkeepers.

Young Horace entered Pratt's office and looked into the stove. The coals had flamed and burned a few bits of trash on the grate, but the letter had barely been touched.

He took it out and examined it. He knew of no one at school who owned President Madison's signature, but he could think of several who would pay handsomely for it. If he used only the flap, he could still destroy the text of the letter. He heard his grandfather's cane tapping toward the door. He jammed the letter into the back of the ledger on the desk. He would return later to claim his prize.

CHAPTER IV

William Rule tightened his tie and slipped into the gray suit jacket that his servant held behind him.

"Will you be needing the car today?" asked the servant, who was also his bodyguard.

"No, Edward. It's a beautiful day. We'll walk."

"Yes, sir. I'll wait outside." Edward spoke very softly and seemed slightly backward, but his loyalty to William Rule was unquestioning and he stood at six feet four.

Rule went into the kitchen, where his third wife was sipping coffee. She was sitting by an open window, and the breeze was carrying the smell of salt air through the house. He came up behind her, slipped his arms around her waist, and kissed her on the back of the neck. She tilted her head back, and he kissed her on the cheek.

"Good morning, Ruley," she purred.

"Hello, babe," he said softly. "Have your suit on and have the boat gassed up. I'm taking the afternoon off."

She rested her head against his chest. "I'll have champagne on ice."

Rule laughed. "Not so fast, babe. Champagne next weekend."

"You've waited a long time for this, Ruley."

"I can wait a little longer before I start poppin' corks all over town." He lowered his voice and spoke with mock disappointment. "For today, I'll have to be happy with poppin' you in the boat."

"And that's too good for you, you son of a bitch."

Rule laughed merrily and headed for the door. "See you at noon."

"Ruley," she said seriously, "stay cool. Don't let them get to you."

"I've got them by the short hairs, babe. If there's any gettin' to be done, I'll be doin' it."

William Rule was thirty years older than his wife. He had picked her out of a Las Vegas chorus line one night when he was in the mood for a brunette, and she had stayed. She was one more symbol of his success, another beautiful possession, like the Lewis Wharf condominium where they lived, the cabin cruiser moored at their front step, the Rolls-Royce, and the Atlantic Avenue offices of William Rule Imports, Inc.

Rule walked out of his building and gazed across the harbor. When he had first come to work on the waterfront in 1938, Lewis Wharf had been a rundown row of warehouses and shipping offices, a remnant of Boston's former greatness. Today, it was part of the renewed city and the home to some of Boston's richest citizens.

Life had been good to William Rule in the last twenty-five years, and the sun felt warm on his face. Everything he owned he had earned himself in his climb from the tenements of the South End to the top of the business world. Beneath the Brooks Brothers suit was the body of a longshoreman, and beneath the black toupee were the heavy features of a Slavic immigrant. But his face showed little of his struggle. He had enjoyed success, savoring his women, his boats, and today, his walk across town.

Philip Pratt and Mr. Soames arrived at the home offices of Pratt Industries fifteen minutes before Rule. After the red-eye special from Los Angeles, Pratt needed a shower, a change of clothes, and a cup of coffee. He wanted to appear rested and relaxed when Rule arrived. His father always told him that the key to success in business was "Look your best and imagine that your adversary is dressed in paisley boxer shorts, dirty T-shirt, and nothing more." Philip Pratt had extended the axiom to every relationship in his life.

❈

As he strolled with Edward across the Public Garden, Rule could admire the Pratt Building on the corner of Arlington Street and Commonwealth Avenue. Five stories of gray sandstone in the French Empire style, one of the first buildings erected in the Back Bay in the 1860s, it was the perfect home for a venerable Boston corporation. From out of that august structure, the tentacles of Pratt Industries spread into electronics, engineering, chemical production, real estate, and entertainment, and William Rule was about to control it all.

The Pratt Industries sign in front of the building was smaller than a doctor's shingle and so overgrown by shrubbery that it was barely visible from the street. The Pratts seemed to consider themselves too important to attract attention. Typical Yankee stupidity dressed up as good taste, thought Rule, the sort of thing that was bringing him to power.

Miss Alice Allardyce ushered Rule into Philip Pratt's office. Secretary to Artemus Pratt IV and now to his son, she had been guarding the door since 1932, and, as she told every visitor, very little had changed in the president's office in the last forty years. Dark mahogany paneling, prints of sea battles and fox hunts, a mammoth desk, oriental carpets, a model of the *Gay Head* on the mantlepiece, the view of the swan boats down in the Public Garden—they were all the same. Only the portrait of Artemus Pratt IV was new. Rule reminded himself to pull it down the day he moved in.

William Rule and Philip Pratt greeted each other with an artificial warmth that expressed their mutual contempt. Pratt was joined by his cousin Calvin, chief legal counsel and member of the board of Pratt Industries; Christopher Carrington, their nephew and a lawyer in Calvin Pratt's firm; and Mr. Soames. Miss Allardyce served coffee in bone china, and the gentlemen sat on the leather sofas in front of the fireplace.

"She's a fine secretary," said Rule. "Do you think she'll stick around after the fifteenth?"

"I see no reason why she would want to leave, Mr. Rule."

Although Philip Pratt's aristocratic tone always irritated him, Rule resolved not to lose his temper. He considered anger one of his best weapons, but he found greater satisfaction in shattering Philip Pratt's icy calm. Whenever they met, he tried to orchestrate his performance with that in mind.

"There's no need for us to be coy, Pratt." Rule paused carefully and sipped his coffee. "We all know what's happening."

"You need a majority of the stockholders to remove us," said Calvin, a tall, balding man with a Phi Beta Kappa key in his vest pocket.

Rule opened his morocco briefcase and took out a piece of paper. "Which one of you wants to read it?"

Calvin Pratt examined the paper. "It's a list of proxies."

Rule settled back and crossed his legs. "And they're all pledged to me."

The color drained slowly from Philip Pratt's face, but his voice remained calm. "We've seen those before, Mr. Rule."

Calvin Pratt smiled. "The names on this list represent only forty-five percent of the voting stock of this corporation, Mr. Rule."

Philip Pratt relaxed. "Yes, and unless I've forgotten my math, that's not enough."

"I wouldn't get too cocky, Pratt. Since that last quarterly statement, you ought to be out sellin' apples." Rule held out his coffee cup. "Would you pour?"

"The company will rebound, Mr. Rule. It always does," said Philip coldly.

Rule filled the cup himself. "This company hasn't rebounded since 1974. In three years, the stock dropped from forty-eight to thirty-three and an eighth, and you're still in this office makin' stupid decisions every time you turn around. It's not gonna go on much longer."

"Mr. Rule, as any Wall Street analyst will tell you, a reduction in the price of stock over a long period of time may indicate a positive retrenchment on the part of a corporation that has overextended itself badly, as we did in the late sixties and early seventies." Calvin Pratt tried to make failure sound like success. He was an excellent lawyer.

"Bullshit!" Rule exploded off the sofa. When he was angry, he had to move. As he crossed the rug, he reminded himself to keep control. He paused at the far side of the room and decided it was time to recite the litany. He turned back to Philip Pratt.

"After the Vietnam War, Pratt chemicals took a nosedive that hasn't stopped. Then the Apollo Program ends, NASA says good-bye, and Pratt Engineering and Electronics is as useless as the moon it landed on. You start makin' computers and components, and when a couple of guys come to you with an idea for a computer

50

game that you rig up to your television set, you tell them to take a running jump. So what happens? They go over to some other company and make millions." Rule's Boston accent grew harsh.

Philip Pratt studied his manicure and pretended not to listen. Calvin Pratt played with his Phi Beta Kappa key. Christopher Carrington took notes. Bennett Soames looked out the window.

"And real estate!" Rule continued. "You have six blocks of rundown granite warehouses on the waterfront. Some small-time company wants to buy them. A lot of people, including me, say, 'Don't do it, the waterfront's comin' back. Look at Quincy Market.' So you sell the warehouses for next to nothing, just to get rid of the damn city tax bill, and those small-timers buy up half the apartment houses in Boston with the profits. Shall I go on?"

"You've made your point quite ably," said Calvin.

Rule glanced at Christopher Carrington, a handsome patrician in his late twenties. "I'll tell one more story for the young man. All about the movies." Rule knew Pratt was especially sensitive about the movie investments. He smiled and approached Carrington, who remained expressionless.

"Your uncle decided he wanted to be in the movie business. Half the members of the board of directors tell him he's crazy. They say movies are a shaky investment, but he thinks he's another Charlie Bludhorn and Pratt Industries has all the clout of Gulf and Western. Then, he goes out and buys forty percent of American Center Films, which hasn't shown a profit since Adolphe Menjou died." Rule glanced at Pratt. He could see the small vein bulging just below Pratt's left eye. Now was the time to condescend. "It wasn't good corporate management, Pratt. If you couldn't buy a chunk of Universal or Paramount, you shouldn't have bought at all."

Philip Pratt was trying not to lose his temper. He walked over to his desk and picked up the *Wall Street Journal*. "You've had your say, Mr. Rule. Thank you and good afternoon. I'm a very busy man."

"Not for long. After the meeting on June fifteenth, you can take that portrait of your old man and that model ship and your subscription to the *Wall Street Journal* and be on your way."

"You can't remove us without fifty-one percent of the stockholders backing you up," snapped Calvin Pratt.

Rule paused and looked around the room. The announcement was premature, but he couldn't resist. "In ten days, I'll have the six percent, gentlemen. I guarantee it."

Rule was disappointed in the Pratts' reaction. He hoped they would beg to negotiate, but they remained silent. He wanted to see them squirm, but they stared at him, as though they were waiting for him to finish his speech.

Paisley boxer shorts and dirty T-shirt. Philip Pratt would not allow himself to lose control. He would not give this crudity any satisfaction. "Thank you very much, Mr. Rule, and good luck in your hunt for stockholders." Pratt turned to Soames. "Do we have any more appointments this morning, Bennett, or do you think I can sneak in eighteen holes at the country club?"

"You're clear this afternoon," said Soames crisply.

Calvin Pratt and Christopher Carrington stood.

"I'd better be running," said Calvin. "I'm due in court in a half an hour."

Soames picked up the telephone. Carrington began to pack his briefcase. Suddenly, no one was paying attention to William Rule. If he hadn't been its victim, he would have admired the technique.

"I'll call the club and get you a starting time," said Soames.

"Very good." Pratt busied himself with the newspaper.

William Rule would have the last word. He stepped close to Pratt and peered over the newspaper. "Stick around today," he said softly, like an old friend giving advice. "Admire the leather and the mahogany and the picture of your old man. Take a few phone calls. Turn a few down. Try to remember what it feels like to run the show. Ten days from now, you'll have all the time in the world to play golf."

Rule turned to leave.

Philip Pratt lost control. He jumped between Rule and the door. "You listen to me, you ignorant rug merchant. We've controlled this company for two hundred years, and we'll control it for two hundred more." Pratt's voice sounded like a bar fight about to happen. "You back out now, or we'll destroy you. I promise you."

Rule laughed in Pratt's face and left. Infuriated, Pratt started after him. He took three steps into the outer office and stopped abruptly.

"Mr. Pratt, this is Edward," said Miss Allardyce nervously. "He's Mr. Rule's butler."

Edward stood in front of Pratt, and somewhere on the other side of him, Rule was laughing.

"Good day, Mr. Pratt. See you in ten days," said Rule. "And Miss Allardyce, you make excellent coffee."

"Thank you, sir." The old woman was trembling.

Calvin Pratt led Philip back to the inner office. "We can do without an assault and battery charge right now, Philip. Especially if you're the one getting assaulted."

Philip Pratt was the sort who punched people or walls when he lost his temper, but he held back, remembering the broken knuckles from his last tantrum. "That son of a bitch laughed at us. He really thinks he has us."

"I think he might," said Calvin. He was five years older than Philip and much more willing to accept the circumstances of his life, which were enviable, regardless of the fate of Pratt Industries. He had a successful law practice, a home in Lexington, a son on the staff of Massachusetts General Hospital and another in Harvard Law School, and he had been happily married to the same woman for thirty-five years.

"I suggest," said Carrington, "that we determine the nine or ten major stockholders most likely to shift allegiance and begin to work on them. Our family has forty percent of the stock. Rule controls forty-five. That leaves fifteen percent uncommitted. We have a lot of convincing to do in ten days."

"I agree," added Calvin. "The McCafferty block is wavering. And over at Aldrich and Bradfield, Jeff Hendricks tells me they're considering a pullout unless things improve. They might decide to throw their portfolio behind Rule just to see what he can do."

"We can tell all these people that the E. and E. wing has a lock on the NASA Venus program," said Carrington.

Calvin shook his head. "That's our big item, but it's still a year away."

"Gentlemen," said Soames, "I think we're forgetting the most direct way to keep Mr. Rule out of this office."

Philip Pratt had cooled off. "We haven't forgotten, Bennett. Rule has given us a deadline, and we'll meet it. We find that tea set in ten days, he's finished, and we stay right where we are."

"We should be proceeding very carefully in this tea-set business, gentlemen," cautioned Calvin.

"We should be proceeding as businessmen, not treasure hunters," said Christopher. "We're being totally unprofessional."

Philip turned angrily on the young man. "You're the one who discovered Abigail Pratt's diaries, Christopher. You led us into this. You have the most to lose if Rule takes over. So do what we ask you."

"When Abigail Pratt Bentley wrote about the Golden Eagle, she was a crazy old lady filling the pages with daydreams. I'm convinced that the tea set has been found, and William Rule found it."

"If he did, he's going to make us look much worse than we do already." Philip Pratt looked at his father's portrait. Artemus Pratt IV seemed sated, almost serene, like a man who had just finished a good meal. Philip shook his head in disgust. "The old man would just shit."

Peter Fallon hadn't thought of the Golden Eagle, Gravelly Point, or DL in almost twenty-four hours. It was eleven o'clock the next evening when he lurched out of a subway in South Boston and into a quilt of humid air. He needed a shave, he had a black eye, his shirt was filthy, and his pants were torn at both knees. During his ten-minute subway ride from downtown, the first heat wave of the summer had arrived, and that called for a beer.

The Rising Moon, near the union hall on Broadway, was a neighborhood bar with a set of regular drinkers and local drunks who thought of their saloon as a sanctuary, a place for guzzling beer and downing shots, for watching sports on color TV and escaping the wife when she began to nag. It was a narrow, crowded dump, with a row of booths along one wall and a few tables in the middle of the floor. Three fans blew hot air around, and when the Rising Moon didn't smell like stale beer, it stank of fresh piss.

For some reason, Thursday nights were usually slow. Somebody was asleep at one of the tables. A few regulars sat at the bar and watched glumly as Luis Tiant, in pinstripes, pitched against the Red Sox. Jackie Halloran and Denny Murphy nursed their beers and strained to hear a conversation between two men in the corner booth.

Kenny Gallagher stood behind the bar and swatted flies with a wet rag. A smiling balloon of a man with a whiskey-red complexion that looked permanently sunburned, he had tended bar at the Rising Moon six nights a week for the last eleven years. When he saw Peter Fallon in the doorway, he drew a draft and placed it on the bar. "Right over here, Pete. Sit down and beat the heat with a brew on the house. No Yankee fans or beer farts allowed, but anything else is all right with old Kenny."

Fallon approached the bar very slowly. "Hi, Kenny."

Gallagher knew that Fallon was drunk and that Fallons were mean drunks. Whenever he had to handle one of them, he thanked St. Jude that the Fallons didn't drink too often. "Now, Peter, sit down and relax and tell me what you've been up to the last few months." Gallagher had a smile for everyone, but he genuinely liked Peter. He'd known him since the day he was born.

"Has my brother come in here tonight?" Fallon was in no mood for pleasantries.

Gallagher leaned across the bar and placed a hand on Peter's shoulder. If he'd wanted, he could have broken Fallon's collarbone, but Gallagher was always gentle with children, animals, and drunks. "Sit down, Peter."

"Where's my fuckin' brother?" Fallon pulled away.

"Now don't let's have no trouble, Peter," pleaded Kenny. "Every damn time you come in here, there's a fight."

"I'm over here, Peter." The voice came from the corner booth.

"I want no trouble," warned Kenny.

"No trouble," said Fallon.

The man seated with Danny Fallon moved over, and Peter slid into the booth opposite his brother. The Fallons were both Irish, but there the tribal resemblance ended. Peter, with dark hair and wiry build, was one of the Black Irish, as his father liked to say. Danny, at thirty-two, was the beer-and-potatoes South Boston Harp. His face was weathered from years of outdoor work. His hands were large and callused. His body was solid, and even his gut looked like muscle.

Peter smiled drunkenly at his brother.

Danny didn't smile back. He was half-drunk himself. "The rah-rah boy from Harvard, all messed up and lookin' like a goddam rummy. You been on another bender or somethin'?"

Peter continued to smile. He loved to hear his brother's South Boston accent. He imagined the words traveling out of Danny's throat, stopping in his sinuses to drop off all the r's, then squirting out into the air. "Why is it that half the guys in Boston sound like they're holdin' their nose when they talk, Dan?"

"Cut the shit. I asked you a question. Have you been on another bender?"

Fallon was annoying his brother, and that was the whole purpose of his visit. "I spend most of my life looking through the wrong end of the telescope, Dan. Every so often, I like to see life up close. So I go on a bender. I've been drunk, I was almost rolled in the men's room of Kelleher's on Summer Street, and now it's time to go back to work."

"So I ain't stoppin' you. Go back to work. If that's what you call it, sittin' in a library all day readin'."

"Since I spent all my money on Jameson's and beer, I need twenty-five bucks till the end of the month." Peter held out his hand.

The little man sitting next to him in the booth began to laugh. In his maroon double-knit suit, Jerry Sheldon looked like a bookie, but tonight he was the mouthpiece for a local loan shark. "Your brother could use twenty-five bucks himself, kid. He could use twenty-five thousand bucks eight or nine times over."

Danny turned angrily on Sheldon. "You've had your earful. Now shut the fuck up and beat it."

Sheldon squeezed past Peter and headed for the door. "Remember our offer."

"Fuck the offer," said Danny.

"Do what you want."

"I really like your suit," said Peter.

"Your brother's a smartass, Danny. Teach him a few manners." Sheldon left the bar.

For a moment, the brothers stared at each other across the table, each waiting for the other to speak.

As usual, Danny gave up first. "When was the last time you talked to the old man?"

Peter had to think. He didn't enjoy conversations with his father and tried not to remember them. "A month, maybe."

"A month." Danny shook his head. "And you haven't talked to me since the last time you were in here."

"The phone works boths ways."

"If you stuck your nose into the family business a little more often, you'd know that Fallon and Son Construction Company is on the ropes."

"That's happened before." Peter seemed unconcerned.

"Not like this time," said Danny bitterly. "The old man bit off too much, he's got no place to spit it out, and the fuckin' creditors are climbin' down his throat. Things look bad."

"That's for fuckin' sure," said Jackie Halloran from a nearby table.

"Who asked you?" snapped Danny.

"If your old man goes under, I lose a job, and so do most of the guys who come in this bar."

"Well, then you can spend your afternoons in here too, so cheer up."

"Shoot the shit with Jackie later," cracked Peter. "I'm getting sleepy."

"Sheldon's right, Dan. Your brother's still a smartass," said Jackie.

"Nobody's talkin' to you, Jackie. Watch the ballgame." Danny turned to Peter, whose disinterested gaze always made him mad. His brother never seemed to care about anything but his history books, his benders, and the undergraduate girls he went through like beers on Gallagher's bar. "You walk in here stiff drunk, you treat Kenny and Jackie like shit." Danny lowered his voice. "You insult

Sheldon, not that I give a fuck, and you aren't even upset to find out that we're up to our asses in debt. What the hell's wrong with you?"

Peter shrugged. "We all got our problems, Danny." As he spoke, he began to duck. He knew what was coming.

Danny snapped a backhander across the table and caught Peter off the side of the head. Peter tumbled onto the floor, rolled quickly to his feet, and swung. He caught Danny under the chin and almost lifted him out of the booth. Anybody else would be gone for the night, but Danny hit his brother with a shoulder about waist high and the two of them flew halfway across the barroom.

"I told you two, no trouble," shouted Gallagher, while Halloran, Murphy, and the other regulars got out of the way and watched the fight.

Peter clipped Danny with a left that slammed him against the bar. Danny countered with a right that knocked Peter on his tail and knocked the wind right out of him. Before they wrecked the Rising Moon, Gallagher jumped between them and straight-armed Danny to the bar.

"You stay right where you are, Peter," he growled. "Every goddam time you come in here, there's a fight."

Fallon smiled and leaned back on his elbows. "You can relax, Kenny. It's all over."

"Just like that?"

"Once in a while, I need to blow off some steam, Kenny. So I come over to Southie and pick a fight with my brother."

"Well, stop pickin' it in here. I'm gettin' old." Kenny released Danny.

"Bring us two cold ones." Danny seemed as relieved as his brother.

"No sir. If you boys want any more to drink tonight, you take it here where I can keep my eye on you."

The Fallons sat at the bar like a pair of chastened schoolboys, and Kenny drew two drafts.

"I gotta straighten you out," said Danny. "Every couple of months, you go on a bender and get into a fight. You better watch out, because someday you're gonna pick a fight in the wrong bar and they'll carry you home in a plastic bag."

"I don't pick fights with anybody but you, and it's the benders that straighten me out."

For the next half hour, they sipped their beer and talked about the fortunes of the family company. Fallon and Son was a small contracting outfit that specialized in masonry, carpentry, and plumbing. In the last year, with rising costs and lack of work, they had sunk slowly into debt. Now they owed their creditors $150,000, they were facing bankruptcy, and Jerry Sheldon had offered a short-term solution.

It was midnight when Danny finished the story. The ballgame was over, and most of the regulars had gone home. Jackie Halloran was sitting with the Fallons. Kenny Gallagher was cleaning up.

"I'm sorry that you're goin' down the drain, but there isn't much I can do to help, Dan." Peter sounded depressed. His drunk was over. He would have to face his work again. "I feel like I'm goin' down the drain myself."

"Just come around more often, kid. Tell the old man you'll do what you can, even if you can't do anything."

Peter looked into the bottom of his beer glass and laughed softly. "Then he'll say, 'If you want to do somethin', go to law school."

Danny placed a hand on his brother's shoulder. "He's on your side, no matter what you think."

"Always slow on Thursday nights," said Kenny. "I think I'll close 'er up and take a few shots myself."

"You nip all night, Kenny Gallagher," said Jackie.

"I sip beer. There's a difference." Kenny flipped off the neon sign in the window and began to sweep the place out.

A young man of about thirty appeared in the entrance. He was slender, with an angular face, pockmarks, and a receding hairline. Fallon glanced at him briefly and noticed that he was wearing a heavy tweed sportcoat, despite the heat.

"Hey, buddy, we're closed," said Gallagher.

"I'm looking for Kenny Gallagher," said the man.

"You've found him, mister." Kenny approached the man. "What can I do for you?"

Fallon heard a noise like a firecracker going off under a pillow. Kenny Gallagher's body snapped as though someone had hit him in the stomach, then a patch of red appeared just below Kenny's left shoulder blade. Two more muffled explosions, another blossom of red. Even at close range, only two of the .22 caliber slugs made it through Kenny's bulk. The gunman was gone before his victim hit the floor.

The three men at the bar stood in shock until a rush of adrenalin sobered them up. Danny and Jackie went after the gunman. Peter sprang to Kenny's side and rolled him over. Kenny was dead. There was nothing Fallon could do. He sat back on his heels and cursed softly to himself.

Danny and Jackie returned without a clue. No gunman, no gun, no license number.

"Who the hell would want to kill Kenny Gallagher?" said Jackie.

Peter Fallon spent the night at his brother's house in South Boston. Danny, his wife Sheila, and their three children lived in a comfortable semidetached house on Pleasure Bay, with a view of the harbor, the container storage facility on Castle Island, and the Columbia Point Housing Project. Peter's parents, Tom and Maureen Fallon, lived on the other side of the house.

At seven o'clock that morning, little Jimmy Fallon burst into his parents' room with the morning paper. Daddy and Uncle Peter were on the front page, witnesses to a murder. Jimmy didn't notice until later that Kenny Gallagher, who always brought him candy, was the victim.

"Jesus Christ," said Danny at breakfast. "Our pictures and your name."

Peter looked at the photograph. It showed himself, Danny, and Jackie standing over the shrouded body of Kenny Gallagher. "'Peter Fallon of Cambridge,'" he read, "'was in the Rising Moon at the time of the shooting, but he could not provide an accurate description of the gunman.' That's because I was drunk."

"And as far as the cops are concerned, you stay that way. You didn't see a thing, Peter. That guy gets it in his head that you got a fix on him, he may try to fix you."

"What do you mean?" Sheila stopped washing dishes for a moment. She was an ex-cheerleader a few pounds on the wrong side of voluptuous.

"He means nothing," said Peter. "I saw a receding hairline and a tweed coat. There's no way I could pick him out in a lineup, and it says so right in the article. So relax."

That afternoon, the Fallons told two detectives what they knew, which wasn't much, although Danny suggested a motive. He told them that Gallagher had recently begun to book ballgames and races, and he hadn't been cutting "the big boys" in on the profits.

"He never told us who 'the big boys' were," explained Danny, "but I'm sure you fellas have some idea of who he was talking about."

The detectives thought Danny's explanation was sound. The killing had the earmarks of a gangland assassination. The killer worked in the open. He used a .22 caliber pistol, the new gangland signature weapon. And someone had ransacked Kenny's apartment, probably looking for books and betting receipts.

"This is the sort of murder that's rarely solved," said one detective. "We've had hundreds of these cases over the years, but frankly, they're low-priority unless the D.A. has the hots for a few crimefighter headlines. As a rule, as long as they're killing each other, nobody seems to get too excited."

"How can you say that?" protested Peter. "Kenny Gallagher was a good man. He was no criminal."

"Makin' book is a crime," said the detective. "I'm not sayin' we won't find out who killed your friend, but I'm not too optimistic."

Philip Pratt read the morning paper with great interest. At noon, he had lunch with Mr. Soames and Christopher Carrington in his office. He showed Soames the photograph of Fallon. "Harrison is certain this is the man?"

"Yes. He claimed he was some sort of graduate student."

"Then perhaps he is some sort of graduate student," said Carrington impatiently. "Not everyone works for Mr. Rule."

"At the moment, we can't assume that," said Soames. "I've placed him under surveillance."

"Ridiculous," said Carrington.

Soames stared at the young man but said nothing.

"You must admit he's been all over the place lately," offered Pratt. "One day he's worming his way into Searidge, the next night he's at the scene of a murder in a South Boston dive. He leads a very unusual life. I think it would be fascinating to follow him around, simply to find out what else he does with his time. Who knows what he may stumble onto next?"

"The surveillance shall continue, then?" asked Soames.

"Don't let the son of a bitch out of your sight."

Christopher Carrington finished his coffee and left.

In a single apartment overlooking a laundromat in Everett, the man with the pockmarks and the receding hairline read the newspaper. He wondered if he should eliminate the witness. He had never bothered before. Witnesses were always too shocked to describe him, and this guy Fallon was probably no different.

Besides, he killed only for pay. If his employer wanted the witness out of the way, he would know about it.

Jack C. Ferguson found his morning newspaper, as usual, on an abandoned table in Waldorf's. He dressed in khaki work shirt and shiny pants. He had a barrel chest, a huge head, and a mane of white hair hidden under a Red Sox cap. With a shower and a new set of clothes, he might have looked distinguished, but he smelled as if he hadn't bathed in months. He drank whatever coffee was in the cup beside the newspaper and left.

He walked down Washington Street beneath the shadow of the elevated, then down a side street toward a row of derelict apartments, half of them burned out, all of them boarded up. He was in the South End in the deteriorating stretch of buildings between Dover Street and the Cathedral. As he walked, he surveyed the empty wine bottles strewn about, hoping to find a few drops someone had missed, and he glanced over his shoulder every few seconds to make sure that no one was following him. He sneaked down an alley beside the row, then ducked into a cellar door. Inside it was dark and damp, and the sweet charcoal smell of scorched timber mingled with the stench of puke and piss.

He heard something move in the shadows. A switchblade appeared in his hand. He stepped closer. Four rats the size of small dogs scurried away from a body in the corner. Ferguson couldn't tell if the bum was alive or dead. Better off dead, he thought. Carefully, he approached. It might be a trick. He kicked the body in the ribs. The bum groaned, then rolled over. Ferguson kicked again, harder. No reaction. In that condition, the bum was harmless, and Ferguson left him where he was.

Jack C. Ferguson lived four flights up, in an attic room equipped with a Coleman stove, a gas lamp, and a bed made of newspapers. He had booby-trapped the stairways and strung tin-can alarms in all the hallways. No one could get to him without his knowing it.

He scanned the front page quickly and noticed the report of a murder in South Boston. He cut it out and put it into a shoebox that was filled with clippings, all alphabetically arranged, on every murder committed in Boston in the last seven years. Kenny Gallagher, fifty-six, of South Boston, was the victim. Peter Fallon, twenty-six, of Cambridge, was the witness. He memorized the names and ages of both men, then turned to the sports page.

Peter Fallon spent the afternoon with his mother. She and Kenny were childhood sweethearts, and they had remained close friends through the years. Maureen Fallon was a heavy-set woman with eyes that seemed resigned to the inevitable pain of life, and she accepted Kenny's death calmly.

"We know neither the day nor the hour," she said softly, the sound reminding Fallon of whispered prayers in a confessional. "It's God's will. Did he make an Act of Contrition?"

"No, Ma."

"He was a good man. I wouldn't worry." She paused for a long time and thought about Kenny.

Fallon marveled at the strength of Irish women in the face of death or unhappiness. Their faith and fatalism sustained them through anything. The men might go to pieces, but the women were like rocks.

"Would you like a cup of tea, Peter?"

"No, Ma. I gotta go."

"Won't you stay to see your father?"

"I have a lot of work to do."

She smiled. "He still loves you, Peter."

"I know, Ma." He kissed her on the cheek and went next door.

Peter found Danny in the basement playroom. He was sipping beer and watching Bugs Bunny with his kids. "I'm takin' off, Dan."

"Don't you think you oughta stick around and see the old man? He had some paperwork to do. He'll be home early."

"I'm two days behind in my work. I'll see him at the wake."

"Suit yourself. I'll call you when they release the body."

"You think they'll find any relatives?"

"Ma was the closest thing Kenny had to a sister. I don't think there's anybody else, but they'll keep the body on ice and make a search. Should be a couple of days."

"He'll be ripe enough to split open by then."

"Let's hope he's in the box when he does," said Danny, and both brothers laughed at the bad joke. "That poor, fat son of a bitch," blurted Danny, suddenly holding back tears. "I told him there was no future in bookin' numbers."

"Danny," said Peter, just loud enough to be heard over Elmer Fudd, "sometimes I think there's no future in anything." Peter headed for the door.

"Hey." Danny's voice was stern. "Don't be talkin' like that."

No future in anything. The words rattled through Fallon's head once more as he opened the door to his apartment. He had lived in three small rooms near Harvard Yard for nearly four years, and his life had not changed appreciably in that time. He still saw the back of Lamont Library from his front windows. He still lived alone, although a girl from the Law School had shared his bed for over a year. He was still telling himself that the place was cheap, convenient, and he might as well stay because he couldn't find anyplace better.

He thought about going down to the river and taking out a scull for an hour. It was still light, and he could use the exercise to sweat out the last remnants of hangover and get into the mood to write. Fallon rowed every morning, and whenever he had a bad day, he rowed in the afternoon. Without the scull, he knew he'd be on a bender every few days. Rowing was smooth and rhythmic. It helped him to relax. It kept him in condition. But on hot, muggy nights, the Charles River smelled like dead carp. He decided to stay in.

He took a container of yogurt and a can of beer out of the refrigerator. That was his supper.

An hour later, Fallon was trying to say something fresh about Jefferson's Embargo Act. He studied his notes from the Pratt ledger books of 1808 and searched for a theme. All he could see was Kenny Gallagher's body jumping involuntarily as the bullets slammed into it. He couldn't concentrate. He looked through his bookcase for something distracting.

The Day They Burned the White House was a first-person account of the British march on Washington, written by a modern journalist. It was the sort of popular history Fallon never read but people always gave him for Christmas. He opened to the index and ran his finger down the "L" column. Latrobe, Lafitte, Lear, Lee, Lovell. He stopped. Lovell, Dexter, 185. D.L. This is too easy, he thought.

He flipped to page 185 and searched for the name.". . . two servants, Dexter Lovell and Thomas Jefferson Grew, disappeared. . . ." Fallon jumped back to the beginning of the paragraph. "The only treasure that Dolley Madison could not save was Paul Revere's Golden Eagle Tea Set. It disappeared and was never seen again. Two servants, Dexter Lovell and Thomas Jefferson Grew, disappeared along with it. We have often speculated that they made some sort of deal with the British and the work of art is now drunk from regularly in an English country manor where they still think of us as Colonials."

An incident in Pratt's life leaped to Fallon's mind. At a banquet held for President Washington in 1789, Pratt had raised hell because the merchants of Boston had given Washington a Revere tea set called the Golden Eagle. He should have thought of it the moment he saw Dexter Lovell's note.

Fallon was excited. He realized that the Golden Eagle story was simply an interesting footnote to his dissertation, something to brighten up the dull prose. Like most Yankee shippers who founded fortunes, Pratt smuggled, privateered, and traded opium when he smelled a profit. Acting as a middleman in an art theft wasn't unusual. Except that the tea set disappeared and, apparently, had never been found. If it was still out there undiscovered, it was worth a great deal of money to the person who found it. If it was in someone's silver cabinet, its journey would make a great story. Fallon had to know more.

He found Evangeline Carrington's number in the book.

"Hello." It was only nine o'clock, but her voice sounded thick, drowsy. In the background, Fleetwood Mac played loudly.

"Is this Evangeline Carrington?"

She turned down the record. "Who is this?"

"Peter Fallon."

"Who?"

Fallon recounted their meeting and told her he'd like to have lunch with her.

"Why?" she asked abruptly.

"Because I'm interested in your family history and there are a few questions I'd like to ask you." He decided not to mention the tea set.

"I told you, my brother is the family historian. Talk to him."

"I intend to, but I'd like to talk with you first."

Family historians usually knew enough about their ancestors to withhold information that might seem scandalous or potentially profitable to an outsider. Fallon hoped the girl might reveal something unknowingly.

"I don't see why. I'm not at all interested in the Pratts."

"Well, I'm also interested in cars, and I really like your Porsche."

"Then have lunch with my Porsche."

Fallon tried for wit, but he sounded stupid, and she hung up.

At the Book Cellar, an all-night bookstore on Mt. Auburn Street, Fallon bought a copy of Walter Muir Whitehill's *Boston: A Topographical History*. He did not notice that a young man in a dark sweatshirt had followed him on his errand and had written down the title of the book. When Fallon returned to his apartment, the man returned to a black Oldsmobile parked across the street.

Fallon opened his last can of Narragansett and settled in with his book. The man in the Oldsmobile drank coffee and watched Fallon's windows.

Fallon discovered that Gravelly Point no longer existed, but Whitehill provided a series of old engineering maps which traced its fate.

In 1814, Boston was a peninsula connected to the mainland by a narrow isthmus called the Neck. On the west side of the peninsula, a square mile of salt marshes and tide flats stretched along the Charles River Basin. Since the area was on the landward, or back, side of the peninsula, it was known as the Back Bay. Gravelly Point was a deserted spit of land that curled into the Back Bay like a fist aimed at the city. The Easterly Channel, which Lovell had mentioned in his note, sliced through the Back Bay and connected to Gravelly Point at the wrist.

Fallon knew that, at high tide, most of the flats were covered in two to three feet of water. He assumed that the Easterly Channel, formed by a stream that flowed into the basin, was several feet deeper. From the map, he could tell that the channel was anywhere from five to twenty-five feet across, and its boundaries were formed by the mean low-tide lines in the bay. When the rest of the Back Bay was mud, there was still water in the Easterly Channel.

The second map showed the area in 1836. A street now crossed Gravelly Point. A mill dam, which regulated the flow of water into the Back Bay, stretched from Sewall's Point in Brookline to the foot of Beacon Hill. Two railroad lines crossed the marsh. The Public Garden, which did not exist in 1814, now extended west from the city on reclaimed land. The dividing and filling of the Back Bay had begun.

In 1861, the marsh had shrunk by half, new streets stretched toward Gravelly Point, and the Mill Dam had become Beacon Street. By 1888, the marsh was gone. Gravelly Point had been swallowed by the landfill and become part of the Back Bay, Boston's most exclusive section.

When Fallon thought of the Back Bay, he saw Commonwealth Avenue, broad, tree-lined, graced by some of the finest nineteenth-century architecture in America. Or Copley Square, with Trinity Church on the east, the Public Library on the west, and the windows of the Hancock tower above. Or Symphony Hall. Or First Church of Christ Scientist. Or the Esplanade. But, as he finished his beer and turned out the light, he tried to imagine the Back Bay as it had looked on a September night in 1814.

CHAPTER V   *September 1814*

Horace Taylor Pratt's carriage pulled slowly away from his house on Pemberton Hill and headed down Court Street. It was midnight. Except for the saloons and taverns still throbbing with life, the city was still. An early autumn chilled the air. A layer of clouds swallowed the moon and promised rain before morning.

From her bedroom window, Abigail Pratt Bentley watched the carriage swing through a pool of light beneath a street lamp and turn south onto Tremont Street. For three nights, her father, her nephew, and Wilson, the family's footman, had been leaving the house—an hour later each night—and not returning until daybreak. Each morning, her father had become more nervous and irascible.

When she asked him the nature of his nocturnal travels, he told her that he and the boy were fishing the night tides. She laughed and asked him playfully if a one-armed man could bait a hook. He left the room without answering.

She sat on the edge of the bed and wondered if she should follow the carriage. Unlike most young Boston women, she rode well and kept a horse for her weekend gallops into the countryside. She could easily trail the carriage and find out where they were going. She knew that her father was unpredictable, and he had become increasingly volatile as the war quickened his advance into old age. Now that she was mistress of his house, it was her duty to know that he was not endangering his grandson or himself.

She removed her robe and began to dress. Her body was lithe and athletic, with firm, muscular legs and breasts that turned up petulantly, like pouting children. She was proud of her body. Most women of her age and class had already begun to slide away from youth. They ate too much, bore too many children, and never exercised, a practice considered most unladylike. Or they ate too little and spent their days playing the spinet while waiting for their husbands to come home. Abigail Pratt Bentley had waited for one husband who went to sea. She would not wait for another, and she would not see her body grow old before its time.

A knock at the door. Abigail wrapped her robe around herself once more. "Yes?"

The door opened and a dark-haired apparition in a white night-gown appeared at the threshhold. Franconia Hampshire Pratt was tall, slender, and impossibly frail, with the frightened eyes of a deer venturing too close to man.

"Abigail, are you awake?" Franconia spoke to the bed.

"Yes, Franconia," said Abigail gently.

Franconia was startled to hear the voice coming from the shadows. She jumped back.

"Relax, dear," said Abigail. "What's troubling you?"

Franconia took a tentative step. She was the widow of Horace Pratt II. "It's young Horace. He's gone. And so is Father. I'm terribly worried."

Abigail smiled. "Go back to sleep, Franconia. They've gone fishing on the night tide."

"Fishing?" Franconia sat on the edge of Abigail's canopied bed and stared into space. "Then it's true."

"What's true?"

"What Father says about the war. It's ruined us. We can't even afford to buy food. Our men must sneak off at night to bring home what we eat."

Abigail sat next to Franconia and put an arm around her shoulder. "Father pampers young Horace terribly, dear. When the boy said he wanted to fish at night, away they went. I assure you, we're not starving."

"And we'll have food on the table if they don't go fishing?"

"Yes, dear."

Franconia smiled. Almost as an afterthought, she became angry. "Well, I wish Father would tell me these things. He acts sometimes as though young Horace were his son and I a dotty old aunt interfering in the boy's upbringing. I am his mother, and I should know when he's going off fishing at midnight."

"I agree. We shall have a long talk with both of them in the morning." Whenever Franconia was upset, Abigail promised a long talk in the morning. It always soothed her.

"That won't be necessary," said Franconia after a moment's thought. "Father loves Horace. That's all that matters."

Abigail led Franconia back to her room and put her to bed. It was too late to go riding after the carriage now. Abigail herself would have a long talk with Father in the morning. Unless he came home with fresh flounder.

The carriage rocked down Tremont Street, past Gardiner Greene's hillside estate and King's Chapel. When it rolled past the Old Granary Burying Ground, Horace Taylor Pratt tipped his broad-brimmed hat and bowed his head. He owned as much real estate in that cemetery as he did on the waterfront, and he had been paying his respects for forty years. His brother Ephraim, three of his children dead in infancy, and his wife Alicia, who had died in 1805, were all buried there. And headstones above empty graves com-memorated his son Horace and son-in-law James Bentley, both lost at sea. Soon enough, he told himself, he would be taking his place beside his wife and his left arm, which he had buried in the family plot after Bunker Hill, but he did not intend to go into the ground without a fight, and not until the future of Pratt Shipping and Mercantile was secure.

The carriage swept past the new Park Street Church, with its majestic steeple reaching higher than anything else in the city, and then along the Boston Common Mall, recently planted with a row of elms that as yet resembled large twigs stuck in the mud.

Pratt shivered. He pulled his cape tight around his shoulders, but it didn't warm him. The ride down Tremont Street, especially at night, when the new buildings were all in shadow, chilled him deep in the pit of his stomach. He was passing his own gravesite with his grandson at his side. He told himself he should contemplate the renewing cycle of life, but he could think only on its inevitable change.

In his boyhood, Tremont Street and the Common had been rural countryside, and the city had been clustered near the waterfront. A granary had stood on the site of the Park Street Church, and Pratt had bought wheat and rye there for his mother's baking. Pratt's father had been a sailmaker who also kept dairy cows. Each morning, young Horace Pratt had milked the cows, then led them from the family home on Summer Street up to the Common pastureland. Horace had always favored the grazing on Beacon Hill, just above the Common. Although John Hancock's family had owned the land, they rarely bothered if a few cows strayed up from the public pasture. On warm summer afternoons, Horace would lie on top of the hill, stare out to the ships moving through the harbor, and wonder what strange ports they had seen, what exotic cargoes they carried. Today, there were so few cows within the city that it was necessary to import manure each spring to keep the Common green. And the Statehouse, with its gleaming copper dome, sat in Hancock's pasture like a Greek temple above its Athens.

Farther down the street, where the hay scales, a school, and a theatre had once stood, the Colonnade Row, a quarter mile of red-brick townhouses, looked out across the Common toward the Back Bay. And even that was changing. In 1795, its waters had washed against the west edge of the Common. Then, land developers had cut off the top of Mt. Vernon Hill, dumped it onto the flats, and fashioned Charles Street, an approach road to the houses they built on the remnants of the hill.

Pratt's city was changing as quickly and inexorably as his body was deteriorating. He prayed for just a few more years to prepare his company and his heirs for the future galloping toward them. He had worked too hard building Pratt Shipping and Mercantile to see it die when he did. Just a few more years under his direction and the company would last. Just a few more years to train young Horace, and Pratt could pass on in peace, for as long as young Horace or his descendants directed the company, Horace Taylor Pratt would live.

Through the trees on the Common, Pratt could see the dark waters of the Back Bay stretching off toward Gravelly Point. Someplace out there, he hoped to find a few more months for himself and his company. If only Lovell would arrive.

"Do you think the British captured him at sea?" asked young Horace.

"It's possible. Or he might never have left Washington. Not everyone has the stomach to carry out bold plans."

"I thought you had great faith in Dexter Lovell."

"He's getting old, Horace. The spirit of adventure rarely burns bright in old men. You have a very unusual grandfather in that respect. You should be proud that he allows you to partake of his adventures."

"I am, sir. And thank you again for the pistol." He patted the leather pouch at his side. Inside it was a small flintlock, powder, and shot.

"If we should be accosted, don't hesitate to use it. Gravelly Point is deserted, but the war has made brigands of many men, and you never know where they may lurk."

The boy's eyes flashed with excitement, and Pratt smiled indulgently. The old man had not intended to involve his grandson so deeply in his scheme, but he knew that there was little danger despite his warning, and little chance that anyone would discover them out on Gravelly Point. Pratt and Lovell had decided on the point because of its seclusion and relative safety. Along the waterfront, there were military patrols, constables, and a steady stream of drinkers and whoremongers who would find it strange to see a strongbox rowed ashore and placed in the carriage of a noted Boston businessman. In the Back Bay, however, there was only the water, the meadow on Gravelly Point, and the cover of night.

It was time for young Horace to learn that life in the business world demanded more than the ability to balance books and predict the needs of buyers in Boston and China. It required men who relished intrigue and took advantage of every opportunity, even if they had to spend their nights waiting for a rowboat at the edge of a tide flat.

The carriage clattered past the old fortress on Boston Neck and headed inland. The Neck was three quarters of a mile long. At its narrowest point, 130 feet of land separated the Back Bay from the South Boston Channel. During storm tides in the eighteenth century, the Neck was submerged and Boston became an island. But sea walls had been built, and spacious homes, standing bleak, treeless, and unprotected, now lined the first quarter mile of the Neck. At Dover and Washington streets, the Neck began to widen toward Roxbury. Two houses occupied opposite corners of the intersection, and two empty blocks of land stretched out behind each of them. A half mile south, at Washington and Lenox streets, the Neck was nine blocks across, extending from the edge of the South Boston Channel on the east to the mouth of the Back Bay's Easterly Channel on the west.

The distance from Pratt's home to Lenox Street was three and a half miles, and the ride took nearly an hour. A light rain had begun to fall by the time the carriage turned west toward Gravelly Point.

Young Horace Taylor Pratt III felt his heart begin to pound as they moved deeper into the darkness. The south end of the Neck had been cut into neat blocks fourteen years before, but except for the houses along Washington Street, the area was uninhabited, a desert of vacant lots and wild-growing shrubbery waiting for the day when Boston would need more space. Young Horace reached into his pouch and took out the pistol.

Pratt heard the hammer click gently into place. "Leave it uncocked," he said evenly.

"What about the brigands and highwaymen?"

"They'll give you ample time to cock the gun and aim. I'll not have you shooting your leg off in a bouncing carriage. Your mother would be very upset."

The boy uncocked the pistol. "My mother is always very upset," he grumbled. "You can't ever be certain of what she's thinking or why."

"Speak respectfully of your mother, boy. I'll not have you grousing."

Young Horace stared out at the darkness. "Yes, sir."

Pratt studied the boy for a moment, then threw his arm around him. "You can always rely on your grandfather, son. I'm your rock."

Young Horace wanted to pull away from the old man, with his yellow teeth and sour breath, but he endured the embrace. He had learned early in life that his grandfather would satisfy his every whim, if he studied diligently, listened carefully when Pratt spoke, and responded warmly to the old man's affection. Most fifteen-year-olds did not enjoy expressions of physical affection from anyone, much less their grandfathers, but the boy knew of no one his age who carried a new pistol and rode down the Neck each night to await smugglers on Gravelly Point. He was having a most exciting summer, and he managed to smile.

The carriage came to an abrupt halt, and Pratt almost fell on the floor. "Good God, Wilson, drive more carefully or you'll kill us all!"

A wizened face peered into the compartment. A top hat covered a few wisps of gray hair, and the complexion was so pale that it seemed almost iridescent in the dark. "Sorry, sir," he said unconvincingly. "I didn't see the end of the road."

"You saw it last night and the night before."

"Last night and the night before, the clouds weren't coverin' up the moon. How the hell do you expect me to see the end of the road in the rain when you won't let me burn my goddam lanterns?" Wilson had been driving Pratt's coach since 1783, and he paid little deference to a man he knew so well.

"Just get us to the point before the tide turns."

Wilson snapped the reigns and called gently to the horses. The carriage left Lenox Street, which ended a hundred yards short of the Easterly Channel, and forged onto a path just wide enough to pass. The horses tried to stop, but Wilson urged them on. The brush fell away. Wilson climbed down and guided the horses across a footbridge that spanned the narrow channel. They were on Gravelly Point.

"Perhaps tonight," whispered Pratt to his grandson.

The Back Bay spread in front of them like liquid onyx. A mile or so to the east, the outline of Beacon Hill loomed black out of the water, like a breaching whale harpooned by the West Boston Bridge and secured to the Cambridge mainland.

Young Horace climbed out of the coach, gun in hand, and looked about. Satisfied that there was nothing awaiting him in the darkness, he ran to the edge of the water and squinted into the rain. He hoped to see a red lantern. Lovell had promised to light one when he rowed under the West Boston Bridge.

"Do you see anything?" asked Pratt.

"No, sir."

"Then come in out of the rain before you catch cold."

"I don't mind if I do." It was Wilson. He took off his oilskin and climbed into the coach. Once inside, he removed his top hat, shook the water from the brim, and carefully placed the hat on the seat beside him. He looked strong and wiry, though he was about seventy years old.

"I did not invite you to join us," said Pratt.

Wilson pulled a pint of rum, a salami, and several stale rolls from the pockets of his livery and spread them on the seat. "But I'm inviting you to join me." He swigged from the bottle and offered it to Pratt. "If we have to sit out here all night in the rain, we might as well be comfortable, eh, Mr. Pratt? When you come right down to it, there's not much left for two old men but to stay warm and dry and keep a fire cookin' in their bellies, is there?"

Pratt took a drink and handed the pint back to his footman. "You ask very little of life, Wilson. That's why you've spent most of yours driving my coach."

Wilson took another swallow of rum, stuffed a piece of salami into his mouth, and bit off a chunk of bread. "If you expect little, life can't disappoint you."

Pratt smiled. "I've demanded everything and gotten most of it."

"And ten years from now, the only difference between you and me will be the size of our headstones. So drink up."

Pratt laughed and drank again. "Wilson, you are a cheerful son of bitch. You never disappoint me."

"Not like your friend Dexter Lovell, who's disappointed you for three nights in a row. From what I remember of Lovell, he'll continue to disappoint you until we all fall down for want of sleep."

Young Horace shook the rain off himself and climbed into the coach. Wilson offered the boy rum. Horace looked at his grandfather, who nodded. It was not young Horace's first liquor, but the rum burned his gullet all the way down. He gagged it back violently, spat it out the window, and in a moment was standing in the rain coughing the fire out of his gut.

"He ain't quite a man yet," said Wilson merrily.

"But he's learning fast," said Pratt.

"Next time you drink my rum," Wilson ordered, "don't be spittin' it out before it gets to your belly."

Pratt smiled and waited for the boy to stop coughing. "Any sign of the red lantern, son?"

Horace crawled back into the coach and collapsed in his seat. "No, sir," he said between breaths. "But the tide is still coming in. It should be slack in about an hour."

"We'll wait until it turns," announced Pratt.

"And hope we don't catch our deaths in the meantime," said Wilson.

"I did not ask for your opinion," answered Pratt.

"You should. You get it anyway."

Pratt turned to his grandson. "When you grow up, my boy, change servants every five years. Otherwise, they become like old cats—too arrogant for their own good, yet too familiar to throw out in the street."

Wilson laughed.

The rain began to fall more heavily. Pratt stared out toward the West Boston Bridge. There would be no red lantern tonight.

Dexter Lovell was eighty miles away, just off Provincetown and plowing into Cape Cod Bay under full sail. He could smell rain in the wind, but the onshore breeze was still fresh and he had never felt better.

The *Reckless* was making fine distance. She was a fine ship. From the moment he had taken the tiller in Chesapeake Bay, Lovell knew that two men could sail her to Boston. He hated to scuttle her. And Thomas Jefferson Grew had become a first-class seaman in just a few days. He hated to kill such a fine specimen.

For two weeks, they had been traveling at night, holding close to the shore, and hiding in a bay or inlet from just after sunrise until late in the afternoon. The British Navy was spread along the Atlantic Coast, but not so sparsely that Lovell would risk the tea set more than once.

Just out of Chesapeake Bay, a British frigate had stopped him with a shot across the bow, and he had feared that his adventure might end quickly. British officers had been instructed to seize any vessel carrying a cargo and to fine any with an empty hold, on the assumption that the captain had sold his goods or held funds to purchase cargo in another port. The British boarded the *Reckless,* but they found no cargo. Jack Dawson's sloop had been modified for smuggling, and Lovell had hidden the tea set in a secret compartment beneath the hold. The British fined Lovell two hundred and fifty dollars, which he paid with the gold coins he had promised Jack Dawson. Then, they warned him to stay in port and sent him and his slave on their way. Lovell did not challenge the Union Jack in daylight again.

Jeff Grew secured a loose shroud and came aft, moving with the confidence of a lifetime sailor. He took a bottle of Jack Dawson's best rotgut from a chest against the starboard bulwark and sat down to drink. He had been enjoying Dawson's store since the trip began, and Lovell was amazed at his capacity for spirits.

Grew offered Lovell the bottle. Lovell refused; he did not intend to let drink weaken his resolve. He would not leave himself open for Jeff Grew's machete.

"How much longer you reckon, Dexter Lovell?"

"We'll be in Boston tomorrow night."

Grew sucked on the bottle and studied the white man. He did not trust Dexter Lovell. He didn't trust anyone who wouldn't drink with him. Yet, as they drew closer to this place called Boston, Grew realized that his life was in Lovell's hands. He knew nothing of the city or its people or their opinions about freedmen. Lovell had lived there for many years, and he would have friends waiting for him. If his friends were smugglers, they might be the sort who would split a nigger's skull when he asked for his fair share of a stolen tea set. The closer they came to Boston, the less Jeff Grew wanted to see its harbor.

"Hey, Dexter, dis be a fine ship, don't it?"

"Aye."

"You think you could sail dis ship across the ocean?"

"I could, but not with a one-man crew."

"What about Jamaica? Could we sail d'ere?"

"We're goin' to Boston," said Lovell firmly.

"But I have friends in Jamaica, good rich friends." He spoke with the ingratiating tone that was a remnant of his days as a slave. It crept into his voice whenever he asked a white man for a favor, and he hated himself when he heard it. "Maybe dey pay us plenty for dis tea set. And I got another friend, be a silversmith. He know how to melt down silver into bars. Den we sell it for plenty, and no one ever know we took it from Jemmy Madison's parlor." A fawning smile punctuated the speech.

Lovell looked straight ahead, into the clouds that were charging out to meet him. He expected the wind to change any minute. "My connections in Boston will pay us two 'undred times what we can get for a bar of unworked silver in Jamaica," said Lovell. "So stop schemin' and do as you're told."

Grew drank more rum. He felt the numbness in his gums that told him he was almost drunk. He took another swallow and looked up into the sail, blown full and round like a ripe pear. Grew wanted the money that Lovell was promising, but he didn't believe he would get it. Better a few hundred dollars for a few pounds of silver than the promise of thousands and a lead ball in the back of the head.

Grew finished the last of Jack Dawson's rum and slipped the machete from his belt. Dexter Lovell shifted his right hand to one of his pistols and watched the black carefully. Grew took a grindstone from Jack Dawson's deck box, spat on it, and drew the length of the blade three or four times across its surface. The sound was cold and efficient, and Lovell heard its meaning.

Suddenly, the wind changed and the sail went limp. There was a crash of thunder, and for an instant, the great dunes at Provincetown appeared blue and ghostlike off the starboard bow.

CHAPTER VI

The sun was burning through the haze of another heat-wave morning. Peter Fallon rowed his scull under the Harvard Bridge and into the Charles River Basin. He remembered from the maps that Massachusetts Avenue, which ran across the bridge, cut straight through the area once known as Gravelly Point. He tried to drive the thought from his head. When he rowed, Fallon preferred to move without thinking, but the Dexter Lovell note and the maps had been on his mind since he woke.

Inhale, stroke, exhale, backstroke. He concentrated on the rhythm of rowing, on the regular splash of the oars, the steady movement of the body in the scull. He liked rowing in the humidity. It was better than a sauna for opening the pores and loosening the muscles, and today he rowed much farther than usual.

Skimming along the northern edge of the Back Bay, he passed Beacon Street brownstones with river-view windows, commuter traffic on Storrow Drive, the Prudential and John Hancock towers, and all he could see was a tidal flat stretching two or three miles inland to a neck of land. He swept by the Hatch Memorial Shell, where the Boston Pops performed on summer nights, and he calculated that the Easterly Channel had once flowed into the Charles River just beneath Arthur Fiedler's podium. He rowed down to the West Boston Bridge, a span of granite arching gracefully over the water, and he saw it as it had looked in 1814—one hundred and eighty piers supporting three quarters of a mile of planking.

At the West Boston Bridge, known to most Bostonians as the Longfellow Bridge, he turned back upstream. It was three miles home, and he knew that the last quarter mile, from the Weeks Bridge to the boathouse, would flush everything out of his head. It always did.

Under the Weeks Bridge, he lifted his oars out of the water and took a few deep breaths. He challenged himself to reach the boathouse as quickly as possible. Then his sprint began.

After a hundred yards, his lungs started to burn, demanding more oxygen to fuel the engine. His thighs expanded as blood pumped through them. His arms and shoulders throbbed. His head pounded in the heat, and he increased the pace. The oars became a blur. He tried to move faster. His brain screamed to stop. He had reached the threshold. Another stroke and his brain stopped. His body became a machine, a piston pounding back and forth in the boat. He felt nothing. He was there.

He let go of the oars and collapsed.

It was several minutes before he had the strength to row up to the dock. Then he felt the rush that always followed his sprint. Oxygen filled his lungs, and blood sugar poured through him. With a few powerful strokes he brought the scull to its mooring and leaped onto the dock. He felt euphoric, even in the heat. It was the best part of his day.

A skinny man sat on the bank next to the boathouse and wiped the sweat from his face. When Fallon jogged past, the man pulled himself to his feet and followed. He was impressed by Fallon's intense conditioning program, and at the moment, worn out by Fallon's energy.

Henry Dill worked on Bennett Soames's personal staff. He had been with Pratt Industries for twenty years as a bookkeeper, office manager, and industrial spy. At midnight, he had replaced James Buckley in the Oldsmobile across the street from Fallon's apartment. At six A.M., he had followed Fallon to the river. When Fallon's scull headed downstream, Dill tried to keep up with it by jogging along the bank in his sportcoat and crepe-soled shoes, but Fallon had disappeared within minutes. Now, he followed Fallon back to the apartment, recorded his activities in the log book, and collapsed in the Oldsmobile for twenty-five minutes, long enough for Fallon to shower, shave, eat a light breakfast, and head for the subway.

Fallon had decided to spend the day researching the story of the tea set. He intended to speak first with Evangeline Carrington. Despite her attitude toward him, she had seemed deeply upset by the secrecy at Searidge. She was also very pretty. When he'd looked up her phone number the night before, he'd found two listings: one of them connected her with a plant store called the Green Shoppe at the Quincy market. He couldn't think of a better place to begin the day.

At the Quincy Market, three buildings stood parallel to one another like granite ships in drydock. Each 555 feet long, the market and two storehouses had been built on a stretch of reclaimed land between Faneuil Hall and the waterfront in 1826. By 1960, the granite had turned black with soot, an elevated highway separated the buildings from the waterfront, and the storehouses were mostly vacant. Durgin Park, a famous old restaurant, was still anchored in the north storehouse. The central building still housed markets for meat, cheese, fish, and other staples. But behind many windows, dust had been accumulating since the Depression.

In the mid-seventies, however, the Quincy Market was refurbished and became the most popular spot in the city. The buildings were sandblasted to their original granite luster. Plywood and broken windows were replaced by plate glass. Interiors were restored, hardwood floors refinished, brick walls and ceiling beams stripped bare. Plazas, trees, and park benches replaced narrow streets and joined the whole complex to Faneuil Hall. The central building—arched windows, Doric columns, and copper dome—regained its Neoclassical beauty. Old businesses were encouraged to stay. Many did not. Restaurants, cafés, and specialty shops moved in. Boston took the Quincy Market merrily into its pocketbook.

Depending on his mood, Fallon thought it was the most successful piece of urban redevelopment he had ever seen, or the biggest tourist trap north of the Florida line. He missed the straightforward honesty of a butcher slicing steaks from a side of beef, and the smell of greasy food permeating the air reminded him of an amusement park. But the Quincy Market had brought people back to the city, it had helped to rejuvenate Boston, and it was always swarming with happy, festive crowds.

Fallon found Evangeline Carrington's Green Shoppe on the

second floor of the North Market. Already he didn't like it. Any place that spelled "shop" with two *p*'s and an *e* was trying too hard to be trendy. Give the name of a store an old-fashioned spelling, and it becomes a bouncy little place where the customer can listen to rock music on FM radio and smell cheap incense while he spends his money on something he doesn't need.

Fallon stepped into the Green Shoppe and heard music, but it was Mozart. He smelled the aroma of damp earth and new growth. He stood surrounded by Boston ferns, coleii, wandering Jew, and all manner of plants. His cynicism fell away. Like a hothouse in springtime, the Green Shoppe enveloped Fallon and absorbed him.

"Can I help you?" The voice sounded familiar, but softer, more relaxed than the day before. Evangeline appeared from behind a pot of Swedish ivy. She was wearing French-cut jeans and a blue T-shirt beneath a loose smock. Her hair was pinned on top of her head, giving her face a warmth and openness that hadn't been there in the fog at Searidge.

Fallon smiled. "Do you remember me?"

It took her a moment. "I hope you're here to talk about your bad luck with spider plants, because plants are the only thing I'm interested in discussing right now."

"The family tree is a plant." He winced as he spoke. He was beginning to wonder why he said something stupid every time he talked to her.

She turned back to the Swedish ivy.

"I'm really sorry to bother you."

"Then don't," she said evenly.

"I'd just like a few guidelines for dealing with the Pratts and Carringtons," he pleaded. "The other day, I guess I overstepped whatever boundaries your family sets for visitors."

"Apparently, so did I."

Fallon sensed an opening. "Right. They haul me out of the attic. They throw you out of the house when you defend your grandmother's rights. Why are they so damn secretive about everything?"

"Why are you so damn nosy?" Evangeline was losing patience quickly.

"It's part of my work," he said, trying to sound as professional as possible. "Your uncle heads one of the oldest corporations in America that is still run by direct descendants. I'm trying to establish the beginnings of that corporation in order to—"

"He's not my uncle," corrected Evangeline. "He's my father's cousin, which makes him my second cousin. However, since he's twenty-four years older than I, I call him 'uncle' on those rare occasions when I call him anything at all."

However useless it might be, she was giving him information. "It sounds to me as if you don't like him."

"I loathe him. He's rich, patronizing, ostentatious, immoral, and, judging from the current status of Pratt Industries, incompetent. When we had a war in Asia and Pratt Chemicals Division was making fifty percent of the defoliants we used, my uncle was a business giant. But the myth of Pratt genius disappeared right along with the ones about American military superiority and moral rectitude."

Fallon looked around at the jungle encroaching on all sides. "Did you start hating him before or after he started producing chemical defoliants?"

She didn't laugh. A customer entered, distracting both of them from his remark.

Fallon watched her wait on a middle-aged businessman who didn't know anything about plants. He could plainly see her love for the work reflected in her smile and enthusiasm, both of which were as genuine as the displeasure she was showing him. She sold a Boston fern for $11.95 and told the man to come back if he had any problems with his plant. Then she disappeared behind a partition in the corner of the store. Fallon heard her dial the phone and speak briefly.

When she emerged, she was holding a piece of paper. "I do not, as a rule, act as a personal secretary for anyone. However, you seem to need help in budgeting your time, and as you are wasting mine along with your own, I thought I'd do you this favor." She handed him the slip of paper. "Meet my brother at La Crêperie in half an hour." Her French pronunciation was flawless. "I've written it down so you don't forget it."

Fallon had not planned on this. Before seeing Christopher Carrington, he wanted to read everything he could find about the Golden Eagle Tea Set. Certainly there were descriptions of it, speculations on its disappearance and ultimate fate, things he should know about before he started asking questions. If he didn't have all the facts that were available, he might look to Christopher Carrington like a bad historian, and Peter Fallon hated looking bad at anything. "Do you think he'd mind if we did it tomorrow? I have a rather full schedule today."

"My brother's is full all month, or so he tells me. Frankly, I don't care whether you see him or not, but I wouldn't pass up the opportunity."

Another customer wandered in.

"There's nothing more I can do for you," said Evangeline. "Come back when you'd like a good deal on a rubber plant." Evangeline headed for the customer and Fallon for La Crêperie.

Christopher Carrington replaced the receiver and swung his feet onto the desk. His windows on the fifteenth floor of the John Hancock building overlooked the South End; he stared instead at the large print of the Boston Tea Party that hung on his wall. He was disgusted.

Two years earlier, he had rejected an associateship at Hoover and Howell, a Wall Street law firm whose clients included two of the largest banks in the country and whose important cases seemed always to establish precedents in the field of corporate finance. Instead, he had accepted a position in the family law practice.

Pratt, Pratt, and Carrington was a small but prestigious firm established in 1870 specifically to protect the interests of Pratt Shipping, Mining and Manufacturing. Now, the firm represented several New England corporations, but Pratt Industries was still the chief client, and Calvin Pratt, senior partner in the firm, sat on the Pratt Industries board of directors. Since 1870, at least one descendant of the original partners had always been with the firm. Carrington's father and grandfather had been partners; Carrington's mother and grandmother expected nothing less of him.

As a first-year associate with Pratt, Pratt, and Carrington, he had enjoyed no favor because of his name. He hunted references, prepared briefs, and drafted third-party complaints for the senior staff. But the cases had been interesting, and his responsibilities had grown quickly. Beyond that, he preferred Boston to New York. It was small and manageable. It was close to Searidge, where he kept his sailboat. It was three hours from Stowe, where he owned a condominium. When he wanted night life, New York was only an hour away on the Eastern shuttle. For a twenty-nine-year-old bachelor, it was an excellent arrangement. For a young attorney who believed that corporate law played an important part in the smooth functioning of American society, it was the ideal practice. Until he began to explore the family history in his grandmothers's attic.

Since then, Christopher Carrington had spent more time as a genealogist than a lawyer. He had tracked down relatives so distant they neither knew nor cared that they were Pratt blood. He had given their names to Philip Pratt, who had sought out every one.

Now, instead of working to solidify his client's position as the controlling force in Pratt Industries, Carrington was trying to protect the company from the charges of harassment that Fallon would certainly press when he discovered Pratt employees following him day and night. Carrington intended to find out what Fallon knew. If Fallon was innocent, Carrington would tell Soames to suspend the surveillance. If Fallon knew something, if it seemed that he was working for Rule or hunting on his own, Carrington would still suggest leaving him alone. Because Christopher Carrington would compromise himself no further. He knew a breach of ethics when he saw one. He knew that he was committing his time and energy to a scheme that was, if it worked, nothing short of blackmail.

"You're becoming emotional," his Uncle Calvin had told him the day before. "We're simply helping a client to keep his options open."

"You wouldn't endanger our reputation for any other client. If someone else mismanaged a firm the way Philip has screwed up Pratt Industries, you'd let him sink straight into the mire he'd created for himself and hope that the new officers showed more business sense."

"I must remember not to let you handle litigation for a while. You've been making some rather rash statements lately. The current problems of Pratt Industries reflect a bad economy and bad management at several levels of the corporation. You know that Philip doesn't deserve all the blame." Calvin Pratt spoke in the carefully measured tones of his courtroom voice.

Christopher's voice rose angrily. "You wouldn't be trying to help him out of this if his name was Forbes or Fishman."

Calvin Pratt fingered his Phi Beta Kappa key and studied his nephew like an opposing attorney. Then, he smiled. "Certainly not Fishman, and probably not Forbes. But we are Pratts. We owe a good deal of what we enjoy to our heritage. We have been blessed with money, homes, roots that sink deep into the New England soil, a name that commands respect, and inbred confidence in our abilities and potential. As individuals, we must take credit or blame for whatever we achieve, but our name has smoothed the way for all of us. We owe it our loyalty." He spoke softly, and it was clear to his nephew that Calvin believed everything he was saying.

"In your own quiet way, you're becoming emotional yourself, Uncle." Christopher liked Calvin Pratt and respected his intelligence.

"Then let me offer you a more compelling reason to assist Philip Pratt in his battle to remain in control of Pratt Industries." Calvin spoke without emotion. "For two hundred years, the Pratt Company has played an important role in the growth of this country. We have taken our profits, but we have always recognized our social and patriotic mission. In the last few years, however, the old guard, the families who've owned large chunks of stock since we went public in 1876, have begun to drop away. They've been selling out. Now, too much of our stock is controlled by short-run profiteers only too willing to turn their support over to a corporate marauder like William Rule."

"Maybe they've been selling out because the company is losing money. Maybe it's time for an outsider to take over. It's time for some new blood." Christopher spoke casually, pretending to toss out an idea he'd been thinking about for some time.

"If William Rule becomes chairman of the board, the only blood will be Philip's and mine, and it will be spread across that mahogany table in the boardroom like lamb's blood on a sacrificial altar." Calvin stood as though he were making a summation. "The tradition of Pratt Industries will end, and you, my boy, will never be elected to your rightful position on the board of directors. That should be a reason for you to oppose William Rule in every way possible."

It was. As he thought about the conversation, Christopher Carrington agreed with most of what his uncle had said. Unlike his sister, he believed in the tradition of the Pratts and Carringtons. His family was indeed special. His ancestors and relatives had helped to develop the national economy, they had built an important American corporation, and they had done it all with undeniable dignity and style.

He was an elitist, and he knew it. He recognized the moral and intellectual superiority of his kind. In his love affairs and friendships, he gravitated toward people of similar background and inclination, people of old money and Protestant upbringing, from New England prep schools and Ivy League universities, people taught from childhood to appreciate the finer things in life—an exhibition of restored Monets at the Museum of Fine Arts, Bach recitals in the upstairs chamber at the Gardner Museum, Bulfinch architecture, IBM stock, twelve-year-old single-malt Scotch, and slopes of packed powder under Hexcel skis.

Even Philip Pratt, for all his failings and subtle vulgarities, was a Pratt. William Rule was an uncultured thug. Christopher Carrington would do everything he could to help his uncle defeat Rule, but he would do nothing dishonorable. He owed his heritage a greater debt than that.

❊

La Crêperie on Newbury Street was decorated like a French country house, bright and pastel, small enough to be intimate yet large enough to maintain a high volume of business.

When he arrived, Fallon realized that he didn't know what Christopher Carrington looked like. By the window, he noticed a young man reading the *Wall Street Journal.* He approached. "Mr. Carrington? Good morning."

Carrington extended his hand and smiled. "You must be Peter Fallon. I'm glad you could make it."

"You didn't give me much choice." Fallon did not sound annoyed.

"I suggested La Crêperie because they have the best air conditioning in town and a very tasty Belgian waffle," said Carrington.

Fallon studied the menu, and the two men studied each other.

Carrington was all that Fallon had expected—fit and well tanned, in a beige Brooks Brothers suit, button-down blue shirt, and brown knit tie, with a polite manner that was just this side of condescending and a pretentious accent that drew every vowel into at least two syllables. Fallon's first impulse was to dislike him, but he resisted it for the moment.

Carrington was impressed by Fallon's obvious fitness and good looks. Fallon's body was muscular, supple, like that of a gymnast. He didn't look to Carrington like someone who spent his days and nights in the library. Perhaps he wasn't. Perhaps Soames was right. This guy might be trouble. Quick, irrational thoughts. Carrington felt a shot of adrenalin pump through him.

Henry Dill entered La Crêperie and went directly to a table in the corner of the room. He did not look around until he was hidden behind a menu.

Not very subtle, thought Carrington. He knew little about Henry Dill, but he felt no comfort in Dill's presence. If Fallon should turn out to be an unknown quantity, someone dangerous or unpredictable, Carrington didn't think he could rely on Dill's help. Then, Carrington realized that he was beginning to think like Soames. He told himself to relax.

Coffee arrived and Carrington slid the sugar across the table to Fallon. "Tell me about your work."

A little small talk first, thought Fallon, just to loosen things up. He saw a copy of the *Boston Globe* beneath Carrington's *Wall Street Journal.* "Not until you tell me the score of last night's ballgame."

"Five to three, Boston. This year, they're going to win the pennant."

Fallon laughed. "Reading Boston sportswriters and New York

stock analysts before breakfast is the sort of thing that makes manic depressives. The sportswriters fill you with false optimism, then the analysts shatter it, or vice versa."

"In the evenings, I read the *Los Angeles Times.*"

"But the news is three hours old when it gets out there."

"I spent a year in Hollywood between college and law school. I was vaguely interested in the movie business, and Pratt Industries owns a piece of American Center Films. I was able to take a close look at the madness and decide I preferred law. However, I still have a few friends out there, and I like to know what's happening. They say that everything starts in Los Angeles, then moves east. If we're forewarned, we can build a wall along Route 495 and protect the city from the next cultural onslaught."

They both laughed, then Carrington's expression turned serious. "And right now, I'm protecting my family from an unwarranted intrusion. As you have already learned, we are most protective of our privacy. We always have been. I hope that you weren't terribly inconvenienced the other day, but my grandmother is sometimes more trusting that the rest of us. The loneliness of old age, I guess. But she should not have allowed you into the attic without consulting me."

"It's her house," said Fallon. "And when you shroud a place in secrecy, you only succeed in making people like me more curious."

"I don't care whether you're curious or not." Carrington felt his anger. He was glad the waitress appeared just then to take their orders. He didn't like to get angry in a discussion like this. When she left, he continued, "The attic is also the repository for most of the documents of our family history, and we always prefer to know something about the historians who poke through our papers. We're willing to support your work if you're a serious researcher, but we're always getting requests from people who want to snoop through our diaries and letters just to see what sort of dirt they can find to publish about us."

Fallon thought Carrington's reasoning a little faulty. He had been declaring his serious intent for months, and the Pratts had not responded. "I don't want to shatter any illusions for you, Mr. Carrington, but very few people outside of the Pratts really care about the Pratts. You may be an important New England family, but you're not the Kennedys. Any dirt that I may dig out of two-hundred-year-old letters and ledger books isn't exactly what you'd call fan-magazine material."

Carrington realized that he was sounding rather arch. "Agreed. But the later records also cover the lives of people still living or only recently dead. We want to protect their privacy."

Fallon recalled nothing later than 1920, but he didn't argue. He sensed that Carrington was hiding something from him. "My interest is in Horace Taylor Pratt and his immediate descendants."

Carrington smiled. "Then I'll tell you whatever you'd like to know."

"And give me access to his papers?"

"Whatever I can do."

Fallon was surprised and a little disappointed by Carrington's sudden willingness to cooperate. For the next half hour, they discussed the life of Horace Taylor Pratt, and their mutual suspicions fell away. Fallon decided that Carrington was hiding nothing; Carrington decided that Fallon was exactly what he appeared to be. They talked about Pratt's business, his wife, and his relationship to his sons—one a martyr to the cause of Pratt Shipping and Mercantile, the other an apparent idler whose ideas were usually five years ahead of their time. Fallon asked about Pratt's daughter, Abigail Pratt Bentley, and Carrington promised that he would let Fallon see her diaries, a few of which existed from a lifetime of writing.

"When you come right down to it," Carrington concluded at the end of their second cup of coffee, "Horace Taylor Pratt was a smart, tough, grasping son of a bitch. And I'm glad he was." He picked up the check. "I'll call Searidge and instruct Mr. Harrison to take down all the papers I feel are pertinent to your dissertation."

Fallon realized that Carrington was going to get away without discussing the Golden Eagle, which was the whole point of the meeting. He thought of no subtle way to introduce it. "There's one period of Pratt's life in which I'm very interested, and I didn't find any papers covering it."

Carrington glanced impatiently at his watch. "Then they probably don't exist."

"But it was a rather important event in Pratt's life. When George Washington visited Boston in 1789, they gave him a tea set. . . ."

Carrington's body stiffened involuntarily. "Yes, I'm familiar with it. The Golden Eagle Tea Set."

Fallon was surprised that Carrington knew that much. He wasn't sure what else to reveal. "Do you know anything about it?"

"As much as anyone knows about it."

Fallon noted the change in Carrington's attitude. Polite suspicion returned. There was something to this after all. "A book I was reading says that the tea set disappeared when the British burned Washington. It was never found. Do you think Pratt had anything to do with it?"

Carrington studied Fallon for a moment, then laughed softly. He tried not to sound derisive, but he couldn't avoid it. If he had had any doubts about Fallon, they were gone now. Fallon had stumbled across something, but he knew nothing. "Do you know when that book was published?"

"Sometime in the late sixties." Fallon sensed that he was about to feel very stupid.

"That explains it." Carrington stood and buttoned his jacket. "When you have the time, take the Huntington Avenue trolley over to the Museum of Fine Arts. When you get inside, ask the first guard you see to direct you to the section on American Decorative Arts. Halfway down the gallery on the left, beneath the portrait of Paul Revere, you'll find the Golden Eagle Tea Set. It's worth the trip."

Fallon managed to smile and thank Carrington. His treasure hunt was over.

"I must be running," said Carrington. "Please stay and finish your coffee." He headed for the door. "And update that library of yours. You should know that history is rewritten every ten years."

Peter Fallon felt very stupid, and he hated feeling stupid.

The eyes were alert, intelligent. The face was serene and satisfied, without a trace of complacency. The hands were large and muscular, yet with a delicacy that befitted their craft. Paul Revere, painted by John Singleton Copley in 1770, hung in the American Decorative Arts gallery of the Boston Museum of Fine Arts. To his left, a display case overflowed with his work. Directly in front of him, beneath two spotlights, the Golden Eagle Tea Set glistened in a Plexiglas bubble. The end of the story.

Peter Fallon knew the beginning, and he had convinced himself by afternoon that he no longer cared about the middle. His fantasies of discovering buried treasure had burned away. If he stumbled across any interesting bits of information about the tea set, he would file them with the Lovell note, drag them out some day when he had nothing to do, and try to piece them together. He expected that he would have nothing to do the day after he defended his dissertation. Until then, he was forgetting about this tea set.

The American Decorative Arts gallery stretched down a corridor that was deserted, except for a guard fighting sleep at the far end. Its silence provided the medium for contemplation, and Fallon stared at the tea set for twenty minutes. He knew nothing about silver—otherwise he would have known all along that the Revere masterpiece was on display in the museum—but he was transfixed by the beauty of the Golden Eagle.

Tea pot, creamer, sugar urn, coffee urn, waste bowl, tea tongs, spoons. The expanses of silver seemed like satin. The engravings on each piece formed a gossamer pattern just imperfect enough to have been etched by Revere's hand. The American eagle, in delicate gold relief, mesmerized Fallon with its gaze.

"And now, children, we arrive at our last stop."

An army of sixth-graders and their teachers trampled over the silence. The children had reached the end of their tour, and their nervous energy was overflowing.

Mrs. Jane Cooper, a museum administrator in her early forties, tried to finish her talk. Her crisp suit and short hair made her seem businesslike and efficient. She herded the children around Revere's portrait and smiled at Fallon, who moved to the edge of the group.

"This is the American Decorative Arts gallery," she explained. "That means silverware, furniture, and other things we use to brighten our home."

"Only thing would brighten my home is a fire," cracked one black kid, drawing laughter from his friends and angry stares from his teachers.

Unperturbed, Mrs. Cooper continued. "One of America's greatest decorative artists and one of Boston's most famous citizens is the man in the painting behind me. Does anybody know who he is?"

None of the children responded.

Mrs. Cooper tried to help them along with a clue. "Listen, my children, and you shall hear/Of the midnight ride of . . ." She waited for an answer.

"Diarrhea," whispered someone, just loudly enough to set off an epidemic of giggles. The rhyme worked best with a Boston accent.

"Out of bed and onto the floor/For the fifty-yard dash to the bathroom door." Mrs. Cooper smiled. "I was in the sixth grade myself, once. Now if you'll just listen for another minute or so, we'll finish our talk and you can all go outside and play."

The children cheered, and Fallon laughed to himself.

"Paul Revere was a patriot and a silversmith. He also cast some of the cannon and made the spikes for *Old Ironsides*. As you all know from your history books, he led a very exciting life, and we at the museum are proud to have the Golden Eagle Tea Set, his most famous work, on display."

His most famous work. Fallon felt like an ostrich just pulling his head out of the sand.

Mrs. Cooper lowered her voice for dramatic effect. "And there is a very exciting story connected with it." In breathless tones, she recounted the presentation of the tea set to George Washington and its disappearance from the White House. "It was a real mystery. For a hundred and fifty years, no one knew where the tea set was. Then, in 1973, a young art dealer reintroduced it to the world, and we found out where it had been."

Fallon was listening closely now. This was the middle of the story.

"The British Army had stolen the tea set and taken it to Europe. It passed through the hands of several soldiers, all of whom were killed because of it."

Already, she doesn't know what she's talking about, thought Fallon.

"Finally, it came to rest in the hands of a rich English art lover, Sir Henry Carrol. In 1870, when he was a very old man, someone sneaked into his house and murdered him. The tea set was stolen again." She told the story well, and the children listened closely. "It turned up a hundred years later in the hands of a rich family in England. It had been passed down the generations until the family decided to sell it. The art dealer brought it to America, where a rich businessman bought it for a great deal of money. When the businessman died, he left the tea set to the museum."

She paused before her closing remarks. "Not all works of art have such exciting stories to tell, but remember, children, that all art is exciting, and it is always here for your enjoyment."

At the urging of their teachers, the children sing-songed their thanks to Mrs. Cooper, then swarmed for the exits.

Mrs. Cooper turned to Fallon. "I'm sorry we interrupted your study of the tea set, but the sooner we start exposing our children to the drama in art, the sooner they'll start appreciating it."

"Well, it's not *Kojak*, but an interesting story nonetheless."

"Thank you." She smiled and started to leave.

Fallon felt his resolve break down. He wasn't going to pursue the story further, but he was following her down the corridor anyway. "Excuse me, ma'am." He told her a little about himself and his interest in the history of the tea set. He asked her if she would answer a few questions.

She invited him to her office, a cramped basement cubicle. Papers, art books, and manuscripts covered every available space, and an inexpensive print of Picasso's *Blue Nude* was hanging on the wall behind her desk. She cleared a spot and offered Fallon a seat.

"They tell me that the good administrator has one piece of paper on her desk and no distractions in her office. I'm afraid I don't quite fit the bill. This place is such a mess that my boss moved me downstairs out of embarrassment." Jane Cooper was an assistant to the curator of the American Decorative Arts collection. "Still, when something needs to be done, it lands on my desk. Always give the work to the person who looks busy." She poured two cups of coffee.

Fallon liked her. She seemed genuinely friendly, and much less orderly than her cotton suit. "I won't take too much of your time."

She smiled and sat at her desk. "That's quite all right."

"I'd be very interested in the name of the art dealer who brought the tea set into this country. Do you disclose such information?"

"Certainly, I'll disclose anything that's public record. Lawrence Hannaford is his name. He has a very successful gallery over on Newbury Street. Handles a lot of younger artists and makes an occasional sale for someone big."

"I assume that the tea set was his biggest sale."

"Yes. He bought it in Europe from a private family which preferred to remain anonymous, and he has kept their confidence to this day. It's a matter of ethics with art dealers, almost like reporters who won't divulge their sources. Then he sold the tea set in this country to the late Henry Drucker, a well-known collector, for a million and a half dollars."

Fallon whistled softly. "I've heard of a Rembrandt selling for a million and a half, but isn't that a lot for a tea set?"

"Not by today's standards. That sale was made in 1973, and I wouldn't be surprised if the Golden Eagle brought two and a half million today. Of course, we try not to attach dollar values to something that's really priceless."

"When you grow up in Boston, Paul Revere is the only silversmith you ever hear about. Was he that good?"

"Most people consider him the finest American silversmith of the eighteenth century, which is known as the golden age of American silver, although I personally have always felt that the Philadelphians, men like Richard Humphrey and Joseph Richardson, were technically more proficient."

"Traitorous words for someone from New England," said Fallon.

Jane Cooper laughed softly and brushed back the brown hair that was already streaked with gray. She wasn't beautiful in any conventional sense, but there was something about her that Fallon found very attractive. Women from Yankee stock always seemed to age gracefully.

"Don't misunderstand me, Mr. Fallon," she said. "I consider Paul Revere one of the best silversmiths in American history. He had his peers and his betters, but from 1860 on, he had the best public relations of any of them, thanks to Longfellow. 'One, if by land, and two, if by sea, / And I on the opposite shore will be, / Ready to ride and spread the alarm, / Through every Middlesex village and farm.' Heady stuff. The price for his work began to climb immediately after the poem was published. Within a few years, J. P. Morgan was offering a hundred thousand dollars for Revere's Liberty Bowl, an incredible sum in those days. A sort of Reveremania began, and it persists right down to the present."

"Fired up, I would imagine, by the rediscovery of the tea set."

"Oh, yes. People have always brought old silver into the museum to find out if it's Revere. He was extremely prolific, and judging from his daybooks, he made several pieces that have not been seen since he delivered them. Ever since the Golden Eagle went on display, people have been flocking in here with absolutely everything. You'd be amazed at what they ask us to authenticate. Silverware bought at E. B. Horne in 1948, pewter candlesticks, silver plates engraved 'To Mom and Pop on Their Anniversary.' Someone even walked in here once with a golf trophy. The curator almost died laughing."

Fallon was laughing himself. "I can't say that I blame him."

"It is hysterical. But people in New England want to feel that they're part of the glorious past. It's only natural when you live in a city like this, where you can't walk two blocks without running into some sort of historical monument or another. Owning a piece of Revere silver gives us a link with our communal history, even if our ancestors arrived from Lithuania in 1900.

"But once in a while"—a sliver of excitement crept into her voice—"we are presented with something authentic. That's an unforgettable thrill."

"Then you must have been beside yourself when you heard about the Golden Eagle Tea Set."

She thought for a moment. "Actually, we were a bit skeptical at first."

Fallon had been skeptical since he heard the story she told the sixth-graders. His suspicions slowly began to expand. "What would make the museum doubt that the tea set was Revere's work?"

"A couple of things," said Mrs. Cooper. "First of all, it had been gone for a hundred and fifty years. Somewhere along the line, you'd think that whoever held it in Europe might want to make a sale to someone like J. P. Morgan. And of course, Lawrence Hannaford's reluctance to reveal the name of the English owner caused us some hesitation as well."

"But you said that's not unusual."

"It isn't really. People selling works of art like to retain their anonymity, sometimes because they don't want the world to know they're poor, sometimes because they don't want the tax man cutting into their sale. But we always feel a trifle uncomfortable when the last owner is unknown. I'm sure you've heard those horror stories about museums purchasing art works of uncertain lineage."

"You mean forgeries?"

She felt him jumping to conclusions across her desk. "Before we go on, Mr. Fallon," she said evenly, "let me remind you that all our suspicions disappeared when we examined the tea set."

Fallon realized that he was sitting on the edge of his chair. He settled back.

"Lawrence Hannaford was actually a middleman for a middleman. His partner in Europe was an American importer named William Rule."

Fallon had never heard the name.

"Rule is a very reputable businessman with offices on Atlantic Avenue and large holdings in several New England corporations. Apparently, he put Hannaford together with the owner of the tea set and took a share of the profits. Then, not long after Hannaford presented the tea set to buyers at his gallery, an article appeared in a local newspaper, one of those counterculture weeklies that rang up in the late sixties."

"The *Phoenix*?"

"Something like the *Phoenix*. It was called *Hubcap*. It folded several years ago. Anyway, they had a columnist who used to pop off about something different every week—the tax rate, Nixon, the price of hot dogs at Fenway Park, anything that came into his head. If you read him regularly, you were soon convinced that he was certifiably crazy."

"Do you recall his name?" Fallon remembered the *Hubcap*, but he had never read it.

"Jack something or other. A big, burly fellow with white hair. Ferguson. Jack C. Ferguson. He wrote that the tea set was a fraud, that Hannaford and Rule were—I can't quite remember the phrase—

'criminals in the guise of cultured gentlemen.' Something like that. He said he knew the real story, and all he needed was 'the permission of a certain fine lady from a certain New England family,' and he'd tell it all. His column caused quite a stir in art circles. But he was an alcoholic. Before his permission ever came, he started hitting the bottle with both hands. Lord knows what makes a man snap like that." She paused and sipped her coffee.

"In the meanwhile, Hannaford had lined up Henry Drucker. He knew that Drucker was one of those collectors who not only appreciate good art, but also enjoy having a good story to tell when they show their treasures to their friends. If a work of art has been in the possession of famous people or the object of thefts and murders, its value rises astronomically. Any art dealer knows this, and Hannaford made sure that he documented the story of the tea set's travels."

"Where does his documentation begin?" Fallon hoped he would find holes in what she was about to tell him.

"With a British military inquest in 1816. Four British soldiers were robbed and killed while transporting a strongbox to the home of an officer in the Sussex countryside. The officer, a Captain Prendergast, had helped to torch the White House. It has always been assumed that he took the tea set. The British took everything else that wasn't nailed down that night. However, Prendergast's dream of a Revere tea set on the sideboard went a little awry."

"I had always heard that Dolley Madison saved most of the valuable pieces in the White House. It seems unusual that the people on her staff would have left the tea set behind. Did they ever look for it in this country?"

"There was a rather limp investigation by some Congressional appointees, but they were as successful as most Congressional appointees are at anything."

"Which means unsuccessful?" He wondered if they investigated Pratt.

"Exactly. Their main objective was to find two White House servants who disappeared along with the tea set. There was no FBI in those days, so the pair were never found. Since one of them was an Englishman, the investigators speculated that he struck a deal with Captain Prendergast and received passage to England in partial payment for the tea set."

"Did the inquest mention the Golden Eagle Tea Set by name?"

"They asked Prendergast if the tea set was on the wagon. He said it wasn't. However, if he'd said yes, it would have meant trouble. You see, a year earlier, the American government had requested that the British return the tea set. The British government requested that any officer who had knowledge of the Golden Eagle step forward. Prendergast did not."

Fallon laughed. "That's pretty flimsy evidence upon which to assume that Prendergast stole the tea set."

"It's just a theory, Mr. Fallon, but in 1870, the evidence becomes stronger. On December 4, 1870, the *Times* of London reported the murder of Sir Henry Carrol. He was killed in his home, surrounded by his collections of English and American silver. The American silver included, and I quote, 'works by Benjamin Burt, Jacob Hurd, and a handsome tea set by Paul Revere.' Carrol was a reclusive old eccentric who never allowed anyone to look at his treasures. We can't be sure if his set was the Golden Eagle or one of three other Revere services which disappeared during the nineteenth century and were recovered later."

Mrs. Cooper took a phone call, and Fallon refilled both coffee cups. The story was beginning to sound more plausible to him. Perhaps Lovell had been successful, and Pratt had sold the tea set to Carrol's family. When Hannaford's researchers were documenting the story of the Golden Eagle, they hadn't had Lovell's note as a starting point, and whatever evidence they had pointed to Captain Prendergast. In short, a historian's honest mistake.

After she hung up, Mrs. Cooper took off her coat and threw it on a chair. Totally absorbed in the story, Fallon had forgotten the heat. He realized that he was perspiring, despite the air conditioning.

"Where was I?" asked Mrs. Cooper, settling herself again.

"Henry Carrol."

"Yes. The tea set disappeared from his house, and a hundred years later, it reappeared in England. That's where we came in."

Fallon feared this part of the story. If the scientific proof was conclusive, he would have little reason to investigate further.

"In order to prove beyond a doubt that the tea set was genuine Revere," said Mrs. Cooper, "Hannaford offered it to us for inspection. Our silver expert at the time was a brilliant man named Elwood Kendall. He is no longer with us." From the way she spoke, Fallon surmised that the silver expert was a bit of an eccentric.

"Elwood Kendall considered it the crowning glory of his career to examine the Revere masterpiece. After he rendered his verdict in favor of Mr. Hannaford, he quietly retired and died a happy man.

"Kendall's first step was to talk with Mr. Ferguson. Since my own field of expertise is American silver, Kendall asked me to accompany him. We found Ferguson in his South Boston apartment, dead drunk and, for the most part, incoherent. No help at all." She shook her head and recalled the pitiful sight. After a few moments, she continued. "Then, we came back here and Kendall went to work, beginning with Revere's daybooks."

"Are they like ledgers?"

"Exactly. Revere was never very systematic about keeping them, either. Occasionally he made a crude sketch of a piece he was working on. Other times he would carefully enter the height and weight of each piece he made. And sometimes he wrote down nothing but the name of the client and the price he charged. With the Liberty Bowl, he never entered a thing."

"What about the Golden Eagle?"

"The daybook lists thirty-one pieces. He gives us the heights and weights of the teapot, creamer, sugar bowl, and coffee urn, and he adds that he has made the set for 'President G. Washington.' The Hannaford set fit the Revere specifications to the letter."

"Can anyone read through the daybooks?"

"Well, they *are* archive material. Anyone with some serious intent could go through them."

"Is forgery serious enough?" joked Fallon.

"Please let me finish, Mr. Fallon." She was beginning to sound annoyed. "The daybooks are simply the first step. Only the crudest fakes are found out through the daybooks. After the daybooks, we look at the method of production. You can usually tell if the body of a piece was raised, shaped, and engraved by hand, or if machines like the slip-roll former and burring wheel did the work. Revere used rolled silver for his Federal tea sets, but he crafted them with hammer, shears, burrin, and needle. No machines. Mr. Kendall determined that Hannaford's Golden Eagle was worked exclusively by hand.

"Next comes the patina. Over the years, the color of a silver surface changes because of tarnishing, polishing, and interaction with whatever is floating around in the air. The deposit, usually of silver sulfide, is called patina. We display all our silver in cases to keep it as free from patina as possible. A recent forgery will not show much patina, or it will have been chemically applied and easy to detect. Mr. Kendall agreed that the patina on the Golden Eagle was the product of time."

She knew her material well and didn't stop for questions. "Third, we compare a piece against some of the artist's well-known work to determine if he has done anything different. You know, in his hammer patterns, his engravings, his soldering technique, the beading and gadrooning, the general structure of the piece. We decided that Hannaford's tea set looks like Revere's work, and it closely resembles the only drawings of the Golden Eagle that were made before it disappeared."

"Didn't all silversmiths place their signatures on each piece they made?"

"Revere used seven different signature stamps in his career. Sometimes he imprinted his initials on a piece, sometimes his last name in capital letters. Sometimes he put a small pellet in front of his name, sometimes not. Anyone who could copy a tea set would certainly be able to copy a signature stamp."

"What about carbon dating or something like that?"

Mrs. Cooper laughed. "It's easy to see you're a historian and not a scientist. You can't carbon-date something unless it's organic, which silver isn't. At the moment, they're working on some sort of device that reads the density of electrons in a piece of silver and tells you its age. I'm not quite sure how it works, but it isn't operational yet, anyway. In the case of Hannaford's tea set, we analyzed the alloy content in the silver. They used a few, simple alloys in Revere's time. Our alloys are much more sophisticated today. We know that Revere melted down confiscated Tory silver, then rolled it and reworked it. The alloy levels found in the Golden Eagle Tea Set were commensurate with those found in most eighteenth-century silver."

"Could someone have faked the alloy content or the patina?"

"They could duplicate the alloy content, but I don't believe that anyone could fake the patina and fool us." She folded her hands on the desk, as though she had finished. "Patina is usually the key."

"Are you convinced of the authenticity of Hannaford's Golden Eagle?" he asked, the disappointment evident in his voice.

She nodded. "You don't add something like this to your collection unless you're positive."

Fallon studied her for a time, hoping she would add something more. Then, he looked at his watch. It was six o'clock. They had been talking for over an hour, and Fallon's questions had been answered. He was thankful, at least, that he hadn't wasted any more time. He offered to buy Mrs. Cooper a drink. She declined. He made a tentative date for lunch and thanked her for her help.

Outside, it was still hot and sticky. Huntington Avenue was clogged with rush-hour traffic. Fallon wasn't quite ready to fight the crowds back to Cambridge, and he hadn't decided what to do when he got home. The idea of sitting down to work held no appeal, but then, it never did. He was a short walk from Fenway Park. Maybe he could call someone and go to the ballgame. Neither of his college roommates was available. One was a suburban family man who programmed computers during the day and played softball at night. The other was a lawyer in New York. Fallon preferred female companionship.

A dime into the slot. Hello, Miss Carrington. Thank you for putting me in touch with your brother today. I have two tickets to the Red Sox game. You don't like baseball. What about the movies? You have television. Thank you very much goodbye. That was quick. He didn't want to go out with her anyway.

He squeezed his way onto the trolley for Park Street. The car was packed: exhaustion, depression, sweat. Somehow, he found a seat near the window. The trolley lurched forward. Its motion created a breeze that was, at best, flatulent, but better than standing still. The trolley began to move faster and tilted forward into the tunnel. The light dimmed, and the noise deafened.

Fallon stared out at the black wall beside him and thought about Jane Cooper's story. "A certain fine lady from a certain New England family." Katherine Pratt Carrington, perhaps? Fallon realized that he didn't want to drink or write or go to the baseball game with Evangeline Carrington. He wanted to find Jack C. Ferguson.

CHAPTER VII   *September 1814*

Abigail Pratt Bentley slept until nine o'clock. She couldn't remember when the patter of rain and the rumble of distant thunder had lulled her to sleep, but she knew she had not heard her father's carriage return during the night. She wrapped herself in a Chinese silk robe and gazed down at the city, which rolled up from the waterfront to the base of Pemberton Hill. The rain had stopped, and the clouds were straggling off toward the North Shore like an army in retreat. Behind them, the sky was a deep September blue.

Abigail walked quickly down the hallway to the master bedroom. At first, she thought her father hadn't come home. His door was open and the coverlet was pulled tight across the bed.

"I expect my breakfast in five minutes." His face covered in lather, Pratt sat in the sun by the east window while Wilson stropped a straight-edge razor.

Abigail was relieved to see him sitting there and annoyed at her own needless concern. Wilson had been shaving him in that spot for nearly forty years, and the bed was always made before Pratt sat down. She was worrying about him too much.

"I must talk with you, Father," she said firmly.

"Then talk."

Wilson applied the razor to the left side of Pratt's face.

Abigail could hear the scraping halfway across the room. "I'd prefer to talk alone."

Wilson stopped shaving and looked at Abigail like an offended child. "I been in this house longer than you, girl, and not one word have I repeated of anything I ever heard."

"Keep shaving and keep quiet." Pratt turned to his daughter. "What do you want?"

Abigail hesitated. "I'm sorry, Wilson."

The old servant grunted but did not look at her.

She turned her attention once more to her father. "I would like to know where you were last night."

Pratt's eyes grew small and angry behind the lather. "I told you, Abigail, we were fishing."

Wilson stopped shaving and took a step back.

"It was raining last night," she said.

"Rain is a concept that fish do not understand."

"I don't believe you've been fishing, and neither does Franconia. When she discovered that you and Horace were not in your rooms last night, she thought that her world had come to an end."

Pratt stood angrily, threw down the towel wrapped around him, and stalked to the south windows, which looked onto the garden behind the house. "And this morning, Franconia is where she can be found every morning—out there, picking fruit for my breakfast."

The garden rose in tiers toward the top of Pemberton Hill. It was not as exotic as some of the neighboring gardens, but it was filled with flowering plants, shade trees, and toward the top, fruit trees and berry bushes. Clad in a loose-flowing white dress and straw sun hat, Franconia Hampshire Pratt wandered the upper reaches of the property. She was humming a Renaissance air and choosing the ripest blackberries for her basket.

"Does she seem upset to you?" asked Pratt angrily.

Abigail picked up the towel and put it around his shoulders. Her touch always settled him. "Franconia and I were both upset last night, Father. I couldn't sleep at all for worry."

"There's no need for you to worry about me, Abbey."

"But I do."

"Long before you were born, I was riding out at all hours to conduct my business. I don't intend to change my methods at age sixty-four simply because my daughter wants to act like my mother."

Abigail's voice began to rise with her anger. "When my James died and I returned to your home, I understood that I was to become the mistress of the household."

"And you are." Pratt spoke softly.

"The mistress of the house takes an active interest in the comings and goings of her family. You'd never tell Mother the story you've been telling me and expect her to believe it."

"Your mother would never have asked."

"I would like the truth, Father, for my own peace of mind," she said firmly.

Pratt paused for a moment and smiled paternally. "Abigail, you're very bright and you have a fine grasp of most business matters, but unlike your mother you don't understand that in the business world men must be about in the middle of the night without explanation."

"While dragging their grandsons along with them?"

"The boy is my successor, Abigail. He must learn all there is to know. Now stop worrying." Pratt returned to the chair by the window, and Wilson began to shave him again.

Suddenly, Abigail felt like a little girl asking her father for an indulgence he did not intend to grant.

The master bedroom was masculine territory. It had not been wise for her to confront him there. The room ran the length of the south side of the house. It contained a canopied bed, a dresser, a mahogany chest of drawers, a wardrobe, two large chairs, and a desk overlooking the garden, and still it seemed massive. Dark browns and whites prevailed. There were no curtains on the windows and little evidence of a woman's hand. Abigail's mother had slept in an adjoining room for the last twelve years of her life.

Abigail would not be so pliable. "You still haven't told me where you go each night."

Pratt slammed his hand on the arm of the chair and jumped up once more, almost losing his nose to Wilson's razor in the process. "If we are no longer a trusting family, so be it."

"Father, it is you who do not trust me."

"You expect too much, Abigail. You may be the mistress of the house, but I am master of the business, and I do not like inter-ference. We will be going out again tonight, and tomorrow night, and perhaps the night after that. We are conducting important business with a most reclusive gentleman at his home on the Neck. If you wish to follow us, go right ahead, but I will not look upon your actions with favor, and your appearance, however furtive, will endanger our negotiations." Pratt wiped the remaining lather from his face, then Wilson helped him into his cutaway and pinned up the left sleeve. "I trust that I have satisfied your curiosity. I will now take breakfast, then walk to my office." Pratt left the room.

Abigail did not move. She had gotten her answer, but she had been made to feel that she was prying into areas that were not her concern. She had tried to assert herself in her father's house, and he had turned her aside with the belittlement and indignant display that he had mastered so long ago.

As he cleaned up, Wilson studied her out of the corner of his eye. He had been watching Abigail struggle with herself and her father since she moved back to Pemberton Hill. "He still thinks of you as his little girl, you know."

"Yes. That's our problem."

"No it ain't. He still treats Jason like a little boy, and Jason puts up no fuss at all. But you, you're just an apple that fell too close to the tree."

At sunset, Dexter Lovell dropped anchor in five fathoms of water just off Thompson's Island. He was in Boston Harbor. Four miles to the west, he saw the copper dome of the new state house, and he imagined Horace Taylor Pratt just sitting down to dinner in his home on Pemberton Hill. On the horizon to the east, he saw the sails of H.M.S. *Shannon* reflecting the rose-colored light, and he knew there were three more British warships just below the line.

Lovell congratulated himself on his good sense. Instead of navigating the northwest hypotenuse from Provincetown to Boston, which would have taken him into the teeth of the British squadron, he had tacked eighteen miles west across Cape Cod Bay, which the British did not usually patrol. When he reached the white bluffs of Manomet Point, he headed north, clinging to the coast until he was well past Nantasket Roads and within the safety of Boston Harbor.

Now, Dexter Lovell's journey was almost over. In a few hours, he would turn the tea set over to Horace Taylor Pratt and spend the rest of his life as a man of property. He would be glad for a hot meal and a warm bed, but he was unhappy that the adventure had ended. He hadn't felt as young in years. He was standing up straight, filling his lungs with fresh air, and walking on sea legs long unused. His age-yellowed complexion had turned brown in the sun. He took a bottle of port from the deck box and called to Jeff Grew.

"It's time you 'n' me drink to the end of a long voyage," said

Lovell. "You've done a good job." He took a slug of wine and handed the bottle to Grew.

The black bared his teeth. He was smiling, but his eyes were wary. He drank deep, all the time watching Lovell over the upturned bottle.

This was the moment Lovell had chosen to kill Jeff Grew. He no longer needed the black, and two quick shots into Grew's gut would be the end of him. It had been easy to kill the Dawsons, and Lovell thought it would be easy to kill this nigger, with his cocky ways and his leering smile and the machete that he sharpened so carefully each day. It wasn't.

The rain which had fallen softly on Boston the night before had attacked Cape Cod Bay with a violent thunderstorm that united Lovell and Grew against a common enemy. At the height of the squall, a powerful gust had torn loose the staysails. Without them, Lovell had to fight to keep the small sloop on course. She was taking on water, and if she swung broadside into the wind, a single wave could send her to the bottom. With a splicing awl in his hand and a knife between his teeth, Grew crawled out onto the bowsprit, which dug like a rapier into the chest of every wave. The sea crashed over him and nearly pulled him off the ship, but he held on. He secured the sail and saved the *Reckless*, and Dexter Lovell knew he would not be able to shoot Jeff Grew.

The storm cleared Grew's head, and he changed his mind about killing Lovell. He couldn't sail the *Reckless* to Jamaica himself, and even if people in Boston treated blacks like free men, he knew that a Jamaican with a strongbox on his shoulder would look suspicious anywhere. By morning, he had decided to stay with Lovell and keep his hand close to his machete. He trusted no white man. He knew only one. Best to keep him alive.

The black emptied the port into his belly and tossed the bottle over the side. "Dat sure be tasty, Dexter Lovell, and I glad to see you drinkin' some of it with me. I been lately wonderin' if you don't like me or somethin'."

Lovell managed to smile. "I don't, but you showed real balls last night. You saved us both. You'll be treated fair when we get that tea set ashore."

"I don't 'spect nothin' else."

The two thieves took final measure of one another. They had traveled five hundred miles on a tiny ship, but neither could guess what the other was thinking. They felt no friendship, no trust. Only the most grudging respect. A tea set and fear and a thread of decency held them together. It was a very fragile bond.

Grew offered a large paw to Lovell. They shook hands, and Grew closed his around Lovell's like a vise. Lovell felt his fingers and knuckles squashing together, but he showed no pain. Grew was giving him one last glimpse of physical strength, and Lovell would not be intimidated. He squeezed back as hard as he could, just enough to neutralize the pressure from Grew's hand. Finally, as if on signal, both men let go, and Dexter Lovell wished that he had the stomach to kill Jeff Grew.

Three hours later, the *Reckless* was washed in the glow of the full moon. The rowboat was pulling gently on the rope which tethered it to the sloop. The two smugglers were sitting in their private corners of the boat. Lovell perched above the cargo hold which contained the Golden Eagle. Grew nestled in the stern with a bottle of rum and his machete. The tide was turning. It was time to go ashore.

Lovell took an ax from Jack Dawson's deck box and went below. In the cabin, a windowless hole beneath the waterline, Lovell picked a spot on the bulkhead and swung the ax. Ten, twelve times the ax bit into the side. A thirteenth and water began to trickle into the cabin.

"What in hell you doin'?" Jeff Grew jumped down the ladder.

Lovell swung again and cut through the side of the *Reckless*.

"Jesus Christ, man. You gone crazy?"

"Not at all, my dark friend, but we'll 'ave no more thoughts of sailin' this 'ere sloop to Jamaica and no evidence of the *Reckless*."

"You sinkin' us?"

"Bow, stern, and midships. These smuggler sloops is built to sink fast, but I can't find no stern sea cock. That's why I'm swingin' the ax."

Three inches of water already covered the cabin deck, and countless empty bottles, the last remnants of Jack Dawson, were floating about in the wash like toys in a bathtub. Then, above the sound of flowing water, Lovell and Grew heard the squealing noise of fright. Rats appeared everywhere, scuttling across the beams, crawling onto tables and chairs, and swimming toward the two men as though they were trees in a flood.

Grew felt something at his foot. He slashed with his machete and sliced a rat in half. He swung the machete again and again, and the water around his feet turned red. He felt something soft and warm slithering across his neck. He plucked it from his ear and flung it against the wall. He was terrified.

"Stop killin' rats and get the tea set out of the 'old," commanded Lovell.

Grew bounded out of the cabin with Lovell a few steps behind. The black pulled back the grate on the cargo hold and leaped down. Lovell ran to the bow and descended into the small forward hold. He found the bow sea cock, swung at it once or twice with the side of the ax, then pulled up. Salt water bubbled into the compartment.

Back on deck, he saw the strongbox appearing from the hold. He took it from Grew's shoulder and pushed it to the side. He peered into the hold, which was eight feet deep, and saw the black face gleaming with sweat. He realized how easily he could close the grate and leave Jeff Grew to drown on the *Reckless*. He reached for it, but his hand stopped and he heard his own voice. "In the middle of the 'old, you'll find the midship sea cock. Open it and get the 'ell out."

"I ain't openin' nothin', Dexter. Dere's rats in here. I'm comin' out."

Lovell slammed the grate shut.

Grew screamed and swung his machete against the wooden latticework above him. "Goddam you, Dexter Lovell!"

"Open the sea cock, or I'll leave you down there for good."

Reluctantly, Grew retreated into the darkness. A moment later, Lovell heard the rush of water into the hold.

"Now let me out," screamed Jeff Grew.

Lovell watched the water swirl. He heard the rats screech as they were flushed from their hiding places. He saw the black's eyes grow wide with fright.

"You ain't gonna leave me here, Dexter Lovell. You can't!"

Lovell stood slowly. Perhaps he could. He stepped back from the grate, as if to test his own resolve.

Grew cursed the white man. Black hands appeared at the holes in the grate. They pulled violently, helplessly against it, then slipped away. Grew splashed back into the water, now ankle-deep in the hold. He bellowed for Lovell to let him out, then screamed. The rats were clinging to him.

Lovell took another step back and tried not to listen.

"Help me, damn you, Dexter Lovell!"

Lovell grabbed the strongbox by both handles and started to drag it toward the rowboat. If he could endure the black man's wail just a little longer, it would be silenced forever.

"I curse you, Dexter Lovell. I curse with all the bad voodoo I know!"

Just a little longer, a little longer.

"Help me, please, Dexter Lovell. Don't be lettin' me die!"

Lovell couldn't do it. He damned whatever shreds of conscience he still had and opened the grate. "I wouldn't leave you there, you crazy black fool. The rowboat slipped loose, and I 'ad to secure it. You don't want us drownin' because we sank our ship out from under us and didn't 'ave no rowboat."

Half-crazy with fear, Grew climbed out of the hold and slashed at the rats still clinging to his pants. Then he turned the machete to Lovell. Every muscle in his body was quivering. "I oughta be killin' you, Dexter Lovell!"

Lovell didn't budge. "And leave yourself alone in a sinkin' ship in Boston 'arbor? Don't be a fool, nigger. I'm your only friend. I just proved it by lettin' you out of that 'old. Now let's get goin'."

The *Reckless* was filling with water and sinking on an even keel. The deck would soon be awash. There was no time for argument. Lovell and Grew loaded the strongbox into the rowboat and pushed off. A few minutes later the mast slipped straight into the water and the sloop was gone. All that remained were a few rats still swimming for their lives.

"Drown, you dirty buggers," whispered Jeff Grew.

"I never seen such a big, strong man so scared of a few rats."

"I hate dem fuckers, Dexter." Grew shuddered. "And I hate you for leavin' me in dat hold so long."

"Just keep at the oars, Jefferson, my boy." Lovell's voice was gentle. From his days in a whaleboat, he knew well the soothing effects of rowing on panicked men.

"I hate dem fuckers."

"I can't say as I love 'em myself."

"Nobody love 'em, but you try livin' sometime down in Jamaica, in one of dem little huts where dey keep slaves. You be a little boy, four, maybe five years old, sleepin' all peaceful and nice . . ." Grew's voice cracked. He swung the oars four or five times through the water, then continued. ". . . and wake up when your momma scream because your little brother be dead from the typhoid beside you, and the rats is eatin' at his face. And den you scream, 'cause dey runnin' on your legs and tinkin' 'bout eatin' you, too. You don't never forget somethin' like dat, Dexter Lovell. You don't never forget dem rats, or what white men put you in dat hole, or how much you wants to get out. Never." When he was finished, the muscles in Jeff Grew's jaw were taut, his teeth were clenched tight, and there was hatred deep in his eyes.

Dexter Lovell feared that he had struck a dangerous spring in Jeff Grew's past. "You don't ever 'ave to go back. Just keep rowin' for another hour or two, and I'll see that you're set for life."

Grew shipped his oars and glared at Lovell. "You be another white man, Dexter. No different than any other."

"You'll 'ave to trust me."

"Like I said in Chesapeake Bay, you can't trust no one." He dipped the oars once more.

The tide and Jeff Grew's muscle carried them quickly through the outer harbor.

In the bright moonlight, Lovell could see the masts and yardarms of the Boston fleet growing like a winter forest along the waterfront. Behind them rose the dark mass of Beacon Hill; beneath them shone the lights of Boston. Lovell had spent the best years of his life in Boston, and now the city appeared to him as in a dream of shadow and darkness and scattered splashes of light. He hoped that the dream would grow brighter.

"Which wharf you want me aimin' for?" asked Grew.

"None. Swing north around the city. We're meetin' my friends on the other side."

"Dis place an island?"

"Just about."

Horace Taylor Pratt stood on Gravelly Point and waited for the splash of Lovell's oars in the Easterly Channel. It would be tonight, or not at all.

"That drive gets longer every night," said Wilson, sipping blackberry brandy from his flask. "Why couldn't Lovell show up at the waterfront, like any other smuggler?"

"The waterfront isn't deserted," said young Horace.

"Quite so," added Pratt.

A half hour later, Grew rowed through the channel between Boston and Charlestown, then under Craigie's Bridge. Fifty yards ahead, the brightly lit West Boston Bridge.

"Another mile and a 'alf or so, and we're there." Lovell's voice vibrated with excitement.

And Jeff Grew's heart pounded. As he rowed toward the West Boston Bridge, he studied Lovell's face for some hint of what awaited him. Would this white man still try to kill him, this white man who drank with him, then locked him in a hold filled with rats, this white man who spoke so gently and always kept a hand near his gun? Or would this white man keep his word?

A voice deep inside Jeff Grew began to chant, Kill him, kill him, kill him now. He tried not to listen, but the voice grew louder. He concentrated on rowing and fixed his eyes on Lovell.

Suddenly, Lovell's face began to change. His forehead and cheekbones burned bright, like gold. His eyes disappeared beneath black scars that fell to his chin. His cheeks sank to blackness beneath the gold. Jeff Grew saw bad voodoo. He had seen it before, in Jamaica. The witch-doctor's mask of evil. He dropped his oars. The boat drifted into the darkness under the bridge, and the mask was gone.

"What the hell is wrong with you?" asked Lovell.

Slowly, Grew picked up the oars and pulled the boat back into the light. The mask appeared again and the voices chanted, Kill him, kill him, kill him now. But Grew kept rowing. He knew that the lanterns on the bridge were playing tricks on him. Or maybe they were trying to warn him.

He rowed another twenty-five yards before he looked over his shoulder into the Back Bay. But for the moon and the West Boston Bridge, all was darkness. Grew didn't like it. "Where we goin', Dexter? I don't see no wharves, no city. I can't even see no houses."

"Row another thirty or forty yards, then turn ninety degrees starboard."

"Dere's nothin' but black out dere, Dexter."

"Just keep rowin'."

Kill him, kill him, kill him now. Don't let this white man deceive you. The voice was becoming insistent.

The rowboat dug into the mud twice before Lovell found the mouth of the Easterly Channel. The Back Bay was covered in water at high tide, but many areas of it were not navigable. Lovell would try to stay in the channel all the way to Gravelly Point.

He reached under his seat and produced a red lantern. After several tries with flint and stone, he lit the wick and held the lantern above his head. The small cube of darkness around the boat glowed deep red.

Kill him, kill him, kill him now. Grew kept rowing.

"I see it, Grandfather." At first, young Horace's voice was uncertain. The light was only a pinprick in the distance.

"The lantern?" said Pratt from the carriage.

The boy put his grandfather's spyglass to his eye. He could make out two men in a rowboat about a mile away, and one of them was holding a red lantern aloft. "Yes, sir. It's them."

Pratt and Wilson were beside him in an instant.

"He's done it," said Pratt softly, his voice filled with admiration. "The old bastard's done it."

"I'll have to say I'm surprised," added Wilson.

"Horace, get the lantern out of the boot and bring it here."

In the moonlight, Lovell could see nothing but the dark outline of Gravelly Point. In the glow of the red lantern, Jeff Grew saw the face of a demon.

"Pull steady, Jefferson. The channel flows south for about a quarter mile, then swings sou'west. Tonight we sleep in beds," said Lovell triumphantly. "And if you want, we'll get you a fine white woman to stroke your dick."

Grew continued to row. The rhythm of the oars as they clanked in the oarlock lent cadence to the words now pounding in his head.

A light gleamed on Gravelly Point, now about three quarters of a mile away. Lovell squinted into the blackness. If it was Pratt, he would signal.

Young Horace held the lantern, and Wilson passed his hat back and forth in front of it.

"They've seen us," said Lovell.

Grew looked over his shoulder and saw the spot of light blinking like an eye in the blackness. Kill him, kill him, kill him now. The white men are waiting to kill you.

Lovell blew out the red lantern.

Kill him. Now. Grew dropped the oars and reached for his machete.

"He's seen us," said young Horace excitedly.

"Then put out your lantern. He can navigate in the dark."

The first scream of rage took several seconds to travel across the Back Bay. It was followed instantly by an animal cry of pain, then a gunshot.

Dexter Lovell's left sleeve was covered in blood.

Jeff Grew felt a hole in his chest. There was another hole, much larger, where the ball had torn through his back. The shot had knocked him off his feet, and he lay in the bow, wedged between the strongbox and the gunwales. Kill him. You must kill him. Grew spat blood and struggled to his feet in the rocking boat.

Lovell grabbed for the second pistol. He thought he had it out of his belt when he realized that his arm was still hanging by his side. Nerve, muscle, and most of the bone were severed, and Grew's machete was swinging at him again. Lovell ducked. The machete glanced off the side of his head. A flap of scalp dropped open, and

Lovell's right ear came away on the edge of the blade.

Water slopped over the gunwales on both sides of the boat. Grew swung the machete at Lovell's throat. He stumbled and fell on top of the white man. Lovell grabbed the loaded gun with his right hand, jammed it against Grew's stomach, and fired. Grew snapped to his feet. He staggered. He tried to swing the machete. He fell backward, and the boat capsized.

Dexter Lovell plunged through cold velvet blackness. He thought he was dead. His body spun through space, then his head broke the surface and he gulped for air. He felt something flailing about in the water nearby. It grabbed him by the leg and pulled him under. He kicked loose and burst to the surface once more.

Jeff Grew appeared a few feet away. He was screaming something at Lovell, but Lovell did not understand him. Grew was chanting in Mandinka, "Kill him. Kill him. Kill him now," over and over until water choked him and he sank once more.

Lovell tried to fight, but his left arm would not respond. His head went under. He struggled violently to bring it to the surface. Then the seaman's instincts took over. He kicked his shoes off and treaded water.

"Damn it!" screamed Pratt.

"Grandfather, what's happening?"

Pratt had been watching the shadows through his spy glass. Horace and Wilson could hear the struggle echoing across the water.

"The fools are killing each other."

Dexter Lovell grabbed the side of the overturned boat. Then he realized that the tea set was gone. He looked about frantically, hoping that, by some miracle, iron would float. He put his head into the water and tried to see the bottom. Blood poured from the wound in his scalp and the deep slice in his shoulder, but he felt no pain.

He let go of the boat and dove. His brain sent signals to both arms; only his right responded. He touched bottom at six feet. He grabbed a handful of mud and tried to drag himself along in the blackness. His hand hit metal. The strongbox was settled in the ooze directly beneath the boat. He clutched at the handle with his right hand and tried to lift. Too heavy.

His lungs screamed for air, but he would not let go. He would not leave the strongbox.

Air, more air. Go up and take a breath, then dive.

You'll never find the tea set again if you leave it now. Hold on and pull. Too heavy. Use your other arm. But my other arm is hanging off. No it isn't. Try to lift it.

Someplace in the blackness, a familiar voice was speaking to him. Yes, lift it, Dexter. The box is light. You're young and strong.

I need air or my lungs will explode.

It's all right, Dexter. You can breathe. Yes, dear. Breathe.

The world grew bright. Dexter Lovell stood on the stern of the *Gay Head*. The sky was blue, the breeze fresh and fair. On the wharf, his dear Beatrice was waving. He jumped from the ship. They embraced. In the last hallucinations of a drowning man, Dexter Lovell found what he was searching for.

Pratt saw a body appear on the surface. He watched through his spyglass until he was certain that both men were dead. He gave the glass to his grandson. "The poor fool came so close."

"What the hell happened?" asked Wilson.

"I don't know."

Young Horace took the glass from his eye. He had hoped to see real dead men floating out there. He saw only a few indistinct shapes. "What will we do now?"

Pratt did not hesitate or allow himself a moment of grief at Lovell's death. He pivoted on his cane and walked back to the carriage. "We'll let the tide take care of Lovell and his friend, and then we'll figure out a way to get that tea set out of the Easterly Channel."

CHAPTER VIII

The stairwell in Peter Fallon's apartment building usually stank of stale onions and stray cats, but when he came home from the Museum of Fine Arts, he smelled cheap shaving lotion the moment he stepped in the door.

Danny Fallon, dressed in his only suit, was waiting at the top of the stairs. "Balled any students lately?"

"I haven't balled anybody lately."

"Well, as the old man would say, that's better than ballin' boys."

"He's still a philosopher, isn't he?"

"He's a Harp, and I never met one yet who wasn't always tryin' to tell you how to live your life."

"While all the time tellin' you that he wasn't tryin' to tell you how to live your life."

Inside the apartment, Peter gave his brother the once-over and a whistle. "What brings you to Cambridge, all dressed up and smellin' like a tout on Derby day?"

"Kenny Gallagher's wake."

"Already? I thought they were holding the body."

"They only kept him for thirty-six hours. Then Ma called the coroner and said, 'I'm Kenny Gallagher's best friend, and I know for a fact that he has no next of kin.' No arguin' with Ma. They gave her the stiff. All the boys down at the Risin' Moon chipped in, Uncle Dunphy gave us a cloth casket, and we're plantin' him ourselves." Danny followed Peter into the kitchen, which was only slightly larger than most closets. "Ma's been callin' you all afternoon."

"I wasn't here."

"No shit. She figured you were lost or somethin' and wouldn't know about the wake. She starts bitchin' at me to come over and get you so you won't miss the Rosary."

"I thought the Rosary was always the second night."

"Hey, we were lucky to get the home for *one* night, and Pa had to twist Dunphy's arm half off before he gave us that shitty casket."

Peter popped open the refrigerator. Three cockroaches scurried away from the half-eaten piece of apple pie on the bottom shelf. "I can offer you a dish of plain yogurt and wheat germ, a loaf of week-old Bavarian bread—baked by a failing student—a piece of unsavory apple pie, or my last can of Narragansett."

"You know, you live like a goddam nigger" Danny exploded. "Stayin' in a dump like this, with cockroaches in the icebox and crabs in the toilet. Why don't you get the hell out of here? You can't like this place. Sometimes I think you want to be a martyr or somethin' and punish yourself because it feels good."

Peter knew that his brother was probably right. In the last six months, his life as an academic had been something to get through and get behind him. The more painful it was, the better he would feel when he threw it all over for something else.

"Do you need money?" continued Danny. "I'll lend you what I can. Just ask. Or ask Pa. But for Chrissakes, get the hell out of this hole."

"I like independence, and right now, this is all the independence I can afford." Peter held out the beer. "Last call."

Danny gave up. "I'll split it with you."

"That's better. Less talk and more communication." Peter took a dirty glass from the cupboard, rinsed it briefly under cold water, and half-filled it with beer. "The guest gets the glass."

"No, thanks. I have enough problems as it is." Danny grabbed the can. The beer was gone in an instant. "Now c'mon. Some old priest from down the Cape is sayin' the Rosary, and he's startin' at seven-thirty."

"Do you think Ma would be pissed if I said I had too much work to do?" Peter wanted to start digging into back copies of *Hubcap*. He knew he shouldn't miss Kenny's wake, but he was thinking of it.

"Pissed? She'd come over here and get you herself."

"What if I told you that I might be on the trail of some big money, and I needed every extra minute to track it down?"

"What kind of big money?" Danny was always suspicious when people started talking about big money.

"Buried treasure. A tea set worth two and a half million dollars."

Danny looked at Peter for a moment, then began to laugh. "I'd say you were out of your fuckin' mind."

Peter realized how ludicrous he sounded. He began to laugh. "And you'd probably be right."

The Kelleher Funeral Home was a handsome Victorian house on Dorchester Heights, the highest point in South Boston.

Small wonder that Washington chose this hill for his artillery emplacement during the siege of Boston. From Kelleher's front porch, one could see the harbor, the downtown skyline, and the three-deckers and row houses which fanned out in every direction across Southie. Great spot for a funeral home, thought Fallon. Crowded dwellings all about, and a mansion right in the middle of it.

It often seemed to Fallon that among the Irish of Boston the three days after death were as important as a whole life. When he was feeling less cynical, he realized that the wake was among the most humane practices that the Irish had brought to Boston. Peter was always taught that when someone died or lost a loved one, he paid his respects. He shook the hand of the bereaved, he tried to offer whatever consolation he could, and he hoped that the Almighty would watch over the deceased, even if he wasn't sure that the Almighty existed.

It didn't matter that a person suffered through life pinching pennies in a three-room cold-water flat. When he died, his friends and relatives laid him out in the house on the hill and gave him a send-off fit for the mayor. It didn't matter that a person never had had a good word for anyone in life. When he died, his clan gathered and said whatever good there was to say about him.

Danny opened the door, solid oak and beveled glass. The Fallon brothers stepped into the front hall. The door closed behind them on a hydraulic hinge, and they were soothed by cool, conditioned air.

Dunphy Kelleher, their father's cousin, greeted them with a solemn nod. Of average height and build, he was distinguished by black hair recently gone gray at the temples. Although he now left the embalming to his employees, his lips were permanently pursed, as though he were constantly holding his nose beside a dead piece of flesh. "Terrible thing about poor Kenny. Terrible. We know neither the day nor the hour. Neither the day nor the hour."

"Save the sermon," whispered Danny. "When he was alive, you wouldn't give Kenny the steam off your shit. Where is he?"

Dunphy's expression and tone did not change. "I've reserved the second floor for the Gallagher party." He looked at Peter. "I haven't seen you in quite a while, my boy."

Fallon smiled. "Wakes and weddings bring us all closer together."

"We should have them more often."

The Fallons walked into the large, formal entrance hall. A leaded glass chandelier hung above them. A sign, white magnetic letters and red arrows on a black background, directed mourners to the left for O'Hara, the right for Lissel, and upstairs for Gallagher.

"Just like goin' to one of those shopping-mall movie theatres that's showin' three different pictures," cracked Danny.

The syrupy smell of orchids and carnations rolled into the hallway, but Peter looked neither left nor right as he walked past the O'Haras and Lissels. He didn't enjoy the sight of dead bodies. It was bad enough that he had to see Kenny, all made up in heavy pancake and rouge, his face distorted from fluid, his mouth stuffed with cotton and wired shut, wax plugs filling the bullet holes so he wouldn't leak, and Rosary beads, which he hadn't touched in forty years, wrapped in his hands for eternity.

Halfway up the stairs, Fallon heard the familiar prayer. A single, strong voice, "Hail Mary, full of grace, the Lord is with Thee. Blessed art Thou among Women, and Blessed is the Fruit of Thy womb, Jesus." And the mumbled response of thirty or forty voices, "Holy Mary, Mother of God, pray for us sinners, now and at the hour of our death, Amen." The Rosary had already started.

Kenny Gallagher's body lay in the bay window of what had been the master bedroom before Kelleher remodeled. The walls had been painted robin's-egg blue, in keeping with the pastel motif, and the draperies were cream-colored. An enormous American oriental, about three inches thick, covered the floor.

"The Fifth Sorrowful Mystery, the Death Upon the Cross," droned Father Gerry Hale, an arthritic old priest hunched over the kneeler in front of the casket.

116

Behind him, the people knelt, sat, and stood wherever they found space. Fallon hadn't known that Kenny Gallagher had had that many friends. The word had gone out from the Fallon household that one of their own, a good man with no family and a penchant for pouring an extra finger on every highball, was dead. Friends and friends of friends had come to say goodbye.

Fallon recognized Jackie Halloran and his wife; the Murphy family, all three generations; Harry Hourihan, the owner of the Rising Moon; the widows' club, an unofficial army of local ladies who materialized for every wake; and the Andy Capps, as Fallon called them, the Rising Moon regulars who seemed to be at the bar no matter when Fallon stopped by for a beer.

Fallon's parents, Tom and Maureen, knelt near the casket and prayed loudly. Fallon's aunts and uncles, most of whom had never met Kenny Gallagher, were there out of deference to Maureen. Danny's wife, Sheila, sat in a far corner with her three children and six others, and God help the kid who wasn't saying his beads.

Peter stepped quietly into the room, nodded toward his mother, folded his hands in front of him, and stared at the floor. Danny stood in the hallway and smoked.

By the time the priest said the final Hail Mary, Fallon understood once more the power of the Rosary. He took no comfort in the words themselves, but their repetition, fifty Hail Marys separated into five decades by the Lord's Prayer, was almost hypnotic. The rhythm of the words created concentration which led to contemplation and, ultimately, to serenity. Even people like Fallon, the agnostics and non-Catholics who stood silently at the back of the room, were held by the prayer.

"In the Name of the Father, and of the Son, and of the Holy Spirit, Amen." The old priest blessed the body and stood painfully.

It was several moments before anyone else moved. Then, Tom Fallon put away his beads and shook hands with Father Hale. Respects had been paid. Socializing began.

"Why, Petie Fallon!" It was Harry Hourihan. "I ain't seen you in ages." Harry pumped Fallon's hand vigorously. His eyes were red and his face looked puffy. He had been Kenny's boss. "It's such a terrible thing to happen, and what a thing for you to see."

"We'll all miss him, Harry," said Fallon.

"That's right." Denny Murphy joined the conversation. "He made the best damn boilermaker I ever drank."

"For Chrissakes, anybody could make a boilermaker," said Hourihan. "It don't take nothin' to pour a beer and a shot."

"But he poured you up a shot that hit like Marciano's right."

"That's because he poured too much."

"He got good tips," said Denny.

"And cost me money doing it." Harry was forgetting his grief.

"He was the best bartender I ever knew, and nobody could break up a fight faster," persisted Denny.

"I can attest to that," added Fallon.

Harry shook his head and looked at the floor. "I don't know what I'll do without him."

Fallon clapped Harry on the shoulder. "I'd better get over and see my old man, Harry. Say hello to the wife for me."

Fallon took ten minutes to get through the knots of people standing about the room. Every few paces, he was stopped by someone who recognized him and wanted to talk. He chatted with Harry Delehante, the barber who always cut his hair short with a part on the left, no matter what the instructions; Mary Donovan, his old baby-sitter, now thirty-five and looking forty with four kids of her own; Auntie Eleanor, who usually slipped five dollars into his breast pocket whenever she saw him; Benny Greene, his father's old partner, who always counseled Peter to be a dentist; and Tom Hennessey, "with a booze named after me," his father's labor foreman and Peter's first boss.

Fallon managed to smile through all the small talk, and he answered questions about his future as gracefully as possible without revealing too much. He had just about run out of good nature when he reached his parents. They were standing near the casket with Father Hale.

"Good evening, folks," he said pleasantly.

"You missed most of the Rosary."

"Sorry, Ma."

"I'll forgive you," joked Father Hale.

Maureen Fallon introduced her son to the priest, who was well into his seventies and clearly suffering from the pain of his arthritis. When they shook hands, Fallon felt knots of bone grown thick around each knuckle of the old man's hand.

"I'm an old friend of Kenny's late mother," the priest explained. "I knew Kenny when he was just a little shaver. I used to visit them on Sunday afternoons when I was in seminary. He was a beautiful child."

Fallon glanced at the body a few feet away. He could not imagine it as a beautiful child.

"Pity he never married," continued Father Hale. "It would be nice if he had some blood relatives here to say goodbye. But from what his mother used to tell me, he was never very comfortable with the girls."

Maureen Fallon smiled. "We're Kenny's blood, at least in spirit, Father."

"We are, indeed." Tom Fallon admired Kenny Gallagher. He knew that without Kenny's help, he'd probably be dead.

Tom Fallon. Called Black Tom by men who disliked his stern expression. Called Nails by the bricklayers who worked for him because he filed away at his fingernails whenever his hands were idle. He was sixty-four, with crew-cut gray hair, enormous hands, and shoulders so broad that his grandchildren could not touch both of them at the same time.

One day in the mid-fifties, Tom and Kenny Gallagher, who had also been a bricklayer, were working for Norton Construction. It was a pointing job—repairing and replacing old mortar—on the Western Union building. Tom and Kenny had just come back from the Barrister Bar and Grill, where they'd each taken a beer and a shot with lunch. They were working nine stories up, on a swing staging that hung from the roof of the building. Tom stepped out the window first. With the alcohol and hot sun, he forgot to check the rigging.

That was the day the laborer had failed to lock the pump after lowering the staging.

Tom Fallon put all his weight on the staging and it fell out from under him. As he started down, he spun toward the window. Kenny, still inside, was able to grab him. For almost five minutes, Kenny clung to Tom's arm and screamed for help. While he hung nine stories above the street, Tom Fallon got religion. He resolved that he would never drink again, and decided that if he had to risk his neck, he would do it for himself.

After that, Tom Fallon went to Mass every Sunday and prayed every day. He drank nothing but beer and only on weekends. He scraped together some money and started his own contracting company. He worked day and night to build his business, placing such demands on himself that he expected too much from those around him. His business never flourished, but it was his own and he was able to give his family a good life.

Tom Fallon told his sons that all his hard work was for them, and he expected great things from both of them. Danny showed promise of becoming a good tradesman, and Tom encouraged him. Peter had other talents.

When Peter showed excellent grades in grammar school, Tom decided to pay tuition and sent the boy to Boston College High School, where he was taught by Jesuits. When Peter became a champion debater, his father imagined a law career. When Peter was accepted at Harvard, Tom Fallon saw the pattern unfolding— Harvard, Harvard Law School, a solid Boston legal practice, and then, the most important step into respectability for the Boston Irish of earlier generations, a career in politics. Senator Peter Fallon and his father, Tom.

Peter Fallon decided in college that he would not let his life be sledgehammered into shape. He had listened to his father's dreams and fulfilled his father's plans for twenty years. When he had to decide between law and history, he chose as much from a sense of rebellion as intellectual interest. His decision caused a rift with his father which had not closed in four years.

Tom Fallon could not understand why Peter would choose a scholar's life, spent in libraries, to a life in politics or business. He believed that his son had run away from a challenge and hidden in the study of the past. He was deeply disappointed.

"You haven't been around in two or three months, Peter. Can't you stop over here more often?" Tom spoke bluntly.

"I'm busy, Dad. I'm almost to the end of my dissertation."

"Then what?" Tom Fallon asked the question as though he already knew the answer.

"I have several teaching offers in the Midwest." Peter spoke as though his privacy had been invaded.

"Father Hale was just telling me about one of his nephews. It seems the boy graduated from Boston College, went to law school, and is now making a name for himself in the Justice Department down in Washington."

"So what?"

"So people are doing things."

Father Hale sensed the coldness between father and son. He excused himself.

"Do you want to know something, Dad?" Peter lowered his voice. "I don't give a shit."

Tom Fallon turned to his wife. "Nice, isn't it? Forty thousand dollars' worth of education, and that's all he can say."

"Well, if you'd find something other than jobs to talk about . . ."

"What else is there, Maureen? A man's work is his life."

"Speaking of that, I hear that Fallon and Son Construction Company has been having a few problems." Peter was sorry he'd said that. He didn't mean to sound so callous.

"We'll survive. We have before." Tom Fallon did not conceal his anger.

Peter tried to convey his concern. "Has someone put the screws to you, or were you just in the wrong place at the wrong time?"

"I made a bad mistake. I signed a contract with a fella who didn't have any money. Except that I didn't know it. To get his job started, I pumped bricks, blocks, and lumber into it. I used my own money. Then, this fella goes bankrupt and leaves me with my hand up my ass." Tom Fallon spat out the details. "You work hard all your life, then you take the shaft. But I don't guess you'd know anything about that, sittin' up there in your library."

Peter decided he'd had enough. Their meetings always ended in unpleasantness. He had paid his respects. He had no need to stay. Before his mother could change the subject, Peter kissed her on the cheek. "I've got to get back."

"Can't you come back to the house? We'll be having coffee and sandwiches for everyone."

"I don't think so, Mama." He offered his hand to his father. "I hope it all works out for you, Dad."

Tom Fallon shook hands with his son. "Try to come around more often."

They looked at each other for a moment. They had more to say to each other, but they were both too stubborn. Neither would start the conversation again. Peter turned abruptly and left, crossing the room much more quickly on the way out. He felt stifled, closed in. He had to escape. Old, familiar faces smiled everywhere. He brushed past them all. He used to enjoy family gatherings, but he could not recount the last four years of his life for anyone else.

Halfway down the stairs, he bumped into Sadie Halloran, Jackie's mother. She gave him a hug and a kiss. At close range, she smelled like a distillery. They exchanged a few pleasantries, but to his relief, she didn't want to talk about his career.

"I think it's a shame we don't have wakes in the home no more. When my Jack dropped dead at forty-six, we laid him out right in the living room. We had coffee and sandwiches and a few other things"—she winked—"and I don't have to tell you that his old pals did themselves proud for my dear Jack."

"Well, I'd say we're doin' proud by Kenny." Fallon tried to smile.

"We'd all feel a little better if your Uncle Dunphy had himself a tap workin' in the other—" Sadie Halloran noticed someone standing at the top of the stairs. "Why, I know that boy from somewhere."

The young man who had followed Fallon to the Book Cellar the night before was standing at the top of the stairs. He had trailed Fallon to the wake. His name was James Buckley. He had an Irish moon face and the body of an ironworker. He was wearing the coat and tie he kept in the trunk of the Oldsmobile, and he blended easily into the South Boston gathering. Fallon glanced at him. Buckley slipped into the smoking room. Sadie scampered up the stairs. Fallon headed down.

Sadie found the young man quickly. "I know that face."

"I'm afraid not, ma'am." Buckley tried to leave.

Sadie clamped a hand on his elbow. "Let me guess your name."

"Denny Flynn," said Buckley.

Downstairs, Fallon said goodbye to Dunphy Kelleher and stepped into the humidity.

Father Hale was climbing into his car, a Chevy Impala parked in front of the funeral home. "Can I give you a lift?"

"I'm going to Cambridge."

"A bit out of my way, but I can run you up to Broadway Station in my air-conditioned chariot."

"You've convinced me."

James Buckley loosed himself from Sadie Halloran's grasp and hurried out to the front lawn. Fallon was nowhere in sight.

"I wanted to stay longer," said Father Hale. "I like meeting new people. But it's a long drive back to the Cape."

Considering how slowly he drove, it would take him several hours to get home, thought Fallon. "Are you retired down there?"

"Oh, no. That I could never stand. I'm the pastor of a small church near Plymouth. Very quiet in the winter, packed for seven Masses on a summer weekend."

"It must be pleasant."

Father Hale grunted. "It's the last stop."

Fallon understood what the old man was talking about. He did not pursue it.

Father Hale stopped at a red light, then glided slowly into the flow of traffic on Broadway. Brakes squealed and horns blared. Fallon grabbed the back of his neck and waited for the collision. Nothing happened.

"Father, I'm not quite ready to make my last stop, yet."

"I'm sorry. I guess I'm preoccupied these days. My arthritis is getting worse." He held up his right hand. The fingers bent off in four different directions. "I can hardly hold the Host. And handling Rosary beads is agony."

"Maybe you should get workman's compensation." Fallon tried to joke.

The old priest sighed. It sounded like a death rattle. "I guess we all have to come to the end sometime. Kneeling over the body of poor Kenny Gallagher, I am reminded that my own is very close."

"Your faith doesn't sustain you?"

"Even priests fear death, my boy. And when you were never sure that you chose the right vocation in the first place, you're haunted by the might-have-beens when you draw near the end."

They rode for a while in silence.

Then, the old priest sighed again. "It's possible that I might have been Kenny Gallagher's father."

Fallon's head snapped around.

Father Hale realized the ambiguity. He laughed softly. "No, no, not what you think. Had I chosen the other path, Kenny's mother would have been Mary Hale instead of Mary Gallagher, and we would have made a child." He shook his head. "What a wonder it would have been. I loved her so much, my poor, dear Mary Mannion." His voice trailed off. He spoke with new strength as the memories flooded back. "We met in school. South Boston High, Class of 1921. She was beautiful, and I was not a bad-looking sort myself."

Fallon felt that he was eavesdropping, but he listened. He sensed the old man's loneliness and knew that Father Hale needed someone to talk to.

"We went together for two years," continued the priest. "I was working as a clerk in a shipping office. She was just waiting for me to pop the question, but I was afraid to.

"You see, all along I thought I might have a vocation for the priesthood. I felt good inside a church. I liked the priests at Gate of Heaven. When I served Mass, I always felt that I belonged on the altar. And those were bad times, the twenties. Bootlegging and gangsterism, right here in South Boston. My mother would always say, 'We need strong men on the altar in these days. We need good Catholic priests to show the rest of the world how to live. Maybe you should think about wearing the collar.' I guess I agreed.

"When it came time for me to choose a wife, I chose Holy Mother Church. Mary Mannion didn't speak to me for almost a year. She ran off and married Big Jim Gallagher, leaving me to wonder if my mother had been wrong." He spoke without bitterness. He had lived too long for that.

The car arrived at the subway station. Fallon didn't move.

"And you know something?" said the priest. "After fifty years in the priesthood, I'm still wondering."

Fallon studied the old man silently. A life had unfolded in front of him, and he didn't know how to respond. Finally, he reached out and shook Father Hale's misshapen hand. "Thank you, Father. Thanks for the ride." He got out of the car.

"Take care," said the priest. "And son . . ."

Fallon poked his head into the car.

"It's a terrible thing to go through life lookin' over your shoulder. Mothers and fathers are always willing to give advice, but a person must pray for guidance, then do what he thinks is best. Goodnight, now."

Philip Pratt loved Szechwan food, especially on hot summer nights. The Yu Hsiang scallops and Szechwan shredded spiced beef were so hot that the fire in his mouth made him forget heat, humidity, and sinus problems all at once. Pratt had found an excellent Szechwan restaurant—blazing food and relaxing atmosphere—on Commonwealth Avenue, just beyond Kenmore Square.

He was dining with his cousin, Isabelle Carrington Howe. They met often to discuss business, the fate of Pratt Industries, and the mental condition of Isabelle's mother, Katherine Carrington. Philip and Isabelle had grown up together, sharing summers on the tennis court at Searidge, learning to sail in the same boat, entering Harvard and Radcliffe in the same year, and, so the rumors went, teaching each other things beneath the wooden stairs at the beach that second cousins were not encouraged to learn together.

"I'm sorry, Philip. You know how carefully we screen her communications. I sometimes think Mother has no conception of the seriousness of all this." A widow without children, she had lived with her mother for the past five years.

"I think she does, but she refuses to acknowledge it. She becomes more difficult to reason with all the time. As a result, we're forced to follow this young historian around until we're sure he's nothing more."

Isabelle heard the annoyance in Philip's voice. She frowned. Horn-rimmed glasses and hair pulled straight back accented the expression. "I do my best, Philip," she said sharply. "We try to keep her happy. We take her where she wants to go. We see that she has visitors. We do whatever you ask."

"Did you know that the young historian had brunch with Christopher and spent the afternoon talking with an administrator in the Museum of Fine Arts?"

"If you're blaming me for that, you can finish incinerating the roof of your mouth alone. I have little enough taste for this food as it is."

Philip tenderly took her hand in his. "I'm simply relating the events of the day. I really don't have anyone else to discuss them with."

She studied him for a moment. "Then no more talk of this business. It sickens me sometimes to think of what's happened to us."

"It would sicken you more to see William Rule in my office."

She nodded. Her expression softened. The age lines around her eyes disappeared. Philip recalled how beautiful he had once found her.

A phone call for Philip Pratt. He took it in the vestibule.

Christopher Carrington's voice wound tight around the line. "Philip?"

"Christopher, I've been trying to get hold of you all day. Who is that student?"

"He's nobody. I've just spoken with Uncle Calvin, and I want to extend the same courtesy to you. I'm calling the police."

"What are you talking about?"

"The police. I'm going to give evidence of a murder."

"Murder? Whose murder?"

"One of our distant relatives. She's dead."

"I still don't know what you're talking about."

"Because you don't read the right newspapers. Yesterday's *Los Angeles Times* reported the murder of Sally Korbel in her Santa Monica apartment."

Pratt was stunned. Three days ago, he'd been with her. Three days ago, he'd screwed her. He couldn't believe it. "I had nothing to do with this, Chris. We're not killers."

"Somebody killed her, Philip. If you didn't, perhaps it was Rule. You should have no objections if we offer our information to the proper authorities."

Pratt didn't know what to say, but he knew he didn't want the police involved, at least until he had talked to Calvin and Soames. "We have no information of value to anyone."

125

"False." Carrington would not be dissuaded.

"Rule did not know that I was going to California to see a whore about a sampler. If he had, he would have gotten to her first. And if he'd had her killed, there's no way we could pin it on him. He's too smart."

"Genealogy is a very refined science. So is criminology. Anything is possible in either."

"If you go to the police with a false charge of murder against William Rule, you will have to describe everything. Blow the story now, and you'll guarantee that we lose control of Pratt Industries."

"We've already lost control." The words snapped in Pratt's ear.

"You're doing us no good at all, Chris. You can't do anything for that girl. Before you call the police, give me ten minutes of your time. Please."

Christopher Carrington hung up.

Pratt called Calvin and told him to get to Carrington's apartment right away. Then he called Soames, who was not at home, and left a message on his service.

"I'm afraid the meal is over," he told Isabelle. "Christopher has slipped a cog."

Isabelle offered to go along. She was very close to her nephew and might be able to influence him.

Twenty minutes later, they arrived at Christopher Carrington's apartment, a handsome old building on Louisburg Square.

Bennett Soames was waiting for them. "I got your message and headed here straight away."

The hallway was dark and smelled faintly of mothballs and Lysol. Carrington lived on the second floor, apartment 2A. Philip Pratt knocked.

No answer.

He knocked again.

Nothing.

"We've missed him," said Pratt.

"Perhaps we can catch up with him," offered Isabelle.

Pratt paid no attention. "I didn't think he'd do it right away. This is really going to hamstring us."

"Unless Rule in fact killed the girl," she said.

"Very unlikely," said Soames. He took out a pocket knife and probed the lock.

"There's no need to go through the apartment," said Pratt.

The lock popped. The door snapped open. A four-inch chain lock held tight from the inside.

A shaft of light sliced into the hallway, momentarily blinding Pratt. Isabelle screamed. Pratt's eyes adjusted.

A chair was lying on the floor in the middle of the room. Above it, a pair of expensive Italian shoes twisted back and forth like magnets above a piece of steel. The clothesline rope was attached to a curtain fastener in the wall and looped over the oak beam that crossed the middle of the ceiling.

Christopher Carrington had not been hanging there long. His face had not turned black, and the muscles in his legs were still twitching. But he was dead.

CHAPTER IX   *September 1814*

Horace Taylor Pratt III placed a glass-bottomed box on the surface of the water and peered down at the floor of the Back Bay.

"See anything, boy?" asked Wilson.

"It's still too dark."

"Well, as near as I can figure, this is where they flipped over."

Heavy clouds smoldered above Boston and turned the sky ashen gray. It was Sunday morning, a half hour before dawn.

Dexter Lovell and Jeff Grew had killed each other on Friday night. The next morning, Grew's body was washed up on the Neck. It was stripped of purse and personal belongings and would be buried in Potter's Field. Lovell's body had not been found. The tides had hauled it back to the harbor and thrown it up on one of the islands, where crabs would pick it clean within a few days. The treasure they had died for was still sitting in the mud at the bottom of the Easterly Channel.

Horace Taylor Pratt stood on the edge of Gravelly Point and peered through a spyglass. They had perhaps three hours to find the tea set. After that, Sunday boaters would begin crisscrossing the Charles River Basin, and two men salvaging a strongbox would certainly attract attention. The strongbox itself, if left beneath the few feet of water that covered it at low tide, might easily be seen from a passing dory and hauled up by some cobbler on holiday.

They were lucky that no one had noticed the strongbox at low tide yesterday, thought Pratt. They had to find it today.

Again, he squinted through the spyglass. Wilson was still circling. Pratt wished that he were out there with them, but an old man with one arm wasn't much good in a rowboat. Best to stay on shore. Wilson was as reliable as the tides, and Pratt had every confidence in young Horace.

He stepped away from the glass, which stood on a tripod, and he began to pace the bank as though he were waiting for one of his ships from China. He figured that the tea set would fetch twenty thousand dollars in England. His ships had brought greater profits, but he had invested thousands on their voyages. He had ventured almost nothing on the Golden Eagle, and now that Lovell was dead, he would pocket almost everything it earned. He congratulated himself on his good judgment. He had picked a valuable tea set to steal and an accomplice obliging enough to drown before he took his share of the money.

Of course, Pratt told himself, he would never have engineered the theft of another tea set, no matter how valuable. He was an honest man. Pragmatic and opportunistic, but honest nonetheless. As he paced, he poked holes in the mud with his cane and repeated to himself his justification. He had protested the creation of the tea set from public treasure, and his livelihood had been threatened by the Presidents to whom it was given. He was simply declaring a private war on the stupidity of his peers and political leaders and saving his business in the process.

In the back of his head, Pratt heard his father—Calvinist, sailmaker, honest man—disapprove of such reasoning. Jason Pratt the elder had raised his sons to believe that a man deserved nothing for which he didn't work. Horace Taylor Pratt had always tried to embrace his father's teachings, especially when negotiating salaries with underpaid supercargoes or confronting representatives of Boston charities. But the world was very different from the days when Jason Pratt set up a sailmaking establishment on North Street and worked day and night to build his business, his reputation, and a comfortable life for his family. This was the nineteenth century. Life in the business world was difficult enough without war and blockade further complicating it. A businessman had to be careful. He took his profits where he found them and speculated when the odds were in his favor. After all, John Calvin himself had encouraged such prudence and praised commerce as a righteous path for all men.

The rowboat stopped cutting on the gray fabric of the Back Bay. Pratt stepped to the telescope again. He saw Wilson throw a sackful of bricks into the water.

They've found it, thought Pratt. A few more minutes and we'll have it in the safe on Merchants Row. A few more days and Hannaford's agents, as trustworthy as old Henry himself, will arrive from Halifax to take the tea set on its way to England.

Wilson watched the sack of bricks sink into the mud. It made a good anchor. From the length of the rope connected to it, he guessed that the water was about six feet deep. The tide was high and would soon be turning.

"No trouble at all, son," he said.

Young Horace was stripped to his underbreeches and trembling with excitement. He picked up the rope harness he had fashioned to lift the tea set and started to slip into the water.

"Why don't you try liftin' her without the harness, boy? Might be the damn thing's as light as a feather and we won't have to waste no time foolin' with a lot of knots."

The boy looked at the black chunk of iron sitting in the mud below the boat. "The box is quite large, Wilson. I'm sure it's too heavy."

"You can't ever tell how big a thing is by lookin' through the water at it. Water plays tricks on the eyes. If it ain't all that heavy, the air in your lungs'll pull it up like a beer belch poppin' outa your gut. Soon as you get close enough, I'll take it off your shoulder, and we'll get the hell outa here."

Young Horace placed his hands defiantly on his hips. He intended to use his harness.

Wilson raised his hand. "If you can't lift it, we'll use the damn harness."

Horace turned and dove. As soon as he broke the water, adrenalin flooded through him and he forgot his anger. He was diving for sunken treasure. He was living an adventure that most boys only read about. Kicking down through six feet of murky water, he barely felt the cold or the sting of the salt in his eyes. He reached the strongbox in a few short strokes.

131

Wilson is right, he thought. It isn't as large as it looks, but it's settled into three or four inches of mud.

He slipped his hand through one of the grips and pulled. The strongbox didn't budge. He grabbed it with both hands, steadied himself by digging his feet into the ooze on the bottom, and tugged again. Nothing. Until the mud let go, the buoyancy of the water couldn't help him. He needed the harness.

Fifty-five, fifty-six, fifty-seven . . . he's been under for nearly a minute, thought Pratt. He must need air by now. The boy's head appeared within the telescope circle of Pratt's vision. The old man realized that he had been holding his breath for nearly a minute.

"It's stuck in the mud and too heavy to move." The boy managed to sound triumphant as he caught his breath. "Give me the harness."

Wilson flung him the coil of rope.

The boy gulped down a few drafts of air and dove again.

Nothing worse than a fifteen-year-old kid who goes to a fancy school, thought Wilson.

The day before, Wilson had noticed the boy weaving ropes together and asked him what he was doing.

"I'm figuring out a way to get that tea set into the boat."

"What's to figure?"

"Suction."

"What's that?"

"You remember the *Henrietta*? She ran aground off Gloucester last fall."

Wilson nodded.

"Master Johnson explained to the class that she was stuck because of suction. One thing is held tight to another because there's fluid in the space between them."

"So what?"

"To get the *Henrietta* loose, they didn't just pull on her like dunderheads. They pried up different sections of the ship and let little air pockets get in underneath her. Then they used the air pockets like rollers and pulled her right out of the mud."

"Sonny, it ain't a ship. It's a steel box two feet long, three feet wide, and two feet deep. It probably weighs sixty or seventy pounds."

"The same physical principles apply to everything." The boy held up the harness. It looked like a large noose with four hangman's knots arranged to form the corners of a rectangle. Two long pieces of

132

rope passed through each noose, one for adjusting the width of the rectangle, the other for the length. Horace would place the noose around the strongbox, tighten the knots at each corner, then return the long pieces of rope to the surface. By placing tension on each of the ropes individually, they could pull the corners loose and bring the tea set to the surface.

Wilson was unimpressed. "What does your grandfather say to all this foolishness?"

"My grandfather respects the opinions of educated men. He told me to make the harness in case we need it."

"Well, I don't guess we'll be needin' it. I think your grandfather must be gettin' soft. All he needs to do is hire a longshoreman and send him out there at low tide, when the water in the channel is just a few feet deep. A big fella could wade back with the strongbox on his shoulder."

A day later, Wilson still felt the contempt with which the boy had regarded him.

"You apparently do not realize that my grandfather wants to involve as few outsiders as possible in the recovery of the tea set. Consider yourself fortunate that you're trusted enough to be included."

Samuel Wilson had no patience with such disrespect. He grabbed the boy by the scruff of the neck and hauled him to his feet. "I know it's hard for a boy who don't have no daddy teachin' him right from wrong. Granddads is mighty lax in that area. So right now, I'm startin' to teach you a few manners." He clenched what few teeth he had and brought his face close to the boy's. "If ever you talk to me like that again, I'll wallop the daylights out of you, and I don't give a damn who your grandfather is. Now apologize, and we'll forget it."

"I'm . . . I'm sorry." The boy sounded sincere, or at least sincerely frightened.

"Sir."

"Sir," the boy grunted, and Wilson let him go.

Now, an uneasy truce prevailed. The family servant was giving orders to the grandson of the patriarch, who resented orders from anyone.

Wilson gazed over the side. The boy's white body seemed to glow through the murk, and the strands of rope swirled around him like a tangle of roots beneath a water lily. Gracefully, he collected two strands and fitted them to a corner of the strongbox. He put the ropes in his mouth and sprang to the surface.

He caught his breath and handed the ropes to Wilson. "Lash them to the oarlock." Before Wilson could speak, Horace filled his lungs with air and dove again.

For the next ten minutes, Horace struggled with the harness, but he could not secure it. As he broke the surface a fifth time for air, Wilson caught him by the hair.

"Into the boat," commanded Wilson. "We'll have no more games."

The boy tried to pull his head out of Wilson's grasp, but Wilson held tight.

"Let go of my hair," demanded the boy.

"Into the boat."

Horace grabbed Wilson's arm with one hand and tried to tread water with the other. "Let me go!"

"Time for a little rest, sonny." Wilson started to pull him out of the water.

Horace grabbed Wilson's arm with both hands and struggled free. For a moment, his head slipped below the surface. He swallowed several great gulps of salt water and began to choke.

Through his telescope, Pratt was watching the scene, but he couldn't tell what was happening. He squinted hard and cursed his old man's eyes. Then he saw the boy's body emerge from the water and, with Wilson's help, climb into the boat.

Young Horace collapsed in the stern. He was coughing up water like the town pump.

"Spit it all up, Horry, my boy," said Wilson. "There's better things in this world to be drinkin' than muddy water from the Back Bay." He took his flask from his pocket and offered it to the boy.

Horace stopped gasping long enough to refuse.

"Suit yourself." Wilson tilted his head back and emptied half the flask.

Wilson pulled on the set of ropes wrapped around the oarlock. The harness, which had not been secured, slipped off the strongbox and floated to the surface. He held it up for Pratt's telescope. Pratt understood the meaning when Wilson made a gesture of disgust and flung the harness into the bow of the boat. Pratt removed his hat to wave them in but changed his mind. If the boy was too weak, Wilson would know enough to bring him ashore.

Young Horace had finished coughing and sat shivering beneath a blanket in the stern. Wilson was pulling up the anchor rope in the bow.

"I told you, I'll be all right, Wilson," said the boy. "Drop the anchor, and I'll try again."

"I'm just checkin' the depth." He let the rope slide through his fingers and watched the bag of bricks hit bottom. "Still a bit over six feet. About as deep as it ever gets. What's your height?"

"Five foot three."

"Tall for your age. Kids is growin' bigger all the time. Too bad you ain't about a foot taller." Wilson took a fresh coil of rope from under the bow seat and flipped it into the boy's stomach. "First, get your breath, then go down there and tie it to the handles on that strongbox."

The boy threw the rope back at Wilson and reached for the harness. "I'll do it my way. The harness was working perfectly."

A slap cracked across his face and knocked him into his seat. "I'll teach you to respect your elders, whether your granddad's watchin' or not. Now we don't have no time to waste with foolish contraptions like that harness."

"It's not a foolish contraption," said Horace, stroking his cheek.

"And we don't have no time to waste arguin'. Because if you take a look over toward the bridge, you'll see a rowboat headin' up the Charles. Prob'ly fishermen. And upstream, there's two sailboats skippin' down from Cambridge. Harvard boys out for a nice Sunday on the river. And here we sit, in full view of all of them, tryin' to raise the strongbox your granddad lately stole from President Jemmy Madison himself. Now in you go."

Horace didn't budge. The excitement of diving for treasure was gone. He was cold, frightened—although he wouldn't admit it—and angry. He had never been struck by an adult before, and his pride was stinging more than his cheek. He glared at Wilson. "I intend to tell my grandfather that you raised your hand against me."

"You tell him anything you want, but he made me captain of this here rowboat, and I'll take no more of your backtalk."

"You'll get no more talk of any kind." Horace pulled the blanket tightly around himself and stared out at the sailboats. He wasn't moving.

Wilson leaned close to him. "It's all right, Horace," he said softly. "Most boys tryin' to be men acts more like boys than men. A few years from now, you'll be a man with a little bit of boy left in you. Then I'll rightfully expect you to act like a man." He fitted the oars and prepared to leave.

Horace threw off his blanket, stood angrily, and snatched the rope from Wilson's seat. "I promise you two things, sir—the tea set within ten minutes, and your job by this afternoon." He dove, purposely rocking the boat and splashing water all over Wilson.

This time, the chill of the water aggravated his anger. Adolescent fury, aimed at Wilson and anything else that irritated him, rolled off Horace in waves. The cold was one more persecution. His dive brought him straight to the bottom. He grabbed one of the handles on the strongbox. He passed the rope through it twice, snapped the rope across the top of the strongbox, and pulled it through the other handle.

Wilson watched from above. He saw the boy's anger reflected in his uncontrolled, jerking movements. Horace's whole body was pouting. He was a child forced to perform an unpleasant task. The footman tugged on the rope, signaling for the boy to surface.

Horace paid no attention. The air in his lungs was getting thin, but his anger was unabated. Wilson was stupid and primitive. Horace would follow his orders to the letter but take no blame if they failed to raise the tea set before low tide.

The boy needed slack to make a knot in the second handle. He pulled gently. Nothing played out from the rowboat. He focused all his anger in the rope. He pulled at it violently and two feet uncoiled into the water. He jammed the rope through the handle, then jammed it again. The second time, his hand slipped completely through the handle, and he tore the skin off his knuckles. He pulled up. The hand didn't move. With his left hand, he grabbed his right wrist and tried to pull free, but his right hand was wedged tight. Two twists of thick rope lashed him to the strongbox.

He felt a stream of bubbles escape from his nostrils and roll across his cheek. He had been holding his breath for nearly two minutes. He could not hold it much longer.

Seen from the surface, his movements did not seem unusual. Wilson thought the boy was still angry at the rope. Then Horace turned over and looked up. The terror in his eyes would cut through Samuel Wilson every night to the end of his life. The old servant froze. He could do nothing.

The black bulk of the rowboat almost on top of him. The horrified face peering down from behind the mirror. A hand breaking through the mirror and reaching for him. These were the last things that Horace Taylor Pratt III remembered. He reached for the hand. He called aloud for help. Three obese bubbles carried his cry wobbling to the surface. Salt water rushed in to fill his lungs, and his body rolled back toward the bottom.

❊

Wilson saw the bubbles break on top of the water. He knew he was too late, but he had to do something. He thought the body was tangled. He cut the ropes leading to the strongbox, but the body didn't swim free. For ten minutes he struggled. Finally, he was able to grab the boy by the leg and pull. The body was limp, the muscles relaxed; the hand slipped loose from the grip of the strongbox. Wilson hauled the body to the surface and laid the heir to the Pratt empire in the bow of the rowboat.

The panic had drained out of him. He felt numb, mechanical. His mind disconnected from his body. Shock was already protecting him. Samuel Wilson left the tea set in the mud and made for Gravelly Point.

Three quarters of a mile away, a figure draped in black stood on the shore. Across the waters of the Back Bay rolled a long, loud, wordless cry of pain.

The clouds burned off by noon, and the warm sun of late summer washed down on the garden behind Horace Taylor Pratt's home. As Pratt grew older, he enjoyed the garden more and more. It was one of the few areas of his city that hadn't changed. He could sit in his room, look out across the flowers and trees and vines, and see the world as it looked forty years before, when his son Horace was a boy and their lives were before them.

He sat there now in the deepest despair of his life. He had no thoughts of a golden past, no hopes for the future. All hope for Horace Taylor Pratt lay in the cool, damp basement of Wilbur Hennison's mortuary, and the facts of a boy's death, altered to disguise the purpose of his plunge into the Back Bay, had been duly recorded in the constable's office on Summer Street.

The soft sound of a woman's singing drifted into Pratt's room. Franconia sat beneath the grape arbor at the top of the hill, her voice entwined in "A Summer's Day."

"Who will tell her that her Horace is dead?" Abigail stood behind her father. She held her hand gently on his shoulder, but her voice was soaked in recrimination.

"I have endured more pain in a single day than most men know in a lifetime. I cannot sustain more."

Abigail nervously ran her hands down the sides of her dress, smoothing wrinkles that weren't there. She left her father and appeared a moment later in the garden below. Slowly, reluctantly, she climbed the hill, past the petunias and salvia which had bloomed all summer, past the chrysanthemums which would soon burst forth, past the blackberry bushes, to the arbor.

"'It fell on a summer's day,/ While sweet Bessie sleeping lay/ In her bower, on her bed,/ Light with curtain shadowed . . .'"

Pratt could see splashes of pastel pink and yellow through the coat of leaves around the arbor. When Franconia stopped singing, he leaned forward to listen. Except for the screeching of two bluejays, the hillside was silent. A minute, then two, then five. He wondered if Abigail had not been able to tell Franconia. He worried that he would have to tell her himself.

Franconia began to sing once more. "'Jamie came. She him spies,/ Op'ning half her heavy eyes.'" Her voice quivered. "'First a soft kiss he doth take./ She lay still and would not wake./ Then his hands learned to woo./ She dream't not what . . .'" Another voice rose out of Franconia, at first blending with her song, then choking it in a mother's primeval wail for her dead child.

Pratt couldn't listen. He closed the window and locked the bedroom door, sealing himself from the world. He studied the face reflected in the mirror above the dresser. The brow still arched proudly. The mouth was still firm and unyielding. The jaw jutted forward like the prow of the *Gay Head*. But nothing else remained of his youth.

"I keep no glass in my room, Horace, because it encourages pride, a wanton love of one's own mortal image. Pride is a sin, my boy, and all good men must avoid anything that will bring a stain upon their soul." Pratt's father spoke to him again across sixty years. "Go forth into the world. Conduct business, make goods, teach, or minister, but always remember that what you do is for God, not yourself. When you do only for yourself, you cannot call yourself a Christian." The voice was gone.

Pratt did not take his eyes from the image before him. It spoke to him, or he to it. "Horace Taylor Pratt, you are an evil man. You have spent your life in the prideful pursuit of earthly things. Now you have nothing. Your world is crumbling around you, and your greed has killed what you most loved. You are an evil man."

He was still staring at the mirror half an hour later.

Abigail pounded on the door. "Father, are you all right?"

"I breathe."

"Please open the door, Father. Gardiner Greene is here to see you."

"I don't want to see him."

"He is here as a friend. He's here to comfort you."

"Let him comfort my daughter-in-law. No man can bring me relief."

"He has given a potion to Franconia. She is asleep. Please let us in."

Pratt opened the door and placed his cane across the space. Despair was no longer etched in his face. He seemed intense, determined. "Good afternoon, Gardiner."

Gardiner Greene was a neighbor and an old family friend. His garden on Pemberton Hill was one of the most beautiful spots in Boston. He had the kind face of a man who enjoyed working with the soil, and Pratt couldn't stand him. "Hello, Horace."

"Can we come in, Father?" asked Abigail.

"I'm going to be busy for quite a while, my dear. Send Wilson to me right away."

"Wilson is . . ."

"Drunk?"

"No, Father. He put the carriage away, unhitched the team and fed the horses, and sat down in the carriage. He has not moved or spoken since."

Pratt did not react. "When he is free, send him to my room."

"Is there anything we can do for you, Father?"

Pratt opened the door wide enough to allow Abigail inside, then slammed it on Greene. "The funeral service is to be held at Park Street Church tomorrow. I want the Reverend Mr. Whitehead to preside."

"Yes, Father."

"The boy is to be buried in the family plot, next to his father's monument."

"Yes."

"Now, take down my Bible for me and leave me in peace."

The Pratt family Bible was an enormous leatherbound King James edition published in 1700. It contained the names and birthdates of every Pratt from Richard, born in London in 1626, to Elihu, Jason Pratt's three-year-old son. Pratt asked for quill and ink. He clumsily wrote "September 9, 1814" next to the name and birthdate of Horace Taylor Pratt III. He studied the line for a moment, as though trying to comprehend its finality.

Abigail placed her hand on his brow. She stroked his hair gently. She could not remember the last time she had seen him reading the Bible. "The Good Book will help you, Father. It will give you strength."

He grunted. "Nothing will give me strength now. I'm looking for reasons."

"The Bible will give you what you seek." Her voice was soothing.

"You need not encourage me falsely. I expect to find no balm of Gilead between these pages."

She decided there was nothing more she could do. She moved toward the door.

"Abigail." The sharpness in his voice caused her to turn abruptly. "I do not wish to be interrupted for any reason. You may bring me nourishment at five o'clock, and my lamp is to be lit at six. When I ring my bell, I expect to see you or Wilson. Otherwise, Jason is the only person who may visit me, and I will see him only at the dinner hour. And keep that damned Greene away from me."

Ordinarily, she was infuriated when her father spoke to her like the captain of a ship delivering orders to his cabin boy, but she remained pleasant. She did not wish to upset the equanimity which, at least in appearance, had reasserted itself against his grief. "Is there anything else, Father?"

He shook his head.

She closed the door behind her. In the hallway, she stopped. She could hear her father's voice. She placed her ear against the door. Pratt was reading aloud. "'Genesis, Book I. In the beginning . . .'"

On September 13, Abigail sat down at her writing desk and unlocked the drawer that contained her diary. She had been keeping a diary since her husband James had gone to sea in 1811. On the day he left, she had promised him that she would keep a record of her daily life, so that he might share it with her when he returned. But James Bentley had been lost at sea. After his death, the diary had become Abigail's closest companion. She began to write.

It has been three days since Young Horace was buried, and Father remains in his room reading the Bible. He has not ventured out, even to pay his last respects to his grandson. When I asked if he would attend Horace's funeral, he said he was preparing for the boy's resurrection and others could bury him. Father has always been willing to quote Calvin, Christ, or the Bible when it was to his benefit, but I have never known him to be a deeply religious man.

He eats little or nothing, taking only water and a little fruit in the morning, bread and wine at midday, and broth in the evening. When I try to make him eat more, he tells me that if he weren't so old, he would fast completely.

His behavior has been most unusual. I am worried.

By far the most worrisome episode occurred today. Our dear brother Jason came to offer his comfort and condolences.

When he descended from Father's room, he wore an expression of supreme smugness that was most unusual. For the first time in his life, he resembled a Pratt. He looked like Father after the return of a schooner from China.

Filled with trepidation, I asked him why he seemed so happy on such a black day. He told me, with great fanfare in voice and demeanor, that Father had put him in charge of the company's operations until further notice. A second tragedy in four days.

After he left, I went straight to Father's room and asked why he had made such an ill-considered decision. In response, Father began to read aloud from Exodus. I asked again, and he read more loudly. Eventually, his stubborness overcame my persistence. I left as the Red Sea destroyed Pharaoh's army.

Now I sit here watching night advance westward from the ocean, and I wonder what the future holds for family and company. Father seems to be in a deep trance. Brother Jason, who has long awaited his ascension to the presidency of Pratt Shipping and Mercantile, but done little to warrant it, is now empowered to make decisions affecting us all. Franconia, I'm afraid to say, is more daft than ever. She spends all her time in the garden, where she sings and picks berries with her "Little Horry." She talks to him as though he were three or four years old and still close by her side. It's pitiful. I take some of the blame for her grief. Had I kept tighter rein on Father, the boy would be here today. And poor Wilson! He has not spoken, except to say "Yes, ma'am" and "No, ma'am," since the accident. At least he is doing his chores again. But his eyes are blank. The life has gone out of him.

In the face of all this, it is difficult for me to know what to do. I expect that I now shall inherit fifty percent of the company, since Horace's death has eliminated one strand of Pratt lineage and freed thirty percent of the company, to be split between Jason and me. Upon Father's death, I will have legitimate power within the company. Until then, I must try to force my opinions upon Jason and manipulate him toward ends that I favor.

This war will end soon enough. With Napoleon defeated, England can concentrate its enormous military powers on us. We have no further need to fight the British over our right, as a neutral nation, to trade with whatever country we choose. And our fond belief that we could conquer Canada has long since been dashed.

So, peace will come, and there will be a rebirth in the shipping industry greater than any we have ever seen. Our warehouses are piled high with goods which have been

141

sitting for two years, awaiting shipment to Europe. Our people, long deprived of the luxuries of the Continent, will be waiting breathlessly for the first American ships to return with European goods.

If we can hold out just a little longer, I'm certain we'll be the richest family in New England by next Christmas.

But until Father regains himself, Jason must be carefully watched. I don't expect that he will attempt to do anything foolhardy. He has never taken the initiative in anything. But the smile I saw on his face today gives me pause. When the weak man takes power, his weakness may lead him to act unwisely where the strong man would do nothing. I must be vigilant, lest Jason decide to act and throw our money into textile mills.

It would be so much easier if I were a man!

Jason Pratt did not act for two weeks. While his father remained at home finishing the Bible and moving on to *Paradise Lost*, Jason sat each morning in the upstairs office on the corner of State Street and Merchants Row and tried to decide how best to use the income from the Pratt investments earning money. The Pratts controlled a granite quarry, a foundry on the Merrimack River, and tobacco lands in Connecticut. They were not on the verge of collapse, as his father had led him to believe. The foundry was turning out cannonballs as quickly as the American Navy fired them, and Pratt was charging an exorbitant rate per round. Moreover, Pratt ships had plied the Peninsula trade throughout 1813. The Pratts had been losing money since the extension of the British blockade in early 1814, but with good management, they would survive.

The Merchants Bank still held mortgages on the *Pegasus* and the *Alicia Howell*, two Indiamen that Pratt had built just before the war at the enormous cost of twenty-five thousand dollars per vessel. While most shippers held shares in several ships and shared their risks with others, Pratt believed that the most powerful businessman owned his ships and relied upon no one. Ships formed the lifeline of New England, he said, and the man who controlled them and the blood pumped through them would never be poor. He was always willing to advance loans to small businessmen, simply to keep them in his debt, and he was never afraid to gamble his assets on a mortgage, especially if he could commission Melville Morton, one of the best shipbuilders in America, to construct a pair of beauties like the *Pegasus* and the *Alicia Howell*. Now, the businessmen were folding and defaulting on their loans, while Pratt Shipping and Mercantile barely made the payments on its idle ships and drained liquid assets in the process. It was clear to Jason that something had to go.

The Pratts held a standing offer from Thomas Handasyd Perkins, one of their oldest competitors in the China trade, to purchase the *Pegasus* and the *Alicia Howell* for thirty-five thousand dollars. Horace Taylor Pratt laughed at the offer, but Jason was inclined to listen. Although they would take a loss on the ships, he could pay off the mortgages and have ten thousand dollars left over, with which to buy into Francis Cabot Lowell's mill.

Jason Pratt believed that textile manufacturing would one day replace shipping as New England's prime industry. For years, he had overseen Pratt operations on Long Wharf, and hundreds of miles of English textiles had been unloaded. He knew the market existed in America, and he had confidence in the ingenuity of men like Lowell, who had managed, in his travels across England, to learn enough about English looms that he could rebuild one in Boston from memory.

Ten shares of preferred stock in Lowell's Boston Manufacturing Company would give Pratt Shipping and Mercantile one of the largest holdings in the organization. For a week, Jason tried to persuade himself to do it.

"Of course you should do it," said his wife one night before they went to sleep.

Sarah Lowell Pratt, a cousin of Francis Cabot Lowell, was small and petite, with delicate features and a voice that sounded like a rusty well wheel, even when she whispered. "After years of treating you like a little boy, your father has given you the chance to show that you have the same initiative and intelligence that your brother had. Take the chance."

"But what if the mill fails and the British lift the blockade next week? The *Pegasus* leaves harbor with a full hold and Perkins makes the profits. Father would be infuriated."

Sarah rolled toward the window and gazed out at the ocean, just visible from their Fort Hill home. "I sometimes believe I married a coward."

"Don't say that." His voice was feeble.

She rolled toward him again. "Then act aggressively. If not for yourself, for me and for your sons. Aren't Artemus and Elihu as bright as little Horace ever was, and in no way so spoiled? Don't they deserve affection and respect from their paternal grandfather? Make their grandfather recognize their father's brilliance. For once, act like a man."

"You're always ready to attack me, aren't you?" His voice was soft but filled with malice.

"You invite it," she rasped. "Act strong, and the world is yours. Otherwise, not even your wife can consider you a man." She rolled away from him again and curled into a ball.

The next morning, Jason Pratt dressed in his finest velveteen cutaway and silk cravat. At the office, he dictated a note to Thomas Handasyd Perkins: "Am considering seriously your offer to purchase the *Pegasus*. I must confer before the decision is made, but you shall have an answer the day after tomorrow." Then he called for his father's carriage and rode up the Charles River to Lowell's mill in Waltham.

Francis Cabot Lowell, up to his arms in grease, was supervising the installation of a new loom. He was short and bald, with a broad forehead, receding chin, and supercilious gaze. He did not welcome interruptions. "Yes, what is it, Pratt?" His high-pitched voice matched his appearance.

Jason ignored Lowell's curtness. He smiled. "I've come to discuss the subscription you offered me. I'm prepared to put up ten thousand dollars."

Lowell stopped working. "If your father was not quite so stupid, if he had acted when we first made the offer, the stock would be yours. However, the ten original investors exercised their options on the second offering, and there are no more shares available. Perhaps in a few years."

Jason tried to hide his disappointment. "If my father is so stupid, why did you invite us to join the company in the first place?"

"Because of my relationship to your wife." Lowell returned to work.

Jason Pratt could think of no rejoinder. He rode back to Merchants Row, went into his father's office, put his hands on the seat of the leather armchair in the corner of the room, and sat on them.

Abigail Pratt Bentley opened her diary that evening, after a horseback ride down the Neck.

My worst fears were almost realized today, and I was
powerless to stop the perpetrator. For two weeks, I have
watched Jason, and he has done nothing. Today, he sent for
Wilson, and I was immediately suspicious. When Wilson
returned, he told me—he has begun to speak, thank God, but

only when spoken to—that he had taken my brother to the Waltham mill.

I dressed and went directly to the office, where I learned, to my relief, that my brother had failed. He looked quite despondent. May he remain despondent until Father returns!

When I interrupted Father's reading to tell him what his son had done, he seemed unperturbed. "Jason must learn to face crisis," he said. "Wisdom is gained only through error."

With those words, so uncharacteristic of the Horace Taylor Pratt in whose home I was raised, I close this entry.

One October morning a few weeks later, Horace Taylor Pratt ended his retreat. He had Wilson dress him in his best breeches and black frock, then he rang for Abigail. When she entered, he was standing in front of the east windows, in a corona of bright sunshine.

"Today, I return to my worldly labors." His voice was stronger and more confident than Abigail had heard it in years.

She smiled. "I feared that you would never again move from this room. You've been here a long time."

"Forty days, to be exact. Forty days seeking answers, like Jesus in the desert."

Abigail said nothing. She could always respond to his cynicism. She wasn't prepared for piety.

"You look at me as though I were mad," he said evenly. "I assure you I am not. Nor do I intend to don sackcloth and ashes and prostrate myself before the pulpit of the Park Street Church. I shall pursue my life and career as I have always done, because I am no hypocrite." He paused. "And in the eyes of man, I am past redemption."

"Father, don't be so dramatic."

"The Lord will save me if he so desires. I acknowledge my sins. I repent of them. But I know that it is my nature to commit them again."

"You talk as though you were a murderer." Abigail laughed gently and started toward her father.

"I am."

She froze halfway across the room.

The sun glared in over Pratt's shoulders. His features were indistinguishable. He seemed suddenly like an apparition. "I am more than a murderer, Abigail. I am Satan."

She didn't know whether to laugh or call for Wilson. She detected no change in voice or expression, and his shadow did not move from the window. She decided that any reaction was worse than none.

Pratt flipped open the copy of *Paradise Lost* on the table beside him. He read the blank verse with a powerful voice. "'Satan with thoughts inflam'd of highest design,/ Puts on swift wings, and toward the Gates of Hell/ Explores his solitary flight; sometimes/ He scours the right-hand coast, sometimes the left,/ Now shaves with level wing the Deep, then soars/ Up to the fiery concave tow'ring high./ As when far off at Sea a Fleet descri'd/ Hangs in the Clouds, by Equinoctial Winds/ Close sailing from Bengala or the Isles/ Of Ternate and Tidore, whence Merchants bring their spicy drugs: they on the trading Flood/ Through the wide Ethiopian to the Cape/ Ply stemming nightly toward the Pole. So seem'd/ Far off the flying Fiend.'"

Pratt closed the book. "Milton compares Satan to a merchant shipper, and this merchant shipper sees himself in Milton's Satan."

"It's only a poem, Father."

"It carries truth, Abigail. I am Satan. I am proud, acquisitive, vengeful. I answer to no one, and I have fought every day of my life to advance my own interests against the Molochs, Belials, and Mammons of my world, against the Appletons, Cabots, and Perkinses who have been my competitors for forty years. I have gloated when I won. I have schemed revenge when I lost."

He stepped away from the windows and put his hand on his daughter's shoulder. "And I have led my innocent children into sin, as Satan led Adam and Eve."

"You have given us nothing but love." Abigail threw her arms around him and held tightly, like a mother comforting her child.

Gently, he pulled away. "I doubt that Franconia would agree with you. I invested her husband and son with the same drives that infect me, and they're both dead."

"My brother was lost at sea, and so was my husband," blurted Abigail. "It is in the nature of men to endanger themselves in the pursuit of riches."

"And apparently, it is the nature of grandfathers to endanger their grandsons, if it be profitable." Pratt's voice was losing its strength.

Abigail stepped back slowly. "Then the boy was not trapping crabs when he slipped into the channel and took cramp?"

"Blueclaws have not been found in that area since I was a boy," said Pratt softly. "I devised that story to protect the real purpose of our nightly trips to Gravelly Point."

Instinctively, Abigail sat down on the edge of the bed.

Slowly, softly, Pratt unraveled the story of the tea set, from its presentation in 1789 until young Horace's death. When he finished, Abigail did not move or speak for several minutes. She simply stared at her father's face, which now seemed serene, composed.

She stood slowly and walked to the fireplace at the end of the bedroom. A model of the *Alicia Howell,* made for Pratt by the shipbuilder himself, rested on the mantelpiece. The large mirror hanging above it reflected the length of the room and the dark figure at the other end.

"I cannot believe," she said, just loudly enough for his reflection to hear, "that one of the most important merchants in America, one of the lions of the China trade, one of the symbols of Federalist opposition in Massachusetts, would indulge himself in such a scheme and involve his grandson, as well."

"Satan must follow his nature, Abigail. I must answer my instinct to survive."

"By stealing a national treasure?"

"The nation and its leaders wronged me, Abigail. They wronged every merchant in Massachusetts. Satan is vengeful. I sought revenge." He stated his position as though it required no further explanation.

She could not argue with such logic. "Where is the treasure now?" she asked weakly.

"Still sunk deep in the mud of the Back Bay. This morning, I rowed out with Wilson. We saw it there, where we left it forty days ago. I thought someone would have noticed it by now, but the water is murky, and the currents have covered it with a thin coating of silt. I am pleased that no one has found it."

"No!" She turned on him. Out of pity, she had restrained her anger for weeks. Now it poured out of her. "You will not go out there again. You have no more grandsons to waste. Use the business brain that made you a rich and respected man. Save your company before your son destroys it. For the sake of us all, leave that strongbox where it is and return—"

He raised his hand to silence her. "Save yourself, Abigail. I agree with you. The tea set will remain where it is."

"You've been lying to me for months. Why should I believe you now?"

"Other than Wilson, you are the only person alive who knows the story."

Abigail turned back to the mirror. She replaced a few strands of hair and composed herself. "I have your solemn word on this matter?"

"I am returning to my office to confront our problems." He paused to separate his thoughts. "And I am making you the custodian of our family secret."

"It is a secret better forgotten."

Pratt's black eyes flashed fire, and he advanced on his daughter. She watched him walk toward her, and out of the corner of her eye, she could see his reflection growing in the mirror. When he stood beside her, he surrounded her.

"Would you forget twenty thousand dollars? Twenty that will one day be a hundred, then two, then a million?"

"We will all be long dead before anything made by Paul Revere is worth a million dollars." She could not help but sound cynical.

"But our children will live on."

"I am a childless widow. I am now the sister-in-law of a childless widow."

"You are also a Pratt!" he exploded. "You have a duty to your blood. You have a responsibility to the ages."

"Rubbage." She tried to walk away, but he blocked her path with his arm.

He spoke softly now, but his voice was strung tight, like a mainsail shroud in a stiff breeze. "I have led my children into sin. I have led them to death. But I leave them a promise of redemption. I leave it in your hands." He pulled a large envelope from his breast pocket. "Contained herein are quotes from *Paradise Lost*. Studied carefully, they will reveal the exact nature and location of the treasure." He held out the envelope.

She didn't want it. She did not want to partake of the madness she saw in his eyes. But she did not wish to upset him further. She had no choice. She took the envelope and started to open it.

He snatched it back. "It is not to be opened until you deem it absolutely necessary. You may never need to open it."

"What harm can there be in reading your little puzzles?"

"They are not puzzles. They are the promise of Christ." His face flushed, and he fanned himself with the envelope.

"Your apoplexy, Father."

"Damn my apoplexy." He crossed the room and sat down. After a moment to catch his breath, he spoke. "You may open the envelope and read the quotes, but no one else is to see them until after I am dead. Perhaps no one will see them until after you are dead, until after Artemus and Elihu and their children are dead, until well into the twentieth century." He gazed out the window for a moment, as though he were trying to imagine what his hillside would look like in a hundred years.

"If I am to be the custodian of your wishes, a duty I do not happily accept, you must explain yourself fully. Why are these lines to remain secret?"

He looked at her like a minister lecturing in Sunday School. "Because, Abigail, redemption is earned only through suffering. If we never face a crisis that threatens to destroy us, we will have no need for the Golden Eagle, and we will have no right to it. But it is there, always."

She waited, expecting more, but he was finished. He had spent so long with his new beliefs that he felt no further explanation was necessary. He gazed out at the garden again.

She crossed the room and stood in front of him. She would end this foolishness right now. "Why is it there always?"

"Dammit, girl!" Pratt slammed his hand on the arm of the chair and leaped to his feet. "I raised you to be as smart as your brothers. Why must you be so damn obtuse? The tea set is our second chance. Pray God that we never need it. But if He decides that the death of my son and my grandson is not enough payment for my transgressions, if He decides to visit the sins of the father upon future generations, He has at least left us the promise that His Son brings to all mankind. If He takes our fortune, He leaves us hidden treasure upon which to build again. If He rends us with familial strife, He leaves us the quotations. Distributed one each to disputing brothers or cousins, the quotations will bring us together again."

"In greed to find the tea set."

"Do not be disrespectful!"

"I am simply being truthful."

Pratt approached his daughter and put his hand on her shoulder. "Abigail, we are living an allegory. Birth, death, resurrection. But within our story, everything has two faces, dual meanings, and it is up to us to find the face of goodness and hope. I am Satan, but I am also God the Father, who has given his grandson for future generations. The tea set is the symbol of my greatest sin, my greed, but it is also the promise of resurrection, bought by my grandson with his life. My descendants are mankind. They will be good and bad. We must always hope that they will build their fortunes by God's light, but we must be ready to forgive them if they fail."

Abigail knew now that her father was mad. "Why have you made me the guardian of this secret?"

"Because you are the most trustworthy of my descendants, and you are a woman. You will never be plunged into the maelstrom of business life. You will always be apart from our worldly struggles and able to judge our needs in detachment."

"When you die, Father, I shall take active control of the stock you leave me. I do not intend to shrink away from the world."

"To that, I have two responses. First, I do not plan to die for many years. There is too much undone. Second, the thirty percent I have promised you is the thirty percent you will get. I am giving young Horace's share to Jason. I will settle any disputes between you and your brother before they start. I will teach Jason all that I can, and when I die, he will take my place at the head of the company. He is, after all, my son."

"And I am your daughter." Abigail felt the rage welling from deep within her. He wanted her to exchange her fair piece of Pratt Shipping and Mercantile for an envelope of worthless quotations. She refused. "I am entitled to the same privileges as my brother. I will not settle for less."

"You are entitled to what I give you. Jason has produced two heirs. You have none. The responsibility I have given to you is as great as any I give my son." He forced the envelope into her hand and headed for the door.

"Father!"

He kept walking. "I'm late for work. My final word has been given. Reject that envelope and you reject me."

Abigail marched back to the fireplace. She looked at the coals still glowing on the grate. She looked at the envelope.

It is now midnight. Father and Wilson have ridden off to the Back Bay for the third night in a row. Each night, they dump dirt and gravel onto the strongbox, further obscuring it from view. Father says he will bury it under three or four feet of mud so that no one will see it.

What a picture they must make by the full moon! A one-armed madman and his near-mute servant scooping dirt into the water.

Of course, Father is careful about his madness. He has exposed it to no one but me, as though he wished to relieve himself of it by transferring it onto his daughter. I am its only victim.

He has robbed me of my birthright. He has given my brother ultimate control of the company. He has left me with nothing but his vision for the future. I do not want it. If I could, I would destroy that envelope of quotations and leave this house tonight. Forever.

But I know that if I am to have any impact on the destiny of

Pratt Shipping and Mercantile, I must remain within the family.

So I will stay. I will carry the burden of responsibility I owe to Franconia, whose son might be alive if I had been more diligent; to this house, which my mother loved so well; and to the man whose seed gave me life.

I will protect the secret unless it becomes advantageous for me to use it on my own behalf.

CHAPTER X

In earlier days, suicide was considered a sin. No such stigma attaches itself to Christopher Carrington. In a moment of black despair, he lost control of the precision instrument that is the human mind, and he decided to escape the problems which so brutally oppressed him. In the eyes of God and man, he is blameless."

Suicides make for difficult eulogies, but Father Henry Henison had been a friend of the Pratt family for years, and he did his best to comfort them. The funeral was held at Emmanuel Episcopal Church in the Back Bay, two days after the discovery of Carrington's body.

Evangeline Carrington sat in the first pew, her mother and stepfather to her left, her grandmother to her right. She had seen her brother seldom in the last few months; they had little in common beyond their name. But she found it difficult to believe that he would kill himself. He was too full of the sense of his own importance, and he enjoyed life too much.

However, the police investigation had revealed no evidence of homicide, and when she had last seen him, she had sensed that something was deeply wrong. He had told her that he was sick of his work and disillusioned with his uncles' efforts to retain control of Pratt Industries. She had suggested to him that he quit. He had refused; he was a member of the family company, and he would not desert.

Now he was dead. The stupid sense of family pride and loyalty, which had been hanging around the family neck for two hundred years, had killed him. When he could no longer help the corporation, when he could no longer do the things that Pratts and Carringtons had always done against their business adversaries, he had committed suicide.

After their father's death, their mother had shielded Evangeline and Christopher from the realities of life. She had protected them and overprotected them. She had never prepared them for failure or tragedy. Now, Evangeline had retreated into a world of plants and tranquillity; Christopher had taken his life.

Father Henison's voice droned on. "His mother's love expanded to fill the void left by his father's death. His education and upbringing prepared him for a life filled with promise. But something was missing in Christopher, something that none of us saw."

Evangeline wished that it had been Philip Pratt whose sense of loyalty and idealism had overwhelmed him. She wished that Philip Pratt were lying in the bronze box next to her. He had presided over the demise of Pratt Industries. It was all his fault. But his sense of survival was too strong.

Philip Pratt was sitting right behind her, staring at the stained-glass windows and listening with one ear to the eulogy. He was not religious. He didn't need to embrace the hope of an afterlife when he could experience everything in this one. To him, the body in the casket was all that remained of his nephew, and he was convinced that Carrington had committed suicide.

When he had first seen Carrington twisting at the end of the rope, Pratt had thought only of William Rule. He had wanted to tell the police that Rule had killed his nephew, but Soames reminded him that Rule was too smart to be killing people, either in Boston or California. Rule was too close to his goal to endanger it now. He was too sensible to make a mistake.

Pratt had agreed. Rule hadn't killed Christopher Carrington. The young man's sense of family duty had run straight into his conscience, and the collision had destroyed him. A conscience was a dangerous thing, thought Pratt. In his world, he couldn't afford to have one.

Father Henison had reached the end of his eulogy. "He was a young man of high ideals, who heeded the words that have motivated so many in his family to greatness: 'Of those to whom much is given, much is expected.' He gave us all a great deal."

A sob shook the pew. Evangeline's mother began to cry softly. She had taken it well enough to this point, but Evangeline knew that she might come apart at any moment.

A hand closed tightly around Evangeline's wrist. Evangeline took the hand gently in her own.

"Another generation, another tragedy. I could have stopped it." For two days, Katherine Pratt Carrington had repeated the words like a dirge while sitting in her rocking chair and staring out at the ocean. This morning, when she had viewed her grandson's body for the last time, she had neither spoken nor cried, and she had been silent since. The periodic tightening of her hand was her only expression of grief. Her shock was deepening.

Evangeline hoped that the police investigation would end quickly. Whatever the cause of her brother's death, she knew that a long inquest would be too much for her mother and grandmother to bear. For their sake, perhaps it would be best to accept the verdict of suicide.

Calvin Pratt stepped into the pulpit and straightened his tie. His complexion was ashen, his voice weak. "Ladies and gentlemen, a young man of high ideals has passed from our midst, but as he would remind us, there can be no time for mourning." His voice cracked, and he fought back his emotions.

William Rule sat with his wife at the edge of the large group of mourners. "Pratts always have something to say," he whispered, "but all the talk in the world won't bring their nephew back. Damn shame, a smart kid like that knockin' himself off."

"Why do you think he did it, Ruley?"

"Because he couldn't bear to see an outsider take over the family company."

"You?"

A smile curled the edges of Rule's mouth.

"We must always remember his love of life, his love of excellence, his love of family. They far outweigh whatever momentary aberration caused him to take his own life." Calvin Pratt's voice was strong at the end. He had overcome his emotions like a good lawyer and a good Pratt.

The church shook with the solemn tones of a Bach requiem.

Peter Fallon felt the vibrations in his shoes. He was sitting in the last pew, directly beneath the organ. He had visited this church often to hear the Bach Mass sung on the third Sunday of every month. He had come today because he was confused, but not over the questions of faith and morality that usually brought people into churches. His concerns were more mundane: an ancient note that no one knew about; a Revere tea set worth two million dollars or more; the art dealer who rediscovered it after a hundred and fifty years and refused to reveal his source; the writer who claimed it was a fake, then disappeared into a pint bottle of Old Mr. Boston; and now, the suicide of Christopher Carrington—seemingly as secure as the First National Bank—who had discussed the tea set with Fallon over brunch and hung himself after dinner.

Fallon had spent the day after Carrington's death analyzing their conversation at La Crêperie. He wondered if Carrington's death was connected to the tea set. He remembered Carrington's stiffness when the tea set was mentioned and Carrington's relief when he realized Fallon's ignorance, but Fallon drew no conclusions. He wasn't thinking very clearly. Two deaths in seventy-two hours had left him numb.

The following day, Fallon had tried to find two people who might answer a few of his questions. Lawrence Hannaford was in London on business and wouldn't be back for five days. Jack C. Ferguson had vanished. Fallon combed through the records of alcoholic hospitals, Skid Row drunk tanks, and the city morgue, but found nothing about Jack C. Ferguson.

Now, Fallon was filled with questions, but he didn't expect to find any answers in the church. He had come today to pay his respects. He wanted to shake Katherine Carrington's hand, say a few comforting words to an old woman in her grief.

The Episcopal Mass was over and the bronze casket was rolling down the aisle toward Fallon. Philip and Calvin Pratt led the pallbearers. Carrington's mother and her husband led the line of mourners that trailed out behind them like the train of a black gown.

As Evangeline and Katherine Carrington passed, Fallon tried to attract their attention. One look at the blank expression on the old woman's face and he knew she wouldn't recognize him. But Evangeline saw him. She glanced briefly at his seersucker suit and looked away. Her eyes neither thanked him for being there nor criticized him for intruding upon the family's private grief.

Expressionless in a black dress—and she was still beautiful.

Fallon's eyes tracked her out the door. He wished that he had met her under different circumstances, and he realized that half his interest in the Pratts was in her. When the end of the mourning line passed his pew, he stepped into it. Outside, the group was already dispersing in the eighty-five-degree humidity. The coffin had been slipped into the hearse and was speeding toward Marblehead. Interment would be private, and there would be no brunch for family and friends. Socializing after the funeral was a Catholic custom.

Fallon noticed Evangeline helping her grandmother into the limousine at the curb. She stepped into the car, the door closed, and the black Cadillac whisked away before Fallon reached the sidewalk.

Across the street, a drunk wearing a Red Sox cap sat on the curb and sipped sauterne from a pint bottle. It was Jack C. Ferguson, and he wasn't quite as drunk as he looked. He rarely ventured so boldly into the open, especially when he thought that Bill Rulick's men would be around. But Ferguson had to pick up whatever bits of information were dropped at the funeral. He was a good reporter, and he never shied from an assignment.

Ferguson saw Katherine Pratt Carrington for the first time in twenty-six years, and he thought she looked pretty good. Her granddaughter wasn't bad either. He saw Isabelle, Philip, and all the rest of the Pratts as they ducked into their limousines. He saw Rulick, paying his respects to people he hated. Then, he noticed a young man crossing the street toward him.

Jack Ferguson recognized the Irish face, but he couldn't place it. Maybe this was one of Rulick's men, and here was Ferguson caught like a bookie on the toilet with the cops at the door. Ferguson reached into his jacket and grabbed the handle of his switchblade. This guy gets too close or makes one wrong move for a shoulder holster, and he'll be picking his nuts up off the street.

The young man did not even glance at Ferguson. Most people never made eye contact with a drunk on the street; they always looked the other way or pretended he wasn't swilling his wine right in front of them. Ferguson knew it was the best way to avoid a panhandle. He relaxed the grip on his knife and studied the face as the young man walked past.

He still had a reporter's eye for detail. He noticed a pattern on the crimson tie, and the connections came quickly. The pattern looked like a Harvard coat of arms. Harvard led to Cambridge, which led to an address he had recently memorized, which led to a name and a picture in the newspaper. Ferguson's detective work had paid off.

Peter Fallon, witness to the murder of a rumdum bartender in Southie, was a family friend of the Pratts and Carringtons.

Maybe it meant nothing, maybe everything.

About the time that Christopher Carrington's body was lowered into the earth, Peter Fallon was riding an elevator down to the microtext room buried deep beneath Harvard's Houghton Library.

He was no longer telling himself that this was a scholarly pursuit, that he was investigating the story of the tea set in order to illuminate the character of Horace Taylor Pratt. He knew enough about Pratt already. He was looking for satisfaction. He had to be certain that there were no connections between the death of Christopher Carrington, the disappearance of Jack C. Ferguson, and the crumbling note sent by Dexter Lovell on August 24, 1814.

For the good of his work, for the four years he had already invested in a master's degree and a doctoral dissertation, he hoped that his research turned up nothing. Fallon knew that if the story became more convoluted, if Jack Ferguson's charges against the authenticity of the tea set were convincing, he would not be able to turn back to the disciplined work of writing a dissertation.

He stepped off the elevator into the concrete bunker that housed the microtexts. He hoped that he might find new leads among the old newspapers, and almost simultaneously, he wished that he had never found Dexter Lovell's note.

He showed his card to the librarian at the entrance and asked if copies of *Hubcap*, Jack C. Ferguson's weekly, were kept on film.

The librarian shook his head.

Fallon recalled that they didn't even keep back copies of the *Boston Globe* at Widener, Harvard's enormous main library. He would have to look in the Boston Public Library for Ferguson's articles. But just as important to him were copies of nineteenth-century newspapers, which the Houghton Library had on film. He requested films of the *Boston Gazette* from August and September 1814.

In the darkness of the reading room, Fallon threaded the microfilm into one of the machines. The blue projecting lamp illuminated his face, and the *Boston Gazette*, dated August 3, 1814, appeared on the screen in front of him. He rolled the film ahead to late August, about the time that Lovell had promised the arrival of the tea set.

He was glad that newspapers of the period were only four or five pages long, because the *Boston Gazette* wasn't indexed and he didn't know what he was looking for. He was simply hunting. He skimmed across headlines screaming alarm at the burning of Washington, editorials summoning Bostonians to the protection of the city, advertisements for felt hats and barrels of salt cod. He paid close attention to the articles usually found on the bottom of the front page. They described the murders, robberies, and other crimes which, even then, sold newspapers in Boston.

On the last page of the September 9 edition, a small article attracted Fallon's attention:

BLACK BODY ON THE NECK

The body of a Negro man, about thirty-five years old, was found washed up on the Neck yesterday morning. He had met with foul play, having been shot twice. One ball tore a fist-sized hole in his back as it exited. The other entered near his navel, traveled upward, through a lung, and left the body beneath his shoulder blade. He has no papers of identification and is unknown to Negroes on the hill. Hence, he will be buried in Potter's Field if his body is not claimed before tomorrow sunset. God have Mercy on his Soul.

Fallon noted the date and copied the article onto an index card. He knew that Lovell had disappeared with a black freedman. Perhaps Lovell had killed him when the black was of no further use, which meant that Lovell had made good his promise and brought the tea set to Boston.

He rolled the microtext ahead. Nothing Saturday or Sunday, but a headline Monday stopped him cold.

PRATT GRANDSON DROWNS IN BACK BAY

Horace Taylor Pratt III, eldest grandson of the founder and president of Pratt Shipping and Mercantile, drowned yesterday morning in the Back Bay. His death was reported to the constable's office by his grandfather, Horace Taylor Pratt I.

The lad, only fifteen, was foraging for blueclaw crabs in knee-deep water when he stepped into the Easterly Channel, which is about six feet deep at flood tide. Said to be a strong swimmer by his bereaved grandfather, young Pratt nonetheless panicked and drowned.

The rest of the story described the boy's schooling, his family's background, and the arrangements for his burial. It sounded to Fallon as though it had been written for last night's deadline. The past drew closer. The sense of danger, vague and imperceptible after his first trip to Searidge, drawn into focus by Christopher Carrington's death, was growing on the blue screen before him.

In his excitement to copy the article onto an index card, Fallon broke the tip of his pencil. He stepped out to the main desk to sharpen it. When he returned, a big man wearing a Red Sox baseball cap was studying Fallon's viewer.

The man finished his reading, then smiled at Fallon. "Excuse me, but I couldn't help noticing the *Boston Gazette* in your machine. When I was an undergraduate, about forty years ago, I wrote my honors thesis on journalistic styles in the nineteenth century, and I always loved the old *Gazette*. Great reading."

It was too dark to see the man's features, but Fallon noticed a fringe of white hair beneath the baseball cap. "They have almost every issue on film," he offered. "Do you want this one after I'm through?"

"No, thanks. Too many other things to be doin'." The man said goodbye and returned to a viewing machine in a distant corner.

Fallon had rarely seen an old grad look so tattered, but he didn't give him another thought. He was too preoccupied with the death of a young boy in 1814 to know that the man who had just been standing beside him was Jack C. Ferguson.

No Harvard graduate, Ferguson was familiar enough with the systems to get a pass into any private library in Boston. He had followed Fallon down to the microtext room, seated himself at a nearby machine, and pretended to read wartime copies of the *New York Times* until he could look at Fallon's screen.

Fallon was certain now that Lovell had gotten the tea set to Boston, and he was willing to believe that something had happened to it in the Back Bay. The death of Horace Taylor Pratt III, the week that the tea set was supposed to arrive and the day after the death of an anonymous black who was probably Jeff Grew, could not be a coincidence. Fallon rattled through another month of the *Boston Gazette* and found nothing else. He couldn't concentrate, anyway. He had to talk to someone about his findings, his theories, his suspicions. He packed up his things and left.

Professor James Hayward lived with his books and his clocks in a comfortable old house just off Brattle Street.

He had come to Cambridge in 1941 from an impoverished ranching family. The eighteen-year-old Harvard freshman brought with him an acute case of asthma, which made ranch life miserable and military service impossible, and a fascination with the people who had forced the American frontier from the Appalachians across his own Wyoming to the Pacific.

At Harvard, he found rich soil in which to nurture his passion. He spent eight years earning degrees, while earning money as a dishwasher in student dining halls, a cab driver in Boston, and a history tutor in Kirkland House. His first book, *Manifest Destiny and the American Spirit*, was expanded from his dissertation. It was nominated for a National Book Award and secured James Hayward a tenured position on the Harvard faculty.

He bought his house, opened its doors to his students, and settled into a life which had continued to challenge and satisfy him. Or, as he told Peter Fallon one night, after three bourbons had left him especially cynical, "It took me eight years to scrape the cowshit off my shoes and find myself a nice soft spot in all this academic bullshit."

Over the years, he had lost his hair and the hard edge on his Wyoming accent, while growing a paunch that looked like an air bubble expanding out of his slender body. However, he was still a commanding figure at the podium, a brilliant guide in seminar, and a friend to most of his students. His lecture course, "The West, 1803 to 1890," began with the Louisiana Purchase and ended with the massacre at Wounded Knee. In his seminar, he turned to the East. "The War of 1812: New England and the Nation" explored the national problems created when Northern Sectionalism clashed with Southern Expansionism. It was always oversubscribed.

James Hayward's work was his life. He had never needed anything else.

In his ninth book, Hayward was studying the effects of Eastern press coverage on the conduct of the war with the Plains Indians. He was reading an account of the Battle of Little Bighorn when the doorbell rang.

Peter Fallon was standing on the porch with the afternoon sun broiling in around him.

"Come in, Peter. Come in and sit down."

Fallon stepped into cool darkness, and Hayward went to fetch iced tea or something stronger, depending on his mood.

The shades in the living room were drawn tight to keep out the heat. A lamp next to Hayward's easy chair provided the only illumination. Fallon found his way to the overstuffed sofa and sank into relaxing gloom. The only sound was the gentle ticking of Hayward's eighteen antique clocks, each beating with a different pitch and rhythm. They soothed like so many massaging fingers. When Hayward returned with two glasses of Molson's Canadian, Fallon's head was thrown back and his eyes were closed.

"Wake up and have a beer," said Hayward.

"I'm not asleep."

"Have a beer anyway. It's after four, and I've been reading all day. A positively fascinating book written in 1933 by a doctor who lived with the Sioux and the Cheyennes. It's called *Save the Last Bullet for Yourself*. He got to know the old warriors who fought Custer at Little Big Horn. They told him that the men of the Seventh Cavalry panicked, and better than half of the troops committed suicide. Imagine. The vaunted Seventh Cavalry!"

Their meetings had always begun like this—Fallon catching his breath while Hayward rattled on about some new book or especially good student paper. Hayward had been the senior reader of Fallon's undergraduate thesis and had advised Fallon all through graduate school; Fallon was Hayward's teaching assistant. A solid friendship had developed between them, although enough formality remained that Fallon never considered addressing his teacher as anything but Professor Hayward. First-name familiarity would come with the doctorate.

"I'm having a few problems with the dissertation," said Fallon. "I could use a little guidance."

Hayward smiled. "That's what I'm here for. Of course, if I had seen the last three chapters when you promised them, I could be of more help now. Any idea of when I can expect to be reading about Horace Taylor Pratt?"

"I don't know. I've come across so much information about him that I really don't know what I'm going to do with it all."

Hayward sensed a note of defeat in Fallon's voice. "I've never met a historian before who was disappointed when he ran across new information."

Fallon did not respond directly. Instead, he described Dexter Lovell's note and everything that followed it, including the news stories he had just read. "The point of all this," he concluded, "is that someone is lying, or at least mistaken, about the story of the tea set, either Hannaford or the facts which I have uncovered in the last week."

"So what?" Hayward had little patience when he thought a student was wasting time.

"I want you to tell me what you think of all this. Should I keep digging? Should I forget about it? Should I try to find this Ferguson guy?" He realized he was whining. He took a swallow of beer and lowered his voice. "I'm confused. I know it's almost out of the question that the tea set in the museum is a fake, as this Ferguson claimed before he disappeared. I'm fairly certain that Hannaford's researchers just made a mistake when they blamed the original theft on Captain Prendergast. I'm probably the only person who knows for certain that Lovell took the tea set."

"Peter," Hayward interrupted, "what bearing does any of this have on your contention that New England emerged from the War of 1812 with more political and economic power than any other section of the country?" He didn't wait for an answer. "None! What bearing beyond a footnote or two does any of this have on your analysis of Pratt Shipping and Mercantile? None! I don't know what's come over you lately, but whatever it is, get out from under it. Week by week, your discipline deteriorates, the quality of your work diminishes, you disappear for days on end, and now this! Tea sets when you should be trying to draw serious conclusions about four years of work."

Fallon tried to defend his activities as important research. "If Pratt saved his company or bought himself a little extra time by fencing the tea set in Europe, I think that knowledge has bearing on my dissertation."

"Then use it! Don't come wandering in here like Little Boy Lost and ask me what you should do. You're a big boy. Plug your information in and get on with your work."

"But right now I can't prove that Pratt sold the tea set. I'm sure it reached Boston, but I don't know what happened to it after that."

"Then speculate, for God's sake. What do you think historians do? We aren't lawyers. We're interpreters. If you can't find specific evidence to support a conclusion that the tea set saved Pratt's ass, take a stand on the basis of what you have, then be prepared to take the heat." He was on his feet now, gesturing grandly to make each point, as though he were giving a lecture. "It's all part of the process. You make a judgment, and somebody says it's bullshit. You argue, and pretty soon, you've both learned something. The dialectic of history."

Fallon smiled at that last phrase. It was one of Hayward's favorites, and he found a way to sneak it into every lecture.

The Seth Thomas on the mantelpiece struck five o'clock. The grandfather in the entrance hall and the banjo in the kitchen began to sound, and within a few seconds, every clock in the house was chiming. The symphony lasted about a half minute, just long enough for Hayward to sit down and cool off.

"Peter, you're too bright to need guidance on something like this. You're not having trouble deciding what to do with this note. Your problem is a lot deeper. It's been boring its way to the surface since last fall, when you started applying for jobs."

Peter nodded. His professor knew him well. "I've been second-guessing myself lately. When you realize you've spent four years at something that offers you no immediate future, you begin to wonder if you've wasted your time."

"You've wasted it only if you've learned nothing, and if you've been listening to me for four years, I can guarantee that you've learned something. Moreover, you have two job offers, which is more than most history Ph.D.s can say. This is a damn tight job market, and you should be glad you have anything, regardless of tenure. Go home and finish your dissertation, then accept one of those positions, no matter what you think of the schools." He took out his pipe, scraped the bowl, and packed it with tobacco. In a moment, his head was enveloped in a cloud of blue smoke. "If you want somebody to solve your problems for you, I've just done it."

"Stop trying to make me feel stupid." Fallon rested his elbows on his knees and folded his hands. "Every time I see my old man, he tells me I should have gone to law school. Lately I've begun to agree with him. That in itself makes me feel about as stupid as I can get."

Hayward shook his head. He hated to see one of his best students so confused. "I told you four years ago that law was a practical choice, a sensible alternative to a career in history, where there's no guarantee that you'll be able to find work. I also told you that the historian has a very important role in our society, a position of tremendous responsibility. Whether he's a university professor, a high school teacher, a writer, he is the controlling voice in the events which have shaped our society and our national character. When he writes about the American Revolution or the *Federalist Papers*, the Dred Scott Decision or the campaign against the Plains Indians, he decides for the rest of us what is significant. He's the window through which we see our past, the mirror in which we see ourselves."

"You were always the master of the aphorism," cracked Fallon.

"I've been lecturing for thirty years," answered Hayward a bit crankily. "I've given that speech before. Next time I deliver it to a prospective student, I'll emphasize the hundreds of hours of research and the loneliness of the work. Somehow I thought you were mature enough to know that the glamour came after the drudgery."

"I always knew it," said Fallon. "I embraced your philosophy, and I believed that what I was doing was vital. I still believe it. But something's wrong. The jobs I've been offered promise no excitement, no prestige, and damned little money. The daily routine of classes, writing, and research has dulled me, made me feel flaccid . . ." He hunted for a better word. ". . . emasculated. I sometimes wish I'd been drafted and sent to Vietnam. I could at least feel that I'd seen a little bit of life before retiring to the library." He finished his beer.

Hayward began to laugh. "You make all scholars sound like eunuchs. We lead very active lives, my boy. Just ask my old colleague Mr. Kissinger. Not everyone gets to be Secretary of State, but we serve on presidential committees, we participate in political demonstrations, and we write excellent angry letters to the *Times*. Some of us who are balding, paunchy, and charismatic also have wonderful luck with female graduate students."

"I'm not talking about you."

"You're not talking about too many people I've ever known here, either." Hayward stopped joking and leaned forward. "If you have the brains, aggressiveness, and ego to get into this program and perform well for four years, I don't understand how you can feel emasculated at the end of it."

Unconsciously Fallon bounced his legs up and down on the balls of his feet. He sensed that Hayward wasn't going to be much help. "Can I have another Molson's?"

"Help yourself."

Fallon sucked down half the beer in the kitchen. He always felt more eloquent when he had a buzz going in his head.

"I hate to admit failure," he said as he sat down again. "I hate to accept my father's prediction that 'all this history bullshit,' as he calls it, will be useless. But the study of the past has been losing its fascination for me. Until I stumbled onto this note, I was working on nothing but stubbornness. Now, I'm excited again. I'm tracking down clues to an ancient mystery."

"And who cares if you solve it?" Hayward grunted.

"I care." Fallon finished the second beer. "What if that tea set in the museum isn't the real one? What if I figure out where it is, just by being a good historian? And what if I find it?" Fallon's voice rose with excitement.

Hayward cleaned and packed his pipe. Whenever he needed a moment to think, the pipe became his prop. "Peter, I think you're crazy." It wasn't quite the answer he'd been reaching for.

Fallon laughed. "The more I listen to you, the more you sound like my father."

"Look, there's nothing more I can offer you, Peter. Your choices seem fairly obvious. You can quit right now and start collecting material for law-school applications. You'll have a helluva time explaining why you left graduate school a few months away from the doctorate, but I'm sure you'll think of something. Or you can take whatever time is necessary to satisfy yourself about this tea-set business, but when it's over, you'll still have to confront your disillusionment with your work. Harvard puts no time limit on the completion of dissertations, so you can come back and finish it any time in the next fifty years. Of course, those two schools out west won't be too interested in hiring you this September if you don't have your doctorate. Or you can go home, sit down at your desk, put all your problems out of your head for three months, and finish. You'll have a much better perspective when it's over."

Hayward lit a match and sucked the flame into his pipe. "I know what I'd do."

Peter Fallon brooded his way home beneath a summer downpour that lasted ten minutes and left everything steaming. He could almost drink the rancid air in his apartment, and the floor beneath the front windows was soaked from the rain.

He took a Narragansett from the refrigerator and sat down at his desk. Hayward had made it simple enough. Drop out and go to law school. Drop out and look for the tea set. Or be responsible.

His copy of *Boston: A Topographical History* was on his desk, open to the map of the Back Bay in 1814. He had outlined the path of the Easterly Channel in red ink, and as he stared at it, he began to sense that something was not quite right. The night before, he had been reading the last chapter, a hundred and fifty pages away.

At first, he thought the wind had turned the pages. However, on the rare occasions when he enjoyed a breeze, it came through the windows. To turn the pages backward, the wind would have to blow through the bathroom wall.

Someone had been in the apartment.

He yanked open the bottom drawer. His Nikon was still there. He spun round in his chair. KLH receiver and turntable remained bolted to the wall. It wasn't a ripoff. Why were they here?

Something fell in the kitchen. Fallon froze, his heart pounding in his ears. Quickly, he calculated the distances between himself, the kitchen door, and the closet, where he kept a baseball glove and a thirty-four-ounce Louisville slugger. He sprang for the bat.

The noise again. He stopped in midair. Across the alley, Mrs. Luskinski was closing her kitchen windows. She worked nights at Elsie's and always locked her windows, even though she lived on the third floor.

Hayward's right, thought Fallon. You *are* crazy. No one's been in here. Your imagination is getting the best of you.

He sat down at his desk. He sipped his beer and looked around. The whole place seemed slightly askew. He noticed little things, subtle indications that his apartment had been searched. A feeling of revulsion crept over him. His privacy had been violated.

He wasn't much of a housekeeper, but he was compulsive about keeping his work material and books carefully organized. He kept twenty-six piles of notecards on the coffee table, and he noticed several cards lying on the floor. They had not been there when he had left. As he picked up the cards, he saw traces of mud and water, the remains of a Cambridge mud puddle, drying on the braided rug. They were not his footprints. Desk drawers were open by an inch or two. The filing cabinet, which protected his bankbook and the completed portions of his dissertation, showed scratches around the master lock. Someone had tried to get in. He couldn't tell if they had been successful, but he knew now that he wasn't crazy.

Excitement quickly replaced revulsion. There was only one reason why anyone would break into his apartment and go through his papers—the Dexter Lovell note.

He had hidden the note in an old geology textbook. He jumped to the bookcase. The note was still there, but a few shelves away, he noticed that one of his pewter mugs, which he used as a bookend, was out of place. The handle of the mug was scratched and bent. It had been knocked to the floor when somebody explored his bookcases.

Had they seen the note and decided to leave it there? Had they missed it? Or had they inspected only a few books? On the shelf with the mug, Fallon kept works from the Elizabethan Renaissance—*The Pelican Shakespeare, Seventeenth Century Prose and Poetry, The Complete Plays of Christopher Marlowe*, Milton's *Paradise Lost*, and *Bartholomew Fair* by Ben Jonson. He knew the intruders weren't interested in Shakespeare. They had been looking for the note.

Fallon heard footsteps in the hallway. He locked the door and took the baseball bat out of the closet. The footsteps drew closer, passed his door, and stopped near his fire door. Fallon kept his hand tight around the bat. The footsteps started back down the hall and stopped at his front door.

Fallon could tell from the heavy step that whoever was out there weighed more than two hundred pounds. Fallon felt the adrenalin rush through him. After several minutes, the person began to move again. The footsteps receded down the hall.

Fallon ran to the window and looked down into the street. A big man wearing a Red Sox baseball cap stepped out of the building and mixed into the pedestrian traffic on Massachusetts Avenue. It was the old grad in the library. Big, burly, white hair, and the smell of cheap wine. Fallon remembered Jane Cooper's description of Jack C. Ferguson.

There he was—alive, well, and right on Fallon's doorstep.

Fallon raced out of the apartment and down Mass. Ave., but Ferguson had already disappeared. For the next half hour, Fallon searched the subway stations and the local bars. But Jack C. Ferguson was a master of concealment. He would pick the time and place that they met.

CHAPTER XI   *June 1825*

The breeze floated down Pemberton Hill and bathed Horace Taylor Pratt in rose perfume. The sweet smell reminded him of the rose on another June morning, and his mind drifted back.

The bombardment had kept up since first light, and the ground shook with each load of grapeshot that slammed into Breed's Hill. Horace Taylor Pratt was twenty-four, and he had never known exhaustion like this in his life. He slumped in the trench, his brow caked in perspiration and dust, his arms throbbing. He had shoveled all night, and he didn't think he would be able to lift a rifle, much less aim and fire one, when the attack came.

"It's a great bright day for the battle of Bunker Hill, eh, little brother?" Ephraim Pratt, three times as big as Horace and bursting with energy, stood atop the earthworks.

"We're on Breed's Hill," Horace objected.

"Well, wherever we are, we're here to give the British a damn good drubbing. Stand up and see the best-dressed army in the world."

Horace picked himself up and looked down toward the water. An endless line of longboats swept across the harbor from Boston, each of them carrying a cargo of scarlet coats and bayonets.

"From up here, they look like autumn leaves in a stream, all red and pretty," said Ephraim.

At the base of the hill, the scarlet coats formed ranks and spread out. Ordered, efficient, deadly. The finest army the world had ever seen.

Pratt looked up and down the earthworks. A jagged line etched across the hills above Charlestown, and seven or eight hundred men huddled behind it for protection against the British wind.

"Ephraim," said Horace, "I've dug all night. I've done a share. Right now, I'm of a mind to be leaving."

Ephraim jumped down from the parapet. "You'll do nothing of the sort. I'll not have my brother disgracing himself and me and the name of Pratt. The call went out, and we answered it. We'll stand and fight like good honest yeomen."

"We're not yeomen, and we're not soldiers. We're shippers."

"And our only ship, bought with every nickel we could muster, sits down there at Hancock's wharf, impounded by the damn British because the Pratts and men like them would take no more abuse. Stand and be a free man, brother. Leave and take no title to the nation we build."

"A speech like that'd bring Gen'ral 'owe 'imself up 'ere." A young Cockney with broad shoulders and high cheekbones was standing next to Horace Taylor Pratt. His name was Dexter Lovell.

"What puts an Englishman up here aimin' to shoot down his own countrymen?" asked Ephraim.

"Well, sir, some would say we're all Englishmen."

"Amen to that," added Horace Pratt.

"But I've got a girl in Boston town, and she said she'd marry me if I stood with her dad against the British Army. Ol' Dad is nowheres in sight, but 'ere I am, true to my word like a damn fool." Lovell laughed nervously.

"Some would say we're all damn fools." Horace Taylor Pratt laid his fowling piece atop the redoubt.

Ephraim smiled at his brother. "If that means you're stayin', amen to that, too."

The British bombardment ended and Breed's Hill fell silent. A cool breeze, the last of the day, idled up from the water. Then the cadence began. Fifty drums beat like one and the scarlet lines lurched forward.

All along the earthworks, they took their places, farmers and merchants, doctors and shopkeepers, boys and men. Horace Pratt smelled the sweat of fear. He rubbed his palms dry and gripped the flintlock. To his left, Ephraim had already chosen a target. To his right, Dexter Lovell was shaking. Pratt realized that Lovell was only seventeen, perhaps eighteen.

"Ephraim," said Horace, "stand between the Cockney and me. A strong branch to hold two trembling leaves." The Pratts exchanged places.

The scarlet machine ground forward, driven by gears that revolved to the beat of the drums. Unhurried, imperious, relentless it came, and Horace Pratt thought again about running.

Down the line, someone fired. Pratt heard the pop of the rifle, then another. And another. Random sounds hurled weakly against the pounding drums.

"Hold your fire, men. Hold your fire. Wait till they reach that big stump settin' out there about fifty yards." Captain Prescott walked past, settling the men who anchored the right flank. "Hold your fire."

Pratt could see figures now in the scarlet line. Men made up the machine. He didn't think he could shoot, but he chose a target.

"Keep comin', keep comin'," whispered Ephraim. "A few more steps and we'll send you all back to England for good. C'mon, my lobsterback bully boys. Keep marchin' like damn fools, right into our guns." He turned to his brother. "Did you ever see anything so damn stupid?"

Horace Pratt did not answer. The drums were pounding in the pit of his stomach. He was terrified. He pulled back the hammer and aimed at a red coat.

The first line reached the stump.

"Fire!"

Pratt closed his eyes and pulled the trigger. A mighty explosion overpowered the drums. He opened his eyes to see the line broken and staggering but still advancing through a thick blanket of smoke. He reloaded quickly.

"Fire!"

The scarlet line withered. The mightiest army on earth fell back.

On Breed's Hill, the men cheered wildly. Lovell leaped to the top of the earthworks and shook his fist at the enemy. Horace Pratt threw his arms around his brother.

"We've won! We've stopped them!" he exclaimed.

"Don't get so excited," said Ephraim. "They'll come again."

A half-hour later, they did, and the Yankee fire drove them back once more.

The third British charge came in the late afternoon. The Americans fired their final volley, but it was too weak to break the British line. There was no more ammunition.

"I'd say we've done our share," announced Ephraim. "Stay close, brother."

"If we're separated, we meet at Mills's Tavern in Cambridge."

"Aye."

"Can I run with you gents?" asked Lovell.

"If you can stay with us," answered Ephraim.

The scarlet line breached the earthworks and the retreat began. A few Colonials stopped to fire a final shot. Others stayed and fought hand to hand.

The Pratts and Dexter Lovell ran with the rest. They were into the saddle between Breed's and Bunker hills when a British musket ball slammed through Dexter Lovell's shoulder. He fell on his face and cried for help.

Ephraim stopped and turned back.

Horace grabbed his brother by the arm. "Forget him. He'll slow us down."

"He fought beside us. We'll help him if we can." Ephraim pulled away and ran back against the tide of retreating farmers.

Lovell was on his knees, staring at the hole in his shoulder. Ephraim put a hand under Lovell's arms and tried to lift him. Lovell offered no help.

"Give us a hand, damn you!" screamed Ephraim at his brother.

Horace grabbed Lovell under the damaged shoulder. He felt a warm pool of blood filling the armpit.

"Now let's go, boy. We've got some runnin' to do." Ephraim shook Lovell's shoulder lightly.

Horace was not so gentle. He throttled the other shoulder, and the pain that shot through Lovell snapped him out of his shock. Lovell stood under his own strength.

"I think I can make it," he said.

At that instant, Ephraim Pratt's head exploded, covering his companions in a shower of blood and brain.

"Sweet Jesus! Help me! I can't see!" screamed Horace. He dropped his rifle and tried to wipe the blood from his eyes. His left arm was torn away from his face. A musket ball shattered his elbow and lodged in the middle of the broken bone.

Lovell grabbed Pratt by the arm, and they began to run.

Pratt's vision cleared, but still he did not comprehend what had happened. "My brother? Where is he?"

"He's gone ahead," screamed Lovell. "We'll meet him at Mills's Tavern."

Another British volley raked across the saddle. Men fell everywhere. Pratt and Lovell hurtled up Bunker Hill, over the crest, and then down toward Cambridge. They ran and ran, never looking back, never pausing. They ran after the British had stopped pursuing. They ran until they could run no more, then they collapsed by a stream.

It was near nightfall. The aroma of wild-blooming roses hung thick in the air. Horace Pratt drank his fill and breathed deep, cleansing his nostrils of the stench of gunpowder, sweat, and blood. He closed his eyes. When he awoke, he was screaming. The saw had cut halfway through his arm.

His scream brought Abigail rushing into the room. "Father, what's the matter?"

Pratt heard the doctor call for rum. He felt it pouring down his throat. He gagged but kept it down.

"Father, it's all right. It's all right."

Pratt mumbled and gurgled and tried to speak while the stump of his left arm flailed wildly about. He had suffered a stroke six weeks before. His right side was totally paralyzed, his speech almost incomprehensible, and the cruelest of ironies, his left side still functioned.

The coolness of Abigail's hand at his temple drove the memories from his head. He was soothed. She brought a glass of water to his lips. He managed a few swallows before the water dribbled down his chin. He turned his head away like a child who refused to eat.

She followed his mouth with the glass. "More, Father?"

He didn't look at her.

"Father?"

His eyes filled with tears. He mumbled something that she took to mean no.

She brushed back the few strands of gray hair around his face and kissed him on top of the head. "Poor child."

He pulled his head away. He did not want sympathy. He

mumbled and gestured with his head toward the window.

She rolled his wheelchair into the sunlight. "Is that better?"

The sun was intense, but he seemed content in the heat. He put his head back and closed his eyes.

Six weeks earlier, he had been known as the toughest old man in Boston. He had survived the War of 1812, and, by 1824, had built a granite foundation for Pratt Shipping and Mercantile. When the Treaty of Ghent was signed and the blockade lifted, Pratt ships poured out of Boston, their holds brimming with New England goods. They returned laden with the products of Europe and the Orient. Pratt bought off the creditors waiting to pounce on the *Pegasus* and the *Alicia Howell*. Then, he leaped into competition with Thomas Handasyd Perkins in the Chinese opium trade.

Pratt had avoided opium before the war, but not because of scruple. The risk had simply been too great. When the Emperor of China announced a new campaign against smugglers, Pratt knew the profits would be enormous for the smugglers who succeeded. Soon, captains under the Pratt flag were plowing from Turkey to the China coast and selling their opium to Chinese dealers, while Pratt agents in Canton bribed government officials to look the other way.

"If the heathen Chinee care so little for their souls," Pratt told Jason, "it is upon their heads, not ours, that the blame for their addiction shall rest. We'll not let Perkins and his Forbes nephews take all the profit."

In 1822, Pratt decided that textiles were worth his attention after all. Associates of the late Francis Cabot Lowell offered the Pratts, specifically Jason's wife, an opportunity to purchase preferred stock in the Merrimack Manufacturing Company, which was building a textile-producing town at the fork of the Concord and Merrimack rivers. Pratt invested fifty thousand dollars at two hundred dollars a share, which gave him nine percent of the company. Two years later, the town of Lowell was thriving, and the stock was returning a yearly dividend of a hundred dollars a share.

Jason Pratt saw vindication, eight years late, in his father's textile investments, but Horace Pratt gave no credit.

"You don't invest in a company when it has shown nothing. That's too risky," he explained. "You wait. You let others take chances, and then you strike, but you never sell ships. Never. If we had sold the *Pegasus* and the *Alicia Howell* when you counseled it, we would have lost thousands in revenue, which we have since invested in the Merrimack Manufacturing Company. In 1814, we

174

were weak. We had to be conservative. Our conservatism made us strong. Now we can profit from the daring of others."

"You forget that my wife's relatives exacted large penalties from us before allowing us the privilege of investing," said Jason.

"The penalties were not so large as the monies earned for us by *Pegasus* and *Alicia Howell*. Do not jump when you have weak legs, my boy."

When Pratt fell ill, he was planning to build four new ships to haul Merrimack Manufacturing products around the globe. American textiles were one of the fastest-selling commodities on the world market, and he intended to assure his family's dominance in every facet of production and distribution.

"I will present the Merrimack board of directors with four fast new ships," explained Pratt to his son. "I will offer them special transport rates, since I am a stockholder, and I will become the sole shipper transporting textiles from Merrimack mills."

After he had built the ships and arranged the contracts, he said his legacy would be assured. The company would be secure. Jason had grown in experience and competence. Jason's son Artemus, a seventeen-year-old freshman at Harvard, promised brilliance in the third generation. The tea set remained buried in the Back Bay. Pratt planned to reach one more goal, then retire.

Now, thought Abigail, he was little more than a plant turning constantly toward the sun. It would have been merciful if he had died the day he fell ill. He had lived almost seventy-five years. There was no need to prolong his life. Abigail hoped that he died before winter, when plants withered for want of sunlight and warmth.

Pratt had been stricken on the first warm Sunday in April. He and Abigail were walking along Western Avenue, atop the Mill Dam, which stretched west from the city to Brookline. The dam controlled the flow of water from the Charles River Basin into the Back Bay and used the power of the tides to operate mills on Gravelly Point and along its own length. As the tide rose, the water flowed into a full basin on the west side of Gravelly Point, then ran through sluices into the receiving basin, the area on the east side of the point that included the Easterly Channel.

Before the tea set had sunk into the channel, Pratt had supported the building of the dam and had considered investing in the Roxbury Mill Corporation. When he later realized that only a foot or two of water would cover his tea set at low tide, he became a vociferous opponent of the dam. The Mill Dam was built nonetheless.

It was low tide when Pratt and Abigail stopped above the sluice gates that day. The water across most of the receiving basin was no more than ankle-deep. A few feet filled the Easterly Channel. But a fresh breeze was snapping down the river and blowing the low-tide stench out to sea. Children were scampering about. Carriages packed with families clattered out toward Brookline and the countryside. Lovers arm in arm promenaded along the dam.

Abigail could not recall when her father had looked so well. She had finally convinced him that, in 1825, gentlemen no longer dressed in the frock coats and broad-brimmed hats that he had been wearing since the turn of the century. He now sported a pearl-gray cutaway, crimson silk cravat, and beaver hat.

"You look positively resplendent, Father, and twenty years younger."

He grunted. His attention was on something else, out in the bay. "I must be getting senile to be buying new clothes at my age."

Abigail smiled. "I no longer care to be seen in public with a relic of the past." She offered her arm. "Shall we walk?"

He didn't respond. His eyes were fixed on the Easterly Channel. A quarter mile away, four boys were sloshing across the flats, poking sticks into the mud as they went. They looked tiny to Abigail. She marveled that her father could see them. Usually, he couldn't read the newspaper.

"They're probably just looking for clams, Father."

"Sewage killed the clams years ago, and I don't care what they're looking for. It's what they might find that bothers me."

"You've worried about that tea set since the day they started building the dam. Why don't you go out and dig it up and be done with it?"

He slammed his cane into the sidewalk. "Do not say that! I will not dig it up. I will not deny it to my descendants." He realized that he was attracting the attention of passersby. He looked out across the water once more.

Abigail did not mention the thought that flashed through her head. Perhaps the tea set wasn't there at all. Perhaps someone had tripped across it when the Back Bay was dry and dragged it off to sell. Perhaps, but she refused to consider it. She had become as jealous as her father of their secret.

Abigail told herself that if the tea set had been found, the world would have heard about it. Its disappearance had created international unpleasantness. The tea set was now legendary.

176

When the war was over, Dolley Madison said she thought she had seen the tea set loaded onto one of the carts leaving Washington, but she couldn't be certain. President Madison believed that his wife might have left it behind. He petitioned Great Britain for its return. The British admitted the possibility that one of their officers had taken the tea set, but they pointed out that the Americans had abandoned their own Presidential Palace, leaving everything in it as spoils of war. In a gesture of friendship and honor, the British called on any officer who knew of the tea set's fate to come forward. None responded, and the Crown considered the matter closed.

The American government then turned the investigation, such as it was, onto its own country. Eventually, it led to Pratt, a former employer of Dexter Lovell. Pratt feigned ignorance and indignation, proclaiming that a hero from Bunker Hill did not deserve such treatment. The meek lawyer appointed by Congress soon went his way and no one ever again considered Pratt a suspect in the theft. There was no evidence to implicate him: the military did not keep careful records when delivering a satchelful of dispatches to a city; the courier left the army after the war and had not been seen since. The investigation ended in failure, and most Americans believed that the tea set was somewhere in England.

Abigail saw her father's body grow tense. She didn't know exactly where the strongbox lay, but she could sense from his reactions that the four boys were near it.

Pratt began to tap his cane nervously on the planking. "Get away from there, you little bastards. Get away from there." He spoke softly, almost to himself.

"Father, we're more than a quarter mile away from them. Distance can play tricks on good eyesight. It's certain to affect yours."

"I have visited that spot too often to be tricked. Those boys are moving straight toward it. They're trying to find it." His voice rose suddenly. "See how they splash at the water and poke their sticks into the mud!"

Abigail put her arm around him and tried to move him along. "Shall we walk, Father?"

"No. The sanctuary is threatened."

"Four boys are playing in the mud. Now come along."

Pratt did not take his eyes from the tiny figures out in the bay. They were running, chasing each other about on the flats. Then, three began to chase the fourth.

"You see, Father? They're not trying to find things in the mud. They're playing games."

One boy caught up with the fourth, then all three had him. They picked him up by the arms and legs, swung him back and forth three or four times, and threw him into the air. He landed in the water and disappeared.

"He's in the channel. He can't be more than five or six feet away from it." Pratt choked on the words.

"He isn't looking for it." Abigail tried to soothe him.

The boy appeared again. The water in the channel bed was up to his waist. He tried to splash his way out, but his mates pushed him back again. Abigail heard their laughter echoing across the flats, and she felt her father turning rigid beside her.

"They must not find it!" He was talking to himself again. "They cannot find it."

The tiny figure in the channel stopped splashing about. He bent over and reached into the water.

"No, no, no." Pratt bit his lower lip. "He's found it."

The boy took a handful of mud from the water and flung it at his friends. They scattered. Then he climbed out of the channel, both hands filled with mud, and began to chase them off toward the sea wall at the edge of the Public Garden.

The air hissed out of Horace Pratt as though someone had pricked him with a pin. The threat was over, the tirade just beginning. He turned to the people walking past and slammed his cane into the planking. "This Mill Dam is a disgrace, an abomination. I damn it publicly. We have interfered with the workings of nature and tried to control the flow of God's tides."

Passersby stared at Pratt as though he were mad, then hurried along. A few stopped to laugh, but most were sympathetic to the sight of a well-dressed gentleman making such a scene.

"We have created six hundred acres of reeking filth. For what? So that a few profiteers might run their mills."

"Father, please!" Abigail was frightened by the pitch of his voice and the veins bulging at his temples. She waved frantically to her footman, who had parked the carriage a few hundred yards down the dam.

"I opposed it!" he screamed. "I opposed this invasion of a . . . a sacred place!" Saliva was trickling out of the corners of his mouth.

"Father, your apoplexy."

"Damn my apoplexy." He directed his attention to her. "I was right. If they'd listened to me, our treasure would be safe forever. Now, young boys play upon it each day and will one day dig it up. I opposed it."

The carriage arrived. The footman, a surly Scot named Dunwell, climbed down and opened the door.

"Help us in with Mr. Pratt," commanded Abigail.

They tried to urge Pratt into the carriage, but he did not want to go.

"Let me alone!" he screamed. "We must watch over it."

Abigail grabbed him by the arm. He swung his cane at her. He was enraged.

"Drag him," she said.

The Scot put his hands under Pratt's armpits and hauled the old man into the carriage.

Abigail climbed in the other side and took her father's bony hand in hers. "The tea set is safe, Father. The tides fell this low before the Mill Dam. No one has touched it."

"I opposed the Mill Dam." His voice sounded like breaking glass. "It is a sin against nature."

The box atop the carriage opened. "Where to, ma'am?" asked the Scot.

"Take us home."

The carriage started to move. Suddenly, Pratt stood. He reached for the door and collapsed in the bottom of the carriage.

"The Mannion couple are here, ma'am." Mrs. Dunwell, the maid, appeared at the top of the stairs. She was in her mid-forties and usually as cranky as her husband.

Abigail had given them their release a week before her father's stroke. They had served her well since Wilson had died and Miss Priddam, their maid for thirty years, had retired to Nova Scotia. But with Franconia mercifully dead of pneumonia the year before, Abigail felt that the household no longer needed a couple. Then came the stroke. The Dunwells, insulted by their dismissal, refused to stay. Few couples wished to enter the service of an old man who needed constant attention.

This afternoon, Abigail was interviewing a couple just arrived from Ireland. They had been recommended by the minister from the Park Street Church.

Abigail went downstairs to the receiving room and ensconced herself in her favorite chair. "Send them in."

Delia Mannion, about forty-five, entered the room. She had a round Irish face, hands callused by years of work, and the full heft of middle age widening her girth. "Good morning, ma'am." Delia Mannion extended her hand.

Abigail was impressed by the strength of her grip. "It's a pleasure, Mrs. Mannion."

"The pleasure's mine, ma'am."

Abigail invited her to sit. Abigail did not ordinarily encourage such friendliness with her employees, and if Mrs. Mannion went to work for the Pratts, she would not be invited to sit in the receiving room again.

"I thought your husband would be with you," said Abigail.

Mrs. Mannion smiled nervously. "Well, ma'am, he ain't . . . isn't my husband, exactly."

"Then what is he?"

"He's my son, ma'am."

Abigail was surprised. "I was expecting a husband and wife. How old is the boy?"

"Nineteen."

"Boys of that age tend usually to be unreliable. If he is to work for me, he will be called upon at all hours of the day and night."

"Oh, he'll be a good one, ma'am." It was clear that Mrs. Mannion desperately needed work. "He's a quiet boy, but strong, and he's stayed by his mother ever since his da died four years ago." She was pleading. "He never raises a ruckus or drinks or causes trouble. He likes to write poetry and such."

"Has he had experience in private service?"

Mrs. Mannion looked at her shoes. "No, ma'am. None."

"Have you?"

"I worked for a Protestant minister in Ireland. When we left for America, he gave me the name of the minister at the Park Street Church. Reverend Russell. He gave our name to you. We've been staying in his carriage house."

"You're Congregationalist?"

"No, ma'am."

"A Catholic, then?" Abigail seemed displeased.

Mrs. Mannion nodded.

"Why have you come to America?"

"To work and, I'll be honest with you, to give my boy a chance at a good life. He can learn a mighty lot in the service of a great lady such as yourself." Mrs. Mannion's brogue was thick. An ingratiating smile spread across her face.

Abigail studied the Irish woman coldly. She had already decided to give the Mannions the job, but she wanted the woman to appreciate Pratt generosity and consider it a privilege to care for a Pratt. "You've had no experience in the service of American gentry, you have no references, you're Catholic, and your son is going to grow out of this work very quickly."

"Oh, but he's a fine boy. Wouldn't you like to meet him?"

Abigail nodded.

"Excuse me, then." Mrs. Mannion went into the hallway, where her son Sean was nervously squashing his cap in his hands. "Now be nice and polite. Say 'Yes, ma'am,' and 'No, ma'am,' and the divil grab you by the scruff of the neck if you dare to speak a word before spoke to."

"Yes'm."

When she saw Sean Mannion, Abigail would not admit to herself that he was beautiful. She had fallen in love twice since her husband had died. Each time, her lover was handsome, intelligent, aggressive, and, in the long run, more interested in her father's power than in Abigail herself. One of her suitors now captained a Pratt opium ship. The other, fired by Pratt for abusing Abigail's affections, worked for Thomas Handasyd Perkins. At thirty-five, Abigail no longer permitted herself to respond to men, except as she would to her brother Jason, with his spreading paunch, dullard's eyes, and watery lack of character.

"Good morning, young man," said Abigail, more pleasantly than she had intended.

"Yes'm, good morning." He spoke softly.

Abigail marveled that such a powerful body produced such a gentle sound. He was six feet tall, with broad shoulders and huge hands, the product of his years on a farm, but his features were delicate, almost feminine, and not at all Irish. His face was smooth and unmarked by the pox. His eyes were blue, and his forehead was framed in strawberry-blond hair.

"Your mother tells me you like hard work."

"Yes'm." He twisted the cap in his hands.

"Do you like caring for people who cannot care for themselves?"

"Sean took good care of his da after the mill wheel crushed his legs," said Mrs. Mannion.

"Your son can answer for himself."

"Yes'm."

"Besides tending the grounds, you will have to take care of my father. You will bathe him, feed him, dress him, carry him to bed, and on pleasant days, drive him around the Back Bay. Will you do these things with a smile and a pleasant demeanor?"

"I'll try, ma'am."

"You will have to do more than try."

"He will, ma'am. He's a fine boy." Delia Mannion was trembling. "Please give us a chance."

Abigail looked once more at the young man. "I must also tell you that my father is incontinent."

"Ma'am?" Sean did not understand her meaning.

"You don't have much of a vocabulary for a budding poet. I will put it plainly for the farm boy. My father shits in his breeches and must wear a diaper. Will you change the diaper as readily as you sit down to your verses?"

He hesitated. "I believe I'd prefer the verses." He heard his mother inhale sharply. He'd said the wrong thing.

Abigail smiled. "I like to have honest men in my service." She rang the bell beside her, and the maid appeared in the doorway. "You and your husband are to vacate your quarters in the carriage house by noon. Mrs. Mannion and her son will be taking your place."

Delia Mannion almost fainted.

An entry from Abigail Pratt Bentley's diary, July 2, 1825:

I have chosen well. The last months of my father's life will be spent in the hands of a kind, patient, decent young man. I am greatly relieved. Each morning, Sean rises at six and feeds the horses. Then, he goes upstairs and checks to see if Father's diapers need changing. With great patience and not the least distaste for this most distasteful task, Sean cleans Father, dresses him, and places him in his chair by the east window.

My heart bleeds to see Father as he is now—an infant whose words are rarely understood, who needs spoon-feeding, bathing, and diapering, who cries out for attention and amusement and finds so little to pass the time.

But Sean is there, and his willingness to help is boundless. He drives Father all about town in carriage and each day spends several hours reading to Father in the garden. He reads from the Bible, Milton, Shakespeare, and, on occasion, from his own poetry. He fancies himself a Romantic in the vein of Wordsworth or Shelley. He has some small talent for rhyming and meter, but his images of sunsets, green countrysides, and doomed young Irish heroes do not sit well with Father. Whenever the boy reads his poetry, Father mumbles so violently that Sean goes back to the classics. He will then read for hours from *Hamlet* or *Macbeth*, taking a new voice for each part and reading with such expression that, were he to ask me, I would encourage him to pursue acting rather than prosody.

The boy has taken a great load off my mind and allowed me to focus my attention on the most important problem facing me—my brother Jason, who has once more encamped himself in Father's office. This time he intends to stay.

I must find a way to undermine him. I must find a way to make my thirty percent of stock the equivalent of his seventy. But how? Pratt Shipping and Mercantile prospers and is secure. Only if the company falters and my brother stumbles into financial straits will I be able to exchange my knowledge of the tea set for whatever measure of power I can wrest from his hands.

For ten years, I have waited patiently. For ten years and beyond, I have allowed men to use me. My father has seen me as a convenience, a mistress, a nurse, and a companion for his old age. He has never considered my intelligence worthy of his business confidences. Two men, who shall forever remain nameless within these pages, used my heart and my love to reach the seat of power in Pratt Shipping and Mercantile. I hate them with my life. And my brother has used my womanhood to climb over me into the president's· office. His intelligence is not half of mine, but what he carries between his legs makes him more worthy.

I will find a way to control the destiny of Pratt Shipping and Mercantile. It is my destiny, after all.

A September morning in Boston: the sky a crisp cerulean blue, the sun warming slowly toward noon, the cool air invigorating the city. On such a morning, Abigail Pratt Bentley put a blue dress on over several petticoats, then a flowered shawl, and a green bonnet. She called for her carriage and told Sean to take her to Long Wharf.

Twice a week, she visited her brother Jason at the offices of Pratt Shipping and Mercantile. They discussed, with as much civility as possible, the current business, plans for future investment, the reasons for their perpetual disagreement, and the state of Horace Taylor Pratt's health. The conversations usually began coldly and ended in frigid silence.

Frustration consumed Abigail whenever she left the waterfront and returned to Pemberton Hill. Because she was a woman, her intelligence, her resolve, and her thirty percent of Pratt Shipping and Mercantile meant nothing. She could not remain in the handsome building on the wharf. She could not, without escort, visit the coffee houses along Congress Street, where the Jacksons, the Lowells, the

Perkinses, and the Pratts met to discuss the business of the day. She could not go to the exchanges on State Street, where money, stocks, bonds, and commodities were traded each hour. And worst of all, she could not sit behind her father's desk, with his capital, ships, and investments spread before her, and make decisions which would determine the future of Pratt Shipping and Mercantile.

She could observe and advise, but her father had delegated her no other authority. Today, she planned to talk about a new investment—railroads. She knew that Henry Eaton, a Pratt bookkeeper just back from vacation in England, was going to make his report on railways in Great Britain. She wanted to hear his impressions.

Jason Pratt's new office occupied the third floor of the outermost building on Long Wharf. Windows on three sides opened to the sea. Pine paneling covered the walls. An oriental rug, given to Horace Pratt by the hong merchant Houqua, adorned the floor. Pratt's model of the *Gay Head* sat in drydock on the mantel.

When Abigail entered the office, Jason Pratt, his son Artemus, and James Curtis, his treasurer and adviser, were in conference with Eaton. Jason sat behind his mahogany desk. Artemus, now seventeen, sat in a corner and listened closely to the discussion. James Curtis, whose stern, ascetic look reminded Abigail of a hungry greyhound, sat beside Pratt and took notes. Henry Eaton was sunk deep in the leather chair in front of Pratt's desk.

"Abigail, come in," cried Jason. "Henry Eaton is telling us about the railroad he has seen in England."

"We have a railroad right here in Massachusetts," she said, referring to the Granite Railway, which carried stone from a quarry in Quincy to the Neponset River.

"A horse-drawn railway. Henry Eaton has seen a train pulled by something called a locomotive, a marvelous novelty."

Abigail sat in a straight-backed chair by the southeast window, and the sun poured in around her. She had learned from her father to make others look into the glare.

"A glass of port, dear sister?" offered Jason.

"I do not drink port, except after dinner. It is a custom you would do well to embrace."

Jason finished the glass and poured another. He was only forty-one, but his body was thick and sluggish, his eyes rimmed in red. "Father joined me for a glass each day before lunch, Abigail. I need no censure from you." He turned to Eaton. "Please go on."

Eaton was a tiny man wearing wire-rimmed spectacles. He had never been in the president's office before. "Mr. Stephenson has designed several locomotives, and he is building two for the Stockton-Darlington run. I took it upon myself to express Mr. Pratt's tremendous interest in locomotives and asked if I could see one. He invited me instead to ride the locomotive operating on nine miles of track between a coal mine and the sea.

"What a memorable sight it was! A great boiler rests atop a platform on steel wheels. All manner of pulley, throttle, and gauge surround it, and two men operate it. One manipulates the devices. The other feeds the fire, which creates steam to drive the wheels. We traveled over hill and dale, sometimes reaching speeds of nine or ten miles an hour. All the while, the boiler spewed forth black smoke and sparks and roared like the fires of hell."

Abigail had seen the Granite Railway in operation, and she had read Stephenson's predictions for the future of the steam locomotive. She felt that railroads might be an excellent investment. "What is your impression of this new device?"

Eaton puffed up like a male bird in the mating season; he was rarely asked his opinion about anything. "Well, Mrs. Bentley, I'd invest some Pratt money in Stephenson's work, if the money was mine to invest."

"I agree, Mr. Eaton. High-speed land transportation may mean the future of America."

"Hah!" Jason Pratt finished his port. "Abigail, you've become a dreamer."

"When we have the money to risk, we should be dreamers."

"Let others be daring, then step in after the ground or the investors themselves have been broken. That was Father's advice."

"To you. Because he didn't believe you had the capacity to be daring and intelligent on your own. Father himself never heeded such words when he was a young man. He gambled his fortunes and won. His early voyages to China were the maneuvers of a daring man."

"He didn't invest in the Waltham mills when I suggested it. Ten years ago, textiles were a daring investment."

"Old age brought conservatism. Father and I both should have listened to you then." Abigail gave him his due. She knew that flattery was an excellent tool.

"But you did not, and we paid for it when we finally took our piece of the textile pie. Now, I am the president, and I will not listen to you." Jason glanced at the others. He spoke as much to impress them as to demean Abigail.

"If our brother had lived, you would not be sitting in this office."

185

Abigail did not move or raise her voice. Her response landed like a blow.

For a moment, no one spoke. Eyes shifted from Abigail to Jason, but Jason lacked his sister's acerbity, and he knew she was right. He had no response.

Mr. Eaton squirmed nervously. Jason excused him.

"Do you say no to railroads because you firmly believe they have no future, or because of your feelings for me?" asked Abigail after Eaton had left.

"I confess that my dislike for you colors all our dealings, Abigail, and I agree that there may well be a future for railroads, but at the moment, we do not have the money to invest. We are building ships. I have commissioned Melville Morton to build six instead of the four that father was planning."

"Six?" While other boys his age learned a trade, Artemus studied the books of Pratt Shipping and Mercantile. "Do we have the money to support such an undertaking, Father?"

"Whether we have the money or not," said Abigail, "it is a bad investment. Our shipping revenues have not risen appreciably since 1820. We have steady income from the China trade, but Boston is losing its position as a center of American commerce. The Erie Canal and the Hudson River make it cheaper to ship goods through New York."

"Boston is still preeminent in the field of textile manufacture, Abigail. We have markets around the globe. And one day, we will be able to trade with all of China. We will not have to go through the hong merchants in Canton. Then we will clothe millions. Hundreds of millions." Jason poured himself more port. "We'll build the ships. The Pratt House flag will rule the seas, Abigail."

"We have no exclusive contracts with textile producers, Jason, and you have not been able to secure any since Father took sick. Until we are guaranteed that the Merrimack Manufacturing Company will ship only through us, we cannot expand our fleet."

"We are building ships."

Abigail stood and approached Jason's desk. "Have you ever considered the distance from Boston to Lowell, Jason? And the length of time it takes to travel it?"

"Only when I travel it." Jason laughed at his joke and looked toward his son, who did not react.

"Then consider this: a railroad line from Boston to Lowell would bring textile goods to the waterfront cheaply and quickly, at a tremendous profit to the operators of the line."

Jason tried to dismiss her with a wave of his hand. "Lowell is over thirty miles away, and efficient steam locomotives are still a dream in the heads of a few inventors."

"Have you ever considered the immensity of this country, Jason?"

"No."

She turned to Artemus. "Have you?"

"I've read the journals of Lewis and Clark's expeditions."

"Then you know what riches lie beyond the Adirondacks and Appalachians. Europe will one day beg for all the minerals, foods, and animal furs this country can produce. To bring these goods to Eastern ports, we will need railroads. Let Boston lead the struggle, and we will guarantee that our ships are always full."

Jason was becoming exasperated. "But there is no railroad to invest in."

"Generate one!" Abigail was speaking passionately now. She had forgotten the coolness with which she usually spoke to her brother. "To start with, a line from Boston to Lowell. Go to Stephenson. Give his company money in exchange for exclusive American rights to his locomotives. It's a gamble, but we must be daring. Otherwise the times will pass us by."

"An excellent phrase, Mrs. Bentley. May I use it?" James Curtis rarely spoke except in sarcasm.

Abigail ignored him. "Have you discussed your decision with anyone else?" she asked Jason.

"I've talked it over with Artemus."

"And I disagreed with your decision to build six ships."

Jason turned on his son. His voice was suddenly harsh. "When I was your age, my father rarely spoke to me, and he never included me in his business discussions. Be glad that I think so highly of you."

"I still disagree." He spoke firmly. Already he seemed more confident than his father.

Jason turned to Curtis. "And your opinion."

"I have agreed from the outset that our fleet must be enlarged, regardless of the expense."

Abigail smiled at Curtis. "After all these years, my brother has managed to find himself a sycophant."

Abigail did not like or trust James Curtis. Long before Jason had moved into the president's office, Curtis had latched onto him and held tight. As Jason's responsibilities grew, Curtis's importance was magnified. Now, he was her brother's closest adviser, a man of intelligence and experience who might easily manipulate his superiors. Abigail often felt that Curtis was directing Pratt Shipping and Mercantile through her brother, and she wondered what profit he took beyond his salary and his shares in Pratt ships.

Curtis stared at Abigail for a few moments, then he looked toward Jason. His eyes suggested that Jason finish the conversation.

"Ships are the lifeline of New England, Abigail. They always have been. They always will be." Jason spun in his chair and gazed out at the ocean. He fancied that he conveyed his father's authoriy.

"Jason, you are a fool. I do not suffer fools gladly. And this matter is not closed." Abigail picked up her purse and shawl.

At the door, she turned again. "I pray, for the good of Pratt Shipping and Mercantile, that young Artemus is not so obtuse as his father. Otherwise, we shall not survive another generation."

Abigail had lost. She did not consider it a small defeat. She would have other chances to argue for railroads; they were still in their infancy. But she could not stop her brother's massive investment in new shipping.

If the weak man takes power, his weakness may lead him to act when the strong man would do nothing. Abigail recalled the lines from her diary. And the weak man may refuse to listen when the strong man would welcome advice.

Abigail stepped into the bright sunshine on Long Wharf. Sarah Lowell Pratt and Philip, her two-year-old son, were alighting from their carriage.

"Good day, Sarah," said Abigail coldly.

"Your weekly harassment of my husband?" Sarah's voice had not softened with the years.

"It behooves me to know what the acting president—"

"Acting and future president," corrected Sarah.

"—is doing with Pratt money."

"You have no constructive interest. You visit that office because you hate my husband and want to embarrass him."

Abigail smiled. She usually found Sarah's distrust rather amusing. "There is no fraternal love between us, but I see no purpose in weakening your husband. We are allies in the interests of Pratt Shipping and Mercantile."

Sarah laughed. She was not amused.

Abigail knelt, or squatted in her petticoats, beside her nephew. She loved the child, as she loved all her nephews, in spite of their parents. She thought that Philip, with his blond curls and blue eyes, was the most beautiful child she had ever seen. "How is our little man today?"

Philip played with the buttons on his suit. He was still learning to speak, and he talked only when the mood was upon him.

Abigail embraced him. "Do you have a kiss for your Aunt Abigail?"

He continued to play with his buttons.

"Apparently, the child is a better judge of character than his older brothers, both of whom have lately spoken well of you."

Abigail felt her muscles tense and her hands tighten around the boy's shoulders. Anger screamed in her ears. It was not the first time that Sarah Lowell Pratt had mocked Abigail in front of the children. Sarah knew that maternal instincts burned in Abigail, as they did in every woman. To be without young was a tragedy, to be fertile, a joy. For years, Sarah had been finding ways to remind Abigail that she was childless. It was Sarah's small victory against Abigail's independence.

Abigail stood. She refused to show her anger.

Sarah took her son by the hand. "Come along, Philip. We must be visiting Papa. Good morning, Abigail."

Abigail felt the tears well in her eyes. She wished sometimes that she had never been born a Pratt, that she had been instead a farmer's daughter and a farmer's wife living in Lexington with her twelve children and her loving husband. If a woman was born to bear children and overflow with love at the sight of a little boy, why did Abigail feel that she had been born to control the affairs of men?

She clenched her fists and closed her eyes. She tried to fight back tears of frustration. She cursed Pratt Shipping and Mercantile and all it meant to her. She cursed her fat brother and her mad father and all the men who had used her. She remembered Richard Lawson, the first mate of the *Gay Head II*, with his tanned skin and the white scar across his cheek. He professed his love every day until her father made him master of the *Ephraim Pratt*. She thought of her own James, the man she loved. They had been married just a week when he had left for England. She remembered how she had pleaded with him to stay. He had said he would be gone a few months, but he had never returned. She could no longer control her tears.

Sean Mannion helped her into the carriage and climbed onto his perch. He opened the box and looked down into the compartment. "Where would you like to go, ma'am?"

Mrs. Bentley was huddled in the far corner. She was crying softly. For the first time since he had met her, she seemed vulnerable. Sean

189

wanted to comfort her, to protect her.

"Where to, ma'am?" he said softly.

She did not answer.

He waited until she stopped crying. "Ma'am?"

"Oh Sean," she said. "Life would be so much simpler for me if I were a man."

"And much less enjoyable for the rest of us . . . beggin' your pardon, ma'am."

Abigail smiled. She pulled a handkerchief from her sleeve and wiped her eyes. "That's very nice of you, Sean. Thank you. Please take me home."

"Yes, Mrs. Bentley."

"And Sean, you're a fine young man. I don't know what I'd do without you."

Sean blushed and called to the horses.

The ride back to Pemberton Hill took only a few minutes. On the way, Abigail resolved that she would not allow self-pity to paralyze her. She would not let other men see her crying. She would be strong.

Sean stopped the carriage in front of the house and started to climb down.

"That's all right, Sean," said Abigail. "You may put the carriage away." She wondered later if she had spoken on impulse, or if she had been planning to say that.

The carriage rolled into the barn. Abigail smelled the pungent odor of hay and manure and sweating horses. She liked it. It was a clean smell. It made no pretense. Neither did Sean.

The carriage door opened and Sean extended his hand. "May I help you out, ma'am?" he asked softly.

She saw the admiration in his eyes. Whenever he looked at her, she saw her beauty reflected. Never did she see lust or self-interest. In his presence, she felt like a work of art.

She gave him her hand. Through her cotton gloves, she felt the perspiration on his palm. It flattered her. She climbed out of the carriage and stood in front of him. For a moment, she held onto his hand and looked deep into his eyes. She felt him trembling. They had never stood this close before.

"Sean," she whispered, "you have brought me great relief." She brought her face close to his. "Do you like me, Sean?"

"Yes, ma'am." He could barely speak.

"I think you are the handsomest young man I have ever met." She paused. She was going to enjoy this boy. "I've decided to let you kiss me."

He didn't move. He had kissed only two women in his life, his mother and a farm girl in a haystack. Mrs. Bentley was a fine lady.

"Kiss me, Sean," she urged gently.

He placed his lips upon hers for a moment, then, believing he had gone too far, he pulled away. She put a hand around his neck and brought his face down to hers. She kissed him hard.

"When I tell you to kiss me, that is how I want it done."

"Yes, ma'am."

"Now kiss me," she commanded.

He pulled her against him. When they separated, they were both breathing heavily.

"That's better, Sean."

She kissed him again. She felt his hands around her waist, but they did not stray. He would do only what she instructed. She began to savor her power over him.

"I have other parts," she whispered. "You may find them if you care to."

"Thank you, ma'am." Tentatively, he ran his hands across her breasts, but the top of a tight corset protected her nipples. He moved down her back and tried to caress her buttocks, but her heavy petticoats were impenetrable. He brought his hands more urgently back to her breasts, then across her stomach. He moved toward her loins, but he could feel nothing through the layers of fabric. His hands settled in defeat at her waist.

She smiled. She had frustrated him just enough. With her fingertips, she lightly brushed across his crotch. He shuddered. She felt his penis bulging against his pantaloons. She pressed her palm against it, an act of mercy. He whimpered, and the fish smell of semen mixed with the earthy aroma in the barn. Abigail breathed deep and wiped her hand on her handkerchief. Now, she owned him.

Sean looked at the stain spreading across the front of his pants and turned away. "I'm sorry, Mrs. Bentley. I . . . ."

"Sean, are you free this afternoon?"

"After my chores."

"When you finish, bring your poetry upstairs to my sitting room. I have never listened carefully to it. I may like it well enough to send it to one of my bookseller friends on Washington Street."

❊

That afternoon Abigail reclined on the settee in the middle of her room. She wore a loose-fitting flowered dress over a slip. She did not wear a corset. Sean sat in a straight-backed chair opposite her. He had changed into trousers and blouse. Her sitting room, on the west end of the house, adjoined her bedroom on one side and her father's room on the other.

Sean was reading from "The Ballad of Denny Dundee," his attempt at Byron. "Off in the heather where the cold wind blows,/ Young Denny Dundee was running./ The Brits did pursue him,/ For a brave man was he/ Who fought all his life so that Eire might breathe free."

Sean intended to tell the story of Denny Dundee's life, from his boyhood on a farm in Kerry to his death at the hands of British soldiers on a heath in England. Sean stopped reading after Denny lost his virginity to a farm girl in a haystack. "That's all I've written. I've a long way to go."

"It's a very fine poem, but I wouldn't be telling people you aspire to Byron. You're not writing *Childe Harold*. You're writing an Irish ballad, and a good one."

The boy smiled. "Will you show it to a publisher, then?"

"You must finish it, first."

"I'm straight to it." He started to leave.

"Sean, I haven't dismissed you."

"I'm sorry, ma'am."

She called him over and told him to sit down beside her. "I've enjoyed getting to know you today, Sean. I've enjoyed your poetry and you."

He blushed and looked at the floor. He didn't know how to respond.

She leaned close to him. She caressed his lips with her tongue.

That autumn, she made love to the boy almost every day. In the late afternoon, when the sun slanted low through the windows of her sitting room, she would send for Sean, leave instructions that they were not to be disturbed, and listen to his poetry. Then, she would take him to her bed.

He worshiped her. He came to her each day filled with a sense of adolescent awe and admiration. He did not see Abigail as the daughter of a fortune, as the avenue to her father. He was no suitor or officeseeker, but a guileless Irish boy overwhelmed by her beauty, breeding, and grace. He did not love her; he did not consider himself worthy to love her. Instead, he wondered each day that this woman would listen to his poetry and allow him to enter her body.

Once, he came to her room and, without any pretense at reading, kissed her passionately. It was a Sunday afternoon, and he had been drinking with his friends. He ground his loins against her and pinched her nipples through her cotton dress. She had fantasized all day the feel of his cock, but she pulled away and angrily dismissed him. She did not allow him back to her room for a week.

When he appeared the following Sunday, he carried twenty-five pages of new poetry under his arm. She listened to him for half an hour, then told him to kneel in front of her. She lifted her dress above her waist. She was wearing nothing underneath it, but he did not move toward her temptation. He was docile, submissive.

"Kiss it," she commanded.

He obeyed, for twenty minutes. Then she sent him away still stiff and sore inside his tight pantaloons.

Abigail did not love the boy, but she found him to be the perfect lover. His passion for her body satisfied her lust, and his willing obedience satisfied her passion for control. She used him, in the way that men had used her, as a means to an end. When she began to feel useless, he reminded her that she was not. When she began to wonder if she would ever direct the movement of her life, if she would ever achieve power in the family company, he gave her confidence in her ability to manipulate others. Without it, she could never overcome her brother.

Horace Taylor Pratt died peacefully in his sleep on December 4, 1825. Two day later, as the first blasts of winter shivered the oaks in the Old Granary Burying Ground, he went to his grave. His funeral was not large. His peers respected his brilliance, but few called him friend.

Most of the mourners were members of the family. However, Thomas Handasyd Perkins, Pratt's competition in the opium trade, was there. Gardiner Greene paid his respects. And many of the Lowells stood by the grave, since he was father-in-law to one of their own.

Patrick Tracy Jackson, brother-in-law of the late Francis Cabot Lowell and the major stockholder in the Merrimack Manufacturing Company, paid little attention to the final reading. He stood at the edge of the throng and gazed up toward Pratt's house on Pemberton Hill. He had already begun to think about railroads connecting

Boston to his mills in Lowell, and now he was wondering where he could build a depot. The height of Pemberton Hill gave him an idea; he would not act upon it for five years.

The Reverend Mr. Russell concluded his reading. Jason turned the first shovel of dirt onto the coffin. Abigail wiped a single tear from her eye. The service was over. A dusting of snow flurried down, and the mourners hurried for their carriages.

Jason lingered a moment to watch the gravediggers cover his father's body. He felt a son's grief at his father's passing, but he did not deceive himself. He was glad that his father was gone. Jason Pratt now commanded his own destiny. He no longer stood in his father's shadow. Another cold blast cut through him. He needed a warm fire and a glass of port. He turned to leave.

Abigail, in black cape, dress, and bonnet, was standing nearby. "I find it difficult to cry."

"His death has freed us all of a terrible burden."

"Yes. Now we must press ahead with his business."

Jason took Abigail's hand. He felt a burst of affection for his younger sister, who seemed so pale and vulnerable. "It is our business, Abigail, and I will operate it in our interest."

She brought his hand to her lips and kissed it. "We must trust one another, Jason, in memory of our father."

Jason smiled and offered his arm. Abigail placed her hand on his elbow. The snow was falling more heavily now. Together they walked toward Tremont Street.

"How much would you estimate that the company is now worth?" she asked.

"Mr. Curtis recently reached the figure of nine hundred thousand dollars."

"A fortune."

"Yes, but very little of it in hard specie. Most of our money is tied up in the ships, land, and stocks that produce our monthly incomes."

She stopped. "We are richer than that, Jason. You must promise on your father's grave, never to reveal what I am going to tell you, unless I first give you permission."

He sensed her solemnity. He agreed.

"Someplace in the waters around Boston, there is a treasure. It is worth forty or fifty thousand dollars. Father was the only man who knew its nature and location. I am the only woman. One day, it will be worth as much as two Indiamen. Remember that it is always at your disposal." She watched the astonishment spread across her brother's face. She kissed him on the cheek and hurried to her carriage.

That afternoon, Abigail made one short entry in her diary:

The hook is baited. Now the fish must bite. Pray he grows hungry before I grow old.

CHAPTER XII

It was six in the morning when the heat woke Peter Fallon from a fitful sleep. He wanted to roll over, but the air in his room was too thick and there were too many things on his mind. He was wide awake before his eyes were open. He peeled back the damp top sheet, which stuck to his body like a second skin, swung his legs out of bed, and kicked over the two beer cans he'd left on the floor the night before.

Half a warm Narragansett spread across the linoleum and made the place smell like a brewery. Fallon didn't bother to clean it up. After a cool shower, he threw on a pair of tennis shorts, a blue jersey, and a pair of black high-top sneakers. He grabbed a quart of orange juice from the refrigerator and left.

Fallon looked at the digital clock above the Cambridge Trust: Wednesday, June 17, six-fourteen A.M., eighty degrees, and the air thick with moisture. He was sweating already. He gulped down the orange juice and walked toward the gray Volvo parked on Massachusetts Ave. He didn't notice James Buckley sleeping in a black Oldsmobile across the street, and Buckley didn't notice him.

Fallon rolled down all the windows, opened both vents, and sped across the Larz Anderson Bridge. He had to move, if only to stay cool. He couldn't sit and wait for Jack Ferguson to walk down his hallway again, and the Public Library wasn't open, so he couldn't read Ferguson's *Hubcap* articles.

On sleepless mornings, Fallon often roamed the streets of Boston. He would absorb the quiet, the emptiness, the almost religious stillness of Beacon Hill and the Common. Or he would sit alone in the middle of Government Center Plaza, surrounded by mountains of brick, glass, and concrete. And he would think. If he had been thinking too much, he would simply stare.

Then, he would stop at the all-night cafeteria on Summer Street, have a cup of coffee, and watch the last of the night people filter off into the daylight. He liked the night people. They seemed to belong in an empty city, and they always fitted his early-morning moods. They were janitors, cabbies, and cleaning women, drunks, hookers, and hustlers. They were the losers and near-losers, exhausted by night and by life. Some talked. Some sat and stared. A few fell asleep in their coffee cups. But among the night people at dawn, Fallon sensed a feeling of community that he never noticed during the day. Attracted by the simple presence of humanity, the night people came to the cafeteria after a long night. They had survived the dark and made it through to first light. In the long run, Fallon often thought, that was all that could be said for anybody.

After the cafeteria, Fallon usually strolled State Street, Boston's high road of finance since 1630. He had often imagined the generations who struggled there to build New England and a few enduring fortunes. He saw Hancocks, Pratts, Lowells, and Kennedys as they hurried from waterfront to counting house, from bank to brokerage firm, manipulating and maneuvering, investing capital and ingesting competitors. He could see them battling with history, fighting to control its flow, struggling to direct their own thrust through it, and burning brightly with a passion that ultimately consumed them all.

Sometimes, as Fallon reached the end of State Street and looked out toward the sea, he wondered if, for all their power and success, the men who built the empires knew less about life than the night people after all. He was never sure.

This morning, Fallon parked on Tremont Street and wandered into the Old Granary Burying Ground. He didn't know what he was looking for. He had been drawn there, he supposed, by Horace Taylor Pratt, who had been dead for 150 years and could still wake him on a summer morning. He found Pratt's grave under an oak in a distant corner. He knelt in the grass and read the inscription on the weatherbeaten stone.

"Horace Taylor Pratt, 1750–1825; Beloved Husband of Alicia Howell Pratt, 1760–1805; Father of Horace, Jason, and Abigail." Beneath that was a quotation from Milton's *Paradise Lost*: ". . . and one for all/ Myself expose, with lonely steps to tread/ Th'unfounded deep, and through the void immense/ To search with wand'ring quest a place foretold/ Should be, and, by concurring signs, ere now/ Created vast and round, a place of bliss . . ."

Fallon had expected that Pratt might leave something more substantial on the ground above his head, but at least the old man was consistent. He probably considered monuments as useless as ceremonial silver tea sets, and perhaps he knew that the cemetery itself would become a monument to him. The Old Granary Burying Ground was a rare patch of green in the middle of the city, and it overflowed with Pratt's descendants.

Fallon looked around at the various Pratt tombstones. Abigail Pratt Bentley had turned to earth in one of the last plots to be filled. He was attracted to her grave by another quotation from Milton. "The World shall burn, and from her ashes spring/ New Heaven and Earth, wherein the just shall dwell,/ And after all their tribulations long/ See golden days, fruitful of golden deeds,/ With Joy and Love triumphing, and fair Truth."

Fallon wondered briefly what significance Milton held for the Pratts, but he was more interested in the dates and what they told him about Abigail. "Born 1790, Died 1874, Beloved Wife of James Elwood Bentley, 1789–1811." Abigail had been a twenty-four-year-old widow when the tea set was stolen. Fallon recalled, from one of Pratt's letters, that Abigail had returned to his house after the death of her husband. She had lived with Pratt through the crisis of 1814 and the death of his grandson. Perhaps she knew the truth about the boy's death and other events that took place in the Back Bay.

Although Fallon tried to caution himself that she might never have heard a thing, his mind was beginning to race. He had seen Abigail's diaries in the Searidge attic, and Carrington had said he could read them. If he could get into the house and go through them, he might find something about the Golden Eagle. He headed quickly out of the cemetery, but before he reached Tremont Street, his mind was spinning in reverse. The Pratts might not let him get into the house, and the chances were excellent that beyond Dexter Lovell's note, there wasn't another reference to the Golden Eagle in all of Searidge. He leaned against one of the monuments, jammed his hands into his pockets, and kicked at the grass. He needed help.

It was seven-thirty when Fallon pressed the buzzer at Evangeline Carrington's South End townhouse.

The South End had been developed in the 1850s as an attractive area for Boston's middle class, with blocks of airy red-brick rowhouses on elm-planted streets. But the middle class did not stay. By 1885, the buildings had become boardinghouses and six-to-a-room immigrant apartments. By 1910, the South End was a patchwork of tough ethnic neighborhoods, split down the middle by the steel girders of the Boston Elevated Railway Company. Eventually, the immigrants moved to the suburbs, and the South End became an extension of Roxbury's black ghetto. In recent years, gentrification had begun. Young professionals, both black and white, were buying and rehabilitating old bowfronts, while the poor were being forced out. It was an area in transition.

Fallon heard footsteps on the other side of the door. He picked up the *Globe* and the *New York Times* that lay on the step. He heard a click—one lock was released. Then another—the deadbolt. The door snapped open six inches and a pair of bleary eyes peered over the chain lock.

"Who is it?" the voice was heavy with sleep.

"Paperboy," said Fallon as he held out the newspapers.

"What do you want at seven-thirty in the morning?" she asked groggily.

"I have to talk with you."

For a moment, he didn't think that she would let him in, but finally she closed the door and released the chain lock.

It was dark in the hallway, and Fallon's eyes needed a few seconds to adjust after the bright sunlight. Evangeline was wearing a cotton shift which did nothing to conceal her breasts or the patch of dark within the roundness of her hips. When he got used to the light, he realized he was staring. She pulled the shift more tightly around herself and folded her arms over her breasts.

"Do you have something to tell me, or did you just stop by to look at my tits?"

He apologized. "I couldn't sleep this morning. I had to see you."

She walked into the living room, which overlooked a walled-in patio. Fallon stood in the doorway and admired her home. The walls had been stripped to reveal the brick. Oak beams crossed overhead. Hardwood floors glistened. Plants crept, crawled, and hung everywhere. The furnishings were strictly the most expensive: brown sofa, leather swivel chair, chrome lamps sweeping out of the corners of the room on graceful aluminum arcs, a glass coffee table, modern teak cabinets containing television and music equipment, and colored textile prints swirling across the walls. Everything about the room said taste, money, and careful attention.

Angrily, she paced back and forth. "You couldn't sleep, so you decided to wake me up. Last night was the first night since Christopher died that I've had any sleep at all."

"I'm sorry, but right now, you may be the only person who can help me."

"Mr. Fallon, yesterday my brother was buried. I'm in no mood to be helping anyone today."

"I was one of the last people to talk to your brother. I really wish you'd listen to me for a few minutes."

She stopped pacing and put her hands on her hips. "All right, talk."

It was more than Fallon could stand. He was staring again.

She wrapped the shift around herself once more and headed for the stairs. "I'll be right down. Don't steal anything."

"Can I make coffee?" he asked.

"It's in the kitchen.

When she came down, she was wearing a tight, rose-colored jersey and a pair of cut-off jeans. Her hair was pulled straight back and held with a single barrette. Looking fresh, despite her mood, she sat down, and Fallon poured her a cup of coffee.

"You've made yourself right at home," she said.

"It's a beautiful place."

"Don't get too comfortable."

"I never get too comfortable."

"Now, how can I help you?" From the tone of her voice, she wasn't offering her services.

"I'd like you to come for a ride with me." Fallon sat down opposite her. "We'll go up to the North Shore. Drive through Gloucester and Rockport, stop in Newburyport for some fried clams, and go out to Plum Island for a swim."

She almost liked the idea, but she knew he had come for something more. "Then what?"

"We stop at Marblehead and visit your grandmother."

"No." She stood angrily. "You try to make me think that you're here to see me—not that I care particularly—when all you're doing is just smelling around again. Leave my grandmother and my family alone and mind your business."

"You said you'd help me," he said softly. "I haven't come here to use you or to take advantage of you. I rarely ask anyone for help of any kind, and I know you're still upset about your brother. I'm just asking you to hear what I have to say. Then, if you want, you can throw me out." She sat down again, poured cream into her coffee, and stirred. For a long time, she studied the little eddies which spun through the cup in the wake of the spoon. She was hoping that Fallon might disappear. Without looking up, she said, "I suppose the only way to get rid of you is to listen to you, so finish your speech."

"Thank you." He poured himself more coffee and described the Dexter Lovell note. With growing excitement, he told her about the death of an anonymous black and the drowning of Pratt's grandson in the Back Bay. Then, he paused. He realized that although she was listening closely, the events were too distant to have any meaning for her.

"The tea set disappeared for a hundred and sixty years," he continued. "According to one story, it was floating around in England. In 1973, it reappeared in the hands of a young art dealer named Lawrence Hannaford.

She interrupted. "He's a distant cousin of ours."

Fallon stopped. The surprise sank in, and he laughed softly. "It gets more complicated all the time."

"Maybe you're making it complicated."

"Or maybe it's the phantom newsman, a guy named Jack C. Ferguson. He charged that Hannaford's tea set was a fraud. He couldn't say any more, however, without the permission of a woman I'm willing to bet is your grandmother."

With her left hand, Evangeline began to massage the bridge of her nose as though she were getting a headache.

"I'll be done in a minute." Fallon knew he was losing her. "After the newsman wrote the article, he started drinking heavily, and no one's been able to find him since.

"Then, an innocent graduate student visits the ancestral home. I run across Lovell's note, and a moment later, I'm thrown out of the house, with you close behind. When I see your brother, I ask him about the Golden Eagle, and for just a moment, he's off balance. He steadies himself quickly, but I'm left wondering."

She was following the story closely now, but he couldn't tell if he was convincing her of anything.

"I become more interested, and when I return from your brother's funeral, I find that people are breaking into my apartment, going through the bookcases, and leaving muddy footprints on the floor."

"Maybe some student was trying to find the exam question for next semester," she cracked.

Fallon smiled. "It was the newspaperman. I saw him leave my apartment."

She stood, suddenly angry. "I don't buy any of this. It's all coincidence. Are you trying to tell me that my brother died because of all this nonsense?"

"I don't know." He sipped his coffee. "But I believe there's a connection between what happened in 1814 and what's been going on the last few days."

"And you want me to ask you how I can help?"

He told himself she was entitled to her sarcasm. "I'd like you to come with me to Searidge. Help smooth the way so I can talk to your grandmother. Help me get into the attic again."

She leaned against the sink and folded her arms. "Why don't you go back to your library and stop wasting your time?"

He shrugged. "I was hoping all this would intrigue you."

"What intrigues me is getting from one day to the next with as little hassle as possible."

"That doesn't sound too exciting." He laughed.

"Listen, you don't know anything about me, and I don't know anything about you. I didn't ask you to come in here and wake me up and interrupt my life, and I'll be very happy when you leave." She turned and tossed her coffee into the sink.

He realized he shouldn't have come so soon after her brother's death, or so early in the morning. His own insensitivity surprised him. He got up and walked over to her.

She didn't look at him. She concentrated on the blank brick wall outside her kitchen window.

"I'm sorry," he said. "I guess this isn't the kind of distraction you want just now. I won't bother you again." He started to leave.

"Mr. Fallon."

He stopped.

"Are you still going to Searidge?"

"Eventually, but it can wait." He leaned against the doorjamb between dining room and kitchen. "You know, if you're interested in a drive up to Plum Island, the offer still goes, and I promise I won't mention the tea set."

Her expression softened. She hadn't decided yet that she liked him, but she was beginning to find him less abrasive. She smiled. "You didn't wake me up this morning, because I didn't sleep all night. I started to think about my brother, and I got to feeling pretty bleak. I guess I could use some company right now. The beach sounds nice."

He thought he had wasted whatever chance he might have had with her. He was happily surprised. "If we leave now, we can beat the crowds to Plum Island."

She didn't move. Once she had decided to go with him, it didn't seem so difficult to stop at Searidge. "I promised my grandmother I'd visit her sometime today. What exactly are you looking for?"

He told her about Abigail Pratt Bentley's diaries.

"If I help you get those diaries, and there's nothing in them, will you go back to your dissertation and forget about the Golden Eagle?"

He hesitated. If she was offering her help, he would not discourage it, but he didn't want it to seem that he was using her. "Don't do this unless you're certain it won't upset her."

She had made up her mind. "My grandmother seemed to like you, and she might enjoy a little distraction herself. Tell her your little story about Pratt and the tea set, but no mention of Christopher."

"What about your aunt and the butler? Can you convince them to let me in?"

"On Wednesdays, Harrison drives my aunt to market at ten o'clock, and they come back around eleven-thirty. I can keep my grandmother and the maid occupied while you go through the attic."

They drove to Searidge in Evangeline's red Porsche convertible. On the way, they talked about their occupations, the heat, the Red Sox, and the mutual acquaintances they had at Harvard and Radcliffe. Fallon thought they sounded like two undergraduates making small talk at a college mixer.

They arrived early in Marblehead, so they stopped for breakfast at a restaurant a short distance from the house. Over pancakes and coffee, Evangeline talked about her childhood at Searidge. She had lived there for nine years. In 1952, she explained, her father had been killed by a burglar at Searidge. After that, Katherine Carrington had insisted that her daughter-in-law and grandchildren move in with her. When Evangeline's mother had remarried in 1961, the family had moved to Exeter, New Hampshire, but Evangeline still considered Searidge her home.

As they turned up the driveway to the house, the temperature seemed to drop ten degrees. The lawn, the trees, and the house itself blotted up the humidity, leaving the air on the bluffs crisp and dry.

Fallon felt his stomach muscles tighten. Searidge was as impressive the second time.

They pulled up in front of the house and got out of the car.

"We're in luck so far," Evangeline said. "On Wednesday mornings, the Rolls is parked in front of the house between nine-thirty, when Grandmother returns from her piano lesson, and ten o'clock, when Isabelle leaves. The car isn't here. Isabelle must be gone."

"Are you certain?"

"Most Pratts and Carringtons are creatures of immutable habit," she said. "I broke the mold."

They mounted the porch, and Fallon rang the bell. No one answered. He rang again. No answer. Evangeline was concerned. She didn't like the Harrisons, but they were the most efficient couple the family had ever had. Usually, one of them was waiting at the door before a visitor was out of his car.

She tried the door. Locked. She looked around at the windows. The shades weren't drawn, but there seemed to be no life inside.

"Maybe they've all gone somewhere together," said Fallon.

"My grandmother goes to her lesson at eight, returns at nine-thirty, takes tea and toast in the living room or on the back veranda, and reads the *New York Times* until ten-thirty."

"No variations?"

"Not in the last twenty years."

They walked through the tennis court to the back of the house. The ocean was crashing on the rocks below, but Katherine Pratt Carrington was not on the porch to enjoy the view, nor, it seemed, was she in the house.

"No *New York Times* and the shades are pulled tight," said Fallon. "You don't get too many nosy neighbors driving by back here. There's no sense in letting the sun in the house to fade the oriental rugs."

"This is all very strange," said Evangeline, just loudly enough to be heard above the surf.

"Stranger things have happened in the last few weeks. Let's go inside."

"I . . . I don't know. I feel funny breaking into my grandmother's house."

"You're not breaking in. You lived here for twelve years." Fallon was too close to turn away now.

She hesitated. "I think we should be looking for my grandmother."

"Your grandmother may be off on a cruise or something. There's no reason to think she's disappeared."

"My grandmother hates the water unless she's sitting on the veranda three hundred feet above it. She's not on any cruise." Her voice was suddenly harsh.

Fallon approached her and put his hands on her shoulders. "Give me one hour in that attic, then we'll find out where your grandmother has gone."

As they climbed through a window on the first floor, Fallon noticed a timer connected to the lights in the living room. It was set to turn on at seven and off at eleven.

"They probably have these things all over the house," he said.

On the third floor, they moved the Winthrop desk aside, opened the panel, and climbed the narrow stairs into the attic. If the house was absorbing heat, it was storing it up here. The room was stifling.

Fallon took a few steps toward the corner of the attic and stopped. "Shit."

"What's wrong?"

He looked around the attic. Almost everything was as it had been a week before. The saber still hung from one of the eaves, military uniforms were protected in a large garment bag in the corner, and the rest of the attic junk still clogged the room.

"What the hell is wrong?" demanded Evangeline.

Fallon shook his head in disgust. "I don't know where your grandmother was going, but she took along all the good magazines to read on the trip."

"What are you talking about?"

"The box containing Horace Pratt's papers is gone." He pointed to a space in the middle of the room. "And right there was a metal box filled with letters, papers, and records. Under the eaves was another box that contained the A.P.B. diaries." He paused to let it all sink in. "Tell me now that it's all coincidence."

Evangeline said nothing. Fallon sat down on the floor next to her. He folded his hands on his knees, put his head on his hands, and studied the floor between his legs. Then he looked at the dust-free rectangle of floor where the box had sat for decades. As if to satisfy himself that it was gone, he crawled closer. His eyes brightened. A six-inch opening ran all around the attic between the floorboards and the eaves. Fallon scrambled quickly into the little wedge and jammed his hand under the floorboards.

"What are you doing?" asked Evangeline.

"When they built these houses, they sometimes didn't finish off the attics completely," he explained as he fished around. "When someone in the house needed extra storage space, they'd just drop a few long planks across the beams and nail them down. Sometimes the planks wouldn't be long enough to . . ."

He had found a book. He pulled it out from under the floor and read the title excitedly: *"The Memoirs of Fanny Hill, Woman of Pleasure."* His voice trailed off. He threw the book across the room.

Evangeline picked it up, wiped the dust from the cover, and studied the old print. Suddenly, her eyes filled with tears. She turned her head from Fallon and began to cry very softly. Fallon didn't know what had upset her, but he did not intrude.

She didn't cry long.

"I'm sorry," she said. "You see, Christopher was fifteen and I was twelve." Her voice halted. "There weren't many kids our age in the neighborhood, so, on summer afternoons, we used to sneak up here and give dramatic readings." She managed to laugh at the memory.

"I'm sorry," said Fallon gently.

"It's all right. If we found Fanny Hill, maybe Abigail Bentley's under there too."

Fallon reached around again. He found a few old letters, several buttons, a sprung mousetrap, two pornographic magazines, and an old baseball glove. Then his hand hit another book.

"I think we've got something." He stretched his arm as far as he could under the floorboard and tried to grab the book. With two fingers, he was able to snatch a corner of it. As he started to drag it out, he heard a car arrive in front of the house. He looked at Evangeline.

She stepped to the dormer. "It's the Harrisons."

Fallon pulled the book from under the floorboards. "A.P.B., 1845" was embossed in the dust on the cover, and a metal clasp held the book shut.

"Is it a diary?" asked Evangeline.

"It sure is," he said. "Now, what chance do we have to get out of here?"

"There's only one way down, and Harrison's coming up."

Fallon looked around the attic and noticed a trapdoor in the ceiling. "Do you think you can convince them that you've come here alone to pick something up?"

"Wait a minute." Evangeline put up her hands, as if to refuse something she didn't want. "I've come about as far as I intend to with you. I've had all the cloak-and-dagger stuff I need."

"Doesn't it seem strange to you that your grandmother and these diaries disappear at the same time?"

"Coincidence," she snapped.

Fallon could hear Harrison on the first floor. "Okay, coincidence."

He was whispering now, hoarse with tension. "But somebody doesn't want people reading these diaries. The guy coming up the stairs probably works for that somebody. Help me find out what's in here."

Slowly, she lowered her hands.

He saw an old dollhouse in the corner of the room. He lifted the roof and put the diary inside. He picked up the dollhouse.

She stepped back. She could hear Harrison drawing closer. She remembered how much she disliked his polite manner and the threat of physical persuasion that always accompanied it. She took the doll house from Fallon. "After this, take care of yourself."

"Come back when they leave," he whispered, and his eyes thanked her.

He grabbed the folding stairs connected to the ceiling and pulled them down. They hadn't been moved, he guessed, in fifty years. Dust fell everywhere as they creaked into place. He climbed the steps, released the bolt locks, and pushed his shoulder against the trapdoor.

"He's on the second floor. Hurry up!" Evangeline was listening at the attic entrance.

Fallon pushed again, harder. This time, he felt something reluctantly giving way above him. He knew that the trapdoor must have been shingled over and the shingles were starting to come loose. He squared his back to the ceiling, mustered all his strength, and pushed. His face turned red, the veins popped out on the sides of his head. Then the shingles seemed to give up all at once. The door popped open, and sunlight poured into the attic.

A moment later, Fallon was on top of the house, on the widow's walk. He closed the trapdoor and sat down on the broiling shingles.

After replacing the staircase, Evangeline dragged the dollhouse to the attic entrance and began rummaging for other bits of personal junk. Might as well make this look convincing, she thought.

"I expected we might find you up here," said Harrison, as he climbed into the attic. He was holding a .22 revolver casually in his right hand and seemed very relaxed. "But my wife and I made a thorough search of the rest of the house first."

"What are you doing with that gun?"

He smiled and lowered it. "I'm sorry, but you can never tell whom you may find hiding beneath a bed or in a closet. Are you alone?"

She looked around the attic in mock concern. "I don't see anyone else up here."

"May I ask what you're doing up here?"

"I'm collecting some old toys for the children in my neighborhood. May I ask you where my grandmother is?"

"Mrs. Carrington was very upset by your brother's death. Your Aunt Isabelle has removed her to a rest home."

"Rest home? Isn't this rest home enough?"

"I'm afraid she needed psychiatric attention. Your grandmother is not well."

Evangeline was stunned. Her grandmother was a strong, vigorous woman. She would not need psychiatric care, even after the trauma of another Carrington death. "Where is she? I must see her."

"The doctors have proscribed visitors," Harrison said. "And now, let me ask you once more. What are you doing up here?"

"I just told you," she said.

Harrison studied her as though he didn't believe her. "If you'll please follow me down the stairs, you can be on your way."

Evangeline started to walk toward the opening, then stopped. "Would you mind helping me carry these toys down to the car?"

"Very well," said Harrison. He placed his revolver in the holster on his belt and picked up the dollhouse.

Evangeline picked up a few other things she had collected and started to leave, but before she could step past the butler, she heard his wife thundering up the stairs.

"Harrison! Harrison!" Her voice echoed through the whole house.

Harrison stepped in front of Evangeline and blocked the exit.

Mrs. Harrison jumped the steps two at a time, arriving breathless at the attic entrance. "Mrs. McChesney from across the road says she saw a young man come in here with the girl."

The color filled Harrison's face. He dropped the dollhouse. Evangeline jumped back and dropped the other toys.

Harrison snapped the revolver out of his holster. "That student."

"I don't know what you're talking about," answered Evangeline.

He raised the .22 again and pressed it against the nipple of her left breast, which showed stiff and scared through the material of her jersey. "Where is he?"

Evangeline was trembling, but her voice was strong. "I think Mrs. McChesney's been in the wine cellar again."

Harrison looked around the attic, but Fallon wasn't there.

"He isn't up my sleeve, either," she cracked.

On the roof, Fallon must have moved, or maybe the adrenalin was pumping through him too fast. A loose bit of dust was jarred from the folding stairs and trickled past Harrison's face. Harrison smiled briefly at Evangeline, then reached for the staircase.

When the door began to open, Fallon stepped back. First, he saw the revolver. Then Harrison's face, which had become an expressionless mask, emerged from the darkness. Harrison stopped halfway out of the attic, his belt buckle level with the rooftop.

He pointed the pistol at Fallon. "Please step down."

Fallon didn't move.

"If you want to dehydrate, stay right where you are." Harrison glanced at the sun. "In this heat, you should be fried by two o'clock." Harrison started to close the trapdoor.

Fallon stepped toward him. He didn't think he could handle Harrison in a fight, and he didn't want to find out. He tried not to sound nervous. "Put the gun away, and I'll step down."

Harrison opened the trap again. "That's better."

"But I want your assurance that we'll be allowed to leave immediately."

"I'm afraid not. My employers will want to talk with you." He paused. "Which makes the roof the best place to keep you until they arrive." He started to close the door again.

An hour on those shingles would mean sunstroke at the very least. Fallon wasn't staying. Before he had time to think about it, he was kicking the gun out of Harrison's hands and trying to fight his way down the stairs. But Harrison was too strong. He grabbed Fallon by the legs and flipped him onto his back. Fallon hit the roof like a brick, kicked loose and rolled to his feet. In one motion, Harrison launched himself out of the attic and flew at Fallon.

Fallon kicked hard. He caught Harrison right in the groin. Harrison bellowed and started to fold, but as Fallon leaped for the hole, a huge hand grabbed him by the collar and spun him around. Another hand fastened at Fallon's throat and started to tighten.

Fallon's kick had enraged Harrison. To forget his pain, Harrison poured all his strength into his hands.

Fallon couldn't breathe. He could feel his nostrils dilating, but no air was reaching his lungs. He began to gasp. He heard a rattling noise. It sounded like somebody else, but it was him. He was strangling. He struggled violently to pull Harrison's hands from his throat. He kicked at Harrison's groin and shins. He could feel his eyes bulging out of their sockets and his ears popping under pressure, as they would in a fast-moving elevator. Harrison could feel nothing but cartilage collapsing in his hands.

Fallon's excellent conditioning was keeping him alive, but he couldn't pry Harrison loose. He was beginning to see a large, black spot that seemed to be floating somewhere between his eyes. He was passing out. He straightened his right hand into a hard, flat plane. He jabbed viciously, hitting Harrison a perfect shot in the solar plexus. Harrison's body snapped like a knee joint, and he fired Fallon across the roof.

Fallon hit the railing on the other side of the widow's walk and nearly toppled over it. For an instant, he could see the ocean crashing against the rocks two hundred feet below. As he caught himself, he felt the wood giving way in his hands. It was rotten.

Harrison lunged again. This time, Fallon sidestepped him, stuck a foot between the butler's legs, and with a final burst of strength, swung his left elbow into Harrison's kidney. Harrison caught himself on the railing and tried to pivot back, but the railing disintegrated. He somersaulted twice down the gentle roof. His third tumble spun him to the edge. His heels caught the gutter and his fingernails dug into the shingles. He was stranded.

Fallon took two deep breaths and jumped into the attic. Evangeline was trying to get down the stairs, but Mrs. Harrison had her by the hair. Fallon grabbed the maid, broke her grip, and toppled her into a pile of boxes.

"I've got the diary," said Evangeline. "Let's go."

Ten minutes later, Evangeline and Fallon were speeding down a lonely stretch of road heading for Route 1. Both of them were bruised, and Evangeline was trembling. The adrenalin had worn off.

Fallon looked behind him. "I guess they're not going to follow us."

Evangeline shuddered involuntarily and gripped the wheel to steady herself.

"Are you all right?" asked Fallon.

"Just a bump on the head."

"I don't mean that. I mean right now. You look . . ."

"Why did you fight with him?" she demanded.

"I didn't want to end the day looking like a piece of bacon cooking on the roof. If I'm going to talk with Harrison's employers, I'm going to do it on my own terms."

"My aunt is Harrison's employer." She was beginning to think clearly again. "My grandmother never liked him."

"From the way he talked, Isabelle isn't the only one he works for."

"Isabelle is very close to Philip Pratt," she offered.

"Do you want to talk to him?" Fallon was hoping she would.

"I don't know." For a mile or so, she drove in silence and concentrated on the road. "Grandmothers and family papers disappearing, butlers running around Searidge with drawn guns. Maybe I should be talking to the police."

Fallon shook his head. He wanted no interference, least of all from the police. He was trying to trace a delicate web of events covering two centuries. The police would only make his work more complicated. Beyond that, if the real tea set was still missing, he wanted to find it.

"As you said yourself, this is all still coincidence. We have no reason to be going to the police." He thumped his fingers on the diary. "We nearly got ourselves killed to find this thing. Let's read it, then talk to your uncle."

She looked at Fallon. For a moment, she hated him for dragging her into this. Then she realized that he was probably doing her a favor. At the main highway, she headed north, instead of turning south toward Boston.

"You're going the wrong way," he said.

She didn't answer. She accelerated to sixty and started for New Hampshire.

CHAPTER XIII   *November 1830*

Abigail Pratt Bentley was now forty years old. For five years she had lived alone in the house on Pemberton Hill, attended by her footman poet and his Irish mother. In the eyes of friends and relatives, she was no longer the young widow of James Elwood Bentley, but a middle-aged dowager who would spin out her life sponsoring readings and recitals for struggling artists like Sean.

Let them think what they wished. She had maintained her youth better than any of them. Beside Sarah Lowell Pratt, Abigail still looked like a young woman. She still had her beautiful lover, her dreams of controlling Pratt Shipping and Mercantile, and her secret treasure. She needed little else.

She stood naked in front of the mirror in the master bedroom, now decorated in feminine pastels. She wondered what the Reverend Mr. Russell would say if he saw her admiring her body so blatantly. She didn't care. She had seen him admiring it. Most men admired it, but she allowed only one to have it.

The lines around her eyes and mouth had deepened, and the flesh beneath her chin sagged slightly, but she gave no other indication of her age. Her skin was pale and smooth, like ivory. Her hands were soft, with perfect nails and long, delicate fingers. She traced the outline of her breasts. She lingered a moment at her nipples and felt the flesh respond. She continued in a graceful, luxuriant arc across her belly, down to her thighs, and up across her buttocks. She did not avoid the few rolls of fat she found gathering at her waist. She would not deceive herself. To remain young, one admitted the passage of time and accepted the inevitability of age.

A second time, she followed the contours of her body and rested her hands on her abdomen, just above her pubic mound. A year earlier, her periodic flow had grown irregular. It had stopped completely eight months later. She knew now that her womb would never expand with life, and the thought depressed her. She dreamed often of bearing young, but after the death of James Bentley, she had never met a man she considered worthy to father her children. Once or twice she had thought she was pregnant by Sean. At first, she was repulsed by the prospect of carrying an Irish child, in spite of her willingness to lie with an Irish man. But she thrilled to the idea of a child in her image. Each time she thought she was pregnant, she convinced herself that the child would be hers alone, that it would bear her traits and the stamp of her upbringing, that the father needed only to be physically fit and intelligent, and society be damned. But her belly never swelled, and she wondered often if she was infertile. She would never find out.

No matter, she thought. Her body would never show the marks of childbirth, and she would be the mother of something much greater than a single baby.

Abigail heard his step. She wrapped herself in a silk robe and sat by the east windows. He knocked three times, then once.

"Come in, Sean."

Five years had added to his beauty and bulk but not to his poetical abilities. Abigail had helped him to publish three volumes of verse, none of which sold more than fifty copies. He had been trying to publish a fourth, but Abigail's influence with booksellers no longer helped him.

"The only people who would want to read your poetry," one publisher told him, "are the Irish, and most Irish can't read."

Still Abigail listened willingly to his memories of Ireland and his visions of heroism. She offered criticism and encouragement and told him to keep writing. Sean's mother never questioned Abigail's interest in the boy; she was thankful for Abigail's kindness.

Abigail and Sean no longer made love after each reading. He had begun to practice on other women the skills he had learned between her legs. She did not give him her love, but she was jealous to keep him to herself. When she sensed that he was seeing some Irish girl from the parish, she would speak to him politely but brusquely, as an employer to a servant. When his expression told her that his new love was gone, she would leave him to suffer a day or two, then invite him into her bed.

Today, she wanted him. She didn't care if he had just come from a Canal Street whore.

"How are you today, Sean?"

"Well, ma'am." He was carrying no poetry with him. He seemed nervous.

Abigail stood and approached him. "I've been waiting for you, dear." She slipped her arms around his waist and clasped her hands behind him.

He stepped back, as though he did not want her to touch him.

"What's wrong, Sean?" She thought he was ill.

"Will you marry me, Abigail?" He called her Abigail when they spoke intimately. The rest of the time, she was Mrs. Bentley.

Abigail smiled maternally. "We've discussed this before, Sean. A lady does not marry her Irish servant. It is simply not done. Besides, dear, we are not in love."

"But I love you," he protested.

"That isn't enough, Sean, and if you loved me, you wouldn't spread yourself around like some Irish alley tomcat."

"Then you're going to lose me, Mrs. Bentley," He buttoned his topcoat as a gesture of finality, a symbol of his leaving. "I can't stay in this house."

"May I ask if you've found another young lass to be tickling your fancy?" Abigail was not upset. They'd had this discussion many times.

"No. I've got to leave this house and make somethin' of myself."

"You've already made something of yourself, Sean. You're a fine poet."

He laughed bitterly. "I thought that once, but that was you lyin' to me."

His words cut into her. She hadn't thought he could hurt her. She put her hands on his shoulders and held him at arm's length. "I

215

have never lied to you, Sean. I have always encouraged you and tried to be good to you."

"You've been good to me as long as I gave you what you wanted, and you wanted me to come to you like a nineteen-year-old boy. Well, I'm twenty-four now. I'm a man. I can't be drivin' a lady's coach and readin' poetry to her all my life."

As he spoke, she began to realize that, this time, he was serious. She had always been able to turn his ambitions aside, but she knew that she had no right to keep him in her service any longer. She was using him. She had to let him go. She brought her hands gently to his face.

He stepped back again. He was struggling to maintain his resolve.

"Please, dear." She touched his face. She wanted to remember each feature. "You're so beautiful, Sean. You have given me so much. If this is what you want, I won't try to stop you."

He took her hand. "I wouldn't stay, even if you married me. I must quit this house altogether. As long as you're in my life, I'll be a slave to you."

"You talk like a poet, Sean."

Impulsively, he brought her hand to his lips and kissed it. Then he turned it over and kissed the palm. She caressed his cheek, and they embraced. She wanted to pull away. If he was leaving her, it was best that he go quickly. She had long feared this day, and she had tried to prepare herself for it, but she knew that she could not let him go completely. She had to take some part in his life.

She stepped back and looked him over as though she were inspecting a ship before a voyage. "Where will you go, Sean?"

"I don't know. I suppose I'll be strikin' out on my own."

"What would you say to shipping from Boston under the Pratt House flag?"

He hesitated. It took a moment for the question to sink in.

"I'll speak to my brother about putting you on the *Alicia Howell*," continued Abigail, warming quickly to the idea. "She's bound for Canton in two weeks. Can you wait that long?"

"Yes. Yes!" he said excitedly.

"A trip at sea would be marvelous. Best thing in the world for a young man." She was beginning to feel like a kindly aunt.

"Indeed, ma'am. I'll do anything they ask me."

"And I shall see to it that they ask you to do everything there is." She walked to her settee. "Learn everything there is."

"Yes, ma'am."

"How to fix a bilge pump. How to take a sighting from the north

216

star. How to flatter a hong merchant and get the best price for Pratt opium."

"I'll learn it all. I promise." The excitement was jumping in his throat.

She lowered her voice. "And Sean."

"Ma'am?"

She sat. "I wouldn't do this for anyone else."

He walked over to the settee and knelt down beside her. "I'll be forever in your debt, Mrs. Bentley."

"I know." A smile spread across her face. "You have two weeks to start paying me back."

The next morning, a note from Jason Pratt awaited James Curtis when he arrived for work. "James, I'm off to inspect new mills in Lowell. My sister has made another request, but she has finally asked for something that it is within my power to grant. Her young servant Sean, the brooding Irish poet, has decided to stop brooding and do something worthwhile with his life. Abigail has great affection for the boy, and she has asked that we find him a position. She says he has a mind for numbers and is very bright. I suggest that we make him assistant to the supercargo on the *Alicia Howell* and let him learn a little about the trade. Anson Dabney will be going out on *Alicia*, and he's a most patient sort. He can keep the boy busy during the voyage and introduce him to our people in Canton. Perhaps the horse thief that is said to lurk in the soul of every Irishman will find a comfortable niche with Pratt Shipping and Mercantile, and we can use his heredity to our advantage."

Curtis tossed the letter aside. He knew Anson Dabney to be a cranky, crustaceous old sot. He had been trying to convince Pratt to fire Dabney for years, and now Pratt wanted to give him an assistant. The China run needed no supercargoes. Pratt Shipping and Mercantile maintained its own agency in Canton, and the agency performed the duties of the supercargo. But Anson Dabney had spent forty years in the service of the Pratts, and Jason couldn't fire him.

Curtis sometimes wondered how the company continued to make money under Jason Pratt. Income had reached a peak by 1825 and leveled off. It had taken a year at sea before Jason's six new Indiamen had become profitable, and their income had never fulfilled Pratt's expectations. After he had built the ships, Jason had stopped making decisions and let the company run itself. Or so it seemed to James Curtis.

217

If Pratt didn't have men like himself, thought Curtis, Pratt Shipping and Mercantile would be slipping slowly into Boston Harbor. Jason Pratt's father had built an efficient organization in Boston, London, New York, and Canton. He had found men like Curtis to support his operation and assure its smooth functioning. Such men freed Horace Pratt from the daily problems of directing his company and allowed him to devote his time to speculations. Such men were the backbone, and the president was the brain. Under Jason Pratt, the brain had functioned sporadically, and James Curtis had been forced to do most of the thinking. He had enjoyed the power he wielded and the rewards it brought him, but he had always resented serving a lesser man.

He would see to it that the Mannion boy was given a position on the *Alicia Howell*. Curtis did not consider it in his interest to antagonize Abigail Pratt Bentley. She was suspicious, distrustful, and nuisance enough as it was.

He called for his morning cup of tea and the company books. Keeping everything balanced was a complicated task.

The packet *Sea Gull* arrived from New York on the afternoon tide. The cabin boy had the job of delivering important dispatches straight off the ship. Before the *Sea Gull* tied up, he was galloping through the crowd on Long Wharf with a dispatch in his hand. He hoped he was carrying good news; it always meant a big tip.

"Dispatch for Mr. Jason Pratt," he announced. He was ushered into James Curtis's office, through which one passed to see Pratt. He presented the envelope to Curtis and waited.

Curtis broke the seal and read the signature. The dispatch came from Roger Hamilton, second mate on the *Ephraim Pratt*, an East Indiaman.

> Sir, It is my unhappy duty to inform you that the *Ephraim Pratt* sank in heavy seas off the coast of Brazil (10° 4' South, 36° 8' West) on September 1, 1830. We carried a crew of eighteen, including captain and mates. All save four perished. Captain Lasher and First Mate Magee went valiantly down with their ship. I could not save her books, but your agents in Canton will supply you with a strict accounting of the cargo. We carried silk, teas, spices, and a special shipment of jade sculpture valued in excess of $20,000. I will arrive in Boston soon after this letter to provide you with a complete report of the tragedy. Your Most Humble and Obedient Servant.

James Curtis read the letter twice. He couldn't believe it. For fifty years, Pratt captains had maintained a record of safety and good seamanship that was unsurpassed. Curtis had never expected this news.

The cabin boy cleared his throat.

"What do you want?" snapped Curtis.

"Nothing, sir."

"Then be off with you."

Bad luck to be delivering bad news. "Thank you, and good afternoon, sir."

Curtis did not notice the sarcasm. He was already planning his departure. He would leave loose ends, a month's salary, and a houseful of furniture behind, but his deposits in the Boston Five Cents Savings Bank would carry him and his wife a long way. Perhaps back to Scotland and his mother's family, perhaps to Florence or Rome. He placed the dispatch on Pratt's desk, then cleaned out his own. He looked around the office a last time and left with Pratt Shipping and Mercantile in turmoil.

That evening, Abigail reclined in front of the fireplace in her sitting room, a glass of sherry at her side and her diary in her lap. She sipped the sherry, holding it for a moment on her tongue to relish its sweetness. Her senses tingled after a day with Sean, and she was glad for these last two weeks. She would savor him every day until he left. Then she would turn her attention to the more serious matters which had today presented themselves.

She dipped her quill and wrote.

Thursday, November 17, 1830

An unseasonably cold evening. I fear another long winter, and this year, I will not have Sean to keep me warm. However, there will be no time to think about loneliness, because my opportunity has arrived.

James Curtis, my brother's closest friend and associate, has betrayed him and the company. The terrible news we heard this morning was compounded by the discovery that the *Ephraim Pratt* was not insured. Neither is any Pratt ship afloat, or the cargo on any Pratt ship currently between ports.

As the company treasurer, the most trusted man on my brother's staff, James Curtis has been embezzling funds and hiding his perfidy for the last six years. He has altered profit statements in order to clear profit of his own. He has withheld bill payments authorized by my brother, earning pennies from the interest while damaging our credit standing. And he decided that the flawless record of Pratt captains was reason enough for him to pocket insurance premiums for himself. Over the last several years, he has made a tidy sum, collecting the four percent per passage premium. It astounds me that no one with the Boston Maritime Insurance Company ever asked my brother why he had stopped insuring ships. Of course, Curtis would have mustered a defense, and my brother would have believed him.

Now, James Curtis has absconded, and I doubt that we will ever find him. If we did find him, there is little chance that he could pay us what we have lost—twenty-five thousand dollars for the *Ephraim Pratt,* a cargo that would have been worth twenty thousand, had it ever reached Boston, and twenty thousand more for the jade sculptures, to which no true value can be attached.

I always considered James Curtis a despicable man. My feelings were not unfounded. It is ironic, however, that his actions have created the situation for which I have been waiting.

We certainly have the capacity to absorb our loss. We own eleven other ships and have extensive holdings in the Merrimack Mills. But if I know my brother, he will not take this loss with equanimity. He may decide that he needs the treasure, and I will not discourage him in that belief.

My actions in the coming weeks and months will determine the future of Pratt Shipping and Mercantile. I must not falter or fail.

She closed the book. As she reached for the whale-oil lamp, she had another thought. She opened the diary again.

A final observation on the fate of the *Ephraim Pratt:* I pity Captain Lasher, who was making his first voyage on the *Ephraim.* Would that his predecessor had been aboard instead!

A week later, Jason and Artemus Pratt awaited a visit from Patrick Tracy Jackson in Jason's office on Long Wharf. Jason sat behind his desk, sipped port, and tore the front page of the daily paper into small strips. Artemus stood at the window, his hands clamped behind his back, his eyes fixed on the *Gay Head II,* a Pratt schooner entering the harbor.

Jason was now forty-six. His one passion was eating, and the effort required to haul his corpulence about left him little strength for anything but more eating. He did not enjoy the responsibilities he had been born to, and he often wished that his brother Horace had lived to save him from the weight now resting on his shoulders. After his early insights, when he tried to convince his father to invest in textiles, he had become conservative, reactionary. The company made money because the China trade was flourishing. But the company had not grown since Jason had built the six Indiamen in 1826.

"I don't know why Jackson should be coming here to visit me," said Jason. "Ordinarily, when we have business to discuss, we meet at the Exchange, or I go to his office."

"He must want something," answered Artemus. "And you would do well not to look quite so nervous when he arrives."

Jason stopped shredding paper and finished his port. "You must choose your friends carefully, son. It's a terrible thing to be wrong about a man."

"I would never give a man the opportunity you gave Curtis." Artemus Pratt was twenty-two years old, with the patrician demeanor of his Lowell mother and the aggressive intellect of his Pratt grandfather. He stood six feet three inches tall, and he knew already that his great height could intimidate other men.

After distinguishing himself at Harvard in the classics and mathematics, Artemus had taken two years off to travel around the world, shipping from port to port on Pratt vessels. He had stayed seven months in Canton and familiarized himself with his family's Chinese operation. He had visited India and the African Coast. He had spent two months in Rome, another in Florence, and two in Paris. He had concluded his trip in England, where he had stayed at the home of Henry Hannaford II, the son of Horace Pratt's most trusted British associate.

In England, he had met George Stephenson and witnessed a race among Stephenson's new locomotive, the *Rocket*, and those of two other British engineers. Stephenson's engine won the prize of two hundred pounds sterling and the admiration of young Pratt.

Artemus was beginning to realize, as Abigail had five years before, that the future of America would travel on steel wheels. Just before returning to Boston, he rode on the Liverpool-Manchester line, pulled by a Stephenson locomotive. He traveled thirty-one miles in the amazing time of ninety minutes, and he came home determined to convince his father that railroads were a sound investment.

Patrick Tracy Jackson had come today for the same purpose. He exchanged greetings with the Pratts, took a glass of port, and folded himself into Jason's chair by the fireplace. He was almost as tall as Artemus, and wore a constant smile that never brightened the rest of his face. "My regrets, gentlemen, on the loss of the *Ephraim Pratt*."

"A good ship, with a fine captain and a crew composed completely of volunteers," said Jason. "To compound the tragedy, I discover that my closest friend and adviser has betrayed me."

"A great pity," said Jackson.

"You are very kind to make a special visit down to the wharf to bring your condolences." In his dealings with his peers, Jason was never certain where friendliness ended and obsequy began.

Jackson smiled. "We have been associates for almost fifteen years, Jason. It is only natural that I should be here." He leaned forward and lowered his voice, assuming a most confidential tone. "Tell me, what is your financial condition as a result of the loss of your ship?"

Don't tell him, thought Artemus. Don't reveal a weakness.

"Losing the *Ephraim* has cost us a great deal, Patrick. Not only in cargo, but also in confidence. I expect that merchants will be much less inclined to ship with us, now that word about Mr. Curtis is about."

"Indeed," he said solemnly. "I've heard that sentiment expressed on the waterfront and at the Exchange. In light of your losses, I assume you have very little in the way of investment money."

Jason nodded.

"A pity," said Jackson. "Because I've come today to convince you to invest in the Boston and Lowell."

Artemus resisted the impulse to leap into the discussion. At business meetings, a son listened in the presence of his father. He did not undermine his father's authority by speaking out of turn or, in the presence of others, speaking against his father.

"I've seen the latest report of your committee on the Boston and Lowell," said Jason. "A six percent profit someplace down the line is not what we're used to in the China trade. I'd rather gamble my money on ships. We make upwards of fifteen percent clear profit on every ship that returns from China."

"I can't argue with that, Jason, except to remind you that your ships are no longer returning regularly. Look around you. You'll see that all your competitors in the China trade have diversified. Colonel Perkins is interested in the Boston and Lowell. So are the Appletons. Fifteen years ago, you wanted to invest in textiles, but your father preferred to concentrate on ships." Jackson glanced toward Artemus. "Now, from the way he's sitting over there about to burst, your own son wants you to leap into railroads, but his father is content with ships and textiles."

Artemus tried to wipe any expression from his face. If Jackson could show nothing, Artemus would show less.

"You've made a thousand shares available to the public at five hundred dollars a share, but the public doesn't seem interested." Jason's command of the figures surprised his son.

"Because the public has no vision, Jason, and the public has no interest in the Merrimack Mills. Do you think Merrimack stock-holders would have invested if they had expected their only profit from return dividends? Of course not. The train runs to the mill. That is why we must control the line and set the rates. Your interest in Merrimack Manufacturing is as great as any. You must invest."

Make a decision, thought Artemus. Don't waver. Don't give excuses. Accept or reject, but be decisive.

Jason studied his blotter and drummed his fingers on the table. "I'll admit there are advantages."

Jackson rose. "At the moment, members of the Merrimack Manufacturing Company hold five hundred and eight shares. I personally have subscribed for a hundred twenty-four. A hundred more and we will maintain comfortable control of the line."

"You're asking me to put up fifty thousand dollars. In light of my recent losses, that is impossible."

"You know that the subscriptions may never be called in, Jason. You're simply pledging five hundred dollars a share, should con-struction of the line require it."

Jason rested his head on his chin.

"Your sister has invested," goaded Jackson. "Ten shares at the public offering. Five thousand dollars from her own funds. A great deal of money for a widow."

Artemus' respect for his aunt grew tenfold.

Jackson poured himself another port, filled Jason's glass, and sat on the edge of Jason's desk. Unlike many of his peers, Jackson had a likable streak that he often used to his advantage. "I've come today, Jason, because I need your help. Your fellow stockholders need it. We must be sure that the right people are investing money in the enterprises that are building Boston and New England. Why do you think my brother-in-law originally offered you the chance to invest in the Waltham Mills?"

"Because my wife was his cousin," said Jason cynically.

"Untrue." Jackson spoke softly, sincerely. "That's what he may have told you, because Francis Cabot Lowell detested flattery. He told me that he wanted the Pratts involved because the Pratts, like the Lowells, Jacksons, Appletons, and Perkinses, are responsible, worthy men."

Jason grunted cynically. "I recall Francis Cabot Lowell telling me that my father had one saving grace—his missing arm. There was less of him to loathe. I assume we speak of the same Lowell and the same Pratt."

Jackson laughed. "My brother-in-law had many opinions, but he always spoke highly of you. And he believed, as I do, that we are a special group. We are, if you will, a merchant artistocracy, related by blood"—he glanced at Artemus, whose mother was a Lowell—"marriage, religion, and pursuit. We are men of a kind, like-minded, godfearing, aggressive, honest. We must always work together. Otherwise, the heathens of the business world will overrun us all."

Jason was flattered in spite of himself. Rarely was he counted among the worthies. "Give me a few days to think it over. With the loss of the *Ephraim*, I'll have to do some juggling to free a bit of investment capital."

Jackson put a hand on Jason's arm. "You know that your word is enough."

"My father always backed up his word in specie."

"As you will." Jackson shook hands with both Pratts, exchanged a few words with Artemus about his world tour, and headed for the door. Then he stopped.

Artemus sensed the theatricality.

"There is one way that you can subscribe for a hundred shares at half price, or, if you are still timid, fifty shares for nothing."

Artemus smiled to himself. He realized that Jackson was after more than Pratt support. He saw his father perk up.

"Your family owns nearly an acre of land on Pemberton Hill," said Jackson. "Give it to the Boston and Lowell Railroad, and I personally will be good for half your subscription."

"You would pay twenty-five thousand dollars for my father's house?" Jason was quite surprised.

"We need the land. Mt. Vernon Hill was cut down to fill the edge of the Back Bay. Beacon Hill has been trimmed by eighty feet in the last forty years. Pemberton is the only hill left. This city is growing. We need to make better use of that land."

"What do you propose to do?" asked Artemus.

"Cut off the top of Pemberton Hill and dump it into the water on the north side of Causeway Street. We'll make new land for the Boston and Lowell depot, and we can develop a whole new residential area on the remnants of the hill."

"Gardiner Greene owns a great deal more property than we on the hill," said Jason. "And his includes the top of the hill. What is his reaction?"

"He refuses to sell. But if we begin to excavate on your land, he'll have to give in." Jackson did not wait for a reply. "Think hard, Jason. It's impossible to build homes on a hillside, and you'll never sell that land to anyone else for twenty-five thousand dollars." Jackson donned his beaver hat and left.

Artemus stood in front of his father's desk and leaned forward on the palms of his hands. "You must join this venture. I cannot believe that you've ignored it until now. The Boston and Lowell may be just the beginning."

"Gardiner Greene loves that home, and his garden is one of the most beautiful things I have ever seen."

"Progress can't wait for an old man's fruit trees. If the loss of the *Ephraim Pratt* has cost us so much that we cannot make a subscription, then we must give up the land."

Jason didn't need much convincing. "There's one problem: Abigail. Your grandfather left the house to her."

"Aunt Abigail is a very sensible, hardheaded woman. I'm certain that when the facts are explained to her, she will gladly sign over the house."

Abigail steadfastly refused. Jason went alone to Pemberton Hill, he explained Jackson's proposal, and she refused. Then, for two days, she waited. She knew that her brother would come to her again.

On Saturday morning, she climbed into her carriage for her weekly trip around the Back Bay. It was to be the last time that Sean would drive her. As the carriage turned onto Tremont Street, Abigail heard Jason's voice. The carriage stopped and Jason's face appeared in the window.

"Abigail, we must talk." He looked as though he hadn't slept in several nights.

"Very well."

Jason climbed into the carriage. Artemus followed.

"Good morning, Abigail." Artemus kissed his aunt on the cheek and embraced her lightly.

Abigail loved Artemus. She saw her father in his black eyes and tireless intellect. "How are you, dear?"

"He's not well," said Jason. "And neither am I."

Abigail rapped her walking stick on the roof the carriage, and they began to roll down Tremont toward the Neck. "I suppose you still want me to give up my house," said Abigail.

"You are the one who wanted to invest in railroads," said Jason.

"And I have. Without you."

"We should have listened to you, Abigail."

"But you didn't. You listened to James Curtis instead."

"And our ships have shown a profit for the last five years," defended Jason.

"They will show no profit this year, thanks to Mr. Curtis."

"Abigail, you must reconsider," pleaded Jason. "P. T. Jackson is a very influential man. I would prefer not to disappoint him in this matter."

Abigail laughed, a single, derisive burst.

"I don't think that should be your attitude, Father," said Artemus softly.

"That has always been his attitude," responded Abigail. "Your father has never considered himself the equal of those men, and if a man does not think highly of himself, who else will?"

"Dammit, Abigail, this is not the time to be running me down in front of my son. We need to make this investment."

"Then I suggest you sell one of your ships or your stock in the Merrimack Manufacturing Company." She gave the advice because she knew he would reject it. She would never support the sale of their mill holdings.

"I will not sell stock that is making money."

"Then you will not invest in railroads, because I have no intention of giving you my house." Abigail stared out at the tide pools and channels reflecting silver in the morning sun. Jason glared at her.

For a long time, they traveled in silence. The coach rolled down Lenox Street, then turned north and clattered past the mills and foundries on Gravelly Point. Abigail did not intend to speak until her brother spoke. She could see him grappling with his own inadequacy. She knew that he was trying to find the courage to break an oath. She sensed his discomfort; she magnified it by saying nothing.

Finally, Artemus spoke. "Aunt Abigail, the house is quite large. Do you really believe you need all that space?"

"It is the ancestral home, Artemus. I'll not see it destroyed so that the Boston and Lowell Railroad can have a depot. I have greater respect for my heritage than that." She spoke evenly, firmly, and looked out the window again.

Artemus couldn't help but admire his aunt. She seemed soft and delicate, but beneath the damask, she was flint and steel.

The carriage reached the Mill Dam and stopped. This was the halfway point in the trip, and Abigail usually climbed out here to survey the city. A mile to the east, Beacon Hill and Boston rose out of the receiving basin. Off to the west rolled the hills of Brookline, brown and leafless in the November light. On the north side of the dam, the Charles River flowed out to Boston Harbor. On the south side, the waters of the Back Bay spread like a film across the flats. Abigail was making her weekly pilgrimage to the treasure, which sat out there beneath the shallow water, a half mile from any solid land.

Abigail looked at the two men sitting opposite her in the cramped carriage. "I'm here for my Saturday stroll. Would either of you care to join me?"

"Abigail," blurted Jason, "I have decided to break a promise to you that I made on our father's grave."

She smiled. "I expected as much."

He looked at his son. "On the day we buried my father, Abigail told me of a treasure somewhere in the waters around Boston. She told me she was the only person who knew its nature and location, and she said it was always there if ever we needed it." He looked at Abigail. "We need it now. Since you are so adamant about giving up the house and so convinced of the rightness of railroad investments, you must be willing to give up something for the good of the company."

Abigail laughed again. "Sell your ships, Jason. Act like a businessman. Learn that life provides no easy escapes from crisis."

Jason's anger flared. "Do you want me to reveal your secret?"

"You've already revealed it to Artemus."

"It's the Revere tea set," he said triumphantly, "and it's someplace out there." He gestured toward the Back Bay.

Abigail was not surprised. He had enough of the facts, and he had spent five years putting them together.

"I know it's the tea set, because the government investigated Father after its disappearance. I know it is in the Back Bay, because that's where young Horace drowned. There is no longer any secret and no need to keep the treasure hidden." Jason sat back and tried to look smug.

Abigail smiled. "If you think it's the tea set and it's in the Back Bay, you have my permission to look for it."

"Is it the tea set?"

Abigail stared out the window and said nothing.

"Well, whatever it is, it's in the Back Bay, and I'll find it." He tried to speak firmly.

"You have several hundred acres in which to look, dear brother, and you don't even know what you're looking for," responded Abigail.

"I'll drag the bottom of the bay. I'll cover every square inch, if I must. But I will find it. It's a family legacy. It's part of my birthright." Jason spat as he spoke.

"Apparently, our father disagreed with you, Jason. I am the only person who knows what it is and where it is. I shall determine when, if ever, it is to be retrieved. Moreover, dragging the bottom of the Back Bay will be an expensive proposition, and you will certainly attract unwanted attention. Someone may get the right idea and start dragging along with you." She was cool, imperious.

"I can handle anyone I have to deal with," said Jason, beginning to bluster.

"And when they ask one of Boston's leading businessmen what he is looking for out there in a rowboat, what will you say?"

"Nothing. Let them mind their own business."

Abigail laughed derisively again. The breeze changed, and the stink of a mudflat low tide filled the carriage. She held a perfumed silk handkerchief to her nostrils and rapped again on the roof of the carriage. "Take us back to Long Wharf, Sean."

"You can't turn me away so easily," Jason sounded like an angry child.

"However, I can turn away *from* you." Abigail shifted her eyes onto the Back Bay.

Soon, Abigail, Jason, and Artemus were rocking gently down the Mill Dam toward the city. Abigail had said all that she had intended to say, and she stared out the window, as if to discourage further conversation.

Artemus realized that Abigail had beaten his father, who sat with his fists clenched on his knees and his eyes fixed in hatred on his sister. Artemus knew that his father was a failure, an inconsequential man too weak to battle in the holy wars of New England business, too weak to control his own sister.

As he listened to the rhythmic clap of the horses' hooves on the cobblestones, Artemus Pratt resolved never to be weak. Like his grandfather, he would be relentless and unbending. He would brook no opposition from politicians, competitors, or recalcitrant relatives. He would never lose control of himself. And he would learn from Abigail to communicate as clearly through silence as though well-chosen words. He would force an issue when he could and avoid it when he couldn't. He would put his faith in business, in the manipulation of goods, capital, people, and events. Treasure hunting he would leave to men like his father.

The fire burned brightly in Jason Pratt's study that night, almost as brightly as it burned in his belly. He had been drinking port since early afternoon while staring alternately at the logs on the grate and the pile of Pratt ledgers on his desk. He had not even eaten supper, but still, he had no solutions.

Jason Pratt wanted to be part of the merchant artistocracy that Jackson had described. His father or son would have told him that the Pratts were already the first family of Boston merchants, but Jason lacked such confidence. He needed acceptance. To gain it, he would gladly give over the house on Pemberton Hill or the family's secret treasure.

He sent for his sons. Artemus, Elihu, and Philip appeared at the door. Their mother was visiting an aunt in Maine. Elihu, a Harvard sophomore, of rather retiring nature, looked to his older brother for counsel. Philip, seven years old, was a bright, handsome child, the product of one of his parents' last couplings.

Jason loved the youngest boy best of all. "I want to talk to your big brothers, Philip. You may go and play."

Philip retreated into a corner. He kept a large box of wooden soldiers on a bookshelf beside the *Collected Works of Shakespeare*. He took it down and dragged it into the middle of the room.

Jason offered Artemus and Elihu a glass of port. Neither accepted. "Then sit down, sons. We must talk."

Artemus leaned against a bookshelf. Elihu reclined in his father's reading chair. Philip, now engrossed in play, filled the room with the sounds of a child's imaginary battle.

"What do you gentlemen suggest that I do with regards to this railroad business?" When he talked business with his sons, Jason always tried to sound very officious.

Artemus spoke first. "That we sell the *Pegasus* and the *Star of Canton,* cover the Curtis losses, and subscribe for a hundred shares of the Boston and Lowell."

Jason looked at Elihu. "Your brother has apprised you of the situation?"

"Yes, and I agree with his judgments."

"What about Abigail?" asked Jason.

"She refuses to move. There is nothing else for us to do," said Artemus.

"We can find the treasure. I'm certain that it's the Golden Eagle Tea Set, and I'd stake my life that it's in the Back Bay. If we find it, we can do all that you've suggested without selling a single yardarm." Through the port-wine haze, Jason could see no other solution.

The two brothers exchanged glances. Artemus had prepared Elihu for this and had told his younger brother not to respond.

"Well," said Jason, "will you help me?"

"I refuse to involve myself in such foolishness, Father," announced Artemus. "We're businessmen. We're Pratts. I'm sure we can find a way to absorb the loss, keep the ships, and still invest in the railroads. But I would prefer not to invest if we must first hunt for some mythical treasure out on a mudflat."

Jason looked toward Elihu, who cast his eyes toward the fire.

"My own sons refuse me." Jason finished his port and stood as decisively as a drunken fat man could. "I will find it alone."

Artemus could see the obsession on his father's face. Or perhaps it was the flush of the wine. "We refuse you nothing, Father. You have our affection, our respect, and our willingness to discuss this problem in the morning." He casually picked up the decanter, which was nearly empty. "Now, let us see you to bed."

"I carried you both to bed countless times. I don't need either of you to help me into my nightshirt." He flopped into the chair beside the fireplace. "My own sons."

Artemus looked at his brother and gestured toward the door. The young men left the room.

Jason Pratt stared at the flames for nearly five minutes before he felt a presence beside him. He looked into the eyes of his youngest son.

The boy wore an expression of the deepest concern. He didn't fully understand the discussion he had just heard, but he realized that his father was deeply upset. "I'll help you, Papa."

Jason embraced the boy and kissed him on the cheek. Philip smelled the sweet aroma that he always associated with his father, the aroma of port wine.

"You help me by being a good boy."

"I can help you find this thing."

"No, son. It may be dangerous."

"Please, Father?"

"I'll tell you how you can help me." He took his keys from his pocket and handed Philip the one for the wine cellar. "Go downstairs to my wine room. Just to the right side of the door, on the first shelf, you'll find a row of green bottles. Get one and bring it to me."

The boy took the key and bounded for the cellar.

"Why do I hate my brother so?" asked Abigail in her diary that night.

> I wish I knew. It would make it much easier for me to drive him from that office. I have planned for so long, the plans are now in motion, and suddenly, I pity him. He sat in my

carriage today, a drowning man grabbing for the rope which I threw and let fall just out of his reach.

I must not soften! Jason is weak and malleable. I could not destroy him if he had his brother's strength. I would not even try. He does not deserve to direct our affairs. He has done nothing new or aggressive in five years. I will give him the house if he gives me ten percent of his stock and agrees to step down in favor of Artemus. I will consider giving him the secret of the tea set if he gives me twenty percent of the stock and a half interest in the company.

Abigail blew out the oil lamp, removed her robe, and climbed into bed. The sheets were cold. The chill cut through her flannel nightgown, and she pulled herself into a little ball. She considered getting up and filling the bed warmer with hot coals, but in the time it took her to do that, her body would warm the bed. She gazed at the log burning brightly in the fireplace and closed her eyes. In five minutes, she was asleep.

On November nights, the fire would keep the room warm for several hours after she went to bed. By the time it usually burned itself out, she would be deep in sleep. But tonight, a draft woke her soon after she dozed off. She opened her eyes and screamed.

A dark figure hulked between her bed and the fireplace. She screamed again and it moved toward her, its enormous shadow dancing on the ceiling above her head.

Sean was still working in his carriage-house apartment when he heard the scream. He jumped to his windows and looked up toward the house. He saw nothing but the orange glow of the fire in Abigail's room. He heard another scream. He grabbed the brace of pistols which Abigail had given him when he had published his first book, and he bolted for the house.

Abigail tried to jump out of bed and run, but the figure grabbed her by the arm and flung her toward the fireplace. She saw the bags of loose flesh, the glassy eyes reflecting the fire, the upper lip curled in hatred—her brother's drunken face.

"Where is it, Abigail?" The words rasped out of him.

"The tea set?"

"Where is it, you bitch?" He struck her across the face.

She would not enrage him further. "It's in the Back Bay. I'll show you where it is in the morning. I promise."

"I know you too well. You won't tell me in the morning. You hate me." He advanced toward her.

"I don't hate you." She tried to soothe him as she reached for the fireplace shovel behind her.

"You show more affection and respect for your footman than you do for me. I despise you."

Her hand closed around the shovel. He came at her and caught her by the throat. She swung the shovel, but he was standing too close to hit.

"Tell me where it is right now," he commanded.

She couldn't speak. She couldn't breathe.

The door flew open. Sean saw Abigail struggling with a figure twice her size. He heard her muffled cries. Without thinking, he raised one of the pistols and fired. The fingers closed tight around Abigail's throat, then let go. Jason collapsed on the floor, and a pool of blood spread like a flower on the rug beneath his head.

For a moment, Sean and Abigail stood in shock.

"I didn't know it was . . . I didn't mean to shoot him. He's not dead. He can't be."

Abigail tried to speak, but she had no voice. She swallowed hard. "I'm afraid he is."

"I thought he was trying to kill you."

"He was."

Sean's mother appeared at the door. She saw the body and the guns in her son's hands. "Jesus, Mary, and Joseph. What's happened?"

"A drunken merchant has been murdered and robbed in a waterfront alley," said Abigail firmly. "Sean, hitch the carriage. Delia, come over here and clean the rug."

The mirthless November sun gave little consolation as another Pratt was buried in the Old Granary Ground. Jason Pratt was found in an alley off Broad Street, his clothes reeking of wine, his money gone, and a bullet hole in the back of his head.

The words were spoken, and Artemus turned the first shovel of dirt. The crowd of mourners, much larger for Jason than for his father, began to disperse. Artemus did not linger by his father's grave. He offered his mother his arm and led her, past relatives and friends offering condolences, to her carriage. Philip trailed along behind them, and Abigail followed on Elihu's arm.

Before Sarah Pratt climbed into her carriage, she turned and stared at Abigail.

"I'm so sorry." Abigail sobbed and threw her arms around Sarah's neck. Her grief was genuine. She had not loved her brother, but she had never wished him dead.

"I despise you," said Sarah coldly. Widow's weeds made her face look waxen. "You drove my husband to his death, and now you express your hypocritical sorrow. Take your arms off my shoulders and never embrace me again."

Abigail stepped back and brushed the tears from her eyes. "As you wish."

Artemus helped his mother into the carriage, and she called to Philip. As the boy stepped up, Abigail ran her hands through his curls.

He pulled his head away and gazed at her defiantly. "I hate you, Auntie Abigail. You made my Papa die."

Artemus tried to help his little brother into the carriage. Philip pulled away from him, as well, and climbed in on his own.

"I hate you too, Artemus. Papa asked you to help him, and you wouldn't. I hate you and Elihu, and I miss Papa." The boy buried his face on his mother's breast and began to cry.

Artemus led Abigail to her carriage. "Don't pay heed to words spoken in grief," he said softly.

"I try not to, but their hatred hurts me deeply. You must assure me that you have no such feelings."

"You didn't kill my father. His own weakness and too much wine destroyed him. You simply acted for the good of the company."

She was relieved. "I care very much about your feelings, dear, because I know that you have taken the time to understand me."

Artemus patted Abigail's hand. His touch was firm. It gave her confidence in their future.

"I want you to know," he said, "that I have long admired your business sense and your foresight. I hope that you will be ready to offer me your advice and guidance."

She smiled. Those were the words she had been waiting to hear. "At any time, Artemus."

"Then I'll expect to see you in my father's . . . in my office on Monday morning."

"You can rely on it, dear. And I will tell you now that my house and property are at your disposal. You may do with them what you wish."

He had almost expected that. He kissed her on the cheek and helped her into her carriage. Sean closed the door.

"I've arranged for you to sail next week on the *Pegasus*," said Artemus to Sean. "You'll be assistant to the supercargo."

"Well, sir . . ." he began weakly and fumbled for words.

Abigail spoke for him. "Sean is most upset by your father's death. He has decided to stay in my service for a short while longer."

"Very well. I'll cancel his appointment." Artemus saluted and returned to his carriage.

"Take me home, Sean," said Abigail softly.

"Yes, ma'am." His voice rang hollow.

That night, Abigail felt the darkness. To hold it back, she wrote.

Tuesday, November 29, 1830

I have finally achieved my goal, but at what cost! The company has a young Pratt president who will turn to me for inspiration and advice. Our future seems bright. But a little boy no longer has a father.

Jason did not have to die for all this to come to pass. I wanted him to live, to learn from me and his son, to offer whatever advice he had to give. My victory tastes bitter and unsatisfying. There is nothing I can do to make up for Jason's death, except to give my love and leave my legacy to Jason's children, if they will have it.

And Sean will be staying with me, but we will bring each other no joy. He stays not because he wants to, not because he needs my affection and inspiration. He is here because he is powerless to move, guilt-ridden by my brother's death. For his own sake, I hope that he regains himself and seeks the adventures awaiting him beyond the horizon.

Of course, if he gets to the horizon, he may find that his dreams have vanished, the landscape is barren, and the emptiness reaches to infinity.

CHAPTER XIV

Evangeline Carrington didn't stop driving for three states. She picked up Route 95 in Massachusetts, skimmed across the southeastern corner of New Hampshire, and into Maine, where she took Route 1 up the coast. The weather 150 miles from Boston was cool and dry, and after a three-hour drive, they arrived at a village called Dory Landing.

A handful of wood-frame buildings, shingled weather-gray and trimmed in white, clustered around the town dock. A half-dozen fishing boats bobbed on the incoming tide. Dory Landing was a working community where men in slickers and woolen caps stayed out for days to fill their holds with cod, where men in rubber boots and rubber aprons chugged along the coast, baiting lobster traps, cursing shorts, and praying for a two-pounder at the end of every rope.

"Welcome to Winslow Homer country," said Evangeline.

About a mile north of the village ten or twelve small cottages grew among the pines. Evangeline parked in front of a saltbox which looked across a meadow to the ocean. The nearest cottage was a hundred yards away and barely visible through the trees.

"Very nice," said Fallon.

"I come up here when I need to get away from things. No one in the family knows I own it."

"Are all these places summer cottages?"

"No. A lot of craftsmen and artists live around here, would-be Wyeths who sell their paintings to tourists during the summer and starve the rest of the year."

"Not a bad place to be hungry. You can fish and pick wild berries, and when it gets cold, you can chop down a tree and spend the winter by the fire."

"Sounds idyllic," said Evangeline, "until you try it."

The shades were drawn and the cottage was chilly and damp inside. It reminded Fallon of the beach houses that his parents had rented when he was a boy. He recalled the smell of mildew and wet sand and the gloom that burned away as soon as Evangeline raised the shades. The afternoon sun poured in, reflecting off the knotty-pine paneling and maple furniture, filling the room with an amber glow. Fallon could feel himself begin to relax. He sat at the table beside the picture window and placed the diary in front of him.

"Not yet," said Evangeline firmly. "I need a drink and a few minutes to collect myself."

She hasn't said a word between the Massachusetts border and Dory Landing, thought Fallon. She should be well collected by now.

"Then," she added, "I'm going to call my uncle."

She produced two bottles of Miller's beer, a small store of ripe Camembert, and a box of crackers. The beer, in clear bottles, caught the sunshine and highlighted the amber glow with gold. Fallon drank and realized that his throat had been dust-dry since he had stepped onto the widow's walk at Searidge.

Philip Pratt stood at service line, five stories up. Behind him stretched three blocks of Back Bay. In front of him, an attractive brunette named Melissa Pike awaited his shot. She was his woman for the season.

In autumn, he chose ladies who enjoyed gourmet cooking and Harvard football games. Winter brought Nordic types who made love as well and as willingly as they skied. In April, he went to the Bahamas alone to recover. And in early summer, he sought lithe young professionals who played tennis and sailed. Melissa worked as a junior editor for a Boston publisher, she shot a withering backhand, and on weekends she didn't wear underwear.

Pratt shot.

"Fault," she cried. "Game, set, and match."

Pratt didn't like to lose, but Melissa jumped about in triumph and distracted him from defeat.

They were playing on the rooftop tennis court of Pratt's Commonwealth Avenue home, which had been in the family since its construction in 1866. Soon they would be playing in Pratt's circular bathtub, which had not been part of the Pratt tradition for quite as long.

"Another match?" she asked.

"You've got twenty years on me, Melissa. Besides, it's too hot. Let's have a drink instead." He poured two chilled martinis, and the phone rang.

"Philip? This is Evangeline."

Pratt excused himself and took the call in his study on the fourth floor. "Where the hell are you, Evangeline?"

She refused to tell him, but it sounded like long distance. "This morning, I went to Searidge."

"I know," he said coldly. "Breaking and entering is a crime."

"Is that why Harrison pulled a gun on me?" She didn't pause for an answer. "And where is Grandmother?"

"We've admitted your grandmother to a rest home. Christopher's death has had an absolutely devastating effect on her."

"A rest home will have an even worse effect."

"It's for her own good."

Evangeline laughed. She didn't believe that Philip Pratt ever did anything for anyone's good but his own.

"Is that student with you?" asked Pratt.

"Yes. Why?"

"Harrison was trying to protect you from him. We're not certain of his intentions, and your safety may be in jeopardy if you stay with him."

"What's that supposed to mean?"

"Don't trust him."

"Philip, I don't trust anyone."

"You'd better trust me, and get yourself up here as soon as possible. I'll explain everything when I see you."

"Tomorrow at ten."

"We'd prefer to talk to you today."

"Tomorrow at ten." She hung up.

Pratt called Soames and told him about the phone call.

"Is she bringing the student with her?" asked Soames.

"I don't know. I told her he might be dangerous and suggested that she get away from him."

"I think it's imperative that we talk to him. Did she say where they were?"

"No."

"He has more than his share of nerve," said Soames after some thought. "I won't be surprised if he's with her tomorrow. I suggest calling Mr. Hannaford. He may be able to help us."

"What if Fallon doesn't show?"

"We'll go out and find him. Whatever he knows, we can't have his knowledge floating around free."

Pratt hung up and stared down at the traffic on Commonwealth Avenue. He had been fighting depression for weeks, and it was making another assault. Once he had moved through his world like a corsair. He had directed the affairs of the corporation with the supreme confidence that came to him from six generations of leadership. His authority had been unquestioned, his business ability recognized by associates, competitors, and stockholders alike. In the early years, as he worked through the lower levels of management to a vice-presidency, he had been tough, disciplined, ruthless, and the stockholders had agreed with Artemus Pratt IV when he had stated, in his last corporate report before retirement, that his son had earned the presidency and chairmanship of Pratt Industries. For years, Philip Pratt fulfilled their expectations. Now, his future rested on the tea set.

He had to commit his aunt to a nursing home because she was deemed a threat to company security. He had to worry when his niece spent time with a Harvard graduate student. And he relied more heavily on the advice of his personal secretary than he did on himself.

Someplace, he had lost control, first of himself, then of the company. As he had reached forty, the discipline which had brought him to be president and chairman of the board had begun to deteriorate. He had realized that he was not enjoying his life, and the future had no longer seemed limitless. He had turned his attention to new pursuits. He had spent more time sailing, playing tennis, and skiing. He had bought into American Center Films because he wanted a plaything. He had begun to enjoy the company of younger women.

A divorce had followed. His wife had taken the house on Martha's Vineyard and custody of their two sons, aged ten and eight. Pratt had kept the family mansion in the Back Bay and the life-style he was learning to enjoy.

Then, William Rule had mounted his challenge, and Philip Pratt had tried to fight back. He had reached into himself for his old resources and had found them gone. He had called to his old allies, and they had not answered. Philip Pratt had decided that he had enjoyed himself too much. He had resolved that he would not be the first Pratt to turn over the chairmanship, and he had instructed Christopher Carrington to investigate the history of the Golden Eagle Tea Set.

Pratt remembered that Melissa Pike was still on the roof waiting to play another set. He stepped into the hallway and heard running water. He glanced toward his bedroom. Melissa's clothes were piled on the rug, and the bathroom door was open. A whirlpool bath for two. Pratt kicked off his shorts and forgot his problems.

Bennett Soames was in his office when Philip Pratt called him. Since the tea-set business had begun, Soames had been working extra hours just to read and initial the paperwork required to keep the executive office functioning smoothly.

However, Soames had always worked long hours, ever since he had begun work in 1946 as a twenty-two-year-old veteran with a background in military intelligence. He had started as an accountant and was running the department within a few years. In the late fifties, he had attracted the attention of Philip Pratt, who was just out of Harvard Business School. He had become Pratt's administrative assistant and confidant, and he rose with the president's son. His loyalty to Philip Pratt had been rewarded with power, a spacious office, a generous stock option, and a salary on which he lived most comfortably.

Soames had never married and had no family. Women interested him only in passing. When he needed female companionship to fulfill social or sexual requirements, he had no trouble attracting it, but his passions were the opera and trapshooting.

He devoted one room of his apartment to his collection of opera recordings, books, and posters. Every summer, he traveled for three weeks to hear the best companies in Europe, and he contributed annually to the Opera Company of Boston. Opera, he said, allowed one to experience the most extreme emotions and, because of the music, hold them at arm's length, so that they might be admired.

On weekends, Soames traveled to the Kenworthy Gun Club, near Newburyport, and he shot clay disks as they traveled across a range. Trapshooting tested speed, coordination, and marksmanship. The target appeared, it was destroyed, and another was launched at the shooter's command. He considered it an efficient sport: one wasted no motion in the stalking of prey and saw no bloody carcasses.

Soames had devoted himself to Pratt Industries and Philip Pratt, and he had been the first to notice when Pratt began to neglect his duties. He had tried to keep Pratt to his daily routine, but Pratt had refused. Pratt skipped meetings, took longer vacations, failed to read reports which, if seen on time, might have meant thousands of dollars to the company. Bennett Soames watched the stock fall, and he felt betrayed. He had decided that he would help to find the tea set, and that would be the last service he performed for Pratt Industries.

After she had hung up, Evangeline looked straight at Fallon. "Without taking more than fifteen seconds, tell me the name of the American who negotiated the Treaty of Ghent."

"What?"

"Don't waste time. Just tell me."

"There were five. Albert Gallatin, John Bayard, and John Quincy Adams started. They were joined later by Henry Clay and John Russell."

She seemed relieved. "You couldn't come up with an answer like that if you weren't a historian."

"What else would I be?"

"Jack the Ripper, according to Philip Pratt." Evangeline then sketched her conversation. "I told him I'd see him tomorrow in Boston."

"Does that mean we're spending the night together?" joked Fallon.

"Don't push, Peter. You've already invaded my world and, at least for today, turned it inside out. I've been tempted several times in the last few hours to pull over at the side of the road and toss you out on your head. Keep your distance." She spoke carefully, logically. She did not threaten. She knew what she needed to keep her life intact, and she didn't care what he thought about her.

He smiled. "I wasn't serious."

They took their crackers, cheese, and beer out to the yard and sat in wooden lawn chairs. Several hundred feet beyond, past a stand of pines and an open meadow, the land fell away to a rocky beach.

Evangeline closed her eyes and listened to the sound of the waves. Fallon wiped the dust off the diary with the tail of his shirt.

The diary was bound in leather, and Abigail Pratt Bentley's initials were hand-tooled on the cover. The lock, made of brass, wouldn't open. Fallon tried to pry it with his pocket knife, but old leather was weaker than brass, and he pulled the lock completely out of the book.

"It's been a bad day for heirlooms," said Evangeline.

"You wouldn't think a lock like that would still hold after so long." Fallon opened the book. The pages were made of the finest rag fiber, and there was very little deterioration. The date of the first entry was January 1, 1845, the last, December 31, 1845. "We have one year of a woman's life in front of us. How much did you know about her?"

"Not much, although Christopher was fascinated by her. Family history became a hobby of his three or four years ago, and I remember one November, between sailing and ski seasons, he spent every weekend reading her diaries in the Searidge attic."

"They must have contained a lot of interesting stuff." Fallon began to read. " 'January 1, 1845. I begin another chapter in the story of my life, which grows more fulfilling with every year. Young Artemus, now thirty-seven, with three bright children of his own, has invested heavily in the railroads that now wend their way across the American landscape. The Reading Railroad, the Attica and Buffalo, and the Auburn and Rochester are all financed by our Pratt dollars. I am now discussing with him the potential of a line to Chicago that is, as yet, unfinished—the Michigan Central.'

"This was one smart woman," said Fallon. "The old Yankee merchant families were still making good money in the China trade, but the profits had leveled off by the time she was writing this, and New York had outstripped Boston as the center of shipping and commerce. More and more Boston money went into railroads, and the Michigan Central was a huge moneymaker."

He looked at the diary again. " 'I have been well pleased with the qualities and capabilities that Artemus Pratt has displayed in the years since he took over the leadership of Pratt Shipping and Mercantile. He has made the right choices, he has dealt firmly with his competitors, and he has conferred closely with me on every decision. From the day that he bargained away Pemberton Hill for seventy-five shares of Boston and Lowell stock, instead of the fifty Jackson had offered, I knew we were in firm hands. Ever since, Artemus has done nothing to disappoint me. Nor has Elihu, who has been Artemus's right hand and faithful servant. My only regret in my dealings with my nephews is that Philip has never forgiven me or his brothers for his father's death. Philip is now twenty-one years old and the handsomest young man I have ever seen. Although he is civil and decorous at all times, he still hates me. My heart breaks to think that what happened fifteen years ago can color our lives today, and I try, whenever I see him, to touch Philip in some way, to remind him of the greatness of the Pratt past and our mission in the future. I fear that I have not reached him.'"

"This is amazing," said Evangeline softly. "Amazing."

"You can almost picture her, sitting there with her needlepoint in her lap fretting about her nephews. She talks as if they were her sons."

"She didn't have any children of her own, so she lavished all her love and worry on her brother's children. It's only natural."

Fallon continued to read. "'Of course, his father's death was a terrible tragedy, and I have relived it in my mind's eye many times. But I firmly believe that Jason was a victim of himself more than anything else. Artemus and Elihu recognized their father's weakness, but Philip was only seven when Jason died, and he retains a romantic image of the man. I deeply regret his death. Had he lived to accept the terms I was going to offer, he would have become his son's chief adviser, and he would have seen his beliefs about shipping vindicated. Since the Opium War ended five years ago and the British forced China to open all her ports, our ships have hauled enormous quantities of textiles to China, and our profits have been greater than ever.'"

For the next several hours, Abigail entranced her readers. Sitting on the lawn, with the afternoon breeze sifting gently through the pines that surrounded the cottage, Evangeline and Peter were transported to 1845.

Abigail spread her deepest emotions across the pages of her diary and wove them through the narrative of her life. When she was happy, she wrote short, fragmented entries that burst with enthusiasm. When she was depressed, she spent hours filling pages with her ramblings. But one theme dominated her writings—she was obsessed by the passage of the Pratts through history, by the mark they had left on the past and the glories they would enjoy in the future.

"Listen to this," said Fallon. "'May 2, 1845. A beautiful blue day in spring. A ride on the Boston and Worcester with my nephew's beautiful children. We picnicked in the Needham countryside and returned to Boston at sunset. The children squealed with delight as we rode the "Dizzy Bridge," that most frightening structure of trestle and track that crosses the Back Bay Full Basin between Brookline and Gravelly Point.

" 'Lord! How much has changed in thirty years. Two railroad lines now crisscross one another in the middle of our Back Bay, and the flow of water is all but stopped. The mills are completely useless. But no matter. Our legacy is still safe, our future is secure, and another beautiful generation of Pratts has learned to love their aunt. I will teach them all I know, for they will take us into the twentieth century.'

"How the Back Bay has changed in thirty years." Fallon repeated the phrase and tried to inject it with importance.

"Everything changes in thirty years," said Evangeline.

"But Abigail says the changes don't bother her, because her legacy is still safe. She's only fifty-five when she's writing this, and she's always talking about her legacy. What kind of legacy?"

"Her diaries, her collection of old walking sticks, her Herman Melville decoder ring. I don't know. Wait until you read something significant before you start finding meanings. The only thing clear to me is that she wasn't a very happy woman. Anyone who is always thinking about the future or the past can't be enjoying the present too much." Evangeline pulled her chair into a patch of sunlight.

"She was a manipulator. She had a hand in everyone's business and, if I read it correctly, played a role in her brother's demise. It sounds as though she was a real dowager queen."

"Whatever she was, she still hasn't told us anything about your mythical tea set. Read on."

Fallon asked Evangeline to read for a while. He wanted to sip beer and listen.

She read through May and into early June. "Here's something interesting."

"About the tea set?"

"No, but it gives us a nice picture of the old girl. 'June 7, 1845. Today marks the twentieth anniversary of Sean Mannion's arrival at my door. It is hard to believe that he entered my service so long ago. I don't know what I would have done without him. In the early years, he was a source of strength, encouragement, and, yes, love of the purest sort. Now, he and his wife Lillian, whom he married ten years ago, are more like close friends than servants. I remember their son Joseph's birthday as I remember my nieces' and nephews'.

Yesterday, we had a party to commemorate his years with me. Artemus and Elihu and their wives and families all attended, along with many of Sean's Irish friends from the North End.

"'He is still a handsome man. His brawn and muscle have not diminished with the years, and his kindness and gentleness grow greater as he grows older. Would that we all aged so gracefully.'"

"Sounds like she had the hots for him," injected Fallon.

"I doubt it. She was a New England Yankee. She wouldn't look twice at an Irishman."

"Maybe that was her problem."

Evangeline pretended to miss his meaning. She simply continued reading. "'He is now thirty-nine, and I know that he will never strike out on his own, as he wanted to do before my brother's death. The circumstances surrounding that unfortunate incident tormented him for many months. Eventually, he regained something of his old personality, but he never found the strength again to break away from the security he has always had with us.'"

Evangeline looked at Peter. "I wonder what happened."

"It sounds like the guy blamed himself for Jason's death. Maybe he killed him."

She looked again at the diary. "'For selfish reasons, I was happy that he stayed, but I now am haunted by the thought that he wasted his life.'"

"She feels guilty because he felt guilty that her brother died." mused Fallon. "Interesting situation."

"This next entry looks like a short one. 'June 8, 1845. Philip will be graduating next week from Harvard. We have suggested that, like his brothers before him, he take a trip around the world and see the extent of the Pratt empire. I think he would enjoy spending a year at our China office. He is very interested in the prospect of a trip, but he says he won't be stopping in China or coming back to Boston. Now that his mother is dead, he says he has no reason to remain in the city.

"'He is young and fancies himself an adventurer, but I hate to see him go. I have, for many years, imagined him as part of the triumvirate that would lead our company for the next forty years. I may yet try to keep him in the fold. I am considering giving him a clue'"—Evangeline slowed down—"'to our family secret and hope that it holds him here.'"

At first, Fallon did not react. "Read that last sentence again."

She did.

"Damn," said Fallon softly. "Why couldn't she be more specific?"

"Because it's a secret. She knew what it was. She didn't have to be specific. Be quiet and listen. On June 15, she writes, 'After a long, sleepless night, I have made my decision. I am going to give each nephew a quotation. I am going to tell them enough about our treasure to—'"

"The tea set never left this country," said Fallon excitedly.

"She calls it a treasure, not a tea set." Evangeline tried to control Fallon's excitement and her own.

"Let me finish." She found her place. "'. . . enough about our treasure to bind them together.'"

"She's certainly crafty." Fallon was certain that Abigail was talking about the tea set. "She's probably hung on to some of the choicest clues for herself."

Evangeline didn't stop to speculate. "'June 16, 1845. I have failed in my plan. Artemus held a graduation party for his youngest brother at his new summer home in Marblehead, a handsome oceanside dwelling called Searidge. Before dinner, I called my nephews into the study.'" Evangeline stopped reading.

"What's wrong?"

"Nothing." She laughed nervously. "It's just very strange to read about a place where you've spent so much of your life. I used to sit for hours in the Searidge study and play with my dolls or look for sexy passages in the books I'd seen my grandmother reading. Nobody else ever used the study. It was my girlhood retreat. I knew that nothing could hurt me there. I never thought about all the life that went on there before I even existed." She paused. "Of course, my illusions about my special place were shattered when I was sixteen. That's when my mother told me that my father was murdered in the study. I felt betrayed somehow. I kept asking myself, why did he have to die there?"

Fallon remembered Katherine Carrington's reference to her son. "How old was he?"

"His late twenties. My mother was carrying me when it happened."

"Who killed him?"

"We never found out. Apparently he surprised a burglar who had just broken into the house. The burglar escaped." She paused again and gazed out toward the ocean. "Of course, for most of my life, my own father has been as distant to me as Abigail Pratt Bentley. Just another link in the chain of the Pratt-Carrington past, another picture on the wall in the living room."

Evangeline picked up the diary again and found her place.

"Abigail calls her nephews into the study. 'And, without naming it specifically, I told them each about the family treasure, the legacy left to us by my father. I told them that it was buried someplace in the waters around Boston . . .'" Evangeline stopped reading and looked at Fallon.

His jaw dropped. "The tea set. Still in the Back Bay mud. Pratt's grandson must've drowned trying to find it, and Pratt just said the hell with it."

"Now it's in the museum," she said firmly.

"Maybe not. Maybe it's still out there buried under some brownstone."

Evangeline finished the entry. "'I gave each of them an envelope containing a clue and told them that if they ever wanted the treasure, which I now estimate would be worth almost fifty thousand dollars to the right buyer, they would have to stay together. Artemus and Elihu were polite but little interested in my story or the envelopes. Philip read his, then folded it and jammed it into his pocket. I thought for a moment that he was intrigued by my story, but then he gazed upon me with an expression of the deepest contempt and said—how it wounds me to use these words!—that I was a "meddlesome bitch unfit for his company." He said that I had manipulated his father and his brothers, but I would not manipulate him. He then stormed out of Searidge, and we haven't seen him since.'" Evangeline could feel Abigail's pain, and her voice conveyed it.

"'Oh, Lord, how hard I tried to make the boy love me and keep him as part of the family. How miserably I have failed.'"

A few days later, Abigail recorded that Philip had withdrawn the money held in trust for him until his graduation and had boarded a Pratt ship for London. She seldom mentioned him or, to Fallon's disappointment, the family treasure again in 1845. She filled her diurnal with business reports, thoughts about new investments, praise for Artemus and Elihu, and an old aunt's admiration for her grand nieces and nephews.

It was after seven o'clock when Fallon neared the end of the diary. They had been reading for over four hours, and the sun was dropping toward the hills a mile or so away. The breeze had died down, and the air was still. Fallon was sipping his third beer as he read.

On December 30, Abigail began her summation of the year. It usually took her two days to write.

As he reached the last page, Fallon was quite amazed that Abigail could calculate her thoughts to end with such precision. "'All in all, it would have been a very good year, except for Philip Pratt's abdication. A more beautiful and intelligent young man I have never met. His presence with Pratt Shipping and Mercantile would have been invaluable. I did all that I could to keep him in the fold. I even offered him a piece of our treasure. He rejected it. He rejected us. We have not heard from him in six months. I fear that we may never hear from him again. I pray that future generations will not have such disregard for my dreams.

"'Thus ends this Year of our Lord, one thousand, eight hundred, and forty-five.'"

Fallon closed the diary and looked at Evangeline. For a time, they sat in silence, in awe of Abigail Pratt Bentley. She had told them much about the tea set, and more about herself. Her revelations had convinced Fallon that he was moving in the right direction, and Evangeline, almost involuntarily, was becoming less skeptical.

For supper, they drove to a little place in Dory Landing called the Chowder Mug, where they had steaming bowls of fish chowder, home-baked bread, salads straight from the garden, and a pot of coffee. Fallon added a wedge of apple pie with cheddar cheese, and Evangeline paid. Fallon said it was the best meal he'd had in weeks. They drove back to the cottage with the top down. The sun had set, and the night was crisp and cool, without a trace of the humidity that was soaking Boston. But Evangeline was still wearing shorts and beginning to shiver in the open car. She pulled the Porsche up in front of the cottage and ran inside.

Fallon lingered to enjoy the arrival of night. He had not been out of the city at night in months. The stillness, the clean smell of pine and salt, the darkness that seemed to gather near the ground like fog and rise until it obscured the tops of the trees, all seemed new to him once more. He breathed deep and rested his hand on his full belly. He felt satisfied, relaxed.

Evangeline came out again. She was wearing jeans and a hooded sweatshirt, and she was carrying a man's windbreaker, which she handed to Fallon.

"Let's walk." She started down the trail toward the water.

Fallon threw on the windbreaker and followed. "When we get back tomorrow—"

"Stay on the trail. This place is infested with poison ivy."

He fell in behind her and started again to speak.

She interrupted."I don't want to talk about tomorrow or Abigail

Pratt Bentley's treasure for at least an hour. I don't like to upset my digestion."

They crossed the road and walked in silence to the edge of the meadow. Wooden stairs led to the beach, twenty feet below. The lights of Dory Landing gleamed to the south, and a full moon was rising out of the water. Fallon looked at Evangeline. A pretty girl in a sweatshirt, a deserted beach, the familiar tightness in his chest—he remembered it all from the nights of his youth, nights spent in the sand at Falmouth or Martha's Vineyard, nights he would love to relive.

He moved a step closer. He wanted to kiss her, but he remembered the warning about keeping his distance. Beneath the cool exterior, she was skittish and unpredictable, and he didn't want to frighten her off.

She bounded down the stairs. Fallon followed. On the beach, she kicked off her sneakers and started to walk. Fallon took his off, found the sand too cold, and put them on again. As they walked, Fallon lagged a few yards behind, sensing that she did not want to talk. Evangeline sauntered along with her head down as though she were looking for something in the sand. After some distance, she angled toward the water and sat down on the hull of an overturned rowboat. Fallon caught up to her and sat in the sand at her feet.

The evening chill was turning cold. Evangeline jammed her hands into the pouch of her sweatshirt and pressed her leg against Fallon's side. "You're warm."

He wrapped an arm around her legs, and they sat listening to the gentle lapping of the waves against the shore. After a while, she reached out and ran her hand across his arm and shoulder. He didn't move. Then she placed her other hand on his arm and crouched down so that her head rested on his shoulder. He turned his face to her and she sat up quickly.

"I'm sorry," she said. "You're dredging up old memories."

He realized that she was caressing the jacket, not him.

"You're the first man to wear that in almost two years." She slid down into the sand next to Fallon. "I was going to marry him. I met him after my first year of law school, when I was working for Legal Aid."

"I didn't know you went to law school."

"Oh, yes." She laughed softly. "I went filled with purpose. I was going to get all the sophisticated weapons I'd need to fight the battles of the generation. You know—Vietnam, racism, pollution, all the windmills we went tilting after in the late sixties and early seventies. And I hated it. The first year was unbearable. But I got through it and went to work that summer for Boston Legal Aid. Most of the cases I worked on involved landlord-tenant problems in poor neighborhoods and hassles between the Housing Authority and their tenants in the projects.

"That's where I met Cliff. He worked in the D.A.'s office. He was heading a campaign against the drug pushers operating in the housing projects where a lot of our clients lived. He said he wanted to nail the big guys and keep all the little losers out of the public defender's office. I had a few professional discussions with him, and they led to a dinner invitation. We fell in love with each other, and together we fell in love with the Maine coast." She recited it all without emotion, as though it had happened to someone else. "But we never got to enjoy it. He pushed too hard, and someone killed him. They found his body in his garage. Carbon-monoxide poisoning." She stood decisively, as if she could leave her memories in the sand.

"Did you quit law school?"

"I went to law school because I was committed. I thought I could make a difference. After Cliff died, I realized that the problems are all too big to go away, and one crusading lawyer isn't going to make much of a dent in any of them. Without him, the simple act of getting from one day to the next became a major challenge. So I decided to concentrate on me, on living my own life and letting everyone else take care of themselves." She spoke softly, but with conviction. "Now, I grow my plants, I enjoy my work, and I seek whatever tranquillity I can find."

Peter Fallon was beginning to understand her. Behind the defenses, he saw someone he wanted very much to know. He wondered how close she would let him come. He wanted to be gentle with her. He wanted to move carefully, but suddenly, he was leaping up and grabbing her by the shoulders. "Damn the tranquillity, Evangeline!"

She was startled. "What are you talking about, Peter?"

"I'm talking about this morning. About breaking into Searidge, about finding the diary." The words began to pour out of him. "I'm talking about a challenge, something dangerous, like that fight on the roof. When I felt those hands close around my throat, I had to reach down and grab hold of all the guts and instinct inside me, and I had to tell myself I could make it. And I did. We both did. We were pushed to the brink, and we fought our way back. There's nothing in life that feels better than when you know you've made it. The rush intensifies everything."

She felt his fingers digging into her shoulders. She didn't want to admit that he was frightening her. She tried to sound sarcastic. "I really think you'd be willing to risk your life for a few charges of high-grade adrenalin."

"I made a big mistake going into history. I'm no scholar. I never was. I got dry rot from three years in the stacks, and I've killed myself writing a dissertation that nobody except my thesis board will read. In a few months, they'll shake my hand and call me 'doctor,' and it won't mean a thing, because I'm not going to disappear into some little school in Arkansas, and I can't wait around until some bureaucracy offers me a job. I need something now. I need to find that tea set."

She pulled away. In little more than twenty-four hours, she had attended her brother's funeral, broken into her grandmother's house, rifled through private papers, and fought her way out of the attic. She had a bump on her head, her body was bruised, and she had been pouring out her past to a man she hardly knew. All her intellect and experience told her to get away from Peter Fallon. He was potentially dangerous, someone she ought to avoid. But Abigail Pratt Bentley had whet her curiosity, and something inside her wanted what Fallon was offering—a challenge that was physical as well as mental, a test of her instincts and her intuition, a chance to see the edge after seeking so long the soft center. She decided to help him.

"Tomorrow, I'll talk to my uncle and try to find out what's going on, for my own peace of mind and your curiosity. After that, I'll make no promises." She turned and headed back toward the cottage.

CHAPTER XV   *June 1855*

The white obelisk thrust proudly into the Boston sky. The American flag, the flags of the six New England states, and the flags of the Revolution encircled the monument and fluttered in the breeze. Red-white-and-blue bunting festooned the platform in front of the monument, and nearly a thousand people had gathered at its base to commemorate the Battle of Bunker Hill.

It was June 17, 1855, and the abolition of slavery was the issue of the day. After the band played "The Star Spangled Banner" and Dr. Henley of the Park Street Church delivered an invocation, William Lloyd Garrison stepped to the podium. He drew generous applause from his supporters and jeers from the many Bostonians who felt that Southern problems should be solved in the South.

Artemus Pratt, now forty-seven, sat near the stage with his wife Cynthia and his five children—Sarah, Artemus Jr., Jason, Olivia, and Henry. Artemus applauded lightly, and his family followed his example. Artemus Jr., a sixteen-year-old cut from his father's mold but without his father's muttonchop whiskers, leaned toward Artemus. "By applauding the Abolitionists, aren't we supporting a cause that could lead to civil war?"

"Most definitely," said his father.

"Would not a war between slave and free states be injurious to our interests?"

"We would certainly lose our best source of cotton, but a war with the South would definitely benefit a manufacturing area like New England and a company like Pratt Shipping, Mining, and Manufacturing."

William Lloyd Garrison was a balding man with tiny eyes and the angry expression of a country minister preaching hellfire and damnation. He was, by choice, a writer, but the circumstances of his crusade had forced him to become an orator. He began to speak in a thin, high-pitched voice. "Mr. Mayor, Reverend Mr. Henley, ladies and gentlemen, esteemed guests . . ."

Behind him, in the place of honor, sat four ancient men, the last American survivors of the Battle of Bunker Hill. Behind them sat the first-generation descendants, one of whom was Abigail Pratt Bentley.

She was now sixty-five, although she looked closer to fifty. Her face showed few wrinkles. Her hair had only recently begun to turn gray. She was still strong enough to ride almost every week. She was respected by Bostonians as a patroness of the arts, a lover of music and oratory, an aunt and adviser to Artemus Pratt, one of the most successful businessmen in America. She was enjoying the day immensely. She put her head back and imagined that the crowd, the speakers, and the warm June sun had convened just for her.

"If one man in our nation is not free," Garrison announced, "no man is free. And in these United States today, there are thousands, yea, hundreds of thousands, who wear the abominable shackles of slavery."

At the edge of the crowd, well beyond earshot of Garrison, a young woman stood bewildered. Her name was Samantha, and she had never seen so many people in one place before. She approached a young couple who seemed more interested in each other than in the speaker. They were both dressed in the latest fashions, the man wearing a short-waisted coat, vest, and silk cravat, the woman in crinolines, with hoop skirt, bonnet, and parasol.

"Excuse me," said Samantha. "I'm looking for a lady called Abigail Pratt Bentley. I was told she would be here today."

The two young people looked at her as though she had walked

uninvited into their parlor, then they moved away. It was fashiona-
ble to listen to speeches by William Lloyd Garrison, but not to talk
with a woman like Samantha. She was a Negro, and the little boy at
her side was half-white.

Although she wore ragged clothes and a shroud of exhaustion,
Samantha had once been a beautiful woman. Brown eyes still shone
like mahogany against coffee skin, and she carried herself proudly,
but a ruthless cough was squeezing the life from her body.

The boy, about six years old, had his mother's features, but his
skin was shades lighter, his hair streaked with blond, and his eyes
deep blue. He held close to his mother in this forest of people and
tried to ignore the hunger digging a pit in his stomach.

Rows of carriages and coaches, parked three deep, lined the
streets surrounding the monument. Samantha decided to find Mrs.
Bentley's carriage and wait for her there. She asked several footmen
before one of them directed her to a carriage parked on Bunker Hill
Street.

A handsome man of about fifty sat atop the carriage. Beside him
sat a teen-aged boy who was obviously his son. Samantha and her
child drew near and stood by one of the horses.

"Can I help you?" said Sean Mannion. His gentle voice was the
first trace of warmth she had found since she had arrived in Boston
the previous day.

"Is this Miz Abigail Pratt Bentley's carriage, m'sieur?" Samantha
spoke with a slight French accent.

"It is, ma'am."

"Could you tell me where she is?"

"She'll be sittin' up there on the platform in front of the
monument."

Samantha looked across the crowd, but she was too far away to
pick anyone out. "Will she be coming back after the speaking is
done?"

"That she will. But I'll tell you now, so you won't be disappointed,
she needs no servants."

Samantha sensed the man's kindness. She thanked him, then
crossed the street to the shade of a young elm and waited for the
ceremonies to end.

Garrison had reached his peroration. He pulled two scrolls of
paper from his breast pocket and held them up for all to see. "I have
in my hand copies of the United States Constitution and the Fugitive
Slave Law." He struck a match and touched it to each document. "So
perish all compromises with tyranny—let the people say Amen!"

The people said Amen. The people jeered. They watched in shock. They applauded. And Garrison sat down. He was followed to the podium by a representative of a pro-slavery group, who received a loud ovation. After an angry rebuke of Garrison's speech and actions, the mayor delivered an oration on the greatness of the city. Then a local poet recited an ode to the men who fought at Bunker Hill. The ceremonies ended with the playing of "Yankee Doodle," and the crowd began to disperse.

On the stand, Abigail approached Garrison, "An excellent speech, Mr. Garrison."

"Thank you, Mrs. Bentley."

"Although I must admit that I was shocked to see you burning our Constitution."

"I was burning pro-slavery construction. A purely symbolic gesture," he said briskly.

"Whatever your motives, I am your ally. You'll find in the mail tomorrow a small donation toward the benefit of your publication."

Garrison nodded his thanks. *"The Liberator* needs the support of everyone."

"This afternoon I'm having a small gathering at my home on Colonnade Row. Tea for the ladies, something stronger for the gentlemen. Ralph Waldo Emerson has promised to attend, and we should be honored if you joined us." She put her hand on his arm. She enjoyed the appearance of familiarity with famous men.

"I'm terribly sorry, Mrs. Bentley, but even on holidays, there is work to be done if we are to publish *The Liberator*. I must decline."

Abigail smiled. "My guests will be disappointed, but I'm sure they'll understand. The work of *The Liberator* must go on."

Abigail rejoined Artemus and his family, and they started back toward their carriages. Dust rose everywhere as a thousand people hurried to leave and carriages jockeyed for position on the streets around the monument. The smell of fresh horse manure baking in the sun and transported on the soles of Bostonian boots over-powered the smell of the sea breeze and the aroma of wild-blooming roses.

Sean jumped down and opened the carriage door when he saw the Pratts approaching through the crowd. Abigail arrived on the arm of Artemus Jr. Samantha and her child crossed the street.

"Thank you, Artemus," said Abigail. "I'll see you and all the children at Colonnade Row. Your father and I will be discussing business on the ride back."

"It's a holiday, Abigail," said Artemus Sr. cheerfully. "We can't be talking about business today."

"My father did business every day of his life. You would do well to emulate him."

"He would do well to relax. You're a terrible influence on him," said Cynthia. The daughter of a Harvard professor, she was plump, fertile, and, from the day they had met, an admirer of Abigail Pratt Bentley.

"I must discuss the consolidation of the Chicago, Burlington, and Quincy Railroads with your husband." Abigail grabbed him by the arm and tried to push him into the carriage.

Cynthia took his other arm and tried to pull in the opposite direction. Cynthia, Abigail, and the children began to laugh uproariously at the sight of Artemus Pratt turned into a wishbone, and Artemus laughed along with them. Then, he broke loose, straightened his cutaway, and agreed to ride with Abigail.

"Very good," said Abigail.

"Excuse me, madame." Samantha and her little boy appeared out of the rising dust and traffic.

"Yes?" said Abigail imperiously.

"I would like to talk with you."

"I don't need servants." Abigail waved Samantha away and started to climb into the coach.

"I am not looking for work."

"Then what is it?" snapped Abigail.

Samantha glanced at the faces of Artemus and his family, and she felt like an insect studied by hungry birds. "I would rather talk in private."

"This is my family. You may speak in front of them."

She hesitated a moment, then pushed the child toward Abigail and blurted out the words she had been rehearsing for almost three years. "My boy is your great-nephew. He's Philip Pratt's son. I was Philip Pratt's wife."

A cloud of dust billowed past, and Abigail held her handkerchief to her nose. She had not heard from Philip since he had left ten years earlier. She had presumed him dead, but the news was nonetheless a powerful shock. She felt her legs begin to tremble, and she leaned on Artemus for support.

"Philip told me to come to Boston. He said you'd take care of me and my boy." Samantha hoped that Abigail's arms would open to her, but they did not.

Abigail regained her composure and eyed the little mulatto, who stepped back and tried to hide himself behind his mother's skirts. "My nephew has been dead to this family for many years. I have accepted his death. But I do not believe that he would marry a Negress and produce a—"

Before she went further, Artemus intervened. "My aunt has a great many things to do today. Come to her house tomorrow and we will talk to you." He pushed Abigail into her coach.

"But sir . . ."

"Do not persist, young lady, or I shall call the constable."

"I have no money and no place to stay, and my boy is hungry. Please help us."

Abigail relented. "They may sleep in the barn tonight. I'll instruct Mrs. Mannion to make supper for the boy."

"Oh, thank you, madame." Samantha tried to climb into the carriage.

Artemus grabbed the door and stepped in front of her.

"Can't we ride with you?"

"Accept what charity we give, young woman, and walk."

Samantha let go. The carriage eased into the traffic and clattered down Bunker Hill Street.

Samantha nudged the boy and they started to walk.

"Mama, I'm hungry. You said the lady would be nice to us."

"She will be, when we get to her house."

"But Mama . . ."

"Stop your whinin'." She slapped the boy, more in frustration than anger. Then she began to cough. The spasms hacked through her, and when they ended, she was crying. She threw her arms around the boy and held him tight. "I'm sorry, *mon cher*. I'm sorry. You're all that your mama has, and I don't want to hurt you. Never."

"It's all right, Mama. I won't cry. I promise."

She stood and brushed the tears away. "It's a long walk, dear. We must go."

The next afternoon, Sean Mannion ushered Samantha and her son into the sitting room of Abigail Pratt Bentley's home on Colonnade Row. Four stories of Bulfinch brick townhouses stretched along Tremont Street and housed some of Boston's leading citizens. Abigail had lived there for twenty-five years.

Her sitting room, like most rooms in Colonnade Row, was long and slender, illuminated during the day by a single set of windows that overlooked the Common. The ceilings were edged with pine molding, and pine wainscoting covered the lower third of the walls. A brass chandelier hung in the middle of the room. Directly above it was a ceiling medallion of white plaster fruit; small holes in the medallion, artfully placed to look like part of the arrangement, allowed the escape of smoke from the oil lamps on the chandelier. The walls were papered light yellow with crimson stripes. An oriental rug covered the floor. Chairs and settee of mahogany and velvet were arranged about the room. Abigail sat in her favorite chair by the window. Artemus leaned on the marble mantelpiece.

But Samantha was not intimidated. She hadn't coughed since the previous day, and she looked much better after a meal and a night's rest. She was certain that when she told her story, Abigail Pratt Bentley would accept her son.

Abigail gestured to the settee, and Samantha sat gingerly. Abigail spoke without warmth. "I'm sorry I didn't speak to you this morning, but I wanted my nephew to join us, and he's a very busy man."

"Thank you for the meal and a place to stay."

"I'll not see a mother and her son go hungry, even if they are trying to take advantage of me."

Samantha shook her head. "I am not trying to take advantage of you, madame."

"You tell me my nephew is dead. You tell me he married a black woman. You tell me he fathered a mulatto child who has come to claim his inheritance. And I must tell you that I do not believe you."

Samantha felt her little boy's hand close tight around her own. "I tell you the truth. Phil Pratt died three years ago. I nursed him till the end."

"I long ago accepted the fact that I would never see Philip again," said Abigail coldly. "I have wept for him many a night. I wept last night, but I will not believe that you are his wife."

"Maybe you cried for a night. I cried for a month," said Samantha bitterly.

"Where did he die?" asked Artemus gently.

"In Angel's Camp, about a hundred and thirty miles from San Francisco."

"The Gold Rush?" Artemus was amazed and secretly pleased. His younger brother had been an adventurer; he suddenly wished that he'd known Philip better.

"Yes, the Gold Rush," responded Samantha. "Four men came to our cabin one night, liquored and drunk. They wanted . . ." She hesitated and looked at her son. She tried to phrase it delicately.

"They wanted to take me out into the woods. Philip fought them off, but one of them shot him in the stomach. It took him a week to die."

"My poor Philip," said Abigail softly. Even if the story wasn't true, the thought of a lingering death chilled her.

"What did the men want with you?" asked Artemus. He knew the answer already.

Samantha looked at her son, then back to Artemus. Her eyes tried to tell him that she did not want to answer in front of the boy.

"Tell my aunt where you came from and what you did in California," said Artemus.

"I grew up in Martinique, in the home of a gentleman." She offered nothing else.

"And why did you go to California if you lived happily on a Caribbean Island?"

"I was not happy." The anger cracked in her voice. "Slaves are never happy. I was given to a friend of my master as payment for a bet. The friend took me to California."

"For what purpose?"

"To go to the Gold Rush." She shifted uncomfortably on the edge of the settee.

The little boy sensed Artemus's hostility. He turned his body so that he stood between Artemus and his mother.

"Your master certainly didn't drag you to California because you could swing a pick and shovel. From what I know of the Gold Rush, the only women to be found there are whores. Isn't that how my brother met you?"

After a time, she nodded, almost imperceptibly.

"What's a whore, Mama?" asked the boy softly.

"It's a job that women do, dear. Hard work. Bad work."

Abigail would not believe that the woman in front of her had married Philip Pratt. She could accept that Philip would fornicate with someone from the lower classes. She had done it many times herself. But he would not marry a Negress and make a black child heir to the Pratt fortune. "How long had you been with Philip before the child was born?"

"Eight months."

"You mean you were having other men at the time?" asked Artemus, almost gleefully.

"Philip came in almost every night for the whole two months before I moved to his tent. He loved me and he wanted me. Once, when he had a big strike, he bought me for a week. Old Cheverus, my master, he did not want me to go, but Philip gave him two hundred dollars, and that is when we . . ." She glanced at the boy, who was listening closely, understanding little. She embraced him. "That is when we made our baby. I know it. I just know it. And so did Philip."

"How did you get your freedom?" asked Abigail.

"Philip shot Cheverus. A fair fight. After that, no one dared to say that Philip Pratt had no right to me. Men did not challenge such a marksman."

Her nephew a gunfighter, a murderer. Abigail found no romance in the image.

"Were you married legally?" asked Artemus.

"There were few ministers, and most judges appointed themselves. Philip did not see the need."

Artemus advanced on Samantha. "You have no proof of marriage, you don't know who fathered this boy, and yet—"

The boy kicked Artemus squarely in the shin, then jumped back to his mother's side.

Samantha grabbed the boy and shook him angrily by the shoulder. "Don't you dare to kick at people. Say you're sorry."

"That won't be necessary," announced Artemus as he rubbed his shin. "Unless my aunt has any objection, I think we can show you the door."

Abigail said nothing, much to Artemus's relief. He did not relish the possibilities of a new Pratt dipping into his children's inheritance.

The black girl looked at the two faces before her. She realized that they were going to reject her. "You cannot do this. Philip told us that you would care for us. I worked for nothing on a schooner to get to Boston. I cooked the captain's meals and slept in the captain's bed while my little boy sat for five months and listened to sailors' dirty stories and stared at empty sea. You cannot put us out."

"I will not allow a Negro prostitute to join my family simply because she says she had carnal relations with my nephew. You have no proof that you married him, and I—"

Samantha stood angrily. "Damn, you lady. I do not lie. I have proof." She took a greasy, dog-eared envelope from her purse. "My proof is written here. I cannot read, but Philip made me memorize the words. '. . . that fury stay'd,/ Quencht in a Boggy Syrtis, neither Sea,/ Nor good dry land: nigh founder'd on he fares,/ Treading the crude consistence, half on foot,/ Half flying . . . / As when a Gryphon through the Wilderness/ With winged course o'er Hill or moory Dale,/ Pursues the Arim . . .'" She stumbled. Her recall was perfect. Her pronunciation was not. "'Arimaspian, who by stealth/ Had from his wakeful custody purloin'd/ The guarded gold: So eagerly the fiend/ O'er bog or steep, through strait, rough, dense, or rare,/ With head, hands, wings, or feet pursues his way,/ And swims or sinks, or wades, or creeps, or flies.'"

Abigail was shocked. The proof was undeniable. She had given Philip the quotation from *Paradise Lost* ten years before. She looked at Artemus, who never blinked.

"Do you know what any of this means?" he asked.

"Philip said you would trust me after you heard those words. He said you would believe me and take care of us. He said you would give my boy his due."

Artemus gave his aunt no chance to soften. "We don't have the slightest idea what you're talking about."

"But Philip gave me these words. He told me they were the key to a treasure."

"What kind of treasure?"

She hesitated. "I . . . I am not sure. He was dying when he told me. He kept talking about a golden bird and tea for the President. I don't know what he meant."

"It is entirely possible," said Artemus, "that you took this envelope from my brother after he had been waylaid by your accomplices, and now you're trying to take advantage of it." Artemus knew that the girl had been his brother's lover, but that did not entitle her bastard son to a piece of the Pratt empire. "Mr. Mannion."

Sean stepped into the room. "Yes, sir."

"Show this woman out."

"No!" screamed Samantha. "I come to you for help. I have no place to go. No money. No job. You cannot treat me like garbage." She thrust the boy at Abigail. She sensed that, in the long run, Abigail's authority would be greater than the man's. "This is your flesh and blood. One of your kin."

Abigail felt no maternal impulses toward the half-breed boy, who resembled her nephew only in his dislike for Artemus. She felt no warmth for his Negro mother, a whore who had enticed Philip Pratt with the charms between her legs. And yet she pitied them. They looked so pathetic in the elegance of a Boston sitting room. "Can you cook, young lady?"

"My master on Martinique sent me to study with the best chef on the island."

"Sean's wife has been complaining lately of too much work. You have a week in the kitchen to prove your worth. As for the boy, we will help him with his education and see that he learns a trade."

Samantha did not smile or thank Abigail. She had hoped for more. She did not expect them to treat her as an equal, but her son was an heir. He was entitled to more than a few years of education.

"Take this woman and her son downstairs, Sean, and show her the kitchen. You will have to fashion living quarters for them in the carriage house."

"Yes, Mrs. Bentley."

"And what do they call you, young woman?" asked Abigail.

"Samantha. Samantha Pratt."

"They do not call you Samantha Pratt in Boston," commanded Abigail.

"But that's my name. And Philip's."

"Nor do you call the boy Philip."

"I call him that after his father."

"Young woman." Abigail stood imperiously. "I am offering you a position out of the goodness of my heart. I do not look upon you as a niece or upon that boy as a grandnephew. You are not Pratts! Do you understand?"

"But we are," said Samantha weakly.

Instinctively, the little boy wrapped his arm around his mother's waist. She had always been strong, but these two people had worn her down in a single day. He sensed that she needed to hold onto him. His eyes shifted toward Artemus.

"Miss . . . what did they call you before you met my brother?" Artemus spoke softly now. His voice was soothing and gentle.

"Cawley . . . Samantha Cawley."

"Miss Cawley," he continued, "I do not approve of my aunt's generosity. I believe that you should be charged with fraud, because I don't for a moment believe the story you are telling us. But I will respect my aunt's wishes if you do the same and refrain from calling yourself a Pratt."

Samantha was beaten. She had no other choice. She took her son by the hand and followed Sean Mannion down to the kitchen.

Abigail returned to the high-backed chair by the window. The afternoon sun had arrived like an old friend. She sat in its glow, put her head back, and closed her eyes. Dust particles illuminated by the rays of the sun danced about her head like snowflakes in a crystal paperweight. She wanted to think of nothing but the warmth. She wanted to sleep, as she always did when the sun visited her room. But today, she couldn't. Samantha's face stayed in her head—that

261

Negro and Abigail's beautiful nephew, the two of them rutting away in some lice-filled cabin on the other side of the world.

Artemus sat in the shadows and waited for Abigail to open her eyes. Usually, the arrival of the sun was his signal to leave, but he knew that his aunt would not sleep this afternoon.

"She's very beautiful," he said. "And she has one of the keys to your treasure."

"She has a phrase. As long as I keep her in my service and in my debt, I can guarantee that she will have nothing more."

"Purloined gold in a boggy place that is neither sea nor good, dry land. Was my father right? Are we talking about the Golden Eagle Tea Set and the Back Bay?"

Abigail smiled. "We're talking about a dream, dear, a dream of beauty, of riches, of Pratt greatness in every generation."

Artemus smiled. He was always amused by his aunt's vision. "It's good to dream, Abigail. We all need dreams."

"You've had plans, not dreams, and you've fulfilled every one as though you were a machine in your shoe factory cutting out a new pattern for next year's fashion. You must have wild, exciting dreams. You must dream of things you can never achieve. You must imagine things you will never see, hope for things that can never come true."

"Like family purity and superiority, now that Pratt blood runs in the veins of a Negro child?" Before he had finished speaking, Artemus knew the remark was ill-chosen.

Abigail stood in anger. "Do not say that! I have taken that child into our home because I am a Christian. Even if Philip Pratt fathered him, he isn't a Pratt. Philip Pratt left us in hatred. He left us to punish us for what he believes we did to your father. This black child is an extension of that punishment, an attempt to blot our shield. Well, I am not chastised and I do not accept the child."

She turned and gazed out toward the Back Bay, just visible through the trees on the far side of the Botanical Garden. It was high tide, and the sun was reflecting off the sheet of water. "My child is out there, the only part of me that will live after I'm gone." The anger left her voice. "Just once would I like to see it. The box must be heavy iron, with great rivets and heavy chains and inner boxes of wood and copper. Sean could shoot off the chains, and we'd open the box, and there would be the red velvet lining, so smooth and soft. And then, we'd see it shining brilliantly in the sun, the most beautiful . . ." She stopped and looked at Artemus.

He smiled. "You can continue. I'll never tell."

"Then there would be no mystery for you and no secret for me, and I think you like the mystery in spite of yourself."

He smiled. He assumed it was the tea set, and it did not interest him in the least.

"I would like to see it though, just once," she said dreamily.

"Go out and dig it up, have your look, then bury it again."

"I'm afraid I'd be disappointed, dear. I'd rather just imagine it." She paused, and her voice filled with bitterness. "It's better to dream of what your golden children may be than it is to see their black offspring."

Artemus stood by her side and squinted into the sun. "Soon, the filling will begin. One day, there will be enough land on the other side of Arlington Street to build a whole row of houses. Then there'll be another street and another until the flats are filled from the Public Garden to Gravelly Point. The Back Bay will slowly be drained, and, eventually, your golden child will sit under a foot or two of mud and gravel. The scavengers will pick through the area looking for junk in the landfill—"

"I know. I've seen them working through the mud along Arlington Street."

"And one of them will stumble across the most valuable piece of junk since the Holy Grail."

"We will protect it, Artemus. We will protect it from black interlopers and Back Bay scavengers. When its security is threatened, we'll find a way. But until they drain the bay, it is safe."

In 1858, the Commonwealth of Massachusetts authorized the filling of the lands west of Arlington Street. One of the largest engineering operations of the nineteenth century was begun. By 1861, sixteen full blocks had been completed and building had already commenced in the Back Bay.

From her windows on Colonnade Row, Abigail had watched the operation closely. Twenty-five times a day, trains arrived at the Back Bay depot carrying gravel fill from the hills of Needham. Every day, less water was admitted through the Mill Dam gates, and the unfilled portions of the receiving basin became a great open sewer. At the end of 1861, the tea set was still under water, but the landfill moved a few feet closer to it every day.

In April of that year, the Civil War had begun, and at Christmas, a melancholy Pratt family gathered for three days of feasting before the war took them away.

Artemus was bound for England. He had been summoned by Charles Francis Adams, Union ambassador to the Court of St. James's. Artemus was to represent Northern business interests to English textile manufacturers, whose flow of Southern cotton had diminished and whose influence might bring England into the war on the side of the Confederacy. Artemus was taking his wife, his two youngest children, and Sarah, his eldest. He was leaving the operation of Pratt Shipping, Mining, and Manufacturing in the hands of his brother, Elihu. While he did not leave willingly, he went with the knowledge that the war would be profitable, since he and Elihu had secured government contracts for the production of arms, shoes, and uniforms.

Three young Pratts—Artemus Jr., twenty-two; Jason, twenty; and Elihu's son Francis, also twenty—wore the uniform of the Union Army. All three had joined the Twenty-fifth Regiment of Massachusetts Volunteers. Artemus Jr. and Francis, considered by Abigail to be the brightest young men of the new Pratt generation, were lieutenants. Jason, after two years of medical studies, was bound for a field hospital. Five months later, at the Battle of Fair Oaks, Jason would remove a shard of grapeshot from his brother's shoulder and pronounce his cousin dead.

On Christmas Day, the men convened in the sitting room to discuss the unfortunate course of the war and the folly of electing Lincoln over Stephen A. Douglas. The wives and daughters gathered in the kitchen to help Mrs. Mannion prepare the Christmas feast. And Abigail retired to the study.

In front of the fire, she poured herself a glass of port and opened her diary. She was drinking port more often now. It was good for the circulation, and it kept her warm on cold winter nights. As Sean always told her, a woman as active as herself deserved an extra glass every now and then.

Abigail laughed softly. Sean had a little saying for everything. He had been her servant for almost forty years, and she often wondered if she could live without his companionship. Occasionally, on a lonely day, she wondered what her life might have been like had she spent it with Sean Mannion at her side, rather than in her service. She stared at the fire and remembered the feel of his strong arms around her waist. He was a fine man, and Abigail was grateful that he had married a good woman.

There was a knock.

"Come," said Abigail.

Philip Cawley entered the study. He was now twelve years old. In his gait and physique, he resembled Philip Pratt more with every visit. He spent his holidays with the Pratts, and during the rest of the year, he boarded at a trade school in Worcester. Philip Cawley was an orphan. Within a few weeks of entering Abigail's service, Philip's mother had begun to cough blood. At Abigail's urging and with Abigail's support, she entered a home for consumptives, where she had died eight months later.

For a time after his mother's death, Philip Cawley lived in the servant's quarters at Colonnade Row, but he was hostile and incorrigible. When he was eight, Abigail shipped him to Worcester, where his toughness and independence helped him to survive among boys much older than himself.

Whenever he visited the Pratts, he remembered how much he hated them. At trade school, he had earned respect; no one dared mock him for his strange features and uncertain color. In the Pratt household, he felt like a stray dog, tolerated for a few days until his owner came to claim him.

Abigail opened her arms and spoke with a gaiety as transparent as glass. "Come here and give Mrs. Bentley a nice kiss."

Philip pecked her on the cheek and gave her a package wrapped crudely in green paper. "Merry Christmas, Miz Bentley."

"Why, thank you, Philip. You'll find something special beneath the tree in the parlor."

The boy didn't move. He wanted to see her face when she opened her gift.

She fumbled with the ribbon and wrapping and unveiled a copy of Charles Dickens's newest novel, *Great Expectations*. She embraced him and kissed him on the forehead. "Oh, Philip, it's beautiful. I shall treasure it. But it must have cost you a great deal of money."

"I wanted to give you something nice," he said.

"I hope you inscribed it." She opened the book and saw an ornate bookplate on the inside flap. "It's exquisite."

"I did it in engravin' class," he said proudly.

Against a border of laurel and ivy, the boy had etched the words *Ex Libris* and Abigail's name. Below that, in flowing script, he had inscribed the lines from a poem. Abigail read to herself the quotation she had given to Philip Pratt in 1845, the quotation recalled by Samantha Cawley the day she appeared at Colonnade Row. Her expression froze.

Philip smiled. "I learned that poem from my father. I thought you would like it."

Abigail glared at the child. He knew what he had done. She could see the mischievous glint in his eye. She was infuriated.

"Have you printed more of these?" she demanded.

"I made them for all my books. And I lend my books to my friends." He tried to look innocent. He had upset her more than he had hoped.

"Do you know what these words mean?"

"That Satan is all around us. He can swim. He can crawl. He can even fly. And he's always ready to steal our gold and our soul."

"What else?"

"They tell of a treasure. That's what my father told my mother, and my mother told me."

"Yes. The treasure of everlasting life. If you live well and keep your vigilance against Satan. That's what these lines tell you, and that's all. It's a good lesson, one you should learn to live by."

"I live by what my mama taught me—don't ever 'spect people to do nothin' good if they don't have to. Always do for yourself. Merry Christmas, Miz Bentley." Without being dismissed, the boy turned and left the room.

Merry Christmas, indeed, thought Abigail. She had done more for the little mulatto than anyone should. She had buried his mother, housed him, sent him to school, and set up a small trust fund which would be his on his twenty-first birthday. Yet he chose to torment her. She tore the bookplate off the flap and tossed it into the fire.

She could burn it, but she could never erase his knowledge or his hatred.

CHAPTER XVI

The beer always did it. About six in the morning, Fallon had to piss. He staggered to the bathroom door and bumped into Evangeline on her way back to bed.

"Good morning," he croaked.

"Hi." She brushed past him. She was wearing a man's flannel pajama top and nothing else.

Maybe it was the clothes, he thought, but she seemed loveliest in the morning. The ivory skin above the tan line peaked out enticingly as she moved away from him, and he followed her into her room.

She climbed into bed and pulled the covers over her head. "Go away."

"I'm cold," he said.

"Then don't stand in the middle of the room in your jockey shorts."

"Can I come in and talk?"

She lowered the covers just enough to look over them. "Are you kidding?"

He laughed.

She pulled the covers over her head again. "I'll be out in the spring."

"I'd stay around to watch, but I have to piss."

When he came out of the bathroom, Evangeline was dressed and pouring coffee. "Long piss," she said. "Noisy, too."

"That was the shower."

She handed him a cup of coffee and toasted with her own.

"To the end of this foolishness."

"To the beginning."

Route 95 led them back into humidity near the New Hampshire border. As they entered Massachusetts, rain began to fall. Evangeline became tense. Her hands wrapped tight around the wheel and she concentrated hard on the road in front of her. She was driving in and out of heavy rain, but something more than the weather was bothering her. She didn't want the foolishness to end just yet. Last night, she had told Fallon things she had not spoken of in years. The fight at Searidge, the afternoon analyzing Abigail Pratt Bentley, and the walk on the beach had drawn them together. She was afraid that if Fallon went back to his work, the excitement she was beginning to feel in his presence would evaporate. She wanted to give him more time. She wanted more time to get to know him.

Evangeline parked at the Quincy Market, and her mood began to improve.

"You want to help me open the place up?" she asked.

"No thanks. I'll wait here."

"It's a good show. I sing a lot and I talk to the plants."

"Do they talk back?"

"They haven't yet."

"Then I'll stay here."

Evangeline hurried into the North Market and up the circular staircase to the second floor. As she passed the Building Block, a children's store specializing in wooden toys, she did not notice the man with the receding hairline and pockmarked face. He was studying a display of wooden trains in the store window, but he was watching for her.

Evangeline walked to the end of the arcade, where Kathy Kelly, her nineteen-year-old assistant, was waiting for her. Kathy worked part time to help pay for her college education.

Evangeline opened the store and helped Kathy put it in order. A brief chat, a few instructions on the care of the African violets, which had lately begun to droop, a check on the dampness of the Boston ferns, which needed careful watering, and she was on her way.

She walked straight into the tweed sportcoat. She began to apologize, then she saw the face. The pockmarked skin was drawn tight over cheekbone and skull, like a mask through which the eyes studied her.

For a moment, she stared, then stammered, "Excuse me."

He said nothing, and she hurried past.

The man watched her mix into the crowd of morning shoppers, but he didn't let her out of his sight. He followed her down the stairs to the plaza, and she led him, as he expected, to Peter Fallon. He instinctively reached for his pistol. But not yet. He had no orders to use it yet.

The Porsche pulled away, and the man walked back to the pay phones in the plaza. He placed a call. "The student is with the girl."

Evangeline parked in front of her uncle's Back Bay townhouse, on the corner of Commonwealth and Clarendon.

Butler John Holt, a relic from the days of Artemus IV, greeted them at the front door. "Good morning, Miss Carrington."

Fallon and Evangeline stepped into the vestibule, and Fallon was struck immediately by the richness, the quiet, the confident elegance. Since the end of World War II, many of the finest Back Bay homes had been converted to apartments, professional offices, condominiums, and fraternity houses. But the Pratt home, like a handful of others, had endured. Mahogany woodwork, Italian marble, parquet floors, rich carpeting, stained-glass windows, and carved balustrades on the monumental staircase, and all of it existing with a sense of reserve that was uniquely Bostonian. The dining room was to the left of the reception hall. To the right, behind glass doors, the music room ran the length of the house. An office-study was tucked neatly into a corner. The receiving room, a downstairs living room furnished in exquisite taste, overlooked Commonwealth Avenue.

Fallon felt a hundred years of life lived as it should be—serenity, order, and grace on every side, an abiding sense of the past, a confident face toward the future, and all in the middle of the city. As he climbed the staircase and passed the library, the billiard room, and the parlor, Fallon wondered how his knowledge of an ancient tea set could upset the equanimity of this world. Perhaps the full story that Philip Pratt had promised would disappoint him. Perhaps there was no treasure at all.

On the third and fourth floors, the furniture and ambience became more modern, almost as if the house had been decorated from the bottom up over a hundred years. Fallon realized that Philip Pratt spent most of his time on the top two floors. Past and present did not coexist so harmoniously after all.

Pratt's study, which looked across the roofs of Marlborough Street toward M.I.T., was dominated by blond mahogany desk and bookshelves, glass and chrome tables, Eames leather furnishings, and track lighting. Calvin Pratt, looking stolid and unhappy, stood near the windows. Soames sat in the corner with a notepad on his knee. An unfamiliar man reclined on the sofa, and Philip Pratt sat behind his desk.

"Hello, Vange. How are you?" Philip Pratt stood and offered his hand.

Evangeline hated Philip's nickname for her, probably because he only used it when he was trying to charm her. She shook his hand, and he kissed her lightly on the cheek. Then, she introduced Peter Fallon.

"I only wish we'd met under less strained circumstances," said Pratt.

Fallon was surprised by Pratt's friendly handshake.

Pratt gestured to the man on the sofa, who stood. "I'd like to present Lawrence Hannaford. Cousin, friend, and trusted associate."

Hannaford smiled. He was dressed impeccably in a gray Cardin suit and blue tie. He had hair the color of Pratt's desk, a tan, and features that were almost perfect. His attitude proclaimed youth and success. "I heard that you were trying to see me last week when I was out of town, so I thought I'd bring the mountain to Mohammed."

Philip Pratt invited Fallon and Evangeline to sit, then he began. "You two have stumbled onto something very bizarre, and we've decided to explain the details to you, primarily because you know enough already to be in danger, but you don't know enough to stay out of the way."

"Where's my grandmother?" asked Evangeline abruptly.

"She's very upset, dear—"

"Skip the endearment, Uncle. Just tell me where I can find her."

Pratt's smile never wavered. "Show your elders their respect,

270

Evangeline, or somebody may cut off one of your trust funds and you'll end up by selling dandelions on a pushcart instead of greening America from the Quincy Market."

Before Evangeline could respond, Calvin began to speak. "The first thing that you two should know is that we're dealing with a dangerous group of art forgers."

"And the tea set in the museum is one of their products?" asked Fallon.

"The tea set in the museum," said Hannaford firmly, "is the original. The forgery had been completed about the time I was first contacted by the real owner, the anonymous English owner, in September of 1972. We began negotiations soon thereafter."

"Is this the family that supposedly got the tea set after it was stolen from Sir Henry Carrol?"

"You've done your homework well," said Soames.

"While we were talking in England," continued Hannaford, "I was approached by a gentleman who said that he represented a syndicate devoted to the recovery of missing art treasures. He said he had reason to believe that the tea set I was about to buy was a forgery. First he told me politely, then more forcefully. I said that I was convinced of the authenticity of the set I had seen, and he responded by threatening to reveal me if I tried to present the tea set to the world.

"I informed the proper authorities, both in Europe and the United States, about this gentleman, and went ahead with my negotiations. The FBI told me that, in recent years, several important works in silver and gold, works which had disappeared during the last two centuries, had been recovered. Art authorities had not been able to disprove the authenticity of any of the works, but there remained—there remains—a nagging suspicion that all these works have come from the same forge."

"How does the Pratt family fit into all of this?" asked Fallon.

"As you know," said Philip Pratt, "certain elements of fact and legend connect our family to the Golden Eagle Tea Set. This syndicate is aware of the legend and is trying to use it. About the time that Lawrence first showed the tea set to the public, we were approached by the syndicate. We were told that Lawrence Hannaford had produced a forgery, and we were asked if we would help the syndicate locate the real tea set. Being friends and relatives of Lawrence Hannaford, we informed him."

"You see," said Calvin, as if on cue, "part of the legend has to do with a set of clues, supposedly held by members of the Pratt family, that tell the location of the Golden Eagle. By producing the clues and presenting the forgery to Hannaford, the syndicate hopes to black-mail him."

"But if you have the real tea set, you have nothing to worry about," said Fallon.

"Perhaps, but I never have revealed the name of the tea set's English owner. It was one of the stipulations when I first entered into a relationship with him. He still prefers his anonymity, but it has left me in a rather vulnerable position."

"And what about the FBI?" asked Fallon.

"The gentleman whom you very nearly threw off the Searidge roof yesterday is an agent," said Soames.

"I don't believe it," said Evangeline.

"Do you recall when Harrison entered our employment?" asked Pratt.

"Two years ago."

"And two years ago," offered Soames, "all this began in earnest. After the Pratts refused to cooperate in 1973, the syndicate let the matter drop for a while. But a first-rate forgery may cost a hundred thousand dollars to produce. They weren't going to charge that to profit and loss. So they waited a few years, then began to move on Hannaford."

Fallon shook his head. It all sounded convincing, but he didn't want to accept any of it, least of all the part about the FBI.

He recalled the name of William Rule and mentioned it to Hannaford. He felt a momentary hesitation, as though the room had gone over a bump. Then, Hannaford explained that Rule was a close associate who had helped arrange the Golden Eagle deal.

Evangeline was becoming confused by the story and realized they were all forgetting the central character. "Where is Grandmother?"

"Under protective custody in a nursing home," said Philip. "Christopher's death has deeply upset her. That's the main reason she is now under doctor's care. However, she is also a rather easy target for people who would like to extract information from her. You've discovered that yourself, Mr. Fallon. We want to protect her completely."

"When can I see her?" asked Evangeline.

"When the doctor permits. At the moment, he does not want her to see anyone who might remind her of Christopher."

"As for you, Mr. Fallon," Calvin Pratt's courtroom voice rang from the corner of the room, "we would suggest that you get back to your own business. Until we investigated your background—a process not completed until this morning, hence the little scene yesterday—we thought you were working for the syndicate." Calvin calculated a long pause. "Now, we fear for your life. We fear for both of you."

"As long as you keep yourself in the middle of all this," said Philip, "You're in danger. Go back to your pursuits, both of you, and you probably won't have anything to worry about."

"How can we be sure of that?" asked Evangeline.

"By telling us what you know." answered Soames. "Once we've ascertained that, we can determine the amount of protection you may need."

Fallon hesitated. Perhaps this was the whole point of the meeting. He didn't want to give away information. Then he decided that he might learn more by telling them everything. He recounted his research for the last two weeks, from Dexter Lovell's note to Abigail Pratt Bentley's 1845, diary. When he mentioned the diary, he could sense sudden interest. He guessed he had found something they all had missed.

"The diary tells us that in 1845, the tea set was still sitting in the mud in the Back Bay." Fallon looked at Hannaford. "In your history of the tea set, you said that Dexter Lovell probably took the tea set to England after the British burned the White House. How could you be so far off?"

"We didn't have access to Abigail Pratt Bentley's diaries at the time. Our researchers theorized on whatever information they had. You're a historian. I'm sure you've done the same thing many times." Hannaford showed no discomfort.

"But historians shouldn't present their theories as fact." Fallon tried to press him.

Hannaford backed away gracefully. "You'll be pleased to know that we're revising our story to fit more closely with the few Bentley diaries that still exist. We now think that the tea set was found by scavengers digging through the landfill in the 1860s. A smart art dealer bought it for a song from the scavengers, then sold it in England to Sir Henry Carrol."

Fallon dropped the subject and asked no one in particular how the name of Jack C. Ferguson fitted into the story.

Mr. Soames wrote Ferguson's name on his scratch pad, then the words, "FIND HIM."

"At first," said Calvin Pratt, "we thought that he was part of the blackmailing operation."

"The article," said Hannaford, "seemed like the first broadside in the attack. Then, of course, Ferguson disappeared."

Fallon decided not to tell them that Jack C. Ferguson had visited his apartment a few days earlier. Instead, he asked them about Christopher Carrington's death.

For a moment, the room was silent. Fallon could feel them all studying him, all except Soames, whose eyes remained glued to his notepad.

"The police determined that his death was a suicide," said Philip Pratt firmly.

"No possibility that somebody killed him because of his knowledge?"

"What did he know that was so special?" asked Soames without looking up.

"He was the family historian. He knew more about the Pratts and probably more about the tea set than anybody else."

Philip Pratt stood slowly. Evangeline could see him hit one of his internal switches. The glib businessman became the friendly confidant who sat on the edge of his desk, casually swung his legs, and counseled a friend.

"We deeply, sincerely appreciate your concern, Mr. Fallon . . . Peter. But my nephew committed suicide. That's what the authorities believe. That's what we believe." He took Fallon's hand in both of his, the gesture of a comforting friend. "If there's anything that we can do to help you with your work, please let us know. But I urge you to get back to it."

"You're getting the suave brushoff," said Evangeline. "Let's go."

Fallon thanked them politely, which Evangeline found rather surprising, and told them he would be going back to his work. Then, he and Evangeline headed for the staircase.

After they were gone, Pratt turned to Hannaford. "Larry, I want to thank you. I wanted my niece out of danger."

"I'm always happy to convince someone to stop searching for a tea set I found years ago. I wish I could convince you."

Pratt took Hannaford's hand in both of his. "We're doing our best to protect you. I wouldn't want to injure the career of an old friend."

Hannaford smiled. He liked Philip Pratt, in spite of everything. "Save your crocodile tears, Philip, and invite me up to play tennis more often. You must know that it's an absolute bitch to get court time anyplace in this city."

"Take good care, and if any more Dali engravings come your way, remember that I'm at the top of your list."

The rain had stopped. The sun was poking a few tentative shafts down through the trees along Commonwealth Avenue. A southerly breeze had begun to blow, but the air was still thick and moist. The rain had simply aggravated the heat.

Peter Fallon leaned against a lamppost at the corner of Commonwealth Avenue and Clarendon Street and gazed down the arcade of elms on the mall. Autos sped past and the noise of the city was all about.

"Are you really going to go back to your work?" asked Evangeline.

Fallon shook his head. "I don't want to."

"Do you think the scavengers found the tea set?"

He shrugged.

"Well, dammit, do you believe anything they told us in there?"

"They had an answer for everything." He had been convinced of nothing, but the Pratts had created doubts. He realized that he had nearly killed a man the day before, and it didn't matter whether the man was with the FBI. Fallon's excitement wasn't worth anyone's life. Maybe this was like one of his benders, and he should quit now, while he still had the chance. Then he thought about Ferguson and Rule and wondered what they could tell him. He shook his head.

Evangeline was disappointed. She did not expect him to seem so confused. "I don't know what to believe either, Peter. But I can't be standing on Commonwealth Avenue staring off into space. I'm going to see if I can find my grandmother, then I'm going to work. Come to my house for dinner. We'll talk then." Evangeline climbed into her car.

Fallon crossed Clarendon Street and started down Commonwealth Avenue toward Kenmore Square. He remembered that the Red Sox were playing an afternoon game at Fenway.

CHAPTER XVII   *October 1863*

Abigail Pratt Bentley and Artemus Pratt stood on the corner of Commonwealth Avenue and Clarendon Street, at the edge of the Back Bay landfill. New lands—flat, dusty, neatly segmented into lots and streets—stretched from the Boston and Worcester Railroad tracks to the Mill Dam and from the Public Garden to Clarendon Street. Beyond Clarendon, the water receded daily as the landfill moved west. The Back Bay had been covered a third of the way to Gravelly Point in a layer of sand, gravel, and trash twenty feet deep.

This would be the new home of Boston's aristocracy, and Abigail Pratt Bentley was certain that one day it would be a beautiful place. Few of the lots beyond Arlington and Beacon Streets were occupied. The houses on other completed blocks stood like volunteers, with proud fronts and blank brick sides, waiting for their ranks to be filled. And as yet, there was not a tree west of the Public Garden capable of giving shade on a hot day. But the trees would grow, and the homes already built had set a criterion of French Empire elegance that others would follow. Abigail imagined an American Paris.

"This is where we'll build," said Artemus, recently returned from his mission in England. "As soon as the war is over and the land is judged stable."

"My father would have cackled for a week if we had ever told him we were going to build a mansion on the Back Bay flats."

Abigail squinted into the afternoon sun and looked toward the Easterly Channel, now just a few hundred feet away. It was a rut in the mud, covered by three feet of water at high tide, a bare trickle at low. To the south, a mile or so away, she saw landfill stretching out from the Neck to join the new lands in the Back Bay. Southwest of the Neck stood the handsome brownstone bowfronts of the South End, built in the fifties and already doomed to slow decay by the development of the Back Bay. Like her father before her, she shuddered at the changes she had seen in fifty years. They had come so quickly.

"Cynthia and I want you to know," said Artemus softly, "that you will have a bedroom and a sitting room on the fourth floor. You shouldn't be living alone."

Abigail thought that she had come out to see the site of her nephew's home. She was shocked. "Except for Sean and his family, I've lived alone for almost forty years."

"And now we want you to move in with us. Artemus and Jason are grown men now. When they come back . . ." He hesitated. He remembered the death of Elihu's son Francis. "If they come back, they will probably wish to strike out on their own. So there will be plenty of room, and Cynthia thinks you would be a marvelous influence on the younger children. Besides, what use will a Boston mansion be unless it is filled with people?"

She kissed his cheek and brushed a tear from her eye. "I've never had children, but with you to love me like a son, I've never needed them."

"It's our loss that you never had children, Abigail. They would have been extraordinary."

She laughed. "They would also have competed with you for power, so don't mourn too loudly."

"I shan't. Now, are you living with us or not?"

She started to say that she would.

"Good mornin', folks!" Up from the mud of the Back Bay, dressed in filthy clothes, and carrying a sack, crawled a figure of indeterminate age and sex. It hoisted itself onto level land and stood face to face with the Pratts. "I said good mornin'. Are you deaf or somethin'?"

"Good morning," said Artemus coldly.

It curtsied and grinned. Apparently, it was a woman, and she wore her hostility proudly. Layers of dirt were caked on her neck and hands. She dropped her sack in front of Abigail, who stepped back instinctively and held her handkerchief to her nose.

"Stink, don't I?" said the woman. "I smell just like shit, 'cause that's mostly what's left down there on the flats. Shit and piss and stinkin' tidewater."

Artemus took Abigail by the arm. They turned to walk away, and the woman jumped in front of them.

"Don't be runnin' off so soon, folks. Give me a chance. It ain't often rich folks like you runs into somebody like me. I'm what you might call a . . . a curiosity, a Back Bay scavenger. There's hunnerts of us just now, and I'm one of the best. I lives damn good from the junk I dig outa the landfill. Looka here." She pulled a spoon from her sack and wiped it on the sleeve of her filthy sweater. "Gen-u-ine silver from the Crawford House. Got threw out with somebody's dinner and ended up here. Like to buy it?"

'No, thank you." Artemus tried to push past her.

She pulled out a wooden hoop. "For the lady's skirt?"

Artemus led Abigail past the scavenger woman and back toward the carriage.

"So you'll have nothin' to do with a woman of the earth?" she shrieked. She reached into her sack, pulled out a handful of oyster shells, and fired them at Artemus. "Take these. I sell them to the the Chink down on Stuart Street. He grinds 'em into powder and sells 'em to his friends. Says they make your cock stiff!"

"Disgusting," muttered Abigail. "Absolutely disgusting."

"Vermin like that are all over the landfill."

"I know," said Abigail softly. "Something must be done."

In the late afternoon, the winds shifted. By midnight, it was overcast and chilly. Abigail Pratt Bentley's carriage stopped at the corner of Commonwealth and Clarendon, at the edge of the landfill, and she climbed out. She was wearing heavy riding boots, an old tweed skirt, and a loose-fitting jacket that would give her freedom of movement. A strenuous evening lay ahead.

Sean Mannion jumped down from the box. "Are you sure you want to be doin' this, Mrs. Bentley? It's mighty wet and muddy out there."

"It must be done, Sean. By you and me and no one else. And you must promise never to reveal what you see tonight."

Sean promised without question. He took his pistol from the carriage boot, then swung two shovels and a pick onto his shoulder. He was fifty-six, still brawny and strong, but now weighed down by a paunch that hung over his trousers.

They found a switchback path, used by the dumping carts to haul landfill, and started down. A few steps and Abigail tripped over the leg of an old chair protruding from the gravel. She was seventy-three, but only recently had her age begun to slow her down.

"Shall I light the lantern?" asked Sean.

"No. We'll not attract attention. There's light enough."

The lands which surrounded the Back Bay were not as deserted as when Dexter Lovell had rowed into the Easterly Channel fifty years before. Light from streetlamps and homes reflected off the clouds and gave a dim, phosphorescent glow to the mudflats, tidepools, and sheets of water in the distance.

It was low tide. Since the building of the Mill Dam, the tide no longer flowed freely, and much of the bay was kept covered in a few feet of water, which lessened the stink of the polluted flats. However, during certain night tides, the water between the landfill and Gravelly Point was allowed to drain through the Mill Dam gates, so that some of the offending sewage was carried away. Tonight was such a night. There was nothing between the landfill and the Easterly Channel but mud.

Abigail looked out across the flats. She knew the distance from the Mill Dam, along the bed of the Easterly Channel, to the tea set. By walking west across the flats from the foot of Commonwealth Avenue, she could find the Easterly Channel. By following the Channel inland, she could pace out the distance to the tea set. But Abigail was frightened. By the darkness. By the scavengers. By the thought that she would not find the tea set. By the temptation she would face if the strongbox was there, the urge to open it and look, just once, at the Golden Eagle. She resolved that she would not look, then she stepped off the gravel at the bottom of the landfill and sank up to her ankles in mud.

"It'll be slow goin', Mrs. Bentley. You sure you don't want me to go alone and do what needs to be done?" Sean did not know why they were going out there; Abigail had never told him about the tea set.

"I must be present."

So they struggled across the mud until they reached the Easterly

Channel, a gentle depression about fifteen feet across which sloped three or four feet down to a small, putrid stream.

Any marsh produces gases, but the Back Bay had been an open sewage pit for many years, and out here in the middle of it, the stink was unbearable. Abigail gagged and leaned on her shovel for support. Even in the dark, Sean could see the color drain from her face. She was an old woman. She did not belong out here. He begged her to go back, but she refused.

"Follow the channel," she said. "Count off two hundred paces, and take care that each pace covers three feet."

A cold wind swept across the flats, and Abigail shivered.

Sean knew that it would be raining soon. "Please, let's go back, Mrs. Bentley. Nothing can be so important that you should endanger your health."

Abigail tenderly stroked his face. She hadn't touched him affectionately in many years. "Do you love your son, Sean?"

Sean's son Joseph was now a bricklayer with a small company of his own. Sean saw everything that his mother had hoped for in him reflected in his son. When he wasn't tending Abigail's needs—and the old woman had few—Sean worked for his son, pitching in with shovel, hammer, and trowel wherever needed. "More than my life."

"Then try to understand that I am out here because of my child and children yet unborn."

"Your child?"

Abigail smiled. "I speak symbolically, Sean. I learned the habit from a romantic young Irish poet I once knew." For a moment, she thought she saw the old look of admiration reflected dimly in his eyes, the look that had excited her so many years before. She took him by the arm and turned him upstream, toward the tea set. "Two hundred paces, two hundred yards. And we'd better move fast, before the tide turns and we're digging dirty water along with the mud."

They slogged off through darkness, following the dribble which had been a six-foot-deep channel when Dexter Lovell had navigated it. With each step, their boots seemed to sink deeper into the mud, as if something were trying to suck them down and hold them. The mud belched each time a foot pulled free. And each footprint filled quickly with water that obliterated any trace of their passing.

As she battled the mud, Abigail's fears for her own safety and the tea set's presence melted away. The Back Bay flats were cold, foul, depressing, and they led nowhere that was not more easily reached by land. No one but the most foolish schoolboy would cross the quagmire for any reason, and no one would be about on a chilly October night.

Sean stopped after about ten minutes and announced, "Two hundred paces."

Abigail's heart was pounding. In a few moments, it would be in her grasp. She hoped.

She told Sean they were looking for an iron box two to four feet beneath the mud. They staked a twenty-five-foot square of ground around the spot where Sean stopped, then, foot by foot, they drove their shovels into the mud within the square. After fifteen minutes, they heard clank of metal against metal. Sean found the strongbox in three feet of gravel and mud, halfway up the side of the channel bed. The ground above it was raised slightly, as though a log had been buried there.

Sean took off his coat, wrapped his pistol in it, and gave them to Abigail. Then he began to dig. At low tide, no water covered the strongbox, but water seeped into the hole from below, making the work difficult and sloppy.

At least it wasn't buried beneath that reeking stream a few feet away, thought Abigail.

Sean fought with every shovelful of mud. The ooze stuck to itself, to his boots, and to the shovel, but he didn't stop until he was scraping the mud from the top of the strongbox.

As he knelt to lift it out of the hole, Abigail swallowed hard and crouched beside him.

Sean scraped the mud from the handles and pulled. Half the box was still buried, and it didn't budge. He picked up the shovel and began to dig around it. Abigail watched for a moment, then she grabbed a shovel and attacked the mud with him.

They were soon standing knee-deep in the hole, with the box free of mud and ready to be lifted. Abigail realized now how large it was. So much iron and so many locks to protect Paul Revere's lost masterpiece. On one of the handles, she saw rotted strands of rope. She remembered how her nephew had died.

"Stand back, Mrs. Bentley."

Abigail stepped out of the hole. Sean grabbed a handle with both hands, grunted, and heaved. The box weighed close to seventy-five pounds, but once he broke the suction, he was able to flip it out of the hole.

Now came the moment that Abigail had feared. She knelt beside the box and ran her hand along its surface. The iron was pitted and caked with mud, but she could almost see shafts of silver light flashing through the cracks and seams. She wanted to touch the tea set. Desperately. She wanted to feel the smoothness, the grace, the solidity. If it was as beautiful as she thought, perhaps the world should see it. She would be revered as a patroness of the arts. She would be famous as the woman who uncovered the Golden Eagle Tea Set. She touched one of the padlocks. She was tempted.

Sean didn't help. He thought they had dug it up to bring it back. He stepped out of the hold and, with some effort, raised the strongbox to his shoulder. "We'd best be gettin' off these flats, Mrs. Bentley. We don't want to be caught here when the tide turns."

She said nothing. She knelt in the mud and watched blankly as he balanced the box.

"Shall we be goin'?"

"No," she said firmly. The world would not remember her. The world would never care that she left the tea set for all to enjoy. Only her father's descendants would think of her. They would remember her as the woman who navigated Pratt Shipping and Mercantile when Jason Pratt was at the helm. They would remember her as the guardian of the family treasure, the protector of the family secret. And the day might come, as her father had predicted, when her descendants would need the Golden Eagle. Then, Abigail Pratt Bentley would live again.

"Put it down," she commanded.

He dropped the box. "What else is there to do?"

"Dig the hole deeper. Another three feet."

Sean was confused. "Are we looking for something else?"

"We've come to protect that strongbox from marauders, to roll a stone across the mouth of the tomb."

"You want me to bury it? Why?"

"We have little time, Sean. I'll explain it all later. I promise."

A scream slashed across the mudflats, followed by the pounding of cylinders and the clatter of forty cars crossing steel rails: the gravel train from Needham. In the dark, the engine looked like an apparition, with the yellow light of the headlamp lancing across the flats, the sparks pouring from the stack, the cockpit glowing hellish orange behind the boiler. The whistle screamed again, and Boston streets arrived at the landfill.

"The next train crosses in forty-five minutes, Sean. By then, the tide will be turning. Please hurry."

Sean made no further argument. Forty-five minutes later, the hole was three feet deeper and three feet square. He leaned the shovel against the side of the hole and used it as a step to boost himself out.

They had an hour before the Easterly Channel was again covered in three feet of water.

"Is it six feet deep?" she asked.

"As near as I can figure."

"It must be exact."

"I'm five-ten. The hole was five or six inches over my head."

"Then we've buried it six feet, three inches below the mud."

"Not yet." The voice growled out of the darkness behind Abigail and felt like the blade of a knife against her neck.

There were three of them. The one who spoke held a Navy Colt revolver at his side. He was tall and scrawny, just barely visible behind an eyepatch and a black beard. His jacket, blue trimmed with yellow piping, belonged to a Union soldier. He was probably a deserter. The other two, smaller and scrawnier, stood behind him in the darkness. One held a club, the other a knife.

"Two old geezers buryin' a box in the middle of the night. You got family jewels or somethin' in there?"

Abigail said nothing. Sean looked toward the pistol, which lay wrapped in his coat on top of the strongbox.

"I'd like to look at what's in that box," said the deserter. "Might be it's somethin' look good in my boodwar."

His mates snickered, as though he'd told a dirty joke.

Abigail took a step to her right, placing her body between the strongbox and the three men. Sean cursed her stupidity to himself. Then she glanced at him, and he realized that she was giving him a shield. He would not use it.

The deserter stepped toward her. "Now which of you folks has the key?"

Abigail looked again at Sean.

A whistle screamed, and the deserter looked toward the tracks. Sean threw Abigail to the ground and grabbed the pistol. He fired twice. The deserter went down. As the man with the club came at him, Sean fired again; the man's face disappeared. The man with the knife leaped. Sean squeezed off another shot, but the man piled into him and they fell to the ground. The knife slashed viciously, expertly, cutting across Sean's rib cage and flying at his face. Sean grabbed the man's throat and held tight. As the gravel train arrived at the depot, the knife pressed against Sean's throat. He could feel the cold blade breaking the skin. His fingers dug deeper into the man's throat. Then he heard a shot, and the man went limp.

Sean flung the body aside and looked toward Abigail. He did not see a gun in her hands. He climbed to his knees, and a bullet slammed into him. He tumbled backward, landing in a sitting position, waist-deep in the water of the Easterly Channel.

The deserter was not dead. The first shot had missed him. The second had grazed his side. He watched for a moment, until he was certain that Sean would not get up. Then he turned to Abigail, who was again standing between him and the strongbox. "I'm sorry to shoot your husband, lady, but he didn't want to show me what's in the box."

"And I'm sorry about your friends." Her voice quivered. Her knees were shaking.

The man smiled. "That's all right. They was scum anyways. Not like me. I'm a reg'lar stand-up gent, and I'm askin' you nice and polite to open that box." He raised his gun. "Or I'll shoot you, too."

"I don't have the key," she said. She was trying to buy time. She didn't know what she would do.

He shoved her aside. "Guess I'll have to do it myself."

His first shot ricocheted off the side of the box and almost hit his foot. The second snapped one of the locks, grown brittle and rusty in the mud. He aimed the pistol at another lock and fired again; it popped open.

"Just one more, and we'll know what you folks been buryin' out here." He aimed the pistol and squeezed the trigger. He heard a shot, but the gun didn't kick. For an instant, he was puzzled. Then he felt the pain above the bridge of his nose. Then he felt nothing.

The derringer had blown a half-inch hole in his forehead and taken the back of his skull clean off. Abigail carried the gun in her boot, but she had never fired it. At close range, it was deadly. She looked once at the vermin she had killed, then dropped the derringer and ran to Sean's side.

He was still sitting in the water with his hand over his stomach. She took his hand away and felt her own insides wither. She tore a clean strip of cloth from her blouse and placed it over the hole in his stomach. Then she replaced his hand. There was nothing more she could do.

"I'm cold," he said feebly.

The tide had turned and the water was rising around him. She put her hands under his arms and pulled him a few feet out of the channel.

"I'll be all right," he whispered.

"Just rest here for a few minutes, dear. Then we'll go."

She had to get Sean to a doctor, but she had to bury the tea set. Abigail Pratt Bentley became a creature of instinct. Although she was seventy-three, she found the strength that comes to a mother protecting her child. She dragged the box to the edge of the hole. She sat down in the mud, put both feet against the box, and pushed. The box toppled into the hole. Abigail grabbed her shovel, and in forty-five minutes, she had buried the strongbox in six feet of mud. She kicked the bodies of the three men into the stream, and she was finished.

"Mrs. Bentley." Sean was whimpering. "I'm cold, Mrs. Bentley." The water had risen again to his waist.

"You must get up, Sean. We have to go."

He looked at her blankly. "I'm cold."

She felt the tears welling in her eyes. She willed them away. If she could get him to a doctor, he might still have a chance. If he was going to die, she did not want him to be found in the Back Bay. "Please, Sean, try to get up."

He moaned and told her again that he was cold. He was in shock.

"If you do not get up, you will never see Joseph and Lillian again." She spoke angrily as she put her hands under his shoulders. "Now get up!"

With her help, Sean Mannion stood. He moaned again, more loudly. Soon the pain would become too intense for the anesthesia of shock, and he would scream every time his heart pumped blood out the hole in his stomach.

Abigail gave him the shovel to lean on. She put her body under his shoulder, and together they lurched across the Back Bay. The coming tide would erase any trace of their presence at the edge of the channel and carry the bodies of the thieves inland toward the South End.

They reached Commonwealth Avenue a few feet ahead of the rising tide. Abigail was supporting most of Sean's weight, and his cries of pain were echoing back at her off the twenty-foot landfill. She tried not to hear. She was exhausted, but she needed one more burst of strength. She felt Sean's body going limp.

She shook him. "No, Sean. You can't give up. Just a little farther."

Somehow, she dragged him up the cart path to the top of the landfill. Commonwealth Avenue stretched out before them, and the carriage was just a few feet away. But Sean couldn't make it. He sank to his knees.

"Just a little farther, Sean." Her voice became frantic. "Please!"

He fell forward on his elbows.

"Don't stop, Sean. You're so close." She knelt beside him. "Please, dear."

His eyes were unfocused. He was moaning rhythmically. He didn't seem to hear her. She rolled him over and cradled his head in her lap.

"I'm cold."

Abigail was helpless. The tears rolled down her cheeks.

"So cold," he said. "So cold."

She had to save him. She tried to lift him. "If we can just get you to the carriage, we can get you to a doctor, Sean. Please."

"Make me warm." Sean took her hand.

"Oh, Sean." Abigail buried her face against his neck. "I'm so sorry, Sean. I'm so sorry."

His moans became screams.

"I never meant to use you. I never meant to hurt you. Never."

The screams subsided. He was losing strength quickly.

"If you'd been born in Boston, or me in Ireland. If I'd been younger. Oh, God, if I hadn't been a Pratt . . ."

His hand clenched tight around hers.

"I love you, Sean." She kissed him. She knew he was going. She screamed, so that he would hear her once more, "I love you."

"Abigail." The word whispered out of him.

Sean Mannion was waked in the upstairs parlor of his son's bowfront on Lenox Street. Abigail offered her home on Tremont Row—it was Sean's home, after all—but Joseph Mannion preferred that his father's body be waked in the home where his grandchildren would grow.

Lillian Mannion, heavy with age and distraught with grief, sat beside the coffin. Abigail Pratt Bentley, in dress as black as the widow's, sat beside her. Mannion friends and family, the Pratts, and the few readers who still remembered the obscure Irish poet came to pay their respects. Even young Philip Cawley journeyed back from Worcester and said goodbye to the only man in the Pratt household he had ever liked.

Some of those who did not know Sean's wife offered their condolences to Abigail by mistake. Lillian was not offended. She considered Abigail a kindly employer and a faithful friend. She did not know that Abigail and her husband had been lovers before she met him. Nor did she know the truth about her husband's death.

Only Artemus knew that Sean Mannion had died protecting the Golden Eagle Tea Set, and Artemus would protect the secret, because he did not care to acknowledge that the tea set existed. He still believed that dreaming of treasure was a frivolous pursuit, something for old women, Irishmen, and hapless businessmen like his father. He wanted his children and grandchildren to learn that they would achieve nothing except through hard work.

Abigail paid for the funeral and made a contribution in Sean's memory to the Cathedral of the Holy Cross, the church where the Mannions had worshiped for forty years. She also enlisted Samuel Blossom, one of Boston's leading silversmiths, to fashion a silver crucifix for Sean's coffin. Abigail was among Blossom's best customers, and he worked quickly. By the second day of the wake, an eight-inch crucifix, with the figure of Christ engraved into the silver, rested on the pillow beside Sean's head.

On the morning of the funeral, Joseph, Lillian, and Abigail stood beside the coffin as it was closed for the last time. Abigail took the crucifix and pressed it into Lillian's hands. "Take this and always cherish it, dear. I loved your husband. Like a brother. I shall never forget him." She looked at Joseph. "And I shall never forget the Mannions."

Joseph smiled tenderly. He was rock-solid in every sense: built like one of his brick walls, good husband, father of two, and a respected member of the community. "There's nothing you could do for us that you haven't done already, Aunt Abigail."

"Your father gave his life to protect me from thieves, Joey. Before I die, I will give something to his children that will show the depth of my gratitude. I promise you."

A year and a half later, with the Union secure and Artemus Pratt's two sons returned from the war, building began on the Back Bay mansion. In the spring of 1866, the Pratts moved into one of the finest homes in Boston, five stories of red sandstone, with high windows, mansard roof, and the most beautiful woodwork, brass, and marble that money could buy. The first floor, with the music room, receiving room, and dining room, was for formal entertaining. The Pratts spent most of their leisure time on the second floor, in the bright parlor, in Mrs. Pratt's withdrawing room, decorated in the latest Parisian furnishings, in a smoking room for the gentlemen, where they played billiards on a fine slate table, or in a library as well stocked as the Atheneum. The family slept on the third and fourth floors, and the servants had rooms on the fifth. The kitchen, service rooms, and wine cellar were in the basement, the carriage house in the alley. The era of gracious living had begun.

Abigail's bedroom and sitting room were on the fourth floor. From her windows overlooking Commonwealth Avenue, she could watch the filling of the Back Bay and the march of the Pratts across the nineteenth century, a parade as sweeping, in its own way, as Sherman's March to the Sea.

The Civil War had proved enormously profitable for Pratt Shipping, Mining, and Manufacturing, and Artemus plowed most of the profits back into railroads, shipping, and the mass production of clothing. But, as he said later, one of the best investments of his life was one he didn't make.

Just after the war, Artemus Pratt had been offered a chance to invest in Crédit Mobilier of America. An offshoot of the Union Pacific Railroad, Crédit Mobilier was to be the Union Pacific's construction contractor during the building of the transcontinental line. Pratt was attracted, but, like his grandfather and father, he had grown conservative as he grew older, preferring to protect what he had built rather than risk the future in an undertaking so enormous. For one of the few times in his life, he did not invest in a railroad when he had the opportunity.

Three years later, the scandal broke. Crédit Mobilier had inflated its contracts to Union Pacific so that both companies could secure government bonds and clear huge profits. To aid their cause with the government, promoters of Crédit Mobilier had enticed Congressmen, Senators, and the Speaker of the House with shares of their profitable stock. When the investigations began, Union Pacific stock tumbled, Crédit Mobilier went into receivership, and Artemus Pratt congratulated his own good sense.

Artemus also had the good sense to listen whenever Abigail discussed business, and he was often rewarded.

Occasionally, Abigail took tea with Louis Agassiz, Harvard's famous naturalist. One afternoon, he told her about his son's recent discoveries at the Calumet Copper Mine in Michigan. Abigail told Artemus, who invested heavily in Calumet and Hecla. A few years later, his stock was returning dividends of a quarter million dollars a year. The Pratts entered their Gilded Age.

Artemus II, who ended the Civil War as a lieutenant colonel, returned to Boston and stepped into the position vacated by his uncle Elihu, who had retired after the death of his son and now traveled the world as an ambassador for Pratt interests. Artemus II possessed all of his father's intelligence and toughness but leavened it with his mother's warmth of personality. Wounded three times and decorated after Gettysburg, he took to the battles of Boston business with the same enthusiasm he had showed leading his first charge at the Battle of Fair Oaks.

Artemus and Abigail were thrilled by his performance, because he assured the continuity of Pratt leadership in the Pratt company. They were further pleased by his choice of spouse. Artemus II married Lydia Hancock Lowell, distant cousin from another first family. As Boston riches grew and Boston money helped expand the continent, Boston society became increasingly insular.

But, as Abigail wrote in her diary, "That merely assures that the right blood is running in the right veins."

Artemus's oldest child, Sarah, married James Hannaford, a descendant of Horace Pratt's closest English associate. Jason, the doctor, completed his medical studies, became the first Pratt to serve on the board of directors at Massachusetts General Hospital, and later retired to teach at Harvard Medical School. He married a Shaw. Olivia, Artemus's younger daughter, fell in love with the son of a Central Pacific Railroad magnate and moved to San Francisco. Henry, the youngest son, joined a Boston law firm after four years of Harvard and two years of yachting, polo playing, drinking, and womanizing which his father called dissipation and Henry called the gentlemanly pursuit of leisure.

Despite the Calvinist roots from which they sprang and the strict regimen to which Artemus Sr. adhered, the Pratts were learning to enjoy their money. In winter, there were dinner parties and soirées, highlighted by the Pratt Winter Ball on Washington's Birthday, which also happened to be the birthday of Horace Taylor Pratt. In spring, the Pratts strolled in the Public Garden and played polo on the grassy fields north of the city. In summer, the Back Bay house was closed and the Pratts went to Searidge, where they sailed, fished, and enjoyed the salubrious salt air. Autumn brought the family back to Boston, back to the business, the dinner parties, the recitals, the afternoon teas.

Abigail had lived to see the prosperity she had helped to ensure, and she saw the Golden Eagle Tea Set buried beneath the city of Boston. By 1871, two new streets, Dartmouth and Exeter, crossed the Commonwealth Avenue axis, and two more were being filled. Abigail could walk to the spot where the tea set lay buried. Each day, she and Lillian Mannion, her personal maid and closest companion, would stroll the Back Bay, past the beautiful new homes and churches, past the shade trees just beginning to grow, to the spot where the tea set lay buried. Abigail would always linger for a while, talk with Lillian about the wonderful future that neither of them would see, then head home.

In April of 1874, Lillian Mannion died, and Abigail commissioned Samuel Blossom to fashion another silver crucifix for another coffin. At the wake, Abigail took Joseph aside and promised him, once more, that she would find a way to express her love for his parents. Joseph smiled and told her that she had already showed the Mannions her love and generosity.

In the next several months, Abigail began to fail. She suffered two heart attacks just before her eighty-fourth birthday, but she would not stay in bed longer than a few days. She said she could not rest until her business had been completed. When she was not sick, she walked almost every day past the site of the church being built above the tea set.

The workmen often wondered about the strange old woman who always greeted them cheerfully and always had a question or two about their work. How deep was the basement? What were the length-by-width measurements? How thick were the outer walls? How deep were the pilings? Was there any chance that the church would settle into the landfill? On several occasions, they saw her pace off the distance from the corner of the building to a spot near the entrance, as though she were taking measurements of her own. Each afternoon, she would go home, record the measurements and other information she had collected, and sit down to hunt through *Paradise Lost*.

In October, she sent for Joseph Mannion again. They chatted for a while about Joseph's family, then she announced that she was going to fulfill her promise to him. First, she made him vow that he would not misuse her gift, give it away, or divulge to anyone except his most trusted child the information she was about to bestow. He agreed, and she presented him with a silver chalice. It was crafted by Samuel Blossom, engraved with three scenes from the Passion of Christ and a single line from *Paradise Lost*. Abigail had chosen a chalice to convey her message because she knew that a Catholic family would cherish it.

"This is my gift to you, Joseph. Protect it. Never let it out of your house. And leave it to your most trusted child when you die. If ever you find yourself in financial straits which you cannot negotiate, if ever you are desperate, bring this chalice to the senior member of my family, and he will help you through your difficulty as though you were one of his own."

"I'll be needing no help, Aunt Abigail," he said softly.

"You may, Joey. You may. And if ever a member of my family requests the cup from you, surrender it."

Joseph smiled. He liked Abigail, but he had always considered her a bit eccentric. "I never say no to my Aunt Abigail."

"One other thing, Joey. I'm leaving you five thousand dollars."

He had been hoping for that. He flashed his Mannion grin, then stood and kissed her on the forehead. "You've always been too kind to us."

"I can never be too kind to Sean Mannion's son."

Her hand was not as steady as it had been, but her mind was still clear and she wrote daily in her diary. She sometimes wondered why she wrote. She never read back over the years, and she knew now that she would never have the chance. Like so much in her life, filling the diary had become an act of self-preservation. Someday, someone would read her journal and know Abigail Pratt Bentley.

November 3, 1874

There are finally enough leaves on the elms outside that their falling seems significant. The wind blows in gusts, tearing them from the trees and blowing them along the street like souls on their way to hell. From up here, three stories above, the trees still seem like little brushes losing their bristles. I suppose that one day, the branches of those elms will scrape against my window pane, but I shall never see it. I have seen enough. I am content.

The baby calls. I must tend to him—

Our little man is now changed into clean diapers, and Great-Grand-Auntie is back to her writing. I am babysitting today for little Artemus III while his parents and grandparents attend a contest of football between Harvard and Rutgers. It is a rather new sport combining all the worst aspects of military strategy and back-alley brawling. I'm told that the ruffians from Yale enjoy it immensely.

But back to my original thought. I am content. Or at least as content as anyone can be when she has outlived all her contemporaries and sees her body, like a sandy neck washed by the waves, growing weaker and smaller each day. But my mission is complete. I have added the codicils to my will and placed ten envelopes in my safety-deposit box. With the help of John Milton and a little common sense, the treasure will be found when the Pratts need to find it. The exact nature of the treasure is contained in a special envelope that will go to

Artemus. Also in that envelope are instructions for the dispersal of the information.

I have also fulfilled my promise to young Joseph Mannion, and that makes me feel wonderful. Even now, I miss his father desperately, although Sean has been gone for more than ten years. If such a thing as reincarnation exists, perhaps we will meet in another life, where there will be no barriers between us, no greater matters to hold my attention. However, I do not expect to see Sean again, except in the hereafter. I will tell him then that I would not have done anything differently. I simply followed my natural inclinations. As my father's old servant once told me, I'm an apple that fell too close to the tree. My only regret is that I bore no fruit.

Little Artemus Pratt III is crying for attention again. He is two years old, blond, and beautiful. (It seems that I have been saying that about Pratt babies for sixty years. Except, of course, for one half-Pratt baby who disappeared, like his father, many years ago. Pray he stays where he went.)

But how I envy baby Artemus. He will see things that I cannot imagine. Already he has the firm Pratt jaw. 'Tis a pity he's not old enough to hear wisdom from the lips of his Great-Grand-Auntie. I could tell him so much! My, how he cries—

There, now. I've bounced him on my knee for ten minutes and fetched him a bottle all the way from the kitchen. I must have a talk with Artemus about the household help. It seems that when the master leaves the house, so do all the servants. I rang three times, and none of those lazy Irish girls answered. Lillian Mannion would have been at my side in an instant. I'll admit it. I'm not quite what I used to be when it comes to climbing stairs. I'm still out of breath.

Baby Artemus. What a span of time is represented here! Me at my writing desk, he in his playpen, a woman born in the eighteenth century, a boy who will live in the twentieth. I would give anything to

The next word was illegible. She knew what she wanted to say, but suddenly, she couldn't hold the pen. Her face went numb. Her right eye closed. The pain at the side of her head was excruciating but lasted only a second.

Artemus Pratt found his aunt seated at her desk, her head bowed on her chest, her left eye open. This time, the stroke had been merciful.

❊

Abigail Pratt Bentley distributed her wealth evenly to her nephews, nieces, and their children. Everyone was satisfied when Henry Pratt, now the family attorney and the executor of Abigail's will, prepared to read the final codicil. Henry cleared his throat and looked around. He had learned already that a large, well-appointed office inspired confidence in potential clients and was indispensable for the reading of a will. In front of his desk, in straight-backed chairs brought from the outer office, sat Henry's wife, his mother, his brothers, his sisters, who had traveled to Boston for the reading of the will, and four spouses.

Artemus Pratt sat to Henry's right, in front of a window, motionless as a lizard in the sunlight.

"'There are ten envelopes contained in a safety-deposit box, and the name of a family member is written on each one. Envelopes shall go to the each of the six couples I assume are assembled here today, the remainder to the four firstborn children of the next generation.'"

As Henry read, Artemus studied the faces of his children. His brothers and their children, except for a single mulatto bastard, were dead. The line of Pratt descent now traced directly through Artemus, and he was pleased that none of his children seemed especially interested in Abigail's envelopes. He knew that most of them would entrust the money that Abigail was leaving them and pay no attention to legends. He had raised them well.

Henry paused for a sip of water, then continued, "'Those envelopes are your means of communicating with me. They are the glue that will hold you together. They are your second chance for greatness. You may not open the envelopes for ten years, and you may never divulge the contents, unless three or more of you agree that the Pratts face a financial or personal crisis that cannot be overcome without a new inflow of funds. If you agree, you must then go to the eldest son of the eldest son and ask him for his permission and opinion. Bide by his decision, for it is my own. Remember that I am with you always in your pursuit of greatness. Signed, Abigail Pratt Bentley, October 9, 1874.'"

Henry put the paper down and folded his hands on his desk. "I'm sorry I couldn't get her to be more specific about all this. But she said that these were the instructions her father gave her, and she was giving them to the future."

"Toward the end," cracked Artemus Jr., "I think Auntie's pigskin needed a bit of air."

"Don't be disrespectful," snapped his mother.

"Father, what do you think of all this?" asked Henry.

"We should do our best to abide by the codicil. It was her wish. The best way to abide by it is to forget about it. Our aunt was an eccentric old woman living in a world of dreams." Artemus stood. "Face reality, and you'll never need to concern yourself with her fantasies."

CHAPTER XVIII

Gin and tonics. Cold cucumber soup. Spinach salad, saffron rice, bluefish steaks marinated in white wine and herbs and grilled over charcoal. California Chablis. Cheese and fruit. Halfway through the preparation of the salad, Evangeline realized that she hadn't taken such care with a meal in months.

She had tried to find her grandmother that afternoon and failed. Now, she wasn't sure how to proceed. Accepting her uncle's explanation of the tea-set business seemed the safe, logical choice, but she did not know what to expect from Fallon. She had been surprised by his reticence after their meeting with the Pratts. If he had decided to go back to work, she wanted to find out quickly if there was going to be anything else between them. She hoped that a relaxed dinner would provide some answers.

Fallon arrived around six-thirty, and they went up to the roof, where Evangeline had built a small patio. It was still hot in Boston; the downtown office buildings, the Back Bay brick, and the green hills of Brookline shimmered through the evening haze. They sipped their gin and tonics and listened to the bluefish sizzling on the grill, and Evangeline asked Peter what he thought of her uncle's story.

He said he'd been thinking all day. He hadn't made up his mind, and he didn't want to think anymore until after dinner. She understood. For the last few years, she had been approaching her own life the same way.

While they ate, Fallon talked about bluefish. He recounted his first deep-sea fishing expedition, when he had hooked into a twenty-pounder that bit through his steel leader. He talked about their voracious eating habits, their migrating pattern, and their incredible strength when hooked.

It was as if they had said everything important to each other the night before on the beach. Now they were talking about fish, and Peter Fallon seemed like a rather ordinary young man. There was nothing wrong with that. Evangeline simply found him more interesting when he was obsessed.

After dinner, he sat back and locked his hands behind his head. He seemed completely at ease. He popped a grape into his mouth and announced, "Bullshit."

"What?"

"Bullshit. Everything they said today is bullshit. I don't believe a single word of it."

She smiled. "When did you decide that?"

"Just now . . . this afternoon . . . on my walk over here from the ballpark . . . I don't know. But I've known since I got out of bed this morning that they weren't going to get me to back out, no matter what they said. They're all tied into it somehow. Pratt, Hannaford, Soames, all of them. They were just trying to get us out of the way with that story. Well, bullshit."

"I had a feeling you'd say that." She seemed pleased.

"But right now . . ." He pushed back his chair and stood dramatically. "I don't give a damn about the tea set, the Pratts, or who-believes-what. You know what I really want to do?"

She shook her head. He had turned unpredictable again.

"I want to go over to that hammock on the other side of the patio, stretch out, and eat grapes. You interested in joining me?"

He grabbed the grapes in one hand and her in the other. She didn't have a chance to refuse. She didn't want one. The suddenness worked in their favor. It was exactly what she needed from him.

They lay down together on the hammock, a balancing act they accomplished with ease. Peter dropped the grapes. They wrapped their arms around each other, and he brought his face close to hers. She had showered before dinner and was wearing a trace of Chanel; he had been sitting shirtless in the bleachers all afternoon and smelled of sunburn and sweat. The aromas mingled. Their lips brushed once, twice.

Then, they hesitated. They looked into each other's eyes and agreed.

She rolled off the hammock, stood, and undressed in front of him. First the blouse, then the sandals, then, in one motion, the tennis shorts and panties. She did not act coy, like a newlywed, or disinterested, like a prostitute. She stood naked in front of him, a vague half-smile on her face, her hands at her sides, the palms turned toward him, inviting him.

He was glad he had waited. He lay on the hammock and let his eyes caress her breasts, her thighs, her blond hair, her brown hair. He noticed a trickle of perspiration glistening between her breasts. Tentatively, he reached out and took her hand.

She pulled it away and whispered, "You, too."

He stood close to her but did not touch her. He removed his jersey, then his sneakers, then his shorts and underpants.

She was surprised. Beneath a shirt, he looked slender, but his body was muscular, explosive, almost an extension of his personality. His erection flattered her. She touched it, and they embraced. Afterward, they lay beneath a blanket on the hammock. It was getting dark, and the breeze had blown out the candles on the table.

"What do you plan to do?" she asked softly.

"Find Jack C. Ferguson, if I can. Also, that Rule guy might know something. And I think we should keep looking for your grandmother."

"You don't give up easily, do you?"

"When nothing else has excited you in months, you just naturally hold onto any idle daydreams that happen to turn you on."

She sat up angrily, exposing her breasts and reminding Fallon that they were both naked. "You need more than daydreams and cheap thrills to get through life."

"I know." He leaned forward and buried his face in the warmth between her breasts. His mouth found a nipple and his hands slid gently down her back.

"Peter . . ." She tried to protest.

His mouth covered hers and he pulled her back on top of himself.

They didn't speak again until several hours later, when, somewhere in his dream, Fallon heard something moving beside him.

Then he heard the pop of a pistol. Someone in the penumbra was shooting at him. He opened his eyes in full fright.

There were three graceful, tulip-shaped glasses on the table next to him, and someone was pouring champagne. At first, he thought it was Evangeline, but she was still asleep and trying to struggle back to consciousness herself. Through the glasses, Fallon saw a barrel chest supporting a head the size of a medicine ball. The body was shrouded in a ragged tweed jacket, shiny pants, and khaki work-shirt. The head was framed in uncombed white hair, and a Red Sox baseball cap was perched on the back of the skull.

Evangeline screamed, jumped up, and wrapped herself in the blanket. The hammock flipped over and pitched Fallon stark naked onto the floor. He rolled to his feet and crouched for a fight, but the barrel chest began to heave and the body emitted a long, low growl. Fallon barely recognized it as a laugh. It sounded lonely and unpracticed.

The man tossed Fallon his shorts and smiled. "Put these on before you catch cold. Then, I want both of you kids to sit down and have a drink with me."

"Who the hell are you," demanded Evangeline.

"Jack C. Ferguson, and I'm pleased to meet you both up close." He still spoke his name with pride.

"Up close? What does that mean?" asked Evangeline. The name hadn't sunk in.

"I've been watching you two for quite a while." He smiled.

"And you liked what you saw, so you decided to join the party?"

He laughed again. The sound got better with practice. "I've been watching you for several days, although I must admit I really enjoyed tonight. It reminded me of my salad days."

"Well, take your limp lettuce and get out of here!"

By now, Fallon was dressed and smiling. "I've been chasing you for the last week."

"You and a lot of folks." Ferguson picked up two glasses of champagne and offered them to Fallon and Evangeline. "I bought this with five bucks I didn't have, which means I stole it. Now let's drink it before it goes flat."

"What the hell is going on here?" said Evangeline.

"I don't know," answered Fallon.

"Well, humor me anyway and drink up." Ferguson stood proudly and held the glass above his head. He was about six-four, two hundred and twenty pounds. "To our new partnership."

"To our what?" screamed Evangeline.

"Partnership." Ferguson clinked his glass against hers, then against Fallon's. "I'm going to help you kids find a treasure and start a happy life together." He emptied his glass, belched, and poured another.

Fallon watched him drink. He liked Jack Ferguson already.

Evangeline was not so impressed. "Listen, Santa Claus, you're six months late."

"You didn't finish your drink yet, dearie," he interrupted. He turned to Fallon. "Nor have you."

Fallon smiled, toasted, and drank.

Evangeline gulped the champagne and slammed the glass down on the table. "Now how did you get in here?"

"All in due time, my dear, all in due time." He refilled their glasses and sat down. "Please, both of you, have a seat."

Fallon pulled up a chair. Evangeline pulled her blanket more tightly around her shoulders and began to pace. "I'd rather stand."

"Sit down," growled Ferguson.

She looked at Fallon, who motioned her to the edge of the hammock.

As she sat, she smelled rotten fruit in the air. She wrinkled her nostrils.

Ferguson noticed it. He didn't miss much. "Sorry, honey. I usually clean up in the men's room at the Public Library every few weeks. But, what with this heat, that ain't nearly enough."

He ran a hand through his hair. In the dark, Evangeline couldn't tell if anything living came off on his fingers.

Ferguson sipped champagne and began to talk. "My name, again, is Jack C. Ferguson. I've been a crack reporter, on and off, for thirty years, I've written two nonfiction books, and for several years I wrote a column in a weekly called *Hubcap*."

Fallon nodded.

"Then, one day, I wrote a scathing article, even for me. I claimed that a certain art dealer named Lawrence Hannaford, his financial backers, led by a guy named William Rule, and his most recent purchase, Paul Revere's Golden Eagle Tea Set, were frauds. The article got me into just a little bit of trouble. I went underground, I started hitting the bottle, and I was reduced to this." He looked at his clothes and laughed to himself. He sounded as though he were clearing his throat before spitting something out. "A threadbare free-lancer trying to stay off the booze and stay alive long enough to find a tea set."

"What do you want with us?" asked Evangeline.

"You're going to help me, and I'm going to help you."

"How did you find us?" asked Fallon.

"I read the death column in the newspaper every day. I'm well marked myself, and every morning when I wake up, I like to make sure I'm still kicking. If I don't see my name in the papers, I know I made it through another day."

"This man is crazy," said Evangeline to Fallon.

"Perhaps, but this is a crazy world. It's the sane ones who end up in trouble, and you two are very sane." Ferguson produced two news photos from his wallet, which, as Fallon noticed, contained no money. He gave one photo to Fallon.

It was a picture of Fallon. The caption described him as a witness to the murder of Kenny Gallagher, a bartender in South Boston.

"Alone, this picture means nothing," Ferguson explained. "You happened to be in a bar fight with your brother when somebody came in and shot the bartender. However . . ."

He opened the second photo. It showed the mourners leaving Christopher Carrington's funeral. Fallon remembered the scene. He had been trying to get to Evangeline before she drove off.

"Here you are at the funeral of another murder victim, and this one is a Pratt. Now, I take notice."

"My brother was a suicide," said Evangeline angrily.

"Believe that if you want to," said Ferguson. "The police do. But that tea set is a very valuable item. In today's market, it's worth two and a half, maybe three million. As a tool for blackmail against Hannaford and his financial backers, it's worth a lot more. There are people out there ready to kill for it, either to find it or to keep it hidden right where it is."

"Are you saying that somebody killed Carrington and Kenny Gallagher because of the Golden Eagle Tea Set?" Fallon was beginning to wonder where Ferguson got his information.

"Carrington most certainly. Gallagher, he's a coincidence. But people have been killed because somebody thought they had information. And you may be killed because you do have information. How much do you know?"

Now we're down to it, thought Fallon. We've finished with the friendly chatter. Ferguson suddenly seemed very dangerous.

"All I know is what I read in the newspapers," said Fallon with a weak smile.

"Not funny." The anger flared in Ferguson's voice, and Fallon decided not to antagonize him again. "When I'm paying for the

302

drinks, I like smart conversation. No bad jokes. Now what do you know about the Golden Eagle?"

No wonder he'd been such a good reporter, thought Fallon. With his huge head, wide-set eyes, and shaggy mane, Ferguson looked like something that ought to be leaving mysterious footprints in the Himalayas.

Fallon decided that whatever he knew, everybody else knew more, so he told Ferguson everything.

When he finished, Ferguson frowned. "That's it?"

Fallon nodded.

"Well, I'll tell you right now that the story the Pratts told you this morning is bullshit. There's no syndicate blackmailing anybody. There's some serious blackmail goin' on, but it's all nice and cozy. Right in the family."

"They told me Harrison worked for the FBI."

"My ass! He works for Soames. From what I've heard, Harrison and the little creep, Dill, have been on the Pratt payroll for years. Company security, industrial spying, that sort of thing. The other one, Buckley, is new. He's just a leg-breaker."

"I don't know anything about Buckley and Dill."

"Look around, and one of them will usually be behind you."

"How do you know so much?" asked Evangeline, a bit harshly.

He glared at her. He considered the question an insult. "I been on this thing longer than anybody. For years. I might be big and ugly, but when I worked, I learned how to make myself invisible and find out what I had to know. You just take my word that what I'm tellin' you is fact."

Evangeline looked at Fallon. They both realized that this was a volatile derelict.

Ferguson turned to Fallon.

"Now, you must know more. What about that famous Renaissance poet and laugh-a-minute gagman for Christ, John Milton?"

Fallon recalled that there was an inscription from *Paradise Lost* on Horace Pratt's tombstone.

"And what did it say?"

"I can't remember."

"You go back and look at it and see if it don't tell you something."

"What?" asked Evangeline impatiently.

"I'll leave it to you to figure. But I'll show you what I mean. You got a piece of paper and a pencil?"

Evangeline gave him her telephone notebook.

He carefully wrote down seven lines and handed her the paper. "What do you see there?"

Evangeline read the lines. "O friends, I hear the tread of nimble feet/ Hasting this way, and now by glimpse discern/ Ithuriel and Zephon through the shade,/ And with them comes a third of regal port,/ But faded splendour wan; who by his gait/ And fierce/ demeanor seems the Prince of Hell,/ Not likely to part hence without contest;/ Stand firm, for in his look defiance lours.' What's this supposed to mean?"

"Don't take any shit from the devil. That's the Archangel Gabriel talking. He's also giving us a clue."

Fallon looked at Evangeline. "This is what Abigail was talking about in her diary."

"You've read the diaries?" asked Ferguson excitedly.

"Only one of them. But in it she talks about giving her nephews clues to the location of her family secret."

Ferguson nodded. "There were two sets. Old Man Pratt made up the first bunch. And after they filled in the Back Bay, his daughter made up a second set. They both had a thing for *Paradise Lost*. Most of the quotes have some moral point to them, but someplace in every one, there's a clue. It might be a number, a direction on the compass. It might be just a word, or it might be the whole idea of the quotation."

"The context," offered Fallon.

Ferguson smiled. "Right. It's easy to see you went to Harvard. Now, with these quotes, you sometimes have to know a little about Boston geography or the treasure itself to know what they're talkin' about. But usually, you can just figure them out by lookin' at them."

"What are we supposed to figure out with this one?" asked Evangeline. "The quotation mentions shade. Are we supposed to look under a tree?"

This time, the sarcasm made Ferguson laugh. "The lady's a skeptic. I can understand that. Until somebody finds the tea set, we're all skeptics. There are specific references in this quotation to a number and a unit of measure. Until we have all the quotations, we can't be certain if she wants us to read 'the tread of nimble feet' or 'a third of regal port' as the clue."

"This is hard to believe," said Evangeline softly.

"Tell that to old Abigail Pratt Bentley. The one who finds all the clues pinpoints the exact spot where the tea set is buried, right down to how deep it's sunk. I have five clues. I been trackin' them down for years, and I got a few I don't guess anybody else has. I even rode the rails out to California and got one from a woman named Mary Korbel, just before she died. That was two years ago. You'll find clues on headstones, samplers, in safety-deposit boxes, and God knows where else."

"This morning," said Fallon, "Lawrence Hannaford told us that the tea set was found by scavengers when the Back Bay was being filled in the 1860s, and it was sold in England, where he bought it. How do you know he isn't telling the truth?" It was a reasonable question, not at all hostile, but Jack C. Ferguson didn't like it.

He rose angrily. "Because I been around, kid. I know Bill Rulick better than anybody. And you can take my word for it—the tea set in the museum is a fake. Until I find the real one, nobody's gonna believe me. Not you, not anybody. But when I find it, they'll all say I wasn't such a dumb sot after all. And not a bad reporter, either. If anybody asks me to work for 'em, I'll thumb my nose, because I'll be rich. I'll be somebody. Just so long as nobody kills me first."

"Who is going to kill you?" asked Evangeline, hoping the concern in her voice would settle him.

"Rulick. Rule. Whatever the hell he calls himself now. If somebody finds the tea set, he's a fraud, because he's the guy who supposedly put Hannaford together with that English owner nobody's ever been able to find. If Rulick is shown up, his pile of stock and Pratt Industries proxies won't mean jack shit. He'll never take over Pratt Industries, and he wants that more than a sixteen-year-old wants pussy."

"He has the votes to win a proxy fight, but my family is trying to stop him by producing the real tea set?" asked Evangeline.

Ferguson sat and poured himself more champagne. "You catch on. Once the Pratts have the tea set, they can threaten him with it. If he don't back out of the proxy fight, they tell the world they've found the real tea set and hope the stockholders decide to dump Rule. It might work. It might not."

"Why not go to the Pratts and make a deal?" asked Fallon.

"Because the Pratts are assholes. They'll deal with Rulick, and if he backs out, they'll deep-six the tea set. They'll promise that if he quits the proxy fight, they'll never reveal the fraud. Since they're Boston gentlemen and Hannaford's in the family, they'll keep their word. I want to see the tea set and feel the money. I got nothing to do with the Pratts."

"Why come to us?"

"Because you're independent." He looked at Evangeline. "And from what I can tell, you're just taggin' along with him."

"Thanks," she said.

"You two can help me, and I can help you. Just find your grandmother, wherever she is, and explain everything to her. She's got six or seven clues in her head, and they're the ones I don't have. We put 'em all together, and we'll be damn close to havin' a tea set."

"How do you know my grandmother?" asked Evangeline.

"Like I said, I been around."

"Why should she help us and not one of her nephews?"

"*We* didn't lock her up just to keep her out of the way. You find her, and I'll find you in a few days."

He picked up the bottle of champagne and gestured toward the Back Bay. "There's a tea set out there someplace. You take my word." He gulped the last of the champagne, strode across the roof, and stepped onto the fire escape. "I'll find my way out."

Fallon ran to the side of the building, just above the fire escape. "You can't take off yet. We haven't finished."

"I have." The iron cage creaked and groaned under his weight. His steps echoed through it.

"You still haven't told me where you got your information," said Fallon frantically.

"I'll tell you more when you tell me more."

"Wait." Fallon stepped onto the escape. He couldn't let Ferguson go.

"Don't follow me, sonny." A metallic snap, and six inches of steel caught the light from a street lamp. "I don't trust too many people, and until I know you better, I don't trust you. Don't follow."

Fallon stayed where he was. Ferguson climbed all the way down and disappeared into the darkness of the alley behind Evangeline's townhouse.

Evangeline stood beside Fallon and looked down into the alley. "What the hell was that?"

CHAPTER XIX   *February 1933*

On Saturday mornings, Sadie Ferguson rose early. She cooked breakfast for her mother, her brother, and her three children. She cleaned the house. Then she baked: four loaves of white bread to last the week, biscuits for Sunday breakfast, brown bread to go with baked beans on Saturday night, and two loaves of Irish soda bread for Sunday-afternoon guests.

After the bread went into the oven, she locked the front door, went up to the attic bedroom, and pulled the gallon can from under little Jack's bed. Back in the kitchen, she took out a funnel and a sack containing thirty-two pint bottles, which she bought from the junkman at a half a cent each. She carefully placed the funnel in the neck of a bottle and filled it with 150-proof grain alcohol, known to her supplier as liquid death. She added water, capped the bottle, and shook it, but not too much, because she was never quite sure if the mixture would explode. When all thirty-two bottles were filled, she poked her head into the freezing February morning and called for Jackie.

The Fergusons lived in the South End, on Decatur Street, a few blocks south of Dover and Washington. A tough neighborhood, and getting tougher now that the Depression covered it like a blanket of dirty snow. The buildings, mostly red-brick bowfronts, had been single-family homes once, but not for long. The upper class had moved to the Back Bay instead, the middle class to the outlying towns. Most of the buildings on Ferguson's block were rooming houses or tenement apartments where immigrant families were always making room for new arrivals. Every fifteen minutes, the elevated train clattered past the end of the street. Kids and dogs hunted rats for sport in the cellars. And outside of the Friday-night basketball game and dance at Cathedral High School, the most popular gathering spot was the Sunday-morning crap game in an alley off Dover Street.

But Sadie Ferguson liked the South End, in spite of the rummies and the rats and the black district a few blocks away. Neighbors still watched out for each other. People were still friendly. The Cathedral was close by. And everyone knew the cop on the beat. The South End was the only home Sadie Ferguson had ever known and the only place in Boston where her whole family could live together and still have room to breathe. Their walk-up was one of the nicer homes on the row, a dowdy old matron whose beauty was gone but who still looked attractive.

Sadie called for Jackie, but a light snow had begun to fall and it muffled the sound. Sadie was a big, beefy woman, but her voice didn't fit her. Built like a tuba, she sounded like a woodwind. She called again. No Jackie. She wondered if he was off stealing coal. She didn't encourage it, but extra coal was always welcome. She called once more. This time, her shrill voice attracted three dogs before Jackie came running out of an alley.

"Jack C. Ferguson, how many times have I told you to stay near the house on Saturday mornings? You have chores to do. You can raise Cain in the afternoon."

"Yes, Mama." Jackie knew never to argue with his mother, especially on Saturday mornings, when the smell of the fresh bread filled the house. He was eleven years old and big for his age, with a high forehead and wide-set eyes that his mother always said were the sign of intelligence. A tough kid, like the neighborhood, but likable and friendly nonetheless.

Sadie put two pint bottles into his outer pockets and four into the pockets she had sewn inside his coat. Jackie went on his first run and came back half an hour later with six dollars. She loaded him up again and he was off. Jackie made two trips on Saturdays. Sadie sold the rest of the booze from the back door.

It was snowing harder now, but Jackie didn't mind. In bad weather, tips were always good. He wrapped his scarf around his neck, pulled his hat low over his ears, and started to run. He galloped down an alley that led to Gloucester Place, past the old Italian fishman pushing his cart from house to house, through the gauntlet of Gloucester Place punks who peppered him with snowballs as he crossed their turf, then on to the Madison Hotel, a decrepit rooming house at the end of the street. He had a stop there, but he always saved it for last. He ran through the walkway under the Madison, a dark tunnel that smelled of piss even in the winter, and he came out on Washington Street. A train screeched on the El above him; it sounded like a thousand fingernails scraping a giant blackboard. He put his hands to his ears and kept running. He dodged a Model A that skidded to avoid him as he crossed the street, and he made his first stop in an old house behind the German Church.

The woman was eighty-five years old and confined to a wheelchair. She left her small apartment only to go to church on Sundays. She took her weekly pint from Jackie, paid for it, and gave him a dime tip. He delivered pints to four other shut-ins, then headed again for the Madison Hotel.

At the corner of Dover and Washington, he ran into Officer Carroll.

"Hiya," said Jackie.

Carroll grabbed him by the sleeve, and Jackie smelled booze. Carroll was one of Sadie's best customers. The policeman winked. "A word to the wise."

Jackie winked back and was off again, moving more cautiously now that he knew the vice men were in the neighborhood.

Jackie went up the back stairs at the Madison to Room 315. He knocked on the door. It opened slowly and an old man peered out.

The bristles of hair on head and brow were white. The eyes were blue. The old man's skin was yellow, like a Chinaman's, but his broad, flat features made him look to Jackie like a nigger. "Come in, little Jack. Come in and sit down."

Jack gave the old man the bottle and took his dollar. Then he stepped into the room. For a fleabag like the Madison it wasn't a bad place, thought Jackie. The old man had a hotplate in the corner to cook on, a Murphy bed, an old stuffed chair that smelled like dirty underwear whenever the weather turned muggy, a table, and a straight-backed chair. The walls had recently been painted gray and were covered with framed engravings of battles, fires, presidential inaugurations, spectacles of all kinds. Corner windows looked east toward downtown, which was dominated by the twenty-five-story Custom House Tower, and north onto the elevated tracks, which ran right past the old man's room.

Jack Ferguson had been delivering his mother's bootleg to Phil Cawley for two years, and the old man had told Jack the story of his life, a life of adventure and excitement that filled Jack's head with daydreams.

Phil Cawley recounted his early years in the California Gold Rush and his trip to Boston on a clipper ship. He told Jack about his stay in the servants' quarters of a rich Pratt family and ten years in a tough trade school where they never gave him enough to eat and he had to fight kids much older than himself to survive. When he was sixteen and about to become an engraver's apprentice, he headed out on his own, too impatient to wait for the small trust the Pratts had promised to give him when he learned a trade. He drifted from job to job for nearly ten years before the lure of another gold rush drew him to the Black Hills of South Dakota. He found no gold, but he learned the territory so well that he became a scout with the Seventh Cavalry. On the morning of June 25, 1876, he broke off with Reno's support column, and two days later, he made the only eyewitness sketch of the Custer battlefield. He sold it to *Collier's*, and for thirty years he was an engraver for American picture magazines. Then his eyesight failed and his work deteriorated. He returned to Boston and tried to collect his trust money and interest from the Pratts. They laughed at him and gave him a few hundred dollars to be rid of a nuisance. His life had never improved after that.

Philip Cawley was now eighty-three years old. He had never married, although he claimed to have a son living on a Sioux Indian reservation. He had no money, and was nearly blind. Little Jack Ferguson, who listened so attentively to his tales, was his only visitor.

The old man opened the window and took a bottle of lime juice and a few icicles from the sill. He put the ice and lime juice into a glass, then added a shot from the pint bottle. An alky split.

"I'd offer you some lime juice," he croaked, "but without somethin' cuttin' it, it's mighty bitter stuff."

"That's all right, Phil. My ma don't like me eatin' other people's

310

food, anyways. She says that, what with the Depression and all, people got trouble enough takin' care of theirselves."

"Damn straight." The old man grunted and threw another piece of wood into his Franklin stove. "Sit down, Jackie. Take off your coat and visit awhile."

"My ma don't like me to stay out with all this money on me, but I guess I can stay for a little while." Jackie sat down by the table at the north window.

"Seein' as how I'm always tellin' you stories, I want you to tell me one." He shuffled over to the bookcase, took down an ancient copy of *Kidnapped*, and placed it in front of Jack. "That book's older 'n you. It's almost as old as me. I've hung onto this one and a few others since I was a kid. If it wasn't for stories, I guess there woulda been nights I'd like to go crazy, bein' an orphan and all. I'm as lonely now, but I can't see to read no more, and I sure would like to hear a little Robert Louis Stevenson again. You get good grades for readin' in school?"

"I get good grades in just about everything."

"Well, this here story's a real corker." Cawley sat in his easy chair and sipped his alky split.

Jackie Ferguson was honored. He considered Phil Cawley a great man. He cleared his throat and flipped to page one. Then he flipped back to the title page. "'*Kidnapped*, by Robert Louis Stevenson.'" As he turned the page, he realized that he hadn't read the bookplate on the inside cover. He turned back to it. " 'Ex Lib-ris.' What does that mean?"

"It's Latin for 'from the books'—it's like saying 'my book.'"

"'Ex Libris, Philip Cawley. . . . That fury stayed,/Quencht in a Boggy Syrt . . . Syrt . . .'" Jack gave up. "What does all this mean?"

Phil Cawley laughed softly to himself. "It means that Satan's all around. He's ready to steal our soul and our gold, and we'd best keep an eye out."

"Oh." Jack studied the quotation. He didn't understand a word.

"But there's more than that," added Cawley. "Right there in them eight or nine lines, there's a buried treasure story as good as any. My mama told it to me when I was a kid."

And Philip Cawley told the story to Jackie Ferguson. It had come to Cawley thirdhand. His mother had heard it from his father, who had first overheard it as a child in his father's study a hundred years before. Still, Cawley had enough of the facts to weave a yarn about a treasure chest sunk in the Back Bay. Contained in the chest, he explained, was a golden teapot shaped like an eagle, and it was worth thousands of dollars. He told Jackie that many men had died trying to find the treasure, and he made up a gruesome story to prove his point.

"All that's right on this bookplate thing?" Jackie was willing to believe whatever Phil Cawley told him.

"No. These lines are only part of the story. They tell about stolen gold in a bog, the golden teapot in the Back Bay. There's other lines around tell exactly where the thing is."

"Did you ever look for it?"

"Never had time. I was too busy livin', too busy drinkin', drawin' pictures, chasin' women. That's all I did for almost sixty years, till I ran out of steam . . . and ran out of light. I never guessed my eyes would go. Now, I wish to hell I did look for that thing. Maybe I might've found it. Now, I wouldn't be just another old man sittin' around waitin' to die." He finished his alky split and made another as the elevated train screeched by the window.

Jackie didn't hear the train. He didn't hear the old man's hopelessness. He didn't hear the prostitute negotiating with a customer in the hallway or the wind driving snow against the windows. He was staring at the bookplate and dreaming about buried treasure. He would stay warm all afternoon just thinking about it.

"Lookit the tits on her."

"Yeah. I wish'd she'd rub 'em all over my face, then sit on it."

"Your face?" Jackie hadn't heard of that before.

"Yeah. She sits on your face and you eat her."

The woman wore a little starched crown, spike-heeled shoes, garter belt, fishnet stockings, and panties which she was about to remove.

"What do you eat?" asked Jackie.

Billy Rulick shrugged. "I don't know. Her buns, I guess."

The bare bulb next to the coalbin cast enormous shadows on the walls in Ferguson's cellar. Jackie always played down here in winter because the furnace wasn't insulated and the cellar was the warmest spot in the house. Jackie and his friend Billy Rulick had come down to the cellar to play checkers, or so they told Jackie's mother. Billy had smuggled a copy of *Gentleman's Fancy* into the house, and the boys were engrossed in "The Maid's Afternoon Daydream."

Jackie turned the page. His hands were sweating and he left fingerprints all over the maid's left breast. In the next picture, the maid removed her panties, turned around and offered her ample rear end to her young admirers. A seam ran down the back of each stocking.

"Shit." Jackie swallowed hard.

"You can practically see her cunt."

The two boys studied the picture in silence, and Billy Rulick's hand drifted slowly toward his crotch.

"King me," whispered Sadie Ferguson.

Jack dropped the magazine.

"A fine game of checkers this is," she said.

Billy grabbed the magazine and tried to shove it into his sweater.

"No you don't." Sadie took the magazine and threw it into the furnace. "Always good to have a little extra heat on cold days."

"That was mine," said Billy Rulick.

"I don't allow things like that in my house," said Sadie firmly. She was not as angry as she wanted the boys to believe.

Billy Rulick scowled at her. He was a handsome child, with black hair, brown eyes, and a perpetually serious expression. He had risked his life for that magazine. He had stolen three oranges from a pushcart in the North End, outrun the Italian grocer and his two sons, and traded the oranges to Teddy Sadowski for the magazine.

"I think it's time you two boys went outside and got some exercise. Shovel our stoop, then go across the street and do Rulick's."

It had been snowing for three days. Jackie had already shoveled the stoop and sidewalk five times, but he was glad for a chance to escape his mother. He grabbed Billy by the sleeve and they headed for the cellar door.

By the time they had finished shoveling Rulick's stoop, Ferguson's was again covered in snow.

"The more you shovel, the more it snows," said Jackie.

"Just like life, my boys." Peter Rulick stood in the doorway. His enormous arms were folded across his chest and his shoulders almost touched the doorframe on either side of him. He had jet-black hair, a bushy moustache, and eyes that betrayed his mood at a glance. He wore a workshirt over his red union suit, and suspenders held up his heavy, woolen pants.

At the moment, his eyes were smiling. "Two fine young workers deserve a good meal." He spoke with an East European accent.

"My ma don't like me eatin' at other peoples' houses," said Jackie, "what with the Depression and all."

Peter Rulick knelt down next to Jackie. He seemed oblivious to the snow and cold. "In my country, when a man invites you into his home, it is an insult to ask if he can feed you. Billy's mama has made beet soup, very fine beet soup. Too many potatoes, maybe, not so much beef as we would like, and milk instead of cream, but real beets." Peter Rulick smiled. "And good friends to celebrate the birth of the great Washington."

"I'll ask my ma." Jackie leaped off the stoop and ran across the street. He envied Billy Rulick. He hadn't seen his own father in seven years.

That night, Jackie filled his belly with beet soup and black bread. He was not the only dinner guest. Rulick's four-room flat was always crowded. Billy had three younger brothers, and Peter Rulick had many hungry friends.

Jack sat between Billy and an Irishman with red hair, grease-stained hands, and the smell of rubber soaked into every pore. During most of dinner, Peter Rulick and Irish Red McDonough talked about the rubber factory where they both had worked until Peter Rulick was laid off.

"They tell me they lay me off because my work is not good and they have no more for me to do. But others still work, men who work slower, men who came later to the plant. They fire me because I want to help start the union. Because I say that workers have rights." He pounded his fist on the table.

Anna Rulick frowned. She was a frail woman wearing a thread-bare dress and two sweaters. "Too much noise, Peter. Your boys know you. Irish Red know you. But little Jack, he no guess why you punch the table."

"Because, little Jack, it is not right that many good people should starve while others live off their labor. It is not right that Mrs. Sadowski upstairs should knock on our door and ask for one potato to feed her husband and three babies. One potato."

"Now, even that is too much to give," said Anna.

Peter nodded. "Now that I have no work, even that is too much. Soon, we will have no potatoes at all."

"Well, Peter," said Irish Red, "you knew right along they'd find a way to nail you when you agreed to be shop steward for a union that don't even exist. They asked me, but I said no. I got a wife and kids to support."

"But you're with me now. You'll be with me tonight."

Irish Red shook his head. "And I'll be regrettin' it in the morning."

"Where are you going tonight?" Anna Rulick had heard nothing of this.

"We are going to a great ball tonight, Anna. Me, Irish Red, and all the men who have been laid off in the last month at Pratt Rubber. We will make our voices heard."

The color drained from Anna Rulick's face. "There will be trouble."

"There will be no trouble."

"It will be bad."

Peter put his hand on her arm. "We are peaceful men, Anna. We simply want a union."

"Men who fight for unions in this country are called Reds, Communists," said Anna. "You leave Lithuania because you hate Communists."

"I hate Communists," he said softly. "I hate hunger more."

Artemus Pratt III always inspected his Back Bay house from bottom to top before the guests arrived for the Pratt Winter Ball.

He started in the kitchen, where the butler, the cooks, and eight servants were preparing the buffet supper that would be served at midnight. The Pratt Ball was one of the few on the social calendar that climaxed with a meal, and the Pratts always lavished great attention on the menu.

Great pans of Veal Orloff—sliced veal layered with mushroom duxelles and soubise of onions and rice, then heated in a light cheese sauce—covered every counter. Two hundred heads of lettuce, enough to make braised lettuce in herbs for two hundred guests, awaited a vat of boiling water. Ice and bottles of white Bordeaux filled a barrel near the door, and a servant hurried in and out of the wine cellar with bottles of Burgundy for those who preferred red with their veal. At a counter, a maid cut lemons, hundreds of them, to accompany the caviar and, later, oysters on the half shell. Another maid sliced hard-boiled eggs and onions. A third sliced hearts of palm with which to garnish the goose-liver pâté. The chef and an assistant whisked away at the cheese sauce for the Veal Orloff. And butler John Holt swooped past Pratt with an armload of champagne bottles which he placed on the dumbwaiter and sent upstairs.

"Good evening, sir," said Holt.

"Everything under control, Holt?" Pratt loved the commotion in the kitchen. He felt like a general watching the preparations for war.

"Yes, sir. And may I say that you look most elegant in black tie."

"Well, we decided to forego white tie and tails this year. Tone things down a bit. This is a depression, after all, and it will be getting worse when that damn Roosevelt takes office. So we must take a tuck where we can."

"Indeed, sir."

Pratt opened the refrigerator. He saw mounds of caviar and fifteen dozen unshelled oysters. "Where's the champagne, Holt?"

"Out in the snow. I elected to buy as little ice as possible. We must take a tuck where we can."

Pratt laughed. "Yes, yes. Very good. Make sure there's plenty of everything. Anyone who'd dig his way through three feet of snow deserves the best and the most."

"Indeed, sir."

Pratt turned and went up the small staircase that led to the pantry. He was sixty years old. His blond hair, which Abigail Pratt Bentley had admired when he was a baby, had turned brown when he was ten years old. Then, on a June night in 1917, it had turned gray when the news arrived that his youngest son, Philip, had been killed on the Western Front. His Pratt features—people said that he resembled the Copley portrait of Horace Taylor Pratt—made him seem stern and resilient. But he was tired. He had planned to retire in 1930 and leave the company in the hands of his sons, Artemus IV and Taylor. The stock-market crash had interfered with his plans.

Artemus Pratt III had remained to supervise the cutbacks and layoffs at various Pratt factories and mines. It had been a difficult time, but the foundation of the Pratt Corporation was strong, and the company had, up until now, withstood the storm. Pratt Rubber, the Pratt Munitions Company, Pratt Engineering, which had joined in the research into vacuum tubes and the transmission of pictures through the new medium of television all had continued to show profit. Freight rates were down and Pratt rail holdings had not been doing well. But Artemus Pratt III was committed to America's future, and he believed that with good Republican management, the economy would bounce back. He would have to wait four years for another Republican administration, but in the meantime, he and his sons would run the company as the country should be run.

He strolled through the dining room, where servants laid out linen, fine china, and silver for the buffet.

He stopped in the music room, a bright hall in the style of Louis Quatorze, all gilt and mirrors and crystal chandeliers. Eleven musicians in black tie, sounding like cats in an alley, tuned their instruments. Within the hour, they would become Henry Blake and His Musicmasters. They would play waltzes, gavottes and, later in the evening, the Charleston and contemporary tunes about overcoming Old Man Depression for the younger set, which rarely gave the Depression a thought.

316

Artemus Pratt ascended the mahogany staircase. The noises of preparation gave way to other sounds—the laughter of children at play, the bawling of three Pratt infants in the third-floor nursery, and the strains of Brahms's Sonata for Cello and Piano in F Major.

Pratt stopped outside the parlor to listen. The cello was, at best, amateurish; his wife Clarissa was playing. The piano was subtle, expressive. Katherine Pratt Carrington's playing was almost as exquisite as her cameo features, her long, graceful neck, her marcelled hair. She was one of the few women Artemus knew who could wear the contemporary female evening dress—bloused satin top over bare breasts—and not look like a slut on Scollay Square. Whenever he thought about her, Artemus heard Bach—cool, rational, detached, yet filled with spirit.

Artemus loved his niece like a daughter. He had cared for her like a daughter since she had returned from Europe in April of 1912, at eleven years old the only Pratt to survive the sinking of the *Titanic*. She knew that her father had stayed on board; she had been separated from her mother and two older brothers and never saw them again.

Artemus and his wife had taken his brother's daughter into their home, nursed her back from her grief, and encouraged her to play the piano. She had eventually studied at the New England Conservatory. She had once played the Tchaikovsky Piano Concerto No. 1 with the Boston Symphony Orchestra, and she performed often at recitals in Boston and New York. At twenty-four, she had married Henry Carrington, a junior partner in the family law firm, and had borne two beautiful children. Jeffrey, eight years old, was deeply involved in mischief someplace on the second floor, and two-year-old Isabelle was squealing in the nursery.

Artemus looked into the room and saw a small, intimate group, a family dressed for the ball. His younger son, Taylor, twenty-six, sat with his wife on the settee. Artemus IV, twenty-nine, stood behind his wife's chair and sipped Scotch. After several years of failure, Artemus IV and Denise Goodby Pratt had finally produced a child, and they seemed at ease with each other for the first time in years. Both sons still lived in their father's mammoth house, although Taylor was preparing to move to Lexington. The luckiest man in the room, thought Artemus, was Henry Carrington, who sat beside his wife at the piano bench and turned the pages of her music like a devoted servant.

Calvin, Taylor's older child, slid down the banister from the third floor and ran toward the parlor. He was still baby-fat, and his tuxedo made him look like a miniature waiter at the Ritz. Artemus grabbed him by the collar before he could disrupt Katherine's performance.

"Where are you going?" he whispered.

"Nanny says that baby Philip is crying, and his mother is the only one who can make him stop."

Artemus smiled. "I'll tell her. You run along."

Artemus went into the room, knelt beside his daughter-in-law, and whispered in her ear, "If there are any women in this house so backward as still to be breastfeeding their infants, those women are needed in the nursery."

Denise smiled. "He's always hungry."

Artemus sat in her chair and looked up at his son. "Aside from Christmas eve, this is the nicest night of the year."

Artemus IV smiled. He was shorter and more compact than his father, with the body of a middleweight and good looks that came from 140 years of careful breeding.

Artemus III was one of the few people who ignored his son's streak of petulance and bad temper, but he noticed tonight that his son seemed unaccountably nervous. He wondered why.

A handful of pebbles rattled against the windows. "Peter. Peter Rulick," came the cry.

Billy and Jack looked out. They saw twenty or thirty men, all roughly dressed and bundled against the cold. Billy recognized men he had seen many times in his father's company. Jackie saw powerful, squat physiques, rugged features, moustaches, and long plumes of steam shooting from mouths and nostrils. They reminded him of draft horses waiting to pull a load.

Peter Rulick threw on his jacket and longshoreman's cap.

"Be careful, Petrov," said Anna.

He kissed her on the cheek. More stones rattled against the window.

"Let's be goin'," said Irish Red.

Peter started for the door, and Billy grabbed him by the arm. "I want to go too, Papa."

"No," said Anna firmly.

"I'm not afraid."

"There's nothing to fear," said Peter, who liked the idea of bringing the boy along. "It is time he saw what a man must do. Besides, where we are going tonight, it will be warm and there will be good things to eat."

Jackie liked the last part. "Can I go too?"

"No," said Anna.

"What will your mother say?" said Peter.

"Oh, she don't mind if I stay out at night," he lied, "just so long's I do my homework."

Peter smiled. "Both of you raise your right hands and repeat after me. 'I will swear to obey Peter Rulick tonight, and I will uphold the laws of the Pratt Rubber Workers Union that we don't yet have.'"

They swore.

"You're honorary members. Put on your coats."

The snow had stopped and the clouds were gone. The sky seemed bottomless and black. The city was never more beautiful or quiet than when it was frozen in snow, and Jackie always roamed the streets after a blizzard. Tonight, he walked with purpose.

He and Billy were in the middle of the group, which moved without form or apparent leadership in silence down the street. Snow crunched underfoot and men breathed hard against the cold. A block away, a snowplow ground along, its blade scraping the pavement. A train rattled past overhead, raining sparks onto the street as it scraped ice from the third rail. Jackie noticed a blackjack in one man's pocket, a length of pipe in another man's hand. He wondered what kind of party they were going to.

The group crossed Washington Street and started up Dover. As they passed an apartment that many of them seemed to know, a man ran out carrying two sacks filled with rocks and several other sacks that were empty. Peter Rulick took one of the empty sacks and hung it around his neck. Then he picked up some snow and made a snowball with a rock at the center. He spat on the snowball and dropped it into his sack. A moment later Jackie and Billy were making snowballs as fast as they could.

"Don't forget to spit on them," said Rulick. "Spit freezes them hard."

They crossed Tremont Street onto Berkeley and approached the Berkeley Street Bridge, which crossed the railroad tracks between the South End and the Back Bay. Jackie noticed lead pipes and blackjacks appearing all around. The group pulled into a tight circle and marched straight down the middle of the street. The men who didn't have weapons moved to the middle of the circle, around the boys, and took as many snowballs as they could hold.

The street was dark and deserted, but Jackie Ferguson sensed the presence of other men. "I'm scared, Billy."

"Me, too."

The boys had not spoken since they crossed Washington Street.

"Wait till they're close and aim for the face," whispered Peter Rulick to the men around him.

The bridge was in sight now. Its four street lamps gleamed brightly above the railroad tracks. Jack heard the whistle of an outbound freight. Then he saw them. They looked like the men he was marching with. They wore the same rough clothes. They had the same immigrant faces. They carried clubs and lead pipes and blackjacks. They appeared from the alleys on either side of Berkeley Street and charged at the marchers.

The union men on the outside of the circle dropped to the ground. The men on the inside unleashed their snowballs and aimed for the face.

A snowball with a rock at its core can lay a face open like a ripe squash, and the union men hit their targets. Blood soaked into the snow. The attackers fell back. The union men outnumbered them by a dozen, but the strikebreakers reorganized and came again. A second barrage of snowballs was followed by a bitter exchange between lead pipe and club. Jackie had seen fights before and been in more than his share, but he'd never seen anything like this. There was no swearing or yelling, none of the noise of a gang fight on the block. This was a silent struggle, punctuated occasionally by a grunt or the scuffing of a boot or the sound of wood slamming into bone.

The union men won and crossed the bridge into the Back Bay.

Company spies at Pratt Rubber had told their superiors about the march, and the information had traveled up the chain of command from the company plant in Brighton to the desk of Artemus Pratt IV. The younger Artemus had hired a few well-known strikebreakers to keep the demonstrators from leaving the South End. The strikebreakers had hired hungry men looking for a night's work and street toughs who did it for fun. Artemus Pratt IV had expected that they would succeed.

The Pratt Winter Ball was in full swirl when the union men arrived. Most of the two hundred guests, some of the richest, most accomplished people in America, were dancing or were clustered around the caviar on the dining-room table. The orchestra was playing Strauss, and the champagne was disappearing as quickly as it was served. Artemus Pratt IV was heading upstairs for a game of three-cushion when he noticed a commotion at the door. Holt seemed to be arguing with someone. Then the door was thrown open and a blast of cold air knocked Holt across the hall.

Thirty men, led now by Peter Rulick and Irish Red McDonough, marched into the house.

320

Artemus Pratt IV was enraged. He leaped off the staircase and jumped in front of the men. "Stay right where you are."

Peter Rulick knocked him back with one punch. Jackie Ferguson had never seen a man hit so hard.

The group marched across the foyer, through the French doors, into the ballroom, and brought the frigid outside air with them. The dancers, perspiring discreetly as they waltzed, froze in their places. The orchestra stopped abruptly.

Peter Rulick began the speech he had been rehearsing all day. "Ladies and gentlemen," he announced loudly, "I am sorry to spoil your party. Parties are good. Everyone should have parties. But tonight, while people are dancing in this house, people are starving in this city. Men who cry out for fair wages and decent working conditions, for unions—"

"Damn your unions!" bellowed the elder Artemus Pratt. Be happy you have jobs in a depression."

Two hundred Bostonians in black tie and evening gown applauded their host.

"I have no job," hollered Rulick. "I tried to organize a union that would be fair to all men, and I was fired. After twenty-five years of service, I was fired. I work like a dog. Me and all these others. We kill ourselves every day mixing the rubber that stinks and burns the eyes, pouring it when it is red-hot, choking on it, smelling it at night. All so we can support our families while you have your great parties and drink the champagne of our sweat."

Artemus Pratt III stepped toward Rulick. "Listen, you Red bastard. My great-great-grandfather built a fortune here with nothing but his brains. His descendants have had the good sense to build upon it. We believe in free enterprise. We believe in business. We believe in an open shop. We will not let our employees hold an ax over our heads. No union."

Jackie Ferguson wasn't paying much attention. He was looking around to see what he could eat. He nudged Billy Rulick, who hadn't taken his eyes off his father. "Let's find the food."

"No. My father needs me."

"He's doin' fine. Let's get somethin' to eat."

"No."

Jackie didn't want to go exploring through the house alone. "Your old man said we should fill our bellies. He'll be pissed if we don't." Jackie grabbed Billy by the elbow and backed him out of the music room.

They moved across the foyer into the dining room. Billy felt traitorous, but Jackie kept telling him that the dining-room table would be covered with roast beef and ham and slices of whipped-cream cake. No one stopped them as they bolted to the table. Even the servants were watching the confrontation. But there was nothing on the table worth eating.

The mounds of caviar sat in glass dishes atop ice-filled silver tureens. The garnishes—lemon, sliced onion, hard-boiled egg, and small squares of toast—were arranged like the petals of a flower around each tureen.

"What the fuck is this?" spat Jackie.

"It ain't roast beef and cake," said Billy.

"Onions and eggs. I eat better 'n this at home. He grabbed a glass of champagne from a tray and drank it down. "Want one?"

"No." Billy Rulick was looking around the corner into the ballroom.

"What the hell are these little black things?" said Jackie. "They look like buckshot."

Billy was paying no attention.

Jackie picked up some of the buckshot and stuffed it in his mouth, just long enough to taste it and spit it out all over the linen table cloth. "That tastes like the balls off a dead carp."

"That's caviar."

Jackie looked up at the most beautiful woman he had ever seen.

"Most little boys don't like it, but I think we might have something for you two down in the kitchen." Katherine Pratt Carrington offered one hand to Jackie, the other to Billy Rulick. "Come along."

Jackie didn't move. He was afraid that if he touched her, she might disappear. Billy wanted nothing to do with her.

"Come along. I won't hurt you." The voice was soft and soothing. She smiled and Jack melted. He hadn't held anyone's hand since he was six years old.

"What about your friend?" she asked.

Peter Rulick's voice boomed from the music room. Billy could see that his father was now facing two men, two Artemus Pratts. He ran back through the foyer.

"I'll give you two pieces of cake. You can save one for your friend," said Katherine to Jackie.

"Yes'm."

Katherine led Jackie down to the kitchen. Three cooks, unaware of the events upstairs, were putting the final touches on the Veal Orloff before it went into the ovens. They stopped and stared when Katherine entered with a street urchin at her heels.

322

"We'll stay out of your way," said Katherine softly. "Go back to work."

She told Jackie to sit at a small table in the corner. She poured him a glass of milk and pushed the pastry cart over to him. It was layered with tarts, Napoleons, and petits fours as beautiful as the woman serving them. Jack decided right then that he would always be a good Catholic, because heaven was probably like this. He studied the pastries carefully and chose a Napoleon—rich, creamy, and thick as his fist. He was about to lose himself in it when he heard the siren. It was like his mother's voice waking him from a dream. He had to go. His mother would kill him if he got himself arrested.

"Thanks, ma'am. See you again sometime." He turned to the back door, then realized that he shouldn't leave his friend. He ran back upstairs.

The police had arrived with five paddy wagons. Their heavy shoes shook the ballroom floor as they closed off the entrance and surrounded the union men. Women in long gowns screamed and fell back toward the music stand; their husbands jumped in front of them.

Peter Rulick told Billy to run.

"No. I'll stay and go to jail with you."

"One Rulick in jail is enough. Go home and be the man of the house. I command you."

Billy Rulick embraced his father, then ran past the police into the foyer. Jackie called to him from the dining room, and Billy followed. A policeman noticed them and gave chase.

Artemus Pratt IV pointed at Peter Rulick. "Be sure you get that one. He's the leader."

"Do not resist," shouted Rulick to the others.

The police grabbed Rulick by the arms.

Jackie led Billy down the narrow stairwell to the kitchen, with the policeman close on their heels. As they flew through the kitchen, Jackie spun a pan of Veal Orloff onto the floor. The policeman hit it at full speed and landed on his tail.

The two boys shot out into the service alley, and Jackie stopped in his tracks. He couldn't believe what he saw. Hundreds of champagne bottles were growing like weeds out of the snowbanks. The policeman wasn't behind him, so Jackie put two bottles in his outer pockets, and four more in the pockets his mother had sewn into his jacket. Then he raced down the alley, with Billy Rulick already two blocks ahead of him.

❄

"Son of a bitch nearly broke my jaw," said the younger Artemus Pratt.

"And spoiled a damn good party in the process," added Taylor.

"It frightens me to think that we're being infiltrated by men like that," said their father, swirling brandy in a snifter.

"The unions are coming, Artemus. There's nothing we can do about it," advised James Pratt, Artemus Pratt's cousin and a member of the Pratt Corporation board of directors.

"But we shan't be bullied," said Henry Hannaford, cousin and stockholder.

The men sat in the oak-paneled office on the first floor and discussed the evening's confrontation. The ball had ended quickly after the police had left the house. Now, it was brandy, cigars, and strategy.

"Indeed, and we won't knuckle under to a group of Bolsheviks and racketeers. That Rulick is a first-class rabble rouser." Artemus III decided his brandy was sufficiently warmed. He brought the snifter to his lips.

"From what I know," said Henry Carrington, "he was approached by the national and asked to help start a local."

"And he's been causing trouble ever since," snapped Artemus IV. "Father's right. In this day and age, the last thing we need is an army of recalcitrant employees telling us how to run our operation."

"So what shall we do?" asked Taylor.

"We see to it that Peter Rulick causes no more trouble. We throw the book at him. Breaking and entering, criminal trespass, unlawful assembly, assault and battery." Artemus IV rubbed his chin. "And whatever else we can nail him on. I'd like you to put someone on it right away, Henry."

"You'll still have to contend with the unions," said Carrington. "People want their unions. You can't escape that."

Artemus Pratt the younger agreed. "We'll have a union, but we'll select the people who organize it ourselves. We won't have Communist outsiders telling us how to run our plants. We could fire every man at Pratt Rubber tonight and fill every position tomorrow with some poor sucker who's been out of work since the crash."

Artemus Pratt III nodded. He liked to see his son take control.

Without knocking, Katherine Pratt Carrington entered the room. The conversation stopped. "I do not, as a rule, interrupt the gentlemen in the midst of important conversation. But I have been eavesdropping on this discussion, and I must speak my mind. None of you seem to realize that you're dealing with more than laborers who want longer coffee breaks. This evening, I met one of the urchins who came with the strikers. He was ravenous." She paused and looked around. "Hungry children, gentlemen. Hungry men and women. We must help those people, or the Pratts and everyone like them will face a grave crisis."

"What do you propose to do?" asked Artemus IV sarcastically.

"At least help to feed them."

"How?" asked Taylor.

"With charity."

"We give too much as it is," said the senior Pratt.

"If my reading of family legend is correct, one of our ancestors left us some sort of treasure to be used when we faced a crisis," said Katherine. "I think we're facing an enormous crisis right now. Our whole society may come apart if we stand by and do nothing."

"Are you talking about that crazy old loon Abigail Pratt Bentley?" Artemus Pratt III began to laugh, and the other men, except for Henry Carrington, joined in. "If you can find that treasure, that tea set, whatever the hell it is, you can give it away to anyone you want. You can even have my quotation from *Paradise Lost*. When I was in college, I had it printed on all my bookmarks. Now if your cousins and uncles will give you their quotations, you'll have a start."

"I have one in a safety-deposit box somewhere," said Hannaford. "I'm not averse to letting Katherine indulge her philanthropic impulses."

"Thank you," said Katherine, masking her annoyance. "What about the rest of you?"

Artemus IV slammed his hands on the arms of his chair. "Dammit, Kate, we're involved in important business here. Those bastards invaded our house, attacked me, and caused general bedlam. We're going to do our damnedest to keep them all in jail, and the hell with charity."

She pretended to ignore her cousin. "If any of the rest of you care to help, you know where you can find me." She closed the door behind her.

"Sorry to be barking like that, Henry," said young Artemus, "but I get madder every time I think of that Rulick bastard catching me with a sucker punch. I want you to make sure he stays in jail."

"Whatever the law provides," said Carrington.

Over the next two days, Katherine Pratt Carrington visited relatives and told them that she was trying to find the old family treasure, the proceeds of which she intended to donate to the South

End Community Club. She collected four sets of lines, most of them kept in envelopes and safety-deposit boxes since the reading of Abigail Pratt Bentley's will.

Her cousin William Pratt, grandson of Jason Pratt, the Civil War surgeon, kept his quotation framed on the wall behind his desk at the Massachusetts General Hospital. It read, in Old English script, "Two of far nobler shape erect and tall,/ Godlike erect, with native honor clad/ In naked Majesty seem'd Lords of all,/ And worthy seem'd, for in their looks Divine/ The image of their glorious Maker shone,/ Truth, Wisdom, Sanctitude severe and pure . . ."

"I like the sentiment. Milton's talking there about Adam and Eve. He's talking about all of us. We all have a chance to be something great. We're all born naked into this world with the same gifts. That's what I always tell my patients."

"You know, of course, that I'm trying to find a treasure that legend says this quotation and several others will lead us to."

Like most of the others, William Pratt laughed softly, patronizingly. "I've heard that it's a Revere tea set."

"That's the legend."

"If you find it, dear, sell it to someone filthy rich and make good use of his money. Then he'll donate it to the Museum of Fine Arts and the world will be able to enjoy it."

After two days of phone calls and visits, Katherine began to realize that not all her relatives were so willing to help.

"Father believes there's nothing to this story," said Artemus IV. "I don't see why I should encourage you to waste your time. Besides, if you do find this mythical teapot, you intend to throw it away on an army of street urchins, socialists, and drunks. No thank you."

Responses like that disappointed Katherine. When she learned that the California branch of the family had disintegrated because of bad investments and divorce, she became discouraged. When she learned that a separate envelope containing Abigail Pratt Bentley's directions had disappeared somewhere between the first Artemus and Artemus III, she despaired of ever finding the treasure.

After two days in the holding tank at the Charles Street Jail, Peter Rulick, Irish Red, and their supporters were officially charged with everything Henry Carrington could think of. The judge released the supporters on their own recognizance, but he held Rulick and Irish Red at a thousand dollars' bail. Peter Rulick was also charged with contempt of court when he announced that the judge was a tool of the Pratts.

Both men went back to their cells while the union tried to raise bail.

On his third day at the Charles Street Jail, Peter Rulick was stabbed twenty-five times while taking a shower.

The knife was discovered in a drain, and, although no fingerprints or witnesses could be found, evidence pointed to a man named Harry Kilcoyne, a small-time gambler and sometime hit man awaiting trial for rape. When asked why he did it, he said, "I just don't like radicals and Reds tryin' to screw up this country."

A few days later, Katherine Pratt Carrington filled her car, a 1928 Buick, with groceries, and told her chauffeur to drive to 31 Decatur Street. Jackie Ferguson was sitting on his stoop across the street when he saw his Back Bay vision emerge from her car and go into Rulick's apartment. He ran across the street and followed her up the stairs.

Katherine Carrington introduced herself through a crack in the door and Anna Rulick let her into the house. The chauffeur and Jackie Ferguson followed.

It was dark and cold in the apartment. The shades were drawn tight and a single lamp illuminated the parlor, where Anna and her four boys sat.

Katherine Carrington told her chauffeur to put the bundles on the table in the kitchen and bring up the rest. She removed her gloves and held them nervously. She sensed the grief, the gloom, the poverty that enveloped the room. She felt ostentatious, even in the tweed overcoat and gray dress that her husband had said made her look like a schoolteacher. She offered her condolences.

Anna Rulick nodded, although she did not seem to hear.

In a soft, wavering voice, Katherine told Anna that she had brought food and blankets and would continue to send food through the winter.

"We don't want it." The voice sounded like the growl of an angry cat. "We don't want charity. My father did not want charity. We will do for ourselves."

Katherine looked at the little boy sitting by the radiator. She recognized him from the Winter Ball. "The food and blankets are not charity. They are assistance from your father's employers. We are very sorry about what happened."

Mrs. Rulick put up her hand, as if to ward off a blow. "I can no take these things. My boy, he's right. We no want your gifts when you take away our . . . our . . ." The words didn't come. She shuddered, sobbed, and began to cry without tears.

Katherine Pratt Carrington watched the forlorn, black-shrouded figure, and she wanted to cry too. In the *Titanic* lifeboat, she had seen shock evolve into grief. In this cold room, with its soot-darkened wallpaper, its worn furniture, its obsessive neatness, she saw despair. Peter Rulick was dead, and his wife's life had ended.

Billy Rulick stood suddenly, marched across the room, and opened the door. He was telling Katherine to leave.

Katherine looked at Billy. His eyes were angry, not the eyes of a child. She smiled tenderly and tried to run a hand through his black hair. She thought that her touch might bring the warmth to his face. He stepped back defiantly.

Katherine turned and headed for the door.

"Excuse me, ma'am." It was Jack's voice.

She stopped and looked back.

"If Miz Rulick don't want this stuff, maybe I'll take it, if it's all right with you."

"Does your mother accept charity?" asked Katherine.

"No, ma'am. I'll just tell her I stole it."

The Carrington house on Beacon Hill was warm and quiet. Isabelle was taking her afternoon nap. Jeffrey was sprawled in front of the fireplace with his crayons and paper.

From the windows of her bedroom, Katherine Pratt Carrington watched the snow falling gently on the city—on the Common, the Back Bay, the South End, on the distant hills of Brookline. Snow stretching to infinity. Fresh snow covering every roof in Boston. It did not discriminate. It made the city look like a village in Vermont.

How deceptive it was. How different were the worlds beneath the snow. How little one person could do to change any of it, even the life of a single boy. Her impulse had been good, but she knew that charity could never remake her city. And no matter what she did, she could never do enough. She took her quotations from *Paradise Lost* and placed them in the living-room safe.

Katherine Pratt Carrington forgot that some people are born with enough stubbornness and strength to survive anything. Maybe she couldn't help the fatherless little boy, but the little boy would help himself.

Billy Rulick stayed in school, but he took any job he could get in the afternoons. He swept floors. He cleaned toilets in a flophouse. He ran numbers for the local bookie. When his family was hungry and couldn't buy food, he stole it. When they were cold and had no coal, he stole it. He forgot his despair. He survived.

And on Saturday mornings, Sadie Ferguson loaded his pockets with liquid death and expanded her business. On Saturday afternoons, Billy Rulick sat with Jackie Ferguson in the Madison Hotel and listened to an old man's stories of buried treasure and the Back Bay Pratts.

CHAPTER XX

Katherine Pratt Carrington had been complaining to her nurse all day about the pain. When the doctor came to her bungalow, she gave him every symptom he asked for.

"Have you noticed blood in your bowels? Coal-black stools?"

"Yes."

"No, she hasn't," said the nurse.

"What about red blood?"

"That, too."

"I haven't seen it," said the nurse.

"They're my stools," answered Mrs. Carrington.

"Where is the pain?" asked the doctor.

"All over."

"You have no temperature. Do you feel nauseated?"

"Yes."

"She hasn't vomited," said the nurse.

The doctor put his hands on her stomach. They were ice-cold. "Relax."

She hardened every muscle.

"Relax," he said again.

"I am."

He frowned. "We'd better take a few pictures. Get her over to X-ray."

The nurse, Mrs. Drexel, put Katherine Pratt Carrington in a wheelchair. Mrs. Drexel had once been a gym instructor, and she was as strong as a man. Except for the dress, she looked like a man. "I know you're not sick. You just want attention."

Katherine Carrington said nothing.

Mrs. Drexel rolled the wheelchair out of the bedroom, across the small sitting room, and out the door of the bungalow where Katherine Pratt Carrington had been living since her grandson's funeral. Mrs. Drexel nodded to the bulky young man by the door. He was one of two private orderlies who kept visitors away from Mrs. Carrington. He was reading *Penthouse* and waiting for the next shift.

The Lynnewood Manor looked like a resort hotel, and only the rich could afford to end their lives there. Dozens of private bungalows, shaded by elms and maples, were scattered across the manor's two acres. The lawn was dotted with old people in robes and pajamas, giant pastel flowers soaking up the June sun. A black wrought-iron fence kept the world out and the occasional wanderer in. Ribbons of clean, bright concrete wound across the lawn and connected the central building to the bungalows. The central building was an old Victorian mansion, all turrets and porches, balconies and bay windows, which had once been the home of a New England shoe manufacturer. The Lynnewood Manor offered full medical care, game rooms, cable television, and, for the healthier guests, shuffleboard and swimming. Katherine Pratt Carrington hated it.

The X-ray technician read the doctor's instructions and helped Katherine onto the table. After she took the X-rays, she told Katherine to stay on the table while she made sure the pictures came out.

For the first time in a week, Katherine Carrington was alone with a telephone. She jumped off the table and ran to the wall phone in the technician's booth. After dialing four digits, she heard the operator's voice. She hung up and dialed nine. This time, she got an outside line. She prayed that Evangeline was home.

It was eight o'clock. Fallon and Evangeline were still in bed.

Instinctively, Fallon reached for the telephone when it rang him awake.

Evangeline grabbed his wrist. "It may be my mother. I'd rather not have to explain you so early in the morning." She reached across his chest and picked up the telephone. "Hello?"

"Get me out of here."

"Grandmother! Where are you?" Evangeline sat up in bed.

"Lynnewood Manor, bungalow sixteen, I can't talk anymore. Lynnewood Manor. And be careful. They have me guarded." Katherine was back on the table before the technician returned to the room.

Evangeline found the address of the Lynnewood Manor in the phone directory. The home was in a rich bedroom community about an hour north of Boston.

Fallon drove. He had been waiting for a chance in the Porsche, and Evangeline trusted him enough now to give him the keys. But instead of heading across the Back Bay to the Mystic River Bridge, he drove toward South Boston.

"Where are you going?" asked Evangeline.

"If you look behind you—and don't—you'll see a black Oldsmobile. I suppose it's followed us before, but this is the first time I've noticed it."

"Who's in it?"

"It must be one of the guys Ferguson was talking about last night."

"One of Soames's men?"

Fallon nodded.

"Why would they be following us?"

"Apparently they didn't believe we fell for their story yesterday."

Fallon pulled the Porsche into a large storage yard near the MBTA car barn in South Boston. A ten-foot chain-link fence topped with barbed wire ran all around the yard, and a sign above the gate read "Fallon and Son Construction Company." A rundown shack, once the office of a used-car lot, sat in the middle of the yard. Behind it was a work shed, and scattered all about was the equipment of a small construction company: mortar mixer, compressor, scaffolding, planks, bags of limestone and cement covered by a tarpaulin, piles of plywood and scrapwood, pallets of bricks and blocks, a railcart the Fallons used when they did a job in the subways, and a frontloader that converted into a snowplow in winter. Tom Fallon believed in owning his own equipment. Peter Fallon thought that his father was a packrat.

Peter parked the car behind the shack and went in the back door.

It was a tiny room—two metal office desks, a filing cabinet, a space heater for winter, and a Playmate calendar on the wall. Danny was reading the sports section behind one desk. Sheila was opening mail behind the other. Although there was little to do, she came in every morning to answer phones, type, and help out in the office.

"Morning, Dan," said Peter. "Where's the old man?"

"Off lookin' at a job. Where the hell did you come from?"

Peter pointed out the door. "From that Porsche."

Danny saw Evangeline sitting in the car. He whistled softly.

"I'll trade the Porsche for your Chevy." Peter held out the keys. "Just for the morning. You can take Sheila for a long spin, but only if she puts on the kerchief in the glove compartment."

"What the hell is going on here, Peter?"

Fallon gestured toward the window, but he did not go near it. "You see a black Olds out there?"

Danny glanced out. "The Cutlass?"

Peter nodded. "I'm trying to lose him."

"You in trouble?" asked Danny seriously.

Peter didn't want to explain. "The guy in that car used to be Evangeline's boyfriend."

"Evangeline." Danny said the name very slowly. He liked it.

"Do me a favor and take him on a little tour of Southie. Then Evangeline and I can get away."

"That's real romantic, Peter," said Sheila.

Danny flipped his keys to his brother. "Anything so my little brother can get laid."

Evangeline looked the other way as her Porsche sped off. Fallon watched it head back toward the expressway with the Oldsmobile a short distance behind.

"If anybody up at that place is expecting us, they won't be looking for a brown Chevy."

Peter and Evangeline swung past the Lynnewood Manor an hour later. A large visitor's parking lot descended in several tiers down from the main house. The only entrances were through the central building or the service gate, where trucks, doctors' cars, ambulances, and hearses passed regularly. Fallon did not stop or pull into the lot. He had already decided that he would go in on foot, avoiding the reception area or the guardhouse at the service gate.

"Why don't we just go in?" asked Evangeline.

"The guy in the black Olds proves they still don't trust us. They're probably watching for us at all the main entrances."

"So what? I don't see why we can't just walk right in. I'll talk to her doctor, or we'll talk to the people in administration, and we'll get her out. She's a responsible adult. They don't have the right to keep her in there."

"If she's still in shock, she isn't responsible. Who's the executor of her will?"

"Her daughter Isabelle."

"Then Isabelle has probably been appointed temporary guardian, and from what I've seen, Isabelle is on your uncle's team.

Fallon watched a bus stop in front of the nursing home. Six people got off. Two were black, one Puerto Rican, three whites. The women wore white dresses, and none of them looked as though they lived in the neighborhood. They crossed the street and the parking lot and went in a side entrance on the basement level of the main building. The midday shift was arriving for work.

Fallon drove the car around the block and back to a bus stop a mile or so away.

"What are you doing?" asked Evangeline.

"I'm going in alone."

"We came here to see my grandmother, Peter."

"If she's guarded, it's going to be hard enough for one person to get near her." He looked Evangeline up and down.

She was wearing an expensive pink blouse, gold neck chain, and Brass Buckle jeans. Fallon had stopped at his apartment for a clean shirt and jeans after borrowing his brother's car.

"I might be able to get in the workers' entrance, but you don't really make it as a member of the proletariat."

She decided to let him follow his instinct.

Fallon got off the bus in front of the Lynnewood Manor along with three nurses, a Puerto Rican man and a white teen-ager who were complaining to each other about the work load for the kitchen help, and a black man dressed like an orderly. Fallon fell in behind the kitchen workers and put his head down.

"Yeah," said the teen-ager, a pimply kid with stringy hair and a bad set of adenoids. "They get real pissed when their tea ain't hot."

"They bitch at me today, man, I tell 'em the bus is late," said the Puerto Rican.

"What if Lard-Ass Loughlin bitches?"

"Ah, I tell her to suck me off, man."

They both laughed.

Fallon decided that if he could get past the entrance, he would follow them to the kitchen. From there, he might have a good chance at Katherine Carrington.

Keeping at the edge of the group, he walked around the side of the main house to the narrow flight of stairs which led to the workers' entrance. He felt his hands beginning to sweat. He wiped them on his shirt. He hoped he didn't have to answer any questions at the door, because he could feel his voice tightening in his throat. He walked down the stairs which led to the cellar and stepped into the air conditioning.

A private security guard sat by the time clock. He was reading the racing form, and he did not look up. Fallon thought about slipping past, but he did not know where he was going. He had to stay with the kitchen workers, who continued to complain as they punched in. Fallon took a time card from the rack and pushed it into the clock. The guard raised his head from the paper, but Fallon didn't miss a beat. He finished punching in, and by the time he put the card back, the guard was again trying to pick the daily double. Fallon realized that the guards weren't waiting for him.

He turned and walked through a pair of swinging doors which led to a new stairwell. He heard the voices of the kitchen men below him. He followed. At the bottom of the stairs, he stepped into another corridor. He was in a subbasement which had been dug when the house was remodeled. At the end of the corridor were swinging doors that led to the kitchen. Two rooms opened onto the corridor, and Fallon could hear the voices of the kitchen workers coming from the room on the right.

He walked down the corridor and looked into a workers' coat-room. There were pegs on the wall, benches and folding chairs scattered about the room.

Fallon stepped in and said hello.

The pair eyed him suspiciously at first, thinking he was another boss. Then Fallon took a white coat off one of the hooks and put it on.

"You new here, man?" asked the Puerto Rican.

"Yeah. My first day."

"You a cook?"

Fallon shook his head. "Loughlin hired me. She said I should start deliverin' food on the noon shift."

The two workers looked at each other.

"You takin' one of our jobs?" asked the teen-ager.

Fallon said he didn't think so and wondered whether the kid would sound any better if he blew his nose.

"She musta found more shit for us to do, then," said the Puerto Rican.

Fallon introduced himself and learned their names. "Mr. Sanchez. You must be the Sanchez that Loughlin told me to see."

The Puerto Rican laughed. "I didn't know that bitch trust me with anything."

Fallon thought he might be going too far. "We don't have to check in with her once we've punched in, do we?"

"Nope. Just deliver the food, then bring the trays back. She find something for you to do then."

Sanchez led Fallon down the hallway. They stepped through the swinging doors into the steam and confusion of the central kitchen. Workers scurried about. Cooks shouted orders. Dishwashers churned away. Institution green and stainless-steel silver were the only colors that cut through the steam. On the far side of the room, behind a glass partition, Fallon saw an overweight blonde shouting into a telephone. He assumed that she was Loughlin.

"Where are the trays?" Fallon wanted to be out of the kitchen before Loughlin was out of her office.

"Take it easy, man. You don't want to move too fast on your first day. You'll wear yourself out," said Sanchez.

"Yeah," added the kid. "Watch us."

They crossed to the corner where the carts were loaded for delivering. Fallon read the notation on the first cart. It listed bungalows one to twelve, the name of each patient, and the meal. There were four carts. Fallon moved to the next and read. "Carrington, number sixteen."

"You choosy, man? You don't like the first cart?"

"It's the first day. Gotta have someone to follow." He glanced at the kid, "And someone behind me to make sure I don't fuck up."

The kid laughed. "You must be pretty stupid if you need me to watch you."

Fallon shrugged and followed Sanchez through another set of swinging doors into a long tunnel which led, eventually, out to the lawn. He pushed the cart past old men playing checkers and soaking up the sun, past old men and women who stared vacantly and others who smiled and hoped he'd stop to talk.

As they reached the walkway that led past the bungalows, Sanchez parked in front of number one.

Fallon kept going. He was doing well so far, but he could see the orderly reading *Penthouse* outside number sixteen. He didn't recognize the orderly, and he hoped the orderly wouldn't recognize him. Katherine Pratt Carrington sat in a lawn chair beside the orderly. She was holding a book, but she wasn't reading. He hoped she noticed him before he got to her. Otherwise he might startle her.

He worked his way to bungalow fifteen, knocked on the door, went in, and placed a tray on a table in the living room. The person sitting there hardly noticed him. He stepped outside again and heard Katherine Carrington's voice.

She was speaking to the orderly. "If you must look at that filth, young man, please do it at a respectable distance from me. Every time I look up, I see pudendae and areoli, and frankly, I am offended. You can keep your eye on me just as well over on the grass."

The orderly said nothing. He closed the magazine, walked a short distance across the lawn, and stretched out.

Fallon wheeled the cart slowly toward her. "Good afternoon, ma'am."

The guard glanced up, as did Nurse Drexel, who was sitting inside the bungalow watching television.

Fallon placed the tray in front of Mrs. Carrington, and she winked at him. Now that he was here, with her protection all around, he didn't quite know what to say or do.

"What do we have for lunch today?" she asked cheerfully.

"Clear soup, ma'am."

"I'm not hungry anyway."

Fallon bent down, as though he had dropped something from the cart.

"Is Evangeline with you?" whispered Katherine.

"She couldn't get in."

Katherine Carrington pulled an envelope from the back papers of her book and slipped it onto Fallon's cart. She hadn't expected that they would have much chance to talk.

"John Milton and *Paradise Lost?*" Fallon spoke in shorthand. He had no time for explanations.

Her eyes narrowed. "You, too?"

"Since my first trip to Searidge."

"Are you with Rule?"

He shook his head.

"Get me out of here, and I'll tell you everything I know."

The orderly looked suddenly in Fallon's direction. Fallon was sure he'd been recognized, although the orderly was ten feet away.

"Good afternoon, ma'am," Fallon said to Mrs. Carrington. Nonchalantly, he took the handle of the cart and started down the path toward bungalow seventeen. As he walked, he looked around for the best escape route. If he had to run, he wanted to know where he was going.

He stopped at bungalow seventeen. He could feel the orderly's eyes boring into him. He told himself to stay cool, to play the role. It had worked for him when he punched in. It could work now. He knocked on the bungalow door, then brought the lunch inside. When he stepped out again, the orderly was eating Katherine Carrington's lime jello.

"I don't see why we should be wasting perfectly edible food," Katherine was saying to him. "And I certainly don't intend to eat that awful stuff myself."

Fallon almost laughed. He wiped the droplets of perspiration from his forehead, delivered the rest of his lunches, and pushed the empty cart back to the kitchen. He returned the white jacket and cap to their hook and left the Lynnewood Manor with another group of workers.

When he got back to the car, Fallon was exhilarated, like a little boy who had just done something on a dare.

"Did you see her?" asked Evangeline.

"Got in and out without a hitch." He was grinning.

"Is she all right?"

"She looks fine. We couldn't talk, but she gave me this note."

"'I write surreptitiously and in haste!'" Fallon began to read while Evangeline drove toward Boston. "'I am here against my will. They tell me it is for my own good, that they want to protect me from danger in this tea-set business. They are lying. They are simply afraid that I might say something to the authorities about Christopher's death. I believe that he is dead because of the tea set, but the Pratts believe otherwise. I do not understand what requires such secrecy, but they have made me its victim, first in my own home, and now here. They believe that my knowledge of the tea set might be helpful to the people trying to find it. They want no one to approach me, not even that Harvard student, a total innocent.'"

"I wish you were," said Evangeline.

"'Please help me to leave here, Evangeline. I no longer love my daughter or my nephews. They have abused my freedom and shown no respect for my wishes. Isabelle tells me that she has been appointed my guardian. It is a lie to discourage me from trying to change my situation. She cannot become my guardian without a hearing. Men are guarding me round the clock, and Philip Pratt is on the board of directors at this nursing home.'"

"I didn't know that," said Evangeline.

"That makes it even harder," said Fallon.

He finished reading the letter. "'But you must do what you can to get me out of here. Bring a suitcase of clothes with you and take me straight to the airport. I still can be of use someplace, but not here. I must leave this tea-seat mess behind. It has already cost me a son and a grandson. I made a mistake twenty-five years ago. I will pay for it no more.'"

Her father. Evangeline was shocked. She looked straight ahead and gripped the wheel. She felt the car accelerate almost involuntarily. Another generation, another tragedy. Evangeline realized that her grandmother had been mourning more than the unrelated deaths of father and son, son and grandson. Her father and brother were both dead because of the tea set and a crazy ancestor who was father to them all.

In the days after Christopher's death, Katherine Pratt Carrington had kept saying that she could have stopped it. And now came this note, with its cryptic reference to a death twenty-five years earlier. Evangeline had to find out what her grandmother meant. An angry buzzing noise rattled Evangeline. She was traveling seventy-five miles an hour, and the speedometer alarm was pulling her attention back to the road.

"We have to get her out," said Peter. "We have to do it quickly and quietly, with no fanfare, no publicity. She can tell us things no one else knows. And with what we know now, I don't think either of us can rest until we end this thing for good."

She was beginning to agree with him.

Philip Pratt had spent most of the day talking on the telephone with major Pratt Industries stockholders. He was trying to convince them not to throw their support behind William Rule. He had not been successful. Former supporters told him that they were disappointed in his leadership and uncertain of the company's future. They said that, in light of the company's drastic losses over the last few years, a change at the top might be a positive move. While many of the old-line stockholders agreed that William Rule was not the sort they would invite to dinner, they all recognized his skill and his toughness. In twenty years, he had built an insignificant import firm into one of the most successful overseas buying operations in the United States.

"We've been very disappointed in your acquisition and diversification efforts," said the head of an investment firm which held a considerable block of Pratt stock. "All you have to show for seven years is a bad movie company. When Rule becomes chairman, he'll bring Rule Imports right along with him, and that's the kind of small, successful operation that makes an excellent acquisition. That alone puts Rule a mile ahead of you. Besides, he isn't making a tender offer. He isn't trying to buy up a controlling interest in the stock. He doesn't have the means. He's simply a stockholder trying to amass enough votes to take over the top corporate office. If the other stockholders don't like the job he does, they can vote him out again. Just as they're doing with you."

Phillip Pratt wanted his tea very strong this afternoon, with nothing but a twist of lemon to cut it. He stared down at the swanboats and sipped the acid, letting it scour his tongue. He did not want to listen to Bennett Soames or his cousin Isabelle.

"Evangeline spent the night with Fallon," Soames reported. "And this morning, they both eluded our observation. I believe that they will try to get to your aunt. They may have tried already. We could handle the problem more easily if your aunt were moved." He paused, then added sarcastically, "Our little charade yesterday didn't work."

Pratt glanced at Isabelle. He did not want to look weak in front of her. "We had only two other options, Bennett. Tell him everything or eliminate him. We're not murderers, and I had no intentions of asking Fallon to join us. He's in it for the adventure and the money."

Soames nodded. "And we couldn't rely on him to cooperate in our negotiations with Mr. Rule."

"Precisely," said Pratt. "Continue to keep him under surveillance and make sure that he doesn't get near my aunt."

"Back to my original point. Your aunt."

"I would prefer that my mother stay where she is," said Isabelle. She sat on the sofa and sipped at her tea. She was wearing a flowered cotton sundress and her hair at her shoulders.

Soames did not move and his expression did not change. He simply stared and waited for Pratt to agree with him.

Pratt realized that he was beginning to feel uneasy in Soames's presence. He had lately been allowing his authority to slip into

Soames's hands. He did not like his secretary giving him orders. "Fallon hasn't gotten to her yet. I don't think we'll have any problems."

"My mother could not stand another move," said Isabelle softly.

Soames did not acknowledge her. He continued to stare at Pratt.

"We're not moving her," said Pratt with sudden firmness. "We put her there for medical and psychiatric reasons. We wanted to shelter her so that she could deal with her shock. Let's remember our responsibility to her, Soames. We're keeping her right where she is. It's your responsibility to make sure that no one gets to her. Not Fallon, not Rule."

Bennett Soames showed no annoyance, but he felt his neck growing hot beneath his starched collar. He did not like to be overruled, especially in matters of security, but he knew that Pratt was beginning to feel the pressure of Rule's deadline and needed to assert himself. Soames could tolerate such displays a while longer.

Philip Pratt turned to Isabelle. "Tell Soames what you've found in the diaries."

Isabelle looked at Soames, whose dispassionate stare always irritated her. "I've been through forty-one diaries, each covering a year of Abigail's life. She kept a diary for over sixty years, but I couldn't find the others. I'm rather surprised that they disappeared. It isn't like us to lose important documents. But from what I read, I could understand Christopher's fascination with the family history. Abigail Pratt Bentley was an amazing woman."

"Did she tell you the whereabouts of the final passage?" asked Soames impatiently.

"If she had," snapped Isabelle, "do you think we'd be sitting here talking about it? If Abigail Pratt Bentley had not been quite so cryptic, we might have the tea set right now. However, as my mother discovered forty years ago, the envelope containing Abigail's instructions was lost someplace between Artemus Pratt and his grandson, Philip's grandfather. No one took Abigail seriously, which is a great tragedy. Fortunately, we saved most of her diaries, and the diaries may lead us to the last clue."

Isabelle took a notecard from her purse. "Just before she died, writing on the last page of her last diary, Abigail Pratt Bentley discussed the final codicil in her will and the ten envelopes she left to her nieces and nephews." Isabelle read, "'I have also fulfilled my promise to young Joseph Mannion, and that makes me feel wonderful.'"

"Who is Joseph Mannion?" asked Soames.

"He was the son of Abigail's servant, Sean, who died defending her from thieves. It seems that Abigail was in love with Sean for most of her life. Considering that and the context from which this quote is taken, it seems quite possible that Abigail gave the last quotation to Joseph Mannion."

Soames wondered why Christopher Carrington had not explored the Mannion descent.

"It's hard to say," responded Isabelle. "He read all the diaries when I first interested him in the family history a few years ago. Maybe he never considered the Mannion reference significant. After all, everything else in the diaries indicates that Abigail was trying to keep the secret within the family."

"Do you think you can track Mannion's descent?" asked Pratt.

"Tomorrow I'm visiting the Massachusetts Genealogical Society, and a friend at the State House will help me research birth certificates. That's the best way to start."

"Let me remind you," said Soames, "that we haven't much time. If our plan is to work with Mr. Rule, speed is of the essence. It is Friday afternoon. We have until Monday morning."

Soames bid them good day and left the office.

"He is a very annoying man," said Isabelle.

"If he wasn't annoying, he wouldn't be Soames." Pratt smiled. "He's been my personal secretary since I joined Pratt Industries in 1957. I'd be lost without him."

Isabelle studied Philip for a time. He seemed smaller, less formidable than she remembered. Once he had fitted perfectly behind the mahogany desk. Now the responsibilities that came with it threatened to engulf him.

"We need all the help we can get, don't we?"

Pratt spun in his chair and looked down at the Public Garden. "All we can get," he said softly. "All because of one crazy old lady who thought she was doing us a favor."

Isabelle stood impulsively and came up behind his chair. She placed her hands gently on his shoulders. "I'll do whatever I can, Philip."

"Thanks, Izzy."

She repeated the name. She hadn't heard it in years.

They both laughed, sharing the memory. Then she began to massage his shoulders. He bowed his head forward. She worked her hands into muscle and tendon, kneading, stretching, relaxing. She enjoyed comforting him.

"I worry about you, Philip. You're so alone in all of this."

"I'm lonely, Isabelle, but rarely alone. There's a difference." His body began to loosen and settle into the chair.

She slid her hands across his chest and clasped them in front of him. "I guess I'm lonely too, Philip. How can people be so lonely with so much?"

He placed his hands on hers. "Do we have anything that matters?"

The buzzer rang. Miss Allardyce told Pratt that a young lady named Melissa Pike was on the phone.

"Tell her I'm out of town on urgent business."

"Yes, sir." Miss Allardyce clicked off.

Pratt looked at his cousin. "How about a game of tennis and a quiet dinner in a lonely Back Bay mansion?"

Evangeline and Peter stopped at Nahant and had lunch on the way back from Lynnewood Manor. They talked about her grandmother. They stared at the ocean for a time. And they returned to Boston around four o'clock. They parked Danny's Chevrolet on Huntington Avenue, cut through an alley, and slipped into Evangeline's apartment.

Jack C. Ferguson, wearing nothing but a wet towel, was seated in the kitchen. He had showered, his white hair was trimmed and neatly combed, and he smelled faintly of Jean Naté.

"Afternoon, kids," he said cheerfully.

Evangeline looked at Peter. "I've been having this nightmare about a white whale in my apartment. Do you think I need to see a shrink?"

"You know, I like your girlfriend, Fallon." Ferguson began to laugh. The rolls of sagging muscle bounced about merrily.

"I wear a thirty-four bra with a C cup," said Evangeline. "You can borrow it any time you like."

Ferguson flexed and the flesh tightened. "I still got it when I need it, honey, especially after a nice bath and a shave."

"How long before the bathtub ring eats through the porcelain?"

"It usually takes about a week." Ferguson laughed. "And I guess you'd better fumigate your washer and dryer when my clothes are finished."

"I may just move instead."

"That's not a bad idea." The good humor left Ferguson's voice.

Fallon took out three beers and offered him one.

"No, thanks. When I shower and shave, I'm on the wagon. I got sloppy last night and nearly got blown away."

"You mean you drank too much?" asked Evangeline.

"I mean a couple of Rule's men were waitin' for me when I got to my flat. I was halfway up the stairs when I heard them movin' around. If I hadn't drunk so damn much champagne, I would've known the minute I stepped into the hallway that somebody was waiting for me."

"How?" asked Evangeline.

"I don't live in a very safe neighborhood, honey. So I have a little security system. But I wasn't paying attention to it."

"What did you do?" asked Fallon.

"I set the place on fire and got the hell out."

"I don't think I can deal with this." Evangeline opened her beer and sat down.

"Don't worry. The place was a boarded-up hovel. I found another one and had a good night's sleep. And I think that you two better find a new place, too. The Pratts are too civilized to go around knockin' people off, but Rulick, he's somethin' else again."

"What do you mean by that?" Evangeline didn't like his tone.

Ferguson flipped a newspaper to Fallon. A small article on the business page was circled. It described the possible takeover of the Pratt Industries board of directors by William Rule, who had been seeking support among the major stockholders for the last several months. It said that Rule would be making an announcement on Monday at the Pratt Industries stockholders' meeting.

"The baseball writers call this nail-bitin' time," said Ferguson. "Rulick can't let anybody find that tea set between now and Monday. If they want to make a dent in his plans, the Pratts have to find it before then. If any of us wants to see the two and a half million, we have to find the tea set before any of them. But we better be careful. Rule's been after me since the day I got sober enough to start lookin' for the tea set. He may just get panicky and come after you, especially if he thinks you're gettin' close."

"I don't think I want this to continue," said Evangeline evenly. "It's getting a little too dangerous."

Ferguson smiled. "It will continue with you or without you until it's found. Now, what about Granny?"

Fallon described his meeting with Katherine Carrington and showed Ferguson the note.

Ferguson read it and smiled. He read it again, then he stared at it, as though it conveyed something more than the message written upon it. "After all these years," he said softly. Then, he stood. He held the towel around his waist with one hand and the note with the other, and he paced back and forth. He seemed suddenly animated and excited.

"This is good. This is very good," he said. "There's one thing you learn when you've been on the run as long as I have—you don't stick your neck out. But for this lady, I'll do it. We get her out. We put her on an airplane. And we'll be damn close to havin' ourselves a tea set."

"How do you know my grandmother?" asked Evangeline.

"It's a long story, honey. You stick around and you'll hear it. Crap out on us, and you'll never know."

"Put some pants on," she said.

That evening, Fallon and Evangeline did not stay at her apartment. Ferguson suggested that they do something to make it seem as though they had given up the search. He told Peter to take Evangeline over to South Boston and have dinner with the Fallons, just like any young man introducing his girlfriend to the family. Ferguson didn't tell them that the presence of several Fallons in one house would probably deter Rulick.

Evangeline went with Peter, although reluctantly. Whenever she considered going to the authorities, he persuaded her to look around one more corner. Each time, she discovered something about her family's past that she did not want to know. But with each discovery, she wanted to know more. Now, she faced the possibility that around the next corner was a man with a gun.

She told herself that she should go to the police and inform them of everything she knew. That would be the rational thing to do. But as Fallon said, if they involved the police, the web might be broken and the tea set never found. Until it was, she could not live in peace. Besides, what could be rational when a mother was imprisoned by her children for her own good and a crazy derelict materialized periodically to dispense information? What was rational about her attraction to Fallon, which grew as the sense of danger deepened?

Danny, Sheila, and the kids ate dinner with Tom and Maureen on Friday nights. Scrod baked in breadcrumbs and milk. They were all delighted to see Peter walk through the door with his new girlfriend. He rarely appeared unannounced, and he'd never brought a girl before. Two more plates appeared and the six helpings of scrod

346

quickly became eight.

The dinner was passed in pleasant conversation. Maureen and Sheila both liked Evangeline, and Danny couldn't take his eyes off her. Tom Fallon thought she was nice enough, although a trifle on the skinny side and altogether too nervous.

When the children went out to play after dinner, Peter told his family the story of the Golden Eagle Tea Set.

Danny was the first to speak after a long silence. "You've gotta be shittin'."

"You know me better than that."

"A tea set worth two and a half million bucks buried under the Back Bay?"

Peter nodded.

Danny rubbed the palm of his hand across his five o'clock shadow. He was hooked already. "Son of a bitch."

"If you can't say something intelligent," said Tom Fallon, "don't be cursin'."

Danny opened the refrigerator and took out a beer.

"Why have you come here with all this?" Tom asked Peter.

"Because we need your help, Pa. Right now, that means a place to stay."

"Are you breaking the law?" he asked sternly.

Peter looked at Evangeline.

"Others have broken the law. I think Peter has bent a few," she said.

"Well," announced Danny, "I don't mind bendin' a few laws for a few million bucks. It sure would get us out of the hole, Dad."

"That thought crossed my mind, too," said Peter.

"Why did you get involved in this, Peter?" asked his mother.

"For a change, I just followed my nose."

"It's not like you to be getting into trouble, Peter," she said.

He smiled and opened a beer. He seemed pleased with himself. "I know."

Tom Fallon looked level at his son. "I'll do what I can for you. I'll never turn away when you ask me for help. But before you do anything else, I think you both should have a good night's sleep."

"And tomorrow," cracked Danny, "we start diggin'!"

That night, Peter Fallon slept in his old room.

Evangeline slept in the guest room. As she climbed into bed, she noticed a crucifix on the wall above her head. She was struck by its beauty. She took it down and examined it. The crucifix was silver, and the figure of Christ was engraved into the metal. The word BLOSSOM was stamped on the back.

Maureen Fallon appeared in the doorway to say goodnight.

"This crucifix is exquisite," said Evangeline.

"Indeed it is. It was the gift of a dear friend."

CHAPTER XXI   *November 1952*

Jack C. Ferguson was thirty-two years old, a tall, muscular man with wavy black hair, an ex-wife, and two suits. Today he was wearing the double-breasted that his friends said made him look like Victor Mature.

He hurried down Beacon Hill, past the courthouse, and into Scollay Square, where the lunchtime crowd was gathering. Lunch in Scollay Square: two drinks in the Domino Lounge watching Shirl the Twirl and her tassles; the midday show at the Old Howard, a burlesque house where your feet stuck to the floor and your pants sometimes stuck to the seat; or a half hour with the lady of your choice in a rundown hotel. Ferguson never spent much time in Scollay Square. He didn't pay for sex, except in the form of alimony, which he called sex on credit. And when he drank, which wasn't often these days, he didn't like pasties distracting him.

He hurried through the square and down Hanover Street. As he passed a Democratic Party Campaign office, a worker thrust a

"Kennedy for Senator" button into his hand and asked for a donation.

"Get it from his old man," Ferguson put the button on his lapel and continued on to the Union Oyster House.

A small sign in the window proclaimed that the Oyster House was the oldest continuously operated restaurant in the United States. Ferguson stepped inside. The first floor hadn't changed in over a hundred years—low ceilings, exposed pipes, pine paneling painted light yellow, raised booths toward the back, the soapstone-and-mahogany oyster bar to the left of the entrance. In the windows behind the bar, oysters, clams, and red-cooked lobsters were displayed on beds of crushed ice and seaweed. Before he walked in the door, Jack had his lobster picked out.

"Jack! Jackie! Over here!"

At the end of the bar, wearing the olive-colored uniform of a sergeant in the United States Army, sat Bill Rulick. The two old friends shook hands and embraced roughly. They had not seen each other since December of 1945, when Rulick had been home from Germany on leave. Ferguson had served, but he had never gone overseas.

"It's been a long time, Billy." Ferguson noticed that Rulick had lost a little hair but still had the build of a wrestler.

"Too long, Jack. What'll you have?"

"A draft."

"No chaser?"

"Nope. Beer's my limit these days."

Rulick recorded that bit of information, then called for two drafts and two orders of oysters on the half shell.

First, Rulick and Ferguson toasted their reunion, then Rulick raised his hand, as though calling for quiet, and focused his attention on the plate in front of him. He squeezed a bit of lemon and shook a drop of Tabasco onto an oyster. He picked up the crusty shell, put it to his lips, and tilted his head back. The oyster slid slowly into his mouth. He slurped the juices from the shell, closed his eyes, and chewed. After another long swallow of beer, he looked at Ferguson.

"Ice-cold American beer and fresh oysters. That's heaven, Jack. Pure heaven. I been stationed in Germany since '46, and I'm sick of kraut food. They cook everything in vinegar, and they drink their beer lukewarm."

"It's always good to come home."

"Yup, and this time, I think it's for good. I'm finishing up my hitch out at Fort Devens. After that, I'll be a civilian for the first time since Pearl Harbor."

"Not interested in seein' Korea?"

"No fuckin' way. I don't think they'll be shippin' my unit out of Germany, but I figure, better to be diggin' ditches in Boston than pickin' gooks off the end of a bayonet in God knows where. Eisenhower keeps talkin' about goin' over to end it if he's elected. My bet is that he'll go at the head of half a million troops."

"So, what are you planning to do here?"

"I'm going into the import-export business. I made some good connections over in Europe. Did a few favors for some influential people."

Ferguson guessed black market.

"Now, I have a nice bankroll and two or three small German companies ready to do business."

"How did you get a bankroll on sergeant's pay?"

"I was always pretty tight, Jack. I saved my money." Rulick smiled.

Ferguson knew it was black market.

"You know much about marketing and trading and finding new clients?"

"Nothing. But I have a lot of balls and some good friends who can help to smooth the way for me over here. Balls and connections. That's a tough combination to top."

"You've always had balls."

"You gotta have balls. I learned that early, thanks to those Pratt bastards. In '33, my old man wants to start a union, and the Pratts tell him to go to hell. They know the unions are comin'. They know they'll have to knuckle under eventually, but they don't give an inch. All through the thirties, whenever the organizers came around—and in those days, some of those organizers were tough bastards—the Pratts would throw them out of the plant. While everyone else was givin' in, the Pratts held on. No benefits, no raises, no afternoon coffee break. Then, the war came, and people were too fuckin' patriotic to be agitatin' for unions. Pratt Rubber wasn't organized until when? 1948 or so?"

Ferguson nodded.

"You gotta admire that. They held out sixteen or seventeen years longer than anybody else. Just because they were tough. It's the way to be."

After the oysters, Rulick had a bowl of clam chowder and Ferguson his lobster. When he wasn't drinking anything stronger than beer, Jack Ferguson always had a little extra to spend, and he liked to buy something special once in a while, just to remind himself how pleasant life could be without whiskey.

"What about you, Jackie? What've you been up to?"

"I started out covering the police blotter for the *Herald* right after the war. You know, 'Two men were stabbed last night during an argument at the Boston Arena.' That kind of stuff. Then, I went to the *Post* and worked my way up through the city room. Now I do mostly features."

"Yeah. I read that thing you had in the Color Roto on Sunday. About the ghost who lives out in the harbor."

"The Lady in Black. She's supposed to haunt Fort Warren. I'm doing a whole series on old New England legends. It's better than listenin' to the police radio, but I'd rather be coverin' the Red Sox."

"Those bums! Always on Armed Forces Radio pissin' the pennant away to the Yankees. They'll never beat New York. Never."

"Maybe not, but I'd rather watch Ted Williams hit baseballs than watch Blaze Starr snap her G-string."

"Don't say that too loud," joked Rulick. "Somebody might get the wrong idea about you. Besides, if things are as hot as I hear they are for airmen over in Korea, the only lumber Ted Williams ever sees again may be on the inside of a pine box."

Ferguson finished his beer.

"Another, Jack?"

"No. One's my limit, especially when I'm working."

"Aw, c'mon. Old times' sake and all that shit. Bartender, two more drafts."

Fresh glasses of beer appeared, and Ferguson gave in. He told himself he wouldn't have a third.

"Old New England legends." Rulick threw the words out.

"Yeah. Salem witches. Old Yankee sea stories. Stuff like that. But it takes time, and I have to research all these things and talk to a lot of old-timers."

"Too bad Phil Cawley's not around."

Ferguson laughed. "Old Phil Cawley and his alky splits."

"He knew a pretty good legend," said Rulick seriously.

"You still believe the stories that old bastard used to tell us?"

"I believe the one about the Pratt teapot. I'll bet you've been thinkin' about it, too."

"It crossed my mind. It's a possibility for an article."

"Do you think it's true? About treasure in the Back Bay?"

"Well, every legend has some basis in fact. A Revere tea set called the Golden Eagle actually did disappear when the British burned Washington in 1814, but . . ." Ferguson shrugged and finished his second beer. "Who knows?"

"I sure would love to find it." Rulick gazed out the window and tried to sound as if he were simply daydreaming. "Figure out where it is and what it's doin' there, then go out and dig it up and tell the Pratts I just took their treasure away from them."

"I'm sure the Pratts couldn't care less."

"I care. I'd love to nail those bastards somehow."

"You still hate them, don't you, Ruley?"

"You're damn right I do," said Rulick quietly.

Ferguson remembered that whenever Rulick became angry, his voice grew soft, almost inaudible.

Rulick put his hand on Ferguson's forearm. The grip was powerful. "When I came home after V-E Day, I had a Purple Heart, a Silver Star, and enough campaign ribbons to open a fabric store. But my papa wasn't there to pat me on the back. My mama threw her arms around me and she said, 'Oh, Billy, your papa, he'd be so proud.' And she began to cry. For the first time since they killed my father, I cried, too. And it was the Pratts who did it."

"They didn't have him killed, Billy, you know that."

Rulick stared at the head on his beer. "They didn't stick the knife in him, but they might just as well. They wanted him out of the way, and somebody knocked him off. They got their wish, and someday I'll get mine."

Ferguson didn't disagree. He remembered how painful Peter Rulick's death had been for Billy. For a time, they ate in silence, two old friends run out of conversation.

Rulick finished his beer and called for the check. "I'd better head back, Jackie. I'll be in touch. And I'm tellin' you, if you want a good story, you ought to talk to the Pratts."

On a Sunday afternoon a few weeks later, Jack Ferguson steered his 1940 Dodge onto the driveway at Searidge. His tires crunched on the crushed stone. An elegant sound, he thought. Others paved their driveways or left them dirt. Only the rich could afford crushed stone. He parked in front of the stately old house and got out of the car. He smelled the fresh salt air. He heard a tennis ball popping between rackets and skipping off clay. Then he heard laughter, applause, and a young woman's voice calling the score.

He looked around the side of the house. Three men and a woman were playing doubles. Two other women, both about six months pregnant, sat on the sidelines and sipped orange juice. Beside them was a pitcher of martinis. Indian summer had lingered far into November. The maples around the court, the last trees of autumn, shimmered orange and gold. It was a day to enjoy, a final burst of warmth before winter, and these rich young people in their tennis whites knew how to enjoy it.

Ferguson rang the bell and wondered if Katherine Pratt Carrington would remember him. He didn't expect that she would. He had been eleven years old when they had last met, and she had made all the impression on him. He remembered an angel of beauty in a satin dress, an angel of mercy in a black limousine.

As a reporter, he had interviewed all sorts of people, from political leaders to bank robbers, and he had rarely felt nervous with any of them. At the moment, his palms were sweating.

The maid ushered him into the study, where Katherine Pratt Carrington was waiting for him. They shook hands, and she offered him a seat. She was not the vision he remembered, but she had reached fifty with grace. Her hair was turning gray and the flesh had begun to crease in the usual places, but in her firm handshake and friendly greeting, Ferguson sensed warmth and confidence that came only with maturity. He realized the difference between a beautiful woman and a handsome woman.

She offered him sherry or tea. He took tea and glanced through the French doors which led out to the tennis court. The maid was pushing an old man in a wheelchair out to the court, and a little boy was bouncing along behind her.

"A son, a daughter, two nephews, and various pregnant wives. The old man is Artemus Pratt III. The toddler playing with the hair in his great-granduncle's ears is our newest addition, my grandson Christopher. My husband and cousin Artemus are off playing golf. I don't expect we'll be seeing them much before dinner. They promised they'd raise a glass or two in honor of Eisenhower's victory. If I know them, they'll raise more than two."

"They haven't had a Republican victory to celebrate since 1928."

"More's the pity. Now, what can we do for you, Mr. Ferguson?"

He explained his series on New England legends, and she said she had been reading it every week. Then he told her the story that Philip Cawley had told him twenty years before.

She didn't look surprised, but she was. "'You heard all that from an eighty-year-old half-blind mulatto engraver who rode with Custer and drank your mother's hootch during Prohibition?"

"I know it sounds bizarre, but—"

She laughed. "I think bizarre is too mild a word for it. Mr. Ferguson. It's downright fanciful." She filled his teacup again.

"You're telling me there's no truth to any of this, not even a little? Every legend has some basis in fact, Mrs. Carrington."

"But not everything that little boys hear from lonely old men can be construed as legend."

Ferguson stared at her. It was one of his more effective techniques when he felt that someone wasn't telling him the truth. But Katherine Carrington stared back and smiled.

"None whatsoever?" he asked.

"Mr. Ferguson, our family has had a very long and exciting history. At the head of the stairs is an excellent Copley portrait of Horace Taylor Pratt, our patriarch and one of this nation's founding fathers. He fought on Bunker Hill, he was one of the first Americans to trade in China, and one of the earliest investors in the New England textile industry. His descendants have been leaders in business, industry, medicine, law, and, when necessary, war. In my son Jeffrey, the blond young man at service"—she tilted her head toward the court—"we may have our first political leader. He intends to run for Congress in two years, and we're hoping that one day he can do for the Republicans what that Kennedy boy has just done for the Democrats." She paused. "The point is, Mr. Ferguson, that an accomplished family, one with a history as broad and exciting as our own, just naturally attracts attention. In this particular case, it seems that a stray legend was looking for a home, and it found us."

"Will you take it in, or must I send it out into the world as an unwanted orphan?"

"Better that you didn't send it out at all. Think of the disservice you'll be performing for the people of the Back Bay." She laughed at the image. "They'll all be rushing out to buy picks and shovels, and before you know it, we'll have holes in every basement from Arlington Street to the Fenway."

Ferguson laughed. "That would make a helluva story."

Her smile disappeared. "I prefer that whatever you write, you leave our name out of it. Please."

"Excuse me, Mother." The female tennis player appeared with her doubles partner in the doorway. Two handsome young aristocrats in their early twenties.

Ferguson thought the slight resemblance between them was a coincidence, because they had the comfortable familiarity of lovers.

Katherine introduced Ferguson to her daughter Isabelle and her cousin's son Philip. The two young people shot a perfunctory greeting toward Ferguson, then returned their attention to Katherine.

"Mother, I'm afraid Jeffrey has crapped out. He'd rather sit with his pregnant wife than play tennis with us."

Philip threw a casual arm around his cousin. "Yes, and Izzy and I are taking all comers. What do you say, Auntie? You and Calvin?"

"Well, at the moment, I'm busy with this gentleman from the *Boston Post.*"

"Oh, he won't mind," said Isabelle. "We can't be wasting the last nice day of the year indoors."

Philip looked at Ferguson. "What about you, old man? How's your forehand?"

"No good unless there's a glass in it." Ferguson stood. "I think we've finished our talk, Mrs. Carrington. I'll leave you to your tennis."

Mrs. Carrington saw him to the door and invited him to come back and visit. He guessed that she was being polite, but he believed that she had been telling him the truth about the tea set, and he always trusted his instincts.

He glanced again at the tennis court. Isabelle, Philip, and Calvin were rallying while they waited for Katherine. Ferguson wondered if they realized that out there, beside that beautiful old house, with that fuzzy ball bouncing back and forth between them, they were enjoying the fruits of two hundred years' labor. He laughed to himself and headed back to Boston.

The following Tuesday, Jack Ferguson received a note from Katherine Pratt Carrington. She said she would be attending an afternoon recital at the Gardner Museum on Thursday, and she wondered if he would meet her there.

At the turn of the century, an extravagant Boston lady named Isabella Stewart Gardner had built Fenway Court on the banks of the Muddy River, at the far edge of the Back Bay. She modeled it after a Florentine villa and filled it with the priceless works of art she had collected in her European travels. She lived in her mansion until 1924 and bequeathed it to the people of Boston as a museum forever.

On Thursday, Jack Ferguson and Katherine Pratt Carrington sat together along the museum's south cloister, overlooking the court. Four stories above, sunshine poured through the skylight. Around the fountains and statues in the court, potted flowers bloomed, as they would throughout the winter. With the fountains bubbling softly in the background, Katherine Pratt Carrington told Ferguson everything that she knew about the Golden Eagle Tea Set. She talked for fifteen minutes. Ferguson didn't say a word or take a note.

"So you see," she concluded, "there may be a basis in fact for the old man's story. But I must emphasize to you that it's still a legend. Uncle Artemus, who was two years old when Horace Pratt's daughter died, has told me that neither his father nor his grandfather really believed the story. But it remained in the family and has been passed down the generations."

"Why are you telling me all this now? On Sunday, I was convinced that the Pratts had nothing to do with the Back Bay treasure. Now I know enough to start looking for it myself."

"I want to convince you not to print it, Mr. Ferguson, and the truth is often the best deterrent. If you were to mention our family with reference to a buried treasure, or if you were to tell your readers that various descendants of Horace Taylor Pratt held clues to the location of the treasure, we would be overrun with crackpots of every species and variety."

Ferguson hated to bury a good story, and from what she had just told him, this one was a winner. He frowned.

She touched his hand.

A man and an older woman engaged in whispered conversation behind a pillar in the Gardner Museum. To someone else, thought Ferguson, they probably looked like lovers. He wondered fleetingly what she would be like.

"I beg of you, Mr. Ferguson, for my peace of mind, put that story in your deepest drawer and forget about it."

"This thing sounds like a real work of art. Shouldn't the world have a chance to see it?"

"I have never had any desire to keep it hidden. In fact, during the Depression, I tried to find it. I was going to give the tea set to charity and be done with it. But I could find only four of the quotations. I think that if a member of the family can't find the tea set, it will not be found. I buried my knowledge of this thing many years ago. For the safety of my family, I'm asking you to do the same."

Jack Ferguson knew he was a good reporter. He also considered himself a reasonable man. "You did me a favor once. I guess I owe you one."

"What did I ever do for you?"

"You gave an eleven-year-old boy the biggest piece of pastry he'd ever seen."

She tried to recall the face or the name. She couldn't.

"The Pratt Winter Ball, February 1933."

She remembered. She smiled, then her expression darkened. "You're not the little boy whose father was killed in jail, I hope."

"No. That was my buddy."

"Then you were the hungry one."

"I still am."

"You ate the Napoleon."

"The cops arrived before I ever took a bite."

"A most frightening night. Whatever happened to your friend?" She seemed genuinely concerned.

"He joined the army and became a war hero." Ferguson didn't tell her about the black market.

"That's wonderful. Wonderful." She looked at her watch. "I must be getting upstairs to the recital room. Can I count on you, Mr. Ferguson?"

"I've given you my word."

She took his hand in hers. "If there's ever anything I can do for you, please let me know."

"How about having dinner with me tonight?"

The offer surprised her. A strange man hadn't asked her to dinner in many years. "Well, I really must be catching the train back to the North Shore. I . . ." She realized that she was stammering like a schoolgirl. "Oh, hell. Henry's off in New York on business. I'd love to."

"Can you meet me at the Parker House? Six o'clock?"

"On the dot."

"See you then." Ferguson put on his topcoat. "What are you hearing this afternoon?"

"I'm playing. Chopin."

Katherine Pratt Carrington and Jack Ferguson did not have dinner together that night. When he returned to his office, Ferguson found a phone message waiting for him on his desk. Katherine Carrington said that she was sorry, but she had overlooked a previous engagement. She said she hoped they could dine together at another time.

Ferguson crumpled the note and threw it in the wastebasket. It was just as well, he thought. He'd look pretty foolish making a pass at a married woman twenty years older.

❄

A few weeks later, Jack Ferguson and Bill Rulick went to a hockey game. The Bruins against the Montreal Canadiens. Halfway through the second period, after a few beers and three Boston goals, Rulick asked Ferguson if he had talked to the Pratts. Ferguson said that he had and that there was nothing to Cawley's story. He was not a good liar.

William Rulick decided to visit the Pratts himself. On the following Sunday afternoon, he went to the Back Bay house, now the home of Artemus Pratt IV, his wife, his ailing father, and his son Philip. Rulick told John Holt, the butler, that he was a serviceman soliciting Christmas contributions for the children of soldiers killed in Korea. Holt told him to wait in the receiving room. Rulick said that he would prefer to sit in the downstairs study. Holt led him into the room where the Pratts had discussed Peter Rulick twenty years earlier.

Rulick didn't stop to admire the oak paneling, the vaulted ceilings, or the fine leather bindings on the backs of the books. He went straight for the copy of *Paradise Lost* on the shelf behind the desk. He opened it and read the bookplate; the book belonged to Artemus Pratt III. At page one, a bookmark fell out. Rulick glanced at it.

"So saying, a noble stroke he lifted high,/ Which hung not, but so swift with tempest fell/ On the proud Crest of Satan, that no sight,/ Nor motion of swift thought, less could his Shield/ Such ruin intercept: ten paces huge/ He back recoil'd, the tenth on bended knee/ His massy Spear upstay'd; as if on Earth/ Winds under ground or waters forcing way/ Sidelong, had push't a Mountain from his seat/ Half sunk with all his Pines." Rulick's eyes fell on "ten paces huge."

Rulick stuffed the bookmark into his pocket and flipped through the book, but there were no other surprises. Rulick had been hoping to find underlined passages or marginal notes, but every page was clean and the binding was stiff, as if the book had never been read.

Holt returned with a ten-dollar bill from Artemus Pratt IV and a half-dollar from his own pocket. Rulick put Holt's coin in a Salvation Army box and had a steak dinner on the Pratts.

Bill Rulick was on leave for five days over Christmas. He spent most of his nights with his mother and brothers, who now lived in the suburb of Roslindale, and afternoons with the attractive young wife of an overaged colonel from Fort Devens.

Three nights before Christmas, he visited Searidge. He had not been invited. He had read in the paper that Katherine Pratt Carrington would be accompanying a choir in a program of Christmas music at Harvard. It would be a good night to tour the library without the interference of the family or the butler, who would probably be in his room watching Milton Berle.

Rulick parked a few blocks from Searidge and walked onto the Pratt grounds. It was a crisp, cold night. He was dressed in dark clothing and black cap. He was not nervous. He had led commando raids during the war. Except for a single light in the living room, Searidge was in darkness. Rulick watched the house for a full fifteen minutes before he decided that it was safe to approach.

He broke into the library through the French doors that opened onto the tennis court. He closed the doors behind him and began to search through the bookshelves for *Paradise Lost*. A light came on in the hallway. Rulick heard someone moving around upstairs. Rulick started for the doors, then decided to gamble. He had come this far, and he'd broken in so quietly that no one could have heard him. He ducked behind a leather chair in the corner of the room.

Someone walked down the stairs, and the lights came on in the library.

Rulick's muscles tensed. He had survived Africa, Italy, and Normandy. In a French barn, he had strangled a Nazi with a length of rope. If threatened, he would survive now.

Jeffrey Carrington, in robe and slippers, strolled into the library. He and his family were spending the holidays at Searidge. They had not gone to the concert because his wife was ill. Instead, they had retired early. But Carrington couldn't sleep. He walked over to the bookcases, which ran the length of one wall.

Rulick was hiding on the opposite side of the room, his body coiled behind the chair.

Carrington was in the mood for adventure. He chose one of the Horatio Hornblower books from his father's complete set and turned to leave. He glanced toward the corner. He wouldn't have noticed anything, except that Rulick was wearing his army-issue shoes, spit-shined every day, and the toe of one of them was showing.

"What are you doing there?" he demanded in the instant before terror turned his stomach inside out.

Rulick followed his instincts. He flew at Jeffrey Carrington. One forearm caught Carrington in the throat, the other behind the head. Rulick brought his arms together quickly and efficiently. He heard the snap of Carrington's neck. He dropped Carrington to the floor. Without finding what he had come for, Rulick left Searidge.

From his years in the military and the black market, Bill Rulick had learned never to make sloppy mistakes. He had been careful to cover his tracks, and the colonel's wife would make an excellent alibi if he ever needed one. He didn't. The police found no evidence and no apparent motive beyond robbery. Jeffrey Carrington's killer would never be apprehended.

Jack Ferguson visited Katherine Carrington a few weeks after her son's death. It was one of those unusual days in January when the temperature pushes past fifty and people begin to wonder if it won't be such a bad winter after all. He parked on the crushed stone and walked around the house.

Katherine Pratt Carrington, wearing a lumberjack's black-and-red-checkered shirt and a kerchief, stood near the edge of the cliff. She was raking leaves. In the middle of January, on the top of a windswept cliff, fallen leaves are scarce, but she had collected a small, crumbled pile.

The leaves, he thought, looked almost as forlorn as the raker. "Hello, Mrs. Carrington."

"Oh. Hello, Mr. Ferguson." Her voice was weak, her expression stiff and lifeless, as though a plaster mold had been made of her features. She stared at him and waited for him to speak.

He could think of nothing to say.

"I know, Mr. Ferguson." She said after a long silence. "You've come to tell me how sorry you are that my son is dead, and if there's anything I need, I shouldn't hesitate to call you." The weakness in her voice was replaced by something else. At first, it sounded like boredom. Katherine Carrington had heard the condolences before. Then, it evolved into bitterness that Ferguson felt was somehow directed at him.

A gust of wind whipped the pile of leaves apart. She watched them swirl about the yard, then she began to rake again.

Ferguson guessed that she had been working on the same pile of leaves all morning.

"Mrs. Carrington." He stepped close to her and took her hand. "You can't explain why a young man dies and his parents are left to mourn him. It's unnatural, as unnatural as a warm day in January. But it happens, and when it does, you can't stop living. I've only met you a few times, Mrs. Carrington, but I respect you and admire you. I know you'll live through this." Jack Ferguson rarely made speeches. He hoped he didn't sound like a damn fool.

"Thank you, Mr. Ferguson. You're very kind," she said coldly.

"But you must permit me the irrationality of grief. You invaded our world a month ago and unearthed something which I had long ago forgotten. You promised that you would not reveal it to anyone."

"I didn't," he said evenly.

"And yet, my son is dead. I know that you didn't kill him, and when I can think clearly, I believe that the burglar was looking for furs or jewels or some other meaningless extravagance. But the feeling persists, deep in the pit of my stomach, that my son died because of the legend in which you seemed so interested. I have no proof, no evidence, and I am accusing you of nothing, but I do not wish to see you again." She began to rake once more.

"Mrs. Carrington."

She did not respond. She had shut him off.

"I promised you that I would never reveal what you told me. I kept that promise. I'll continue to keep it." He returned to his car and drove back to Boston.

Bill Rulick had been discharged, and he was living in an apartment in the Back Bay.

Twenty years earlier, most of the buildings in the Back Bay were single-family homes. But the Depression, World War II, and the slow deterioration of city life had driven many of the finest families off to the North Shore permanently. By 1952, half the homes in the Back Bay had been sold to universities or to landlords who converted the townhouses and mansions into apartments. William Rulick lived on the second floor of a Marlborough Street French Academic.

Although he had been out of the army for two weeks, he was still seeing the colonel's wife every afternoon. It was a discreet affair. She wanted only one thing from him; he had only one thing to give, and he sometimes gave it to her three or four times in an afternoon. Rulick was on top of her, with her fingernails dug deep into his shoulders, when the doorbell rang. Neither of them heard it, but Jack Ferguson could hear them.

He knew that Rulick made a lot of noise; they'd shared a few whores when they were younger. But the girl was a banshee. He waited until they were finished and rang again.

Rulick answered the door in his bathrobe.

"Hello, Bill."

"Hi, Jack. How about comin' back later? I'm busy." he winked.

Ferguson stepped inside. "I just want to ask you something, Bill, then you can get back to work."

Ferguson heard the bedroom door slam. He heard footsteps, then another slamming door.

"You scared her, Jack." He smiled. "She's real skittish."

"I'll be gone in a minute." Ferguson paused and lowered his voice. "What do you know about Jeffrey Carrington's death?"

Rulick blinked once. That was all. "Why are you asking me?"

"Call it my newsman's intuition."

"I call it shit," snapped Rulick. "You think that because I knew a little about the story, I killed one of the Pratts to find out more. You sure don't stand by your friends, do you?"

Ferguson realized he had lit the fuse. "I just asked you a question, Billy. I'm not sayin' you had anything to do with it."

"You're fuckin' right I didn't have anything to do with it." Rulick stepped toward Ferguson. He was six inches shorter, but Ferguson respected his strength and his temper. They were close enough now that Ferguson could smell the scent of the colonel's wife on Rulick's face.

"Listen, you big nobody son of a bitch. If I want to get back at somebody, I don't sneak into their house and kill their son, who wouldn't know me from a pisshole in the snow. I do it in a big way. And that's just how I'll nail those fuckin' Pratts—in public! Maybe I'll find the tea set and wave it in their faces. Maybe someday I'll shoot their company out from under them. Maybe I'll do both. But someday, there'll be a good story about me and the Pratts, and I'll see that you get it first. Now get out of here before I take your fuckin' head off."

By the time he reached the cobblestones, Ferguson felt ridiculous. He'd come across like a bad detective, and he'd insulted a friend. He wanted to go upstairs and apologize, but he knew that Rulick was mad enough already. Ferguson didn't want to interrupt him in the middle of another screw.

One night a week later, Jack Ferguson wandered home around midnight. He had been drinking—four or five beers—and he was close to hitting the hard liquor again. He lived in the West End, in a three-room flat above an Italian grocery store. As he came home, he noticed a light shining from under the door.

Suspiciously, carefully, and, because of the alcohol, a bit clumsily, he let himself into the apartment and saw the mess. His filing cabinet had been pulled open, his papers covered the floor, notes were scattered everywhere, and his typewriter lay smashed. Bill Rulick sat in the middle of the chaos, in Ferguson's armchair, and puffed on a cigar as though he had just finished a good dinner.

Initially, Ferguson felt no rage. He was too shocked.

Rulick stood and walked over to him. "I guess you're clean, Jackie."

"What the hell are you doin' here?"

"Well, Jack . . ." Rule took a long drag on his cigar. "I learned a long time ago that the quickest way for a guy to get himself out of trouble is to blame someone else. So I got thinkin', maybe it was you broke into Carrington's house that night a while back. You know, by actin' real innocent, you're tryin' to get yourself a late alibi."

Rulick blew a few smoke rings and studied the cigar, a long green Havana. "So since you been thinkin' about nailin' me, I thought I'd check around and see if I could get anything on you."

"Like what?" Ferguson took a step toward Rulick and put his hands on his hips.

Rulick was not intimidated. "Like stuff about the tea set. Why else would you kill Carrington? You went up there to hunt around that night, and old Jeffrey surprised you."

"Get out of here before I break you in half."

Rulick laughed and puffed on his cigar. "You might have four or five clues around here, and you don't want to tell anyone about them."

Ferguson looked around at the mess and asked sarcastically, "Did you find any of them?"

Rulick shook his head. "Like I say, you're clean. For now. But if I find out you're lookin' for that tea set and you're not includin' me, I'll be pissed."

Ferguson grabbed Rulick by the necktie. "I don't ever want to see your face again, you prick."

Rulick's hands shot into Ferguson's belly and slammed Ferguson against the wall. "No rough stuff, Jackie," he growled. "Since we been kids, you know who wins the fights." He let Ferguson go and backed off, giving himself room if he needed it. "I didn't come here to punch you out, Jack. I got bigger fish to fry than you. But remember this—don't you ever cross me again."

"Nobody's crossed you." Ferguson didn't move.

"You were thinkin' about it. Where I grew up, that's enough."

CHAPTER XXII

On Saturday mornings, Danny Fallon cooked breakfast. Sheila slept late. The kids watched cartoons. Tom worked around outside. Maureen baked bread. And everyone ate in Danny's kitchen.

Peter filled his plate with bacon and eggs and his mother's bread. Evangeline had an English muffin and coffee.

"No wonder she's so skinny," said Tom Fallon.

Maureen told him to be quiet.

"Hey, Peter," said Danny, "remember when we were kids and Pa would ask us at breakfast what we were gonna do that day to make our first million?"

Peter nodded.

"If he asks you this morning, you might have an answer."

The two brothers laughed, and a smile cracked across Tom Fallon's face. None of the women at the table thought it was very funny.

"Peter." Evangeline's tone was enough to strangle the laughter.

She had not slept well. She had spent the night thinking about her grandmother, her father's death, and her family's involvement with the Golden Eagle Tea Set. She had resolved nothing. "What are you planning for today, Peter?"

"Not much of anything. I'm going over to Cambridge to get a gray suit. Then I'm going to the New England Genealogical Society to look at the Pratt family tree. It might tell us something we want to know. After that, I'm coming back here to wait for Jack Ferguson's call."

"What do you need a suit for?" asked Danny.

"For tonight. And Dad's charcoal-gray suit will fit you. Just make sure you have a white shirt and a dark tie to go with it."

"Why?"

"You'll see."

Evangeline saw a trace of skepticism on Danny's face. She had hoped to see more. She thought that a grown man with a wife and two children might exert a steadying influence on his younger brother. She was disappointed.

Peter turned to his father. "What kind of terms are you on with Uncle Dunphy?"

"The usual. Lousy."

"Well, put the arm to him, because I need a hearse and a coffin for tonight. The biggest coffin he's got."

"What on earth do you want with a coffin and a hearse?" screamed his mother.

"I was thinkin' that myself," said Tom.

Evangeline knew what Peter was thinking, and she didn't like it.

Peter stood. "You said you'd help me, Dad."

Tom Fallon frowned. His bushy eyebrows came together to form an unbroken strip of hair across his forehead. "And I'm not supposed to ask questions?"

"Evangeline's grandmother is being held in a rest home on the North Shore. If we can get her out, she'll give us the key to the tea set's location."

Evangeline shook her head. "There has to be another way, Peter."

"None I can think of that won't take days," he said. "We go in and out. The Pratts won't do a thing to stop us, because they can't afford the police interference themselves."

"I don't know about this," said Tom.

Peter crouched down beside his father. "With you or without you, I'm going through with it. Help me, and I'll help you." He turned to Evangeline. "It's nine o'clock. Ferguson said we should open the

Green Shoppe today, just to make it seem that we're getting back to normal."

Evangeline finished her coffee. She wasn't sure if she would go to the Green Shoppe or the police. She and Fallon left together.

"I don't know about this," said Tom Fallon to his wife.

"What can you do to stop him?" she asked.

"Nothing." Danny slammed his fist on the table. "He's got brains, and he's usin' them. I'm for that."

"I'll admit it's the first time I've seen any initiative out of him in a long time."

"That's a harsh thing to say, Tom," chided Maureen. "He's shown initiative all his life. Now he's just showin' craziness."

"And there's laws against diggin' up people's cellars," said Sheila.

"We'll worry about that when we find the thing," Danny responded. "Peter's doin' somethin' most people wouldn't have the balls to even think of, Dad. That's what it takes, sometimes, if you want to get out of the hole. He deserves some help."

Tom Fallon studied his massive hands. "I told him last night I'd help him."

"You told him last night you'd help him, and I was glad to see you standin' behind him," said Maureen. "But if you don't think this is right, Tom, don't do it."

"Me and Sheila could use the money, Dad." He glanced at his wife. She didn't say anything. She knew that once his mind was set, Danny would do what he wanted.

"Even if we found this thing," said Tom, "the state would probably try to take it away from us."

"They wouldn't take all of it," said Danny. "I was just readin' about a big Spanish galleon they found down off Jamaica or someplace. They had to give the country half the treasure. We do that, and we still have a million and a quarter. Nice work if you can get it."

Tom Fallon thought hard. "It sounds to me like risky business."

"Sittin' in your livin' room catchin' radiation from a color TV is risky business, but if you want to watch the Red Sox, you'll sit."

"Don't be exaggeratin'," said Sheila.

"He may be right," said Tom softly, almost bitterly. "You have to take risks. A man works all his life, tries to build a business and keep to the straight and narrow, and he ends up in a corner. When one son comes along with a chance to turn everyone's life around, and the other son is ready to pitch right in, I guess he'd be a fool not to join them."

"Hail Mary, Mother of God, pray for us sinners." said Maureen.

"Aw, c'mon, Ma. Say an Our Father that we find the thing. Then you can pray the Rosary all winter in Florida."

He was wearing bathing trunks and sunglasses. His wife was rubbing oil into his hairy shoulders. His butler was preparing bloody Marys. William Rule reclined on his balcony three stories above Lewis Wharf and sipped espresso. Behind him, the water of Boston Harbor flashed silver in the morning light. Power boats left tiny trails of foam in the water, and bleach-white sails stretched in the breeze. Later, Rule would be going out in the *Peter*, his twenty-five-foot cabin cruiser, to do some fishing while his wife stripped off her bikini and soaked in the sun. At the moment, he was awaiting a visit he had looked forward to for many years.

The door buzzer rang, and Edward announced the Pratts.

"Send them in," said Rule.

"Good morning, gentlemen. Thanks for stopping by." Rule extended a hand. Calvin and Philip Pratt offered perfunctory greetings.

"Espresso, or something stronger? Not that there's anything much stronger than the espresso I drink."

"It's the weekend," said Philip Pratt expansively. "I guess I can have a bloody Mary before noon." He sat down on a deck chair. He was wearing tennis shorts, jersey, and sneakers. He wanted Rule to believe that he was completely confident about retaining control of Pratt Industries and that he intended to spend all of Saturday on his tennis court. He looked casual, but Rule had outdone him.

Rule was wearing bathing trunks, sunglasses, and a film of tanning lotion. He had the *Globe* sports page in his lap. "A bloody Mary sounds good. I'll have one, too. What about you, Calvin?"

"We haven't come for drinks and friendly chit-chat," said Calvin. "We're bringing you a final offer, and we think you'll want to consider it before Monday."

Rule waved Edward away with the drink orders, then he smiled. "If you've come here askin' me to keep your old man's picture on the wall, forget it."

"On Monday," said Calvin, "we will have the tea set in our possession. I can guarantee it."

"The museum has the tea set," said Rule. "How can you have it?"

Calvin ignored Rule's response. "We are offering you a final chance to back out. Drop your challenge now, and no one but the people seated on this balcony and my cousin's personal staff will ever know that your Golden Eagle is a forgery. If you don't, we'll reveal the fraudulent tea set."

Rule laughed softly. Philip Pratt saw the sweat and suntan oil glistening in the folds of fat around Rule's belly.

"I got two things to say. First of all, you'll have to produce this tea set that's supposed to be buried in the Back Bay before you can prove that mine's a fake. And second," he spoke with feigned, mocking indignity, "I'm really disappointed to think that the sons of Boston's most famous family, and one of them a lawyer, have sunk so low." He shook his head and sucked his teeth. "Whatever happened to integrity?"

"Let's cut the shit, Rule" said Philip Pratt angrily.

Rule leaned back and locked his hands behind his head in an attitude of complete relaxation. He had Pratt mad already.

"Don't lecture us on integrity—"

Calvin interrupted Philip. He preferred to do the talking. In a meeting of this sort, he presented himself with a professional calm that usually unsettled men like William Rule. "We would like to avoid a scandal. The company has been suffering of late, and you know how sensitive the stock market can be when a company is not doing well. If a new board chairman is elected and the stockholders discover that he built much of his fortune on art frauds, the value of Pratt Industries stock might fall even more dramatically."

Rule laughed again. "Then you'd better not tell anybody about it. Just let me take over and run the show the way it ought to be run."

"We don't want to damage any reputations, Mr. Rule—yours, the company's, or Lawrence Hannaford's. That's why we've kept quiet this long and tried other means to convince our stockholders that you'd be bad for the company. If you'll consent to surrender your proxies, we're perfectly willing to keep this matter among gentlemen."

"Gentlemen." Rule repeated the word softly, almost to himself. "I've been called a lot of things by a lot of people, but this is the first time that one of the Back Bay Pratts has ever called me a gentleman."

Edward arrived with the bloody Marys.

Rule took his and held it up. "To gentlemen. At last."

Philip Pratt did not toast.

"We have the utmost respect for you, Mr. Rule." Calvin Pratt tried not to choke on the words.

"As you should." Rule stepped to the balcony railing, folded his hands behind him like a sea captain, and gazed out at the harbor. "You know why I like it here? Because I can look out and imagine the clippers and cargo schooners that used to fill this harbor, and I can feel like a part of history. Yeah, that's right." He liked the phrase. He turned to the Pratts and repeated, "A part of history. An empire builder. Just like the Cabots and the Lowells and the Kennedys."

Philip Pratt sipped his drink and tried not to listen.

Rule smiled. "Just like the Pratts. Except for one thing—my empire's already built. I'm takin' it away from you. On Monday, I'll be elected chairman of the board. On Tuesday, I'll move to have the president replaced. On Wednesday, you'll be playin' golf."

Philip Pratt stood. He had come with a bluff. He would not leave until he was satisfied. "Save your daydreams for someone else, Rule. You're not moving us out."

"Monday morning, I start a new job, and once I'm in that office, don't ever expect to get me out. My old man's picture is gonna hang over that fireplace for the next two hundred years. And you want to know why?" He aimed a finger at Philip Pratt and forty years of hatred rasped out of him. "Because you built your fortunes on the sweat of men like my father, and when they asked you for fair treatment, you cut them down."

Rule looked at Calvin. "Pratt Winter Ball, 1933. You remember it, Cal? You must've been six or seven at the time. You remember the labor demonstration? The leader of that march was my old man." He turned to Philip. "And the man who had him killed was yours."

"I don't know what you're talking about," said Philip Pratt softly.

"But you'll pay for it. I promise you that." It was a moment of triumph, of bitter satisfaction, for William Rule. He folded his arms on his chest and watched the expressions. He saw bewilderment, confusion, and, on Calvin's face, dim recollection. He smiled. "Chew on that for a while, gentlemen."

"We will retain the office," said Calvin firmly.

Rule ignored Calvin's response. "They say the bluefish are making an early run this year, gentlemen. I want to be out of the harbor before the tide turns. Good morning."

The Pratts left.

From his balcony, he watched them climb into a silver BMW parked on the wharf. Then he gazed out toward the harbor and wondered if the Pratts were close. Maybe they had a line through the student. He had been seen with the girl. He had talked to the Pratts. He had snooped around Hannaford. He had even witnessed the bartender's murder. Rule decided not to take any chances. It would not be unusual for the witness of a gangland shooting to be shot himself.

Evangeline drove the Porsche to Cambridge. Peter wanted it to seem that they no longer cared if anyone was following them. They didn't speak until she had pulled up in front of his apartment.

"Do you want me to wait?" she asked.

"No. Go to the Green Shoppe. I'll see you at Quincy Market around one."

Evangeline drove off toward Harvard Square. Then Fallon saw the black Oldsmobile swing past. He was surprised to see that Soames was riding with Buckley in the front seat. The Pratts were getting serious. He looked down Massachusetts Avenue and saw Henry Dill duck into a doorway.

Maureen Fallon answered the telephone in South Boston.

"Is Peter Fallon there?" It sounded as if the caller was in a subway station.

"Who's calling, please?"

"Jack C. Ferguson."

Maureen remembered the name. "He's gone to Cambridge, to his apartment."

Ferguson hung up before he swore. He didn't want to frighten Fallon's mother, but Rulick's men had come after him again, and he figured they would be going after Fallon. He heard a train rumble through downstairs. He was at Park Street Station. It would take him ten minutes to get to Harvard Square. He didn't have much time.

Evangeline circled through Harvard Square and back down Mt. Auburn to Central Square. She parked at a meter near the intersection of Massachusetts Avenue and Western Avenue, near the Cambridge police station. She left the motor running because she didn't know if she was staying.

The black Oldsmobile drove past and parked on the other side of the square. Soames got out of the car.

Evangeline didn't see Soames. She didn't see anything. She was composing the story she would tell Lieutenant Maughan, a Harvard classmate who had studied law enforcement in graduate school and stayed in Cambridge to practice it. Nothing had happened within his jurisdiction, but she knew he could help her.

Soames was across Central Square and moving toward her car. He reached for the handle, and she saw him. The Porsche swung out of the parking spot, turned right, and headed down Western Avenue. She lost the Oldsmobile in the side streets between Central Square and the river, parked near Dunster House, and was back in Fallon's apartment a few minutes after she had left him. He was listening to the tape of his phone messages when she arrived.

"I was followed," she said.

"I know."

"Soames tried to get into my car in Central Square."

"What the hell were you doing in Central Square? I thought you were going to work."

"I was thinking about going to the police." She looked him straight in the eye, but she didn't know him well enough to predict his reaction.

There was none. He simply stared at her. He couldn't believe that she would end it just when they were closing in.

"I couldn't do it, " she said. "At least not until we talked."

"We've talked already, Evangeline. If you end it before we find that thing, don't ever expect to know me any better than you do now, because I won't know myself."

"You can't play a dangerous game with yourself and other people and expect that you're going to learn how to get from one day to the next."

The phone rang. It rang again.

"Aren't you going to answer it?"

Fallon shook his head. "It's probably Professor Hayward. He's been calling for three days. I don't want to talk to him." Fallon hit the button on his telephone recorder, then played the message back.

Even on the tiny speaker, they heard the tension in the voice. "This is Ferguson. You're in trouble. Don't go out of the apartment, and don't answer your door. If you've heard this message, pull down your shades."

The shades in Fallon's apartment snapped down. Ferguson stepped out of the telephone booth and looked across the street. He didn't know the man behind the wheel of the late-model Chevy, but he knew the man who was entering the apartment house. He had seen the slender body, the receding hairline, and the gaunt, pockmarked face before. He knew that under the tweed sportcoat, the man carried a .22 caliber pistol.

Ferguson had to help them. As a rule, he worried about Ferguson first and let other people take care of themselves. He didn't want to cross that street. He wanted a good stiff drink.

Fallon looked at Evangeline. They both heard the footfalls in the stairwell. Fallon took the baseball bat out of the closet. He didn't know what help it would be. He didn't know what was coming up the stairs. He stepped closer to the door. He cocked his head and listened. He shifted his eyes toward Evangeline. She was frozen; tension crystallized in the air around her.

The man with the pockmarks reached the second floor and stopped. He took a silencer from the pocket of his tweed jacket and screwed it onto the muzzle of his Smith & Wesson .22. He looked down the hallway—front doors and emergency escapes for four apartments. Fallon's was the first on the right, and Fallon was the assignment. The man didn't want to kill the girl. He had orders not to kill the girl. But she had gotten herself into the middle of it. If she was in the way, he would have no choice.

Jack Ferguson saw the neck of a long, thin wine bottle protruding from a trash basket. Green Hungarian from a California vineyard, and a few ounces still sloshed in the bottom of the bottle. He held the bottle to his lips. He was tempted to drink, but he didn't. He started across the street.

"Go into the kitchen," said Fallon softly. "Wait until I've got them inside, then open the fire door and run like hell."

She said nothing. Without taking her eyes off Fallon or the door, she backed slowly into the kitchen.

In the hallway, the man began to walk again. Very slowly, very cautiously.

Evangeline could hear the footsteps. She was petrified. She stood with her back hard against the refrigerator door and her arms drawn tight around her. The footsteps grew louder. She dug her fingers into the gasket so she would not tremble.

Jack Ferguson stumbled on the curb beside the Chevrolet. He put the bottle to his lips, but he didn't drink. Then he pulled down his fly and leaned against the car. He was glad he was frightened. He didn't have to wait at all. His stream hit the side of the car and washed down the dust on the rear quarter panel.

A broken nose and a crew-cut skull appeared at the window. "Hey, you fuckin' rummy, stop pissin' on my car."

Ferguson didn't stop.

The man started to get out of the car, and Ferguson smashed the wine bottle into the side of his head. The man was stunned. Ferguson took the bottle in both hands and swung. Two short, brutal strokes. He broke the broken nose again and fractured the block-shaped skull. Then he pushed the body back into the car and reached under the left armpit. He pulled out a .45 caliber automatic pistol. He took the morning newspaper off the seat, placed the pistol inside it, and went into the building.

In the hallway on the first floor, he pulled up his fly. The front of his pants was covered with urine. He looked up the stairs. Something inside him said not to go up. He wasn't fighting for himself. He was sticking his neck out. Only fools stuck their necks out.

The man with the pockmarks pressed Fallon's buzzer. The electric sound snapped through Evangeline and sent chills down Fallon's neck. Fallon positioned himself against the wall by the door. If he released the lock, he'd have a clear shot when the door opened.

Evangeline gripped the refrigerator and wished she could climb inside it. Her whole body was shaking.

The man buzzed again.

From where she stood, Evangeline could see the end of the baseball bat swing slowly through the air as Fallon cocked it. She realized that Fallon was endangering himself for her while she cowered in the kitchen. Something outside the door was threatening both of them. It had entered her world and driven her into a corner, and if she did nothing, it would destroy her.

Fear became anger, then resolve. She released her grip on the refrigerator. She opened a drawer and grabbed a butcher's knife. She appeared in the archway between kitchen and living room with the knife held threatening at her hip.

"Where do you want me?" she whispered.

Fallon studied her for a moment, then gestured to the other side of the door. She took her position.

They heard someone else coming up the stairs. Fallon put his ear to the door. A familiar voice was humming "Sweet Adeline."

The gunman stepped away from Fallon's entrance, picked up the newspaper in front of the opposite apartment, and pretended to read.

Jack C. Ferguson staggered up to the second floor. His left kneecap was vibrating, and inside the newspaper, his index finger was squeezing the trigger. He hesitated for a moment at the end of the hall. He saw that the man was not holding his gun. He stopped staggering and took four crisp steps down the hall.

Rule's assassin recognized another item on his hit list. He reached for his pistol, but he was too late. The *Boston Globe* exploded into his chest and blew him halfway down the hall.

Not one door opened on the second floor.

"It's me, Ferguson."

Fallon peered through the peep hole and opened the door.

"You two all right?" asked Ferguson.

"Yeah."

"Then let's go."

Fallon threw his suit over his arm, Evangeline dropped the knife on the floor, and they stepped into the hallway. They were both trembling—equal measures of fear and relief. As they walked past the body, Evangeline tried not to look. She wanted to think of it simply as a force, not a man. But Fallon stopped.

The shot had spun the gunman around and he lay so that most of his face was obscured. Fallon sensed something familiar about the physique. He started to kneel beside it.

"He's dead," said Ferguson. "Let's not hang around."

They hurried down the fire escape, out of Henry Dill's view, and headed for the subway.

Philip and Calvin Pratt sat beside the tennis court on the roof of the Back Bay house. Philip had wanted to play a set to work off his frustrations, but Calvin had been too distracted to return a serve. Instead, they sipped beers, and Calvin told the story of the 1933 Winter Ball.

When Calvin finished, Philip shook his head. "And now, he wants to pay us back for something that happened over forty years ago."

"He may yet back out. The power of blackmail lies in its threat, in the knowledge that someone has or may have the power to destroy you. As long as Rule fears us—and I'm certain that he does, despite the bluster—there's a chance he'll back out, even if we don't have the tea set."

"A very slim chance."

"Slim, but better than announcing to the world that the tea set is a fraud. Once we've done that, Rule will have nothing to lose by charging ahead, and he still might find enough votes to overthrow us."

"I still think Rule is too seasoned to back out in the face of a few empty threats. He knows that it may well be impossible for us to find the tea set, because he's looked for it himself." Philip laughed. "Or maybe he knows it will be impossible to find because he's already found it. The tea set in the museum has been officially accepted by a lot of people, from Revere experts right down to members of our own family."

None of the discussion was new to them. They were simply talking to fill up the time and distract themselves from the heat. They had forty-eight hours and no solutions. Calvin hoped Rule might crack. Philip was relying on Isabelle to find the missing link in Sean Mannion's family history.

After a while, Philip spoke again. "I think we should be preparing to lose on Monday."

"If it happens, I'll immediately begin to structure a tender offer and we can try to buy a controlling interest in the stock. Christopher wanted us to do that from the outset."

"I've never considered a tender offer, Calvin, and neither have you. It would mean buying outright another twenty percent of Pratt Industries. It would force us into alliances that we've never cared to make with banks and bonding institutions, and they'd end up controlling Pratt Industries."

For a time, they sat silently and listened to the noise of the city traffic.

Philip picked up his tennis racket and a ball and absent-mindedly began to bounce the ball on the strings. "No, William Rule was the first person ever to make a serious challenge against us, and I believed we could turn him back, either by convincing the stock-holders to stay with us or by scaring the bastard out of his hairpiece. So far, we've failed on both counts." He paused. "Maybe the mistake was made back in 1876, when Artemus Pratt decided to go public."

"Then, Pratt Rail and Mining, or whatever it was called back then, would never have grown into Pratt Industries," said Calvin. "Even if we lose, we'll still have all the stocks, bonds, and comforts that Pratt growth has provided for us. And there will be other worlds to conquer."

Philip laughed. "Other worlds to conquer." He bounced the ball higher on the racket and tried to turn the racket over between bounces. "How can we expect to conquer other worlds when we can't even hold onto this one?"

"Philip," Calvin spoke sternly. "If you believe that you've lost, you have."

Philip continued to bounce the ball. "No pep talks, Calvin. I'm just trying to face facts. Twenty years ago, we would've rattled our saber, and a nobody like Rule would've run for cover. Now, we have to try bluff and blackmail."

"Don't start getting philosophical on us, Phil. Not yet, anyway."

"But consider the absurdity. The president of a major corporation, his father's hand-picked successor, and unless he can find some clues from a four-hundred-year-old poem, he'll be out in the street on Monday." He stopped bouncing the ball and thought for a moment. "Maybe that wouldn't be so bad after all. Maybe it's time I remade my life. I've always dreamed of stocking up the *Gay Head IV* and trying to sail her around the world. Maybe this year."

Isabelle appeared at the roof entrance and walked across the court. She was smiling. She seemed excited. "We're closer than ever," she announced. "I've been reading birth certificates all day, and I think I've done it. Sean Mannion's last known descendant is a man from South Boston named Kenny Gallagher."

Tom and Danny Fallon followed Peter's instructions with care. At nine-thirty that night, Danny dressed in a gray suit and dark tie. He and Tom sneaked out the back door of their duplex, made sure that no one was watching them, and walked to Kelleher's Funeral Home. With Tom following in a rented Mercury sedan, Danny drove the hearse to a spot in the South End near the *Herald-American* newspaper plant.

Fallon, Evangeline, and Ferguson were waiting for them under a light rain that added more humidity to the heat. Peter, in a dark suit, and Ferguson, in his usual rags, climbed into the hearse. Evangeline got into the rented car; white shoes, stockings, and the hem of a white dress showed beneath her raincoat. Tom Fallon wished them luck and watched them as they headed for the expressway. Then, he went home to wait.

Peter had tried to prepare Danny for Jack Ferguson, but Ferguson had to be seen to be appreciated. For a moment, Danny stared at the big man on the other side of the front seat. Then Peter introduced them.

"You've got a damn nice hearse here." Ferguson greeted Danny with a friendly handshake and a broad smile, and Danny warmed up to him.

"We had a helluva time gettin' it," explained Danny. "Uncle Dunphy had a shit fit when we asked him to lend us a hearse. So Dad asked Dunphy who gave him the loan to buy the funeral home, and Dunphy came around, although he made us change the plates so the hearse couldn't be traced."

"Nice idea," said Ferguson. "This whole thing's a nice idea. I gave my approval the minute I heard it."

"Your approval?" Danny sounded surprised. "Which one of you guys is the boss?"

"We're partners," said Ferguson. He was beginning to like the concept. He had always been a loner. "Now that you're in it, you're a partner, too. Every partner gets to have a say, but since I been lookin' for five years, and your brother's only been at it a week, I think my say counts for a little more."

Danny smiled. "Just so long as we find it, I don't care who says what."

"That's the way to talk." Ferguson liked a positive attitude. He reached across Peter, who was sitting in the middle, and slapped Danny on the knee.

Danny grinned. "You know somethin', Jack? You don't smell half as bad as I expected."

Ferguson laughed.

Evangeline got to Lynnewood Manor ten minutes ahead of the hearse, at about eleven o'clock. It had stopped raining. She tucked her hair up under her nurse's cap and put on her glasses, a pair of heavy horn-rims which considerably changed her appearance. She took off the raincoat, smoothed out the wrinkles in her nurse's uniform, and headed to the entrance.

The nursing shift changed at eleven o'clock. The central desk would be surrounded with white uniforms and Evangeline might have a chance to slip past.

She stopped at the foot of the steps which let into the reception hall. For a moment, she thought of the madness of it all. But she was committed now. She knew that the only way out was straight ahead. She would recover the tea set and learn the truth about her family's relationship to it. She did not want to spend her life wondering what had killed her father and her brother. She refused to spend her life wondering what might come to her door. She had always relied on herself. She would rely on herself to end it.

She smoothed the uniform once more and reminded herself to act confident. If she looked nervous or self-conscious, she wouldn't have a chance. She took a deep breath and strode up the steps. The reception area was a large, circular room, paneled in gumwood, with comfortable furniture scattered all about, with recreation rooms and library opening onto it. The main desk was located beside the hallway that led to the back of the house. A dozen nurses and orderlies, part of the evening shift, clustered near the desk, and Evangeline had to walk past them to reach her objective.

She stopped briefly just inside the door. No one paid special attention to her. No one seemed to be waiting for her. She knew she could make it. Then she wondered if her grandmother had been moved, leaving no need for a guard at Lynnewood.

A nurse's aide walked past and said hello. Evangeline realized that she was hesitating. She smiled pleasantly to the aide, then crossed the reception area. As she approached the nurses' desk, she looked straight ahead. If anyone stopped her, she planned to tell them she was a private nurse called in on short notice to care for the man in bungalow eighteen; Fallon had gotten the name from the lunch list. But no one stopped her. Although a nurse or two glanced up, they were all busy with clipboards and doctors' reports, and the staff was large enough that new faces were not conspicuous.

Evangeline walked crisply down the hall. She felt her heart pounding as the adrenalin coursed through her. She had passed the first obstacle. She did not look back.

She glided past four patient rooms to the solarium at the back of the house. The solarium was in darkness, but two floodlights illuminated the porch on the other side of the full-length windows. She had been hoping for complete darkness. She put on her raincoat again. It was navy blue and would make her less visible.

She stepped outside and hurried to the end of the porch. One of the floodlights was directly above her, but its beam angled outward so that she was in shadow. Just beneath the floodlight, the telephone wire ran from the main building down to the gatehouse. It was exactly where Tom Fallon had anticipated she would find it, at the corner closest to the gatehouse, about eight feet above the porch.

She carefully stepped onto the railing, which brought her within reach of the wires. She gripped the corner of the building with her right hand and balanced herself precariously on three inches of wood. She didn't look down. She didn't want to see the twenty-foot drop to the doctors' parking lot. With her left hand, she carefully reached up toward the wire. She didn't look up. She was afraid of losing her balance. She found the wire, then brought her hand back down, reached very slowly into her pocket, and froze.

Someplace below her, a door opened and a man walked out of an entrance on the basement level. Evangeline listened as the man moved up the sidewalk a short distance and stopped. It seemed to her that he was standing directly beneath her. She felt her knees begin to tremble. She hoped she wouldn't fall. Then, she heard keys jangle. A car door opened, an engine kicked over, and the man drove off.

Evangeline forgot her fear of heights. She wanted to get down from that railing, and fast. She pulled a set of wire cutters from her pocket, reached up, and snapped the telephone line. She jumped down and hurried to the other end of the porch, where the drop to the ground was much shorter. She climbed over the railing and lowered herself into the shrubbery, where she left her raincoat. She smoothed her dress again and started down the lawn to the gatehouse.

In the gatehouse, two guards were playing gin rummy. They were Lynnewood Manor security people, an old man and a boy of about twenty, both unarmed.

"Excuse me," she said cheerily.

Both men looked up, and both looked as though they liked what they saw.

She smiled."Hi. They sent me down from the main desk to tell you that your phone's out of order. They'll have it fixed in a while. They also want to tell you to be expecting a hearse soon."

"Second one today," said the old man.

"I haven't seen you before." The young man wasn't suspicious. He was trying to be charming.

Evangeline acted interested. She took out a cigarette, and the young man offered her a light. She stepped back into the middle of the driveway. The young man followed her with his lighter. She put her hand gently on his, drew the flame into the cigarette, the smoke into her lungs, and almost choked.

"Nothing like a butt to tear up your lungs," said the young guard.

Evangeline agreed between gasps. She hated cigarettes, but the lighting of the cigarette was her signal for the Fallons. She thanked the guards, turned, and walked back toward the main building. When she was out of sight of the gatehouse, she cut back across the lawn and strolled past bungalow sixteen.

Nurse Harriet Burnham, a carbon copy of her sister, Nurse Drexel, was in Katherine Carrington's bedroom preparing her patient's nightly injection. Katherine Carrington was preparing to make her nightly scene. Katherine Carrington's bodyguards, dressed as orderlies, were watching a *Kojak* rerun on television.

The gatehouse guards waved the hearse ahead, and Peter directed Danny to a small lot near the bungalows. Evangeline saw the hearse pulling through the gate, and she hurried down the walk to meet it.

Peter jumped out of the car. A smile broke across his face when he saw her. He had been worried about her.

"We can do it." She spoke firmly, more to convince herself than Fallon. Then she described the arrangements at the bungalow.

"Were there any Pratt men watching the door in the main house?" asked Peter.

"Not that I could tell."

"Then I guess we'll be up against it with the guys in the bungalow." He sounded as though he wanted to meet them.

"Let's stop shootin' the shit and get goin'," said Danny. "The more I stand around thinkin' about this, the stupider it gets."

They opened the back of the hearse, and the coffin rolled out as smoothly as a drawer in a file cabinet. They placed it on its folding metal cart and started up the path to bungalow sixteen. They walked slowly, almost respectfully, with the cart wheels clicking rhythmically over the joints in the concrete.

An old man peered out of his bungalow to see a white angel leading two dark figures and a coffin through the night. He watched the cortege curiously, then moved toward his door, as though he were thinking about joining the vision.

Danny saw the man outlined in the pale-blue glow of a television set. "We'll be back for you later," he whispered.

"Shut up," rasped Peter.

"He didn't hear me."

"I did," came the voice from the coffin.

"You shut up, too," said Peter.

Evangeline knocked on the screen door of bungalow sixteen.

One of the guards appeared. He studied her from behind his Fu Manchu mustache. "Yeah?"

"Hello. I'm . . ." Her nerves caught the words in her throat. She swallowed. "I'm a special for an old gent next door. He's in the tub at the moment and I can't seem to get him out. I was wondering if one of you gentlemen could help me."

"We're private. Call the main house if you want an orderly."

"My telephone isn't working, and if he stays in the tub much longer, I'm afraid he'll start to pucker up."

The guard glowered at her, then he turned to his partner. "I'll be back in a minute, Benny."

Evangeline heard the Fallons moving into position in the darkness behind her. For a moment, she pitied the guard.

He unlatched the screen door.

"Thank you so much," said Evangeline. She swung the door wide open and stepped out of the way.

The coffin hit the guard full force in the groin and knocked him halfway across the room. Before Benny could react to the sight of a coffin flying through the door, the lid flew open and Jack Ferguson aimed a pistol at his head.

"Move or make a sound and you're dead. And you better believe me, because anybody ridin' around in a coffin is fuckin' crazy to begin with. Got it?"

The other guard rolled to his feet.

"And tell that friend of yours that if he don't stay right where he is, I'll leave you all over the wall."

Benny saw the glint in Ferguson's eye. He believed everything Ferguson said. "Back off, Sonny."

In the bedroom, Nurse Burnham grabbed the telephone. Katherine Carrington reached over and pulled the wire out of the wall.

Peter heard the scuffle. He stepped into the bedroom, and the nurse started to scream. He couldn't let her scream. He came at her and clamped a hand over her mouth. She tried to bite him, to wrestle away from him, but he held tight. He wasn't going to let her ruin everything. She began to swing and kick at him, and he tried to tell her she would be all right.

"Cold-cock the bitch," said Katherine Carrington. Her own language surprised her.

Fallon threw the nurse into a headlock and dragged her into the living room. Wrestling with her wasn't quite as exciting as fighting with Harrison, but he had to settle her down. He hauled her right up to the muzzle of Ferguson's .45. When she saw the man behind the gun, she stopped moving.

"That's better," said Ferguson, still sitting in the coffin.

"Easy work, scarin' women," said Sonny.

"Even easier to keep an old lady penned up when she don't want to be," said Ferguson.

They bound and gagged the guards and the nurse and locked them each in a separate closet. It was easy. Sonny and Benny had both been around long enough to know they didn't argue with a man holding a .45.

Evangeline threw her arms around her grandmother's neck. "I've worried about you, Grandmother."

"I'll be all right, darling. You're so brave to help me."

"Let's save the speeches for later and get the hell out of here," said Danny.

"What about the quotations?" asked Peter.

"When we get to the airport," said Katherine firmly. "How are we going?"

"There's only one way out," said Ferguson.

She studied the strange-looking man sitting in the coffin. "Do I know you?"

"We met a long time ago, and before this trip is over, we'll be best of friends."

"It's tight quarters," said Peter. "But you'll only be in there for a few minutes."

She looked at Ferguson and joked, "I'll have no hanky panky, young man."

"You have my word."

She squeezed into the coffin, the lid was closed, and Katherine Pratt Carrington was smuggled out of the Lynnewood Manor.

At twelve-thirty, she was standing with her granddaughter, Peter Fallon, and Jack C. Ferguson in the Eastern Airlines lounge. She was wearing a powder-blue jumper, bought by Evangeline, accented with a dark-blue scarf. She looked again like the vibrant old woman Fallon had first met at Searidge. She was in her seventies and beginning a new phase of her life.

"I feel like a schoolgirl going off on a great trip." She laughed nervously. "Of course, the last time I felt this way, I was eleven years old, and we were about to embark on the *Titanic*."

Evangeline embraced her. "Oh, Grandmother, I'm so afraid to send you off alone."

Katherine put arms around Evangeline and patted her gently on the back. "I should be worrying about you, leaving you here in the middle of all this." Her hands stopped moving and she looked at Evangeline. "Do you realize I used to pat you like this when you were a baby?"

"Where will you go, Grandmother?"

"Away from here. I had to leave that place." She smiled at Ferguson. "Even if it meant hiding in a coffin with a strange man."

Ferguson smiled back, almost sheepishly. He was still in awe of Katherine Carrington.

Evangeline drew her grandmother to her and held tight. "I can't just let you fly off."

"Nonsense." Katherine's voice was growing stronger as departure approached. "If I were younger, I'd stay and help you clear this up. I'm convinced now that the only way is to find the tea set, and I'm too old to do that."

The public-address system announced departure, and people in the lounge scurried for the plane.

Katherine took an envelope from her purse and put it into Ferguson's hand. She took Evangeline's and Peter's hands in her own and held them tightly. "Find it and rid us of it for good. But be careful, darlings, please." For a moment, she didn't want to leave them in danger, but she knew that until the Golden Eagle was found, they would always be in danger. Let them find it together. She had done all that she could to help them.

She threw her arms around Evangeline again. They held each other silently for a moment, then Katherine broke away and picked up her suitcase. There were tears in her eyes. She turned and started down the tube.

Evangeline ran after her. "Grandmother, where will you go?"

"I'll visit cousins in New York for a few days. Then I'm going to Hawaii."

"Hawaii?"

Katherine kept walking. "Cousin William has invited me a hundred times. He runs a school for the retarded on one of the outer islands." She reached the plane. She stopped and looked back. "I still have my music and my love of children, dear. I can still be of use." She stepped onto the plane and the door was closed.

Evangeline walked back to Fallon and Ferguson. "I never even asked her about my father."

"I can fill in a few of the details," said Ferguson. "It's a long story."

Fallon's attention had already shifted to the envelope in his hands. "Does it have anything to do with *Paradise Lost?*"

"I've always thought so."

It was one o'clock in the morning when the *Peter* returned to Lewis Wharf. Before Rule cut the engines, Lawrence Hannaford jumped from the wharf onto the main deck.

"Hey, Larry. How ya doin'?"

"Terrible."

"Too bad you didn't come out with us. We didn't catch many fish, we got a little wet, but we beat this heat and had a real nice time anyway."

Rule's wife jumped off the boat and secured the stern to the dock.

"Help me tie 'er up, Larry, then we'll go upstairs and have a drink."

"It's late, Rule, I didn't come here to socialize." Hannaford's slender voice cracked with anger. He threw the early edition of the Sunday *Globe*, which came out on Saturday night, onto the table in Rule's cabin. He flipped back the comics and pointed to a story on the bottom of the front page. "Do you know anything about that?"

The headline read, "Gangland Assassin Found Dead in Cambridge Apartment Building." Above the headline was a police photograph of the man with the pockmarks and the receding hairline.

Rule cursed softly.

"You tried to kill the student, didn't you?"

"Anybody I knock off is as much of a threat to you as he is to me." Rule pointed a stubby finger at Hannaford. "Before I came up with the tea set, we were both small-time. I did you a favor, and you did me one. We're partners, right down the line."

"I won't be partners with a murderer. I won't permit you to kill anybody else."

"I've waited too long, Larry. I'm too close."

"You can kill a whore in Los Angeles and a bartender in South Boston and a young lawyer—"

"We didn't kill Carrington," interrupted Rule.

"Somebody did, but the spread among the three of them is wide enough that you can get away with it. Kill any more people, and you'll end up in jail instead of at the head of Pratt Industries."

"You'll be right along with me, Larry."

Hannaford sensed Rule's contempt. He hated Rule. He hated himself. "I have a better solution," he said softly. "We can solve all our problems without killing anyone else, and we can do it once and for all."

Rule studied him for a moment, then leaned against the bulwark. "Convince me."

From the fold of the newspaper, Lawrence Hannaford took a large manila envelope. It contained a sheet of paper, which he unfolded and spread on the table in front of him. Rule studied it quizzically. The paper was covered with floor plans and circuitry diagrams. Lawrence Hannaford explained his plan.

CHAPTER XXIII   *December 1972*

On the last afternoon of 1972, Lawrence Hannaford sat in the office at the rear of his gallery and sipped coffee.

In other years, he had always thrown a New Year's Eve party, and every party had been a resounding success. His theme for the 1971 party had been "Do Your Own Thing." He stripped the white gallery walls, gave all his guests paintbrushes and buckets of bright latex, and let them follow their fancy. The results were so colorful and unusual that, for the succeeding two weeks, he invited the public to view a work of living art, "New Year's Eve, 1971," on the walls and ceiling of his gallery.

This year, there would be no such celebration. Lawrence Hannaford was broke. Since 1969, when he had been politicized by the Vietnam War Moratorium, he had been showing the work of radical young artists who painted their protests. But stark, primary-colored depictions of American B-52s raining bombs on black Americans or of angry Vietnamese peasants trashing Wall Street did not sell to the people who bought art in Boston. Nor had abstracts with titles like "Napalm," or "African Sunrise," in black, red, and green, attracted buyers. Radical liberal sentiments did not reach deep into Boston pocketbooks.

Hannaford's Newbury Street gallery was closing. He would miss his life there, the sophisticated chatter of art lovers at champagne previews, the liaisons with college girls who came to his gallery to research term papers on current American art, and the excitement of discovering a talented young artist. Eventually, he would have to sell his sports car to pay for his beautiful Marlborough Street apartment. His life-style, which remained extravagant despite his support of the Movement, and his tastes in art had cost him most of his savings and trust money. His father refused to lend him any more money. If he declared bankruptcy and allowed his personal finances to be scrutinized, several rather large discrepancies, appearing regularly over a period of five years, would be uncovered in Hannaford's income-tax returns.

Around four o'clock, just as Hannaford was about to close up the gallery for the last time, a man in a chauffeur's uniform appeared at the back door. Twenty minutes later, Hannaford was sitting in the office of a warehouse in East Boston. The coils of an electric space heater glowed at his feet, a pot of coffee steamed on a hotplate behind the desk, and a single hanging lamp threw harsh shadows onto the floor. The chauffeur had told Hannaford that his employer was interested in some art work, but this was not the sort of place where collectors did business. Hannaford was beginning to feel nervous.

Through the windows that separated the office from the rest of the warehouse, Hannaford saw a stocky man with a mustache walking toward him. The man was wearing an expensive cashmere overcoat and brown fedora, and he moved past the crates and boxes like a pit bull looking for trouble.

The office door opened and the cold air rushed in. The man extended his hand. His greeting was more friendly than his appearance. "Good afternoon, Mr. Hannaford. I'm Bill Rule. Thanks for coming over. These damn year-end inventories keep me all tied up, but I wanted to talk to you."

Hannaford smiled. "I'm always ready to talk to a collector."

Rule poured two cups of coffee and sat behind his desk. It was cold in the little office, and he kept his overcoat on. "A little New Year's Eve cheer for your coffee?"

"It might make me a little warmer. Sure."

Rule took a bottle of Jack Daniels from his desk drawer and tossed generous shots into each cup. The men toasted to the new year, and Rule tilted back in his chair. "Mr. Hannaford, I've been watching your career for quite some time."

"I hope you like what you've seen."

"What I've seen is a man trying to do something different. I don't hold with all this radical hippie shit, but I admire a man who has the balls to be a rebel, no matter what he's rebellin' against."

Hannaford was flattered. He liked to think of himself as a rebel. "Thank you."

"But I've also seen a man slipping into debt, a man who's spent all his money, who's borrowed heavily from people in his family, whose father would rather have an alcoholic Communist faggot than an art dealer for a son."

Hannaford put down his coffee and stood. "This has nothing to do with art, mister."

Rule smiled, "I also see before me a man who, according to my private sources, has been jerkin' off the IRS to the tune of ten or fifteen thousand a year since he first started selling paintings."

Hannaford swallowed hard. He was so shocked he didn't have the presence of mind to deny it. "That was a war protest."

"Sit down, Mr. Hannaford, and cut the shit. Can I call you Larry?"

"I prefer Lawrence."

"Okay, Lawrence. I'm not tryin' to be unfriendly by tellin' you all this. I just want you to know that I've had my eye on you for quite a while, and I know you pretty good. I think you and I can do some business."

"I'll tell you right now that I'm not interested."

"The IRS might be interested in you, Larry. Lawrence. So I'd suggest that you listen up."

Hannaford sat reluctantly.

Rule leaned across his desk. "What you need is somethin' to make your name a household word with the people who buy art. You have to build a good reputation before you can sell that gook-and-nigger art. You have to be in the know with those rich Europeans who look for brainy American dealers who can sell their trinkets and junk to stupid Americans at armed-robbery prices. Furthermore, you need money. I'm gonna help you out on all counts."

Rule opened the safe behind his desk and took out a velvet bag. He placed it on his desk, loosened the drawstring, and peeled the velvet away from the contents of the bag.

Hannaford was dazzled.

"You're an art man. What does this look like to you?"

"It's a teapot," he said softly. "Probably Federal."

"Look closer."

Hannaford saw the tiny golden eagle. He carefully turned the teapot over and saw Revere's stamp in block letters on the base. He knew enough about Revere to know the story. "This was stolen from the White House in 1814. It's been missing ever since."

"You want to sell it for me?"

"Where did you get it?" asked Hannaford suspiciously.

"You haven't answered my question, Larry. Lawrence. You want to be my partner?"

"Certainly I want to sell it. But first, I want to know where you got it and what kind of deal you want to make."

"Second question first. You sell the tea set for what you can get. A million, maybe a million and a half. You keep the money. When your father dies—and we all know that Henry Hannaford's had three heart attacks in two years—you sign over to me his fifty thousand shares of Pratt Industries stock, market value of about two million, and I gamble that the stock stays where it is. Big liberal art dealers shouldn't be holdin' stock in a company that produces chemical defoliants, anyway."

"Where did you get it?" asked Hannaford.

"You haven't told me if you're interested in my deal."

"I need time to think about it."

"You got no time. I want to know now."

Hannaford's voice faltered. "I believe that I am."

Rule smiled. "You're a smart boy, smart enough to know that what I'm gonna tell you now goes no further than this room. If it does, I'll destroy the tea set, and then I'll destroy you." He picked up the teapot. It was so delicately balanced that he could hold it with one finger. "This is a fake."

Hannaford was only mildly surprised. In an East Boston warehouse, with an unctuous arm-twister like Rule, he couldn't expect anything else. But the forgery seemed flawless.

"The man who made this tea set is one of the finest silversmiths in Europe. Before he started, he spent months studying Revere's work—his daybooks, his techniques, everything. He used the right alloys for eighteenth-century silver, and he even developed a process that uses chemicals, heat, and infrared light to apply a patina that seems like the real thing."

"Why are you telling me this?"

"When I go into a partnership with a man, I want him to know everything. That way, if he slips up, he's not ignorant, just stupid. And you're not stupid. Besides, the Pratts have been connected into this thing for two hundred years. I think it would be good if one of their own introduced it to the world."

"I'm a distant cousin, and I don't know what the Pratts have to do with this tea pot."

Rule looked at his watch. "I have to get home and get ready for a New Year's drunk. I'll tell you the Pratt story some other time. You have two days to think this over, Larry. If I don't hear from you, I'll know you're not interested." Rule offered his hand.

"Don't you think this is rather dangerous business?"

"Not at all. The silversmith won't talk because he's an old friend. Two of his sons live in this country because of my influence. You won't talk because you're not stupid, like I say. Which leaves me. I can guarantee you I won't talk. Other than that, it's simply a business proposition, a long-term loan. You need money and reputation right now. I want a piece of Pratt Industries, and I'm willin' to wait for it. That tea set cost me a hundred thousand bucks to copy. I'll make twenty times that much when you inherit your stock. I could sell the tea set myself, but I'd rather use someone with family connections." Rule stood. "You see, Larry, I'm going to strangle the Pratts with their own rope, and you're the guy who's pickin' up the slack."

Hannaford was stunned by this man, who seemed to know so much. "What happens if I refuse to turn over the stock when my father dies? You can't go to the police and tell them I didn't pay for your art forgery."

"If you don't give me the stock when your old man bites the bag, you'll get a mouthful of it yourself. And if you don't want to go along with me, you'll be hearin' real soon from the IRS." Rule took Hannaford's hand and shook it. "Happy New Year."

Two days later, feeling something like Faust, Lawrence Hannaford agreed to Rule's deal.

The unveiling of the Golden Eagle Tea Set was the art event of the season. Two hundred people—potential buyers, museum officials, members of the news media, and the usual glamorous hangers-on—jammed the Newbury Street gallery to gawk at one of the most important finds in American art history. Four armed guards protected the Golden Eagle, which was displayed in the middle of the room on a pedestal covered in blue velvet. Four spots highlighted it. The rest of the room was soft lights, background music, the clinking of champagne glasses, and the conversation of people who mattered.

Lawrence Hannaford, coolly elegant in black tie, tuxedo, and studs, glided through the crowd, shaking hands, pecking cheeks, and accepting congratulations. He was enjoying his greatest moment. He tried not to think about the deal with William Rule or the story they had fabricated about an anonymous English owner, the murder of Sir Henry Carrol in 1875, and the original theft by the British Captain Prendergast.

In his office, telegrams of congratulations were piled high on his desk. He had left all but one of the messages out so that friends could read them. He had filed Katherine Carrington's note immediately after reading it.

"Congratulations, Lawrence," she wrote. "We in the Carrington wing of the family are very happy for you. I must tell you, however, that my knowledge of the tea set's history does not coincide with the story you have given to the press. Admittedly, my information comes to me via family legend and fable, while yours is the result of several months of careful research. But I must say that I was surprised to learn that the tea set has been in England since 1814; the legend says that it sank into the Back Bay. But I'll never rain on your parade, as the saying goes. I'm glad that the tea set has been found under any circumstances. The legends can once and for all be laid to rest."

The note comforted Hannaford. Katherine was the only member of the family to mention anything about the Back Bay, and she seemed perfectly willing to forget about it. Hannaford did not know that there was a newspaperman in the crowded gallery that night who had no intentions of forgetting about the tea set.

Jack Ferguson was wearing a rumpled gray flannel suit and bow tie, and he looked conspicuously out of place among the tuxedos. He was elbowing his way toward a stocky figure who looked equally misplaced, despite his evening dress.

"I hear you've changed your name," said Ferguson.

William Rule turned around. He didn't recognize the white hair and the craggy face. He hadn't seen Ferguson in twenty years. His expression darkened for a moment, then he smiled and shook Ferguson's hand. "Jack. How are you?"

"Still kickin'."

"What do you think of this big shindig?"

"I think someone's takin' it in the ass."

Rule's eyes shifted nervously from Ferguson to the people conversing around him. Ferguson's voice hadn't carried. Rule took Ferguson by the arm and led him to the side of the room. "Ease off, Jackie. You talk like that, you'll spoil the kid's big night."

"It sounds to me like you've spoiled his life."

Rule's hand clamped around Ferguson's forearm. His grip was still powerful. "I did him a favor."

Ferguson glanced over at the tea set. "Where did it come from?"

"You mean you didn't get a press release?" Rule was trying to be very smooth.

"Well, I've heard a rumor that isn't in the press release. It says you're the English mystery man." Ferguson looked around at the well-dressed mob. "I think the common man should know about rumors like that."

Rule smiled, he had hoped to keep his name out of it completely, but he knew Ferguson would try to implicate him. "Actually, Jack, I'm a middleman for Hannaford. One of my English contacts is the owner."

"Bullshit."

"The tea set came from England. Old Phil Cawley was spinnin' yarns. You told me that yourself twenty years ago at a hockey game. The tea set never made it to Boston."

Ferguson smiled like a man who knew the truth.

Rule believed that nothing made him nervous. He felt a trickle of sweat beginning just beneath his hairpiece. He told himself it was the heat in the gallery. A waiter came by carrying a tray of champagne glasses. Rule grabbed two and offered one to Ferguson.

"No thanks."

"On the wagon, eh?"

"Not a drop for the last four years. And never another one, if I can help it. Since the last time we talked about that tea set, back in fifty-two, I've been down for the eight count and bounced back more times than Marciano." Ferguson's voice was a sharp edge cutting through the years.

"C'mon, Jack. Bygones. Didn't you ever get the letters I sent you?"

"I got them."

In 1967, when Rule had first begun to think about the forgery, he had written Ferguson several notes, inviting him to lunch. Ferguson had never answered them.

"We all do things we're sorry for, Jackie. When I was younger, I was filled with hate. I always figured people were out to screw me. That's the way I grew up. I was always ready to strike first or take revenge if someone struck me. When you accused me of killin' that

Carrington kid, that really hurt, Jack. Deep in the pit of my stomach it hurt. I had to get back at you."

Ferguson didn't believe a word.

"I had a mean streak, but not any more. I'm a changed man since the last time I got married. She's a knockout. Let me haul her over here." Rule found Cindy and led her back to the side of the room.

Ferguson was gone.

"That son of a bitch," said Rule.

"What's wrong, honey?"

"Nothing we can't take care of."

Jack C. Ferguson's article appeared in the next issue of *Hubcap*. "Look under a rock," it concluded, "and you'll find a Boston businessman named William Rule. He claims to be Hannaford's middleman. I wonder. . . . He's been obsessed by the tea-set legend since he first read about it as a boy. I'm willing to bet a little U.S. cash that this Golden Eagle Tea Set is a fake. I'd tell more, but without the permission of a certain fine lady from a certain New England family, I'd be breaking an oath. So let's let it lie. Just like Bill Rulick."

Lawrence Hannaford was petrified. He denied Ferguson's charges and offered the tea set to silver experts and Revere scholars for examination. He had no other choice. Rule told him he had made the right decision, encouraged him to remain cool, and promised him that Jack Ferguson would cause no further problems.

A few nights later, Rule visited Ferguson at his three-room apartment in South Boston. He brought Edward and a quart of Canadian whiskey with him. Edward waited in the hallway.

"Talk fast, Rule. I'm busy."

Rule looked around the apartment. It was small and dingy. Ferguson's typewriter was on the kitchen table, a pile of papers beside it. The dwelling of a man who'd spent most of his life struggling, alone.

Rule offered Ferguson the bottle. "Let's have a drink."

"Say your piece and get out. I don't want to drink with you."

"That's unfriendly, Jack. I'm here for a peace conference. Show a little class." He handed Ferguson the bottle. He hadn't stopped smiling since he had walked through the door. "Pour a couple over ice and hear me out."

Ferguson put the bottle on the coffee table and went into the kitchen. He came back with a glass and a tray of ice cubes and put them beside the bottle. "Pour your own."

"Good old Alcoholics Anonymous. Even if you haven't touched it for four years, a single shot can touch you off."

Ferguson nodded. "They're right. I've learned that lesson the hard way too many times."

Rule opened the bottle and poured three fingers. He washed the liquor around on the sides of the glass to release the sweet aroma, then he held it out to Ferguson. "They say a drunk can be on the straight and narrow for twenty-five years and still crave a drink every day of his life."

Ferguson stepped back. He didn't need temptation. "I'll give you ten seconds to take that booze and get out of here."

Rule flung the whiskey in Ferguson's face and followed it with a left that clipped Ferguson on the chin and sent him toppling over the coffee table. Rule was fifty years old, but he lifted weights and worked on the light bag every day. Ferguson tried to roll to his feet. Rule kicked him viciously in the ribs and called for Edward.

Ferguson was dazed. He felt something trickling into his mouth. He tasted blood and the old familiar tingle of Canadian Club. He licked his lips and spat. Then Edward's knee smashed into his face.

When he regained his senses, his arms were pinned behind him and Rule was pouring whiskey into his mouth. Ferguson turned his head away. Edward snapped it back.

"Taste good, Jackie?" asked Rule.

Ferguson was weak and confused. He swallowed, and the whiskey burned all the way to his stomach. He wanted more, but he heard himself telling Rule to get out and take his booze with him.

Rule held the bottle in front of Ferguson's face. It was half empty. "There's no use fightin' it, Jackie. It's in you, and you'll need a lot more now to put out the fire."

Rule clinked the glass against the mouth of the bottle. The air pocket popped as the whiskey pumped out. Rule brought the glass to Ferguson's lips. Ferguson turned his head. The glass followed him. Ferguson turned in the other direction, but he couldn't escape the glass. Like a drowning man giving in to the last wave, he drank. He was dead drunk a half hour later.

"Stay with him all night," said Rule to Edward. "See that he keeps drinking. When he wakes up in the morning, give him a drink right away. I'll send someone to help you." He took twelve dollars from his pocket and dropped it on Ferguson. "Just enough for two jugs. That'll hook him good."

Rule was right. There was nothing worse than an alcoholic on a tear after four years sober. Ferguson got drunk. Drunkenness became dejection, then self-pity. He lost his job and continued to drink over a quart a day. For a while, Rule kept him supplied. When he was certain Ferguson was hooked, Rule stopped sending whiskey. Ferguson drank up his small savings and continued to slide. He had no wife or family to help him. His few friends tried to straighten him out, but the addiction was too strong.

In one of his few lucid moments, he recalled a visit from two people who had said that they worked for the Museum of Fine Arts. He couldn't remember what he told them, but they only stayed a few minutes and left looking disappointed. He realized that he had lost his chance to tell the story to the right people. The thought drove him deeper into his pit. His friends deserted him and Jack Ferguson disappeared into the bowels of Skid Row.

On a cold February morning over a year later, he decided to stop drinking. He had been sharing a jug of sauterne with another wino in the cellar of an abandoned South End building. It was snowing outside, and they had huddled in the corner for warmth. After finishing the bottle, they had fallen asleep. When Ferguson awoke the next morning, his toes were numb and his fingers like icicles. He gave his drinking partner a shove, and the man fell over, frozen into the position in which he'd passed out. Ferguson saw the blue face and knew the bum was dead. He dragged himself to his feet and staggered to the warmth of the Salvation Army Neighborhood Center on Columbus Avenue.

With his hands wrapped around a cup of hot coffee and his brain thawing slowly out of its stupor, Jack Ferguson realized that he would have frozen to death if another drunk, whose name he did not even know, had not fallen asleep on top of him. Ferguson sipped the coffee and watched the steam swirling into the air, and he saw Bill Rulick's face. Rulick was to blame. Rulick had robbed him of his job, his reputation, his self-respect. Rulick had tried to kill him.

Jack C. Ferguson resolved that he would not die a derelict in the basement of an abandoned tenement. He might die alone, but not without a fight.

CHAPTER XXIV

Jack C. Ferguson had never stopped drinking, but he had been able to taper off and go for up to three days without a drop. This was the third day. He wanted a drink, but he wasn't going to have one. He had come too close to falter. Too close, but not close enough.

He looked at Fallon and Evangeline, curled up together in a sleeping bag on the other side of the room. He liked them both, and he sensed that they liked him. He hadn't let anybody get close to him in a long time. Even if he didn't find the tea set, he thought, he had helped Katherine Pratt Carrington and these two kids.

Bullshit. If he didn't find the tea set, nothing mattered.

He rolled off his pallet of newspapers and got up. They had spent the night in one of Ferguson's hideouts, a deserted warehouse near Dover Street. If Rulick sent men after them, Ferguson wanted to be in his own territory, and he didn't want to endanger the Fallon family any further.

Ferguson looked out the window. A few blocks away, the modern *Herald-American* newspaper building covered most of his old South End neighborhood. Beyond that, the downtown skyline glinted in the June sun. Another scorcher. Ferguson thought about the snowy days when he had sat in Phil Cawley's room and gazed out at this same view. He remembered that the Customs House Tower, now dwarfed by glass, steel, and red granite, had dominated the city.

Old Phil Cawley and his tale of buried treasure and his quotation from *Paradise Lost*. Damn the quotations, thought Ferguson. Damn the one they didn't have.

They had spent most of the night piecing together the quotations. At an old desk in the warehouse office, with Ferguson's kerosene lamp giving light, they had arranged the quotations before them in ascending order, from Book II to Book XII. Occasionally, a rat would scuttle across the floor, and Ferguson, thinking he heard Rulick's men, would reach for his .45, or a police siren would wail past the warehouse, but sounds served only to punctuate the silence in the mouldering old building.

The first quotation, which Ferguson had gotten from a woman in California, appeared in Book II. It told of a "boiling gulf" over which a bridge stretched from hell to earth. They wondered if Abigail was referring to a bridge. The quotation also mentioned the tracks of Satan, which led them to speculate briefly that the treasure was buried near a bridge over the Boston and Maine tracks.

Evangeline pointed out that it was the only quotation containing a word which might be taken as a homonym for a Back Bay street. "Boiling," she suggested, could easily become "Boylston," Boylston Street, the main commercial thoroughfare in the Back Bay. They agreed.

The next set of lines came from Katherine Carrington. They were part of the prose argument, or introductory synopsis, for Book IV. "Uriel descending on a Sunbeam warns Gabriel, who had in charge the Gate of Paradise, that some evil spirit had escap'd the Deep . . ." The quotation ended in midsentence. Fallon thought that the rest of the lines in Book IV might refer to the depth at which the tea set was buried, since "Deep" was the last word in the passage. They decided to look at the succeeding quotations with that in mind.

Dr. William Pratt's quotation, which had hung over his desk at the Massachusetts General Hospital, came next in Book IV. It referred to Adam and Eve, "two of far nobler shape."

The next set of lines was the quotation Ferguson had shown to Fallon and Evangeline when he had first appeared on Evangeline's roof. In it, the Archangel Gabriel heard the "tread of nimble feet" as three spirits, including Satan, approached him.

"Like I said the other night, are we supposed to read the unit of measure or the number?"

"Use both of them and put this quotation together with the one before it," said Fallon. "You get two feet three, which doesn't help us if she's talking about the depth at which the tea set is buried."

They read the next quotation. It was another which Katherine Pratt Carrington had given them at the airport. "So wise he judges it to fly from pain/ However, and to 'scape his punishment./ So judge thou still, presumptuous, till the wrath,/ Which thou incurr'st by flying, meet thy flight/ Sev'nfold, and scourge that wisdom back to Hell,/ Which taught thee yet no better, that no pain/ Can equal anger infinite provok't."

Evangeline read the context. "It's Gabriel talking to Satan again."

"A Calvinist world view for sure," said Fallon. "Run away from punishment now, and you'll get it sevenfold in the ass when the Lord catches up with you."

"Okay," said Ferguson. "We've now got a 'sev'nfold,' a 'two,' a 'three,' and we think we're talking about feet and depth. Do we put the 'two' together with the 'sev'nfold' and come up with fourteen feet?"

"Not if we're talking about depth," said Fallon. "The average depth of the landfill is twenty and a half feet, and we know the tea set was buried in the mud under the landfill."

"What about 'feet,' 'three,' and 'sev'nfold'? Twenty-one feet?"

Fallon shook his head. "That would leave the tea set in six inches of mud. Even if water did cover it for most of that time, I don't think the tea set could lie there for fifty years and not be found. If Abigail is telling us how deep the thing is buried, I think she wants us to read 'sev'nfold' simply as the number seven. That gives us 'two' and 'seven' sandwiched around the word 'feet.' Twenty-seven feet."

"What about the number 'three' in the 'nimble feet' passage?"

"If the tea set is buried thirty-seven feet down, I don't think anyone is going to find it. The tea set sank into the mud and was covered over by a layer of dirt and gravel. I say that the tea set is buried from twenty-three to twenty-seven feet down."

Another quotation, from Book VII, was more general in its reference. "But they, or under ground, or circuit wide/ With Serpent error wand'ring, found their way,/ And on the washy Ooze deep Channels wore;/ Easy, ere God had bid the ground be dry . . ."

Katherine wrote that this had been her quotation, coming to her through her through her granduncle, Henry Pratt. The reference was obvious—a channel in the ooze before God filled the land. The Easterly Channel.

Fallon, Evangeline, and Ferguson kept working until five in the morning. Anticipation and frustration struggled within them as they deciphered. It was not difficult to draw a single clue from each quotation; Abigail had been careful to make the individual meanings clear. But they were not always certain if they were arranging the clues in the correct order. At times, she seemed to follow a sequence—in Book IV and later, when she gave directional clues—but quotations like the "boiling gulf" appeared to have been chosen without reference to the other lines.

They agreed that the lines on the tombstones of Horace Pratt and Abigail were not clues, but exhortations to succeeding generations. They did not consider them.

They pushed the other clues around until they found a logical sequence for the words and phrases. They thought that the tea set was now within their grasp. They stepped back, like artisans admiring their handiwork, and read, "In the channel beneath the fill; Boylston; twenty-three to twenty-seven feet deep; ten paces east on southwest corner."

Fallon cursed softly.

"Southwest corner of what?" asked Evangeline.

The vital clue was missing. Fallon sank into a sitting position on the floor. He realized that he was too exhausted to be disappointed.

Ferguson looked out the window. The sky was already light. "I rode the rails for three weeks back in seventy-six. I found an old woman named Mary Korbel in a seedy Hollywood apartment, I knew just lookin' at her that she didn't have much time. Cancer. She showed me this sampler that the quotation was embroidered onto, the one about boiling abysses. I tried to buy it off her, but she wouldn't sell. She said her daughter was a godless prostitute, and someday the message on the sampler might lead her to salvation. All along, I've been figuring that this was the clue the Pratts didn't have, and once I had the Pratt clues, I'd find the tea set."

"Maybe they don't have it," offered Evangeline. She didn't care how they found it now, as long as they found it. "Maybe they have another one. They might be willing to make a deal."

"No deals." Ferguson growled.

"No deals," agreed Peter. "There's another quotation out there. Either that or we've deciphered these things all wrong. Let's get some sleep and try again in the morning."

Standing now in the bright sunlight, Ferguson began to wonder if he would ever see the Golden Eagle. He had searched for years, and he was not much closer than he'd been the day Phil Cawley told him the story. He could hear Phil Cawley's rasping voice. He could almost taste Phil Cawley's alky split. He took some money from Evangeline's purse, stepped past the tin-can alarms, and went down the fire escape.

It was eight o'clock. Philip Pratt sat in his study and watched two tree sparrows chase each other about in the elm outside his window. He had been up for an hour, since Soames had called to tell him of his aunt's disappearance. They had already decided that a report to the police would be unwise. Pratt heard the elevator door open down the hall. He was expecting Soames and James Buckley, who had been dispatched onto Fallon's trail the day before and had disappeared for the night. Pratt swiveled around to face the door.

Isabelle walked into the room. She was wearing Philip's terrycloth bathrobe and a gold necklace. She was carrying a tray of coffee, juice, and croissants. She had spent the night in the Back Bay mansion, and there was only one bed for the maid to make up in the morning. "You'll feel better if you have a little breakfast, Philip."

"I'll feel better when I know what's going to happen."

"Soon enough."

He watched her pour the coffee. She seemed serene, unworried. He asked her if she was concerned about her mother.

"Not really. I know where she's gone."

"Where?"

"Hawaii." She sat back on her heels, exposing her muscular thighs. "It's always been one of her fantasies. I'll bet she's on a plane right now."

"Hawaii." He said the word dreamily, then said, "I'm still worried about her."

"We both know that Evangeline got her out with the help of the Fallons, and she's fully competent. She wasn't for a day or so after Christopher died. None of us were. But she knew that we were keeping her there because it served our convenience."

"And her safety."

"She didn't accept that, and I'm not sure I do, either. But in any event, I'm quite certain that she hates us both."

He looked again at the sparrows chattering at each other "Would she hate us more if she knew about last night?"

"She'd give me the same motherly advice she dispensed thirty years ago, when we first started going for long walks on the beach: don't."

"Are we wrong?"

"I suppose." She did not want to think about morality. She simply wanted to enjoy him. "But I'm too old to have children. We're both alone. And I was brought up in such a rarefied atmosphere that I've never found a man outside the Pratt family worth my time, and that includes my late husband."

Isabelle Carrington Howe was not beautiful in the way that Melissa Pike was beautiful. Her hair was turning gray, her nose was rather prominent, and when she was unhappy, her look was stern and severe, instead of pouty and little-girl sexy, like Melissa's. But Isabelle comforted Philip. No one had comforted him in years.

"I have the feeling," he said, "that rather soon I am going to be unemployed."

"You mustn't think that way."

"I'm beginning to enjoy the prospect. I'm thinking of loading up the *Gay Head IV* and just sailing away. I've always wanted to do it. Now that I owe a personal apology to your mother, I think I'll aim for Hawaii."

"In the *Gay Head?*"

"The original *Gay Head* wasn't much larger, and Horace Taylor Pratt built an empire on its keel." He paused for a moment and looked at Isabelle. "If I should turn the empire over to someone else, I'll be free to go where I please and with whom I please. Would you be interested in sailing to Hawaii with me?"

She knew he was serious. She liked the idea, but it frightened her. She didn't know what to say. The sound of the elevator distracted them.

Soames and Buckley entered the study. Buckley looked like a schoolboy come to see the principal.

"Good morning. Bennett," said Pratt.

"He was never able to pick up the Fallons, either in South Boston or the South End, so he called his girlfriend and spent the night with her." Soames spoke as though Buckley were not in the room.

"I hope he realizes that while he was screwing, he might have been providing us with valuable information," said Pratt.

"Give a guy a break," protested Buckley. "I been so damn busy followin' that Fallon around I ain't been on the rack in three weeks."

Pratt smiled. He was in no position to criticize. "One break is extended. Two weeks ago, you followed Peter Fallon to a wake. It is very important that you tell us everything that you remember about it."

"Can I have a cup of coffee?"

Isabelle poured, and James Buckley took a small notebook from his pocket. It contained names, addresses, and extra notes on Peter Fallon's activities.

Evangeline felt something crawling on her leg. She kicked violently, knocking Peter awake.

"What? What's wrong?"

"A cockroach!" She jumped up from the sleeping bag, and the cockroach streaked off into a corner. She would have stepped on it, but she wasn't wearing shoes. She had slept in T-shirt, panties, and socks.

"Be glad it wasn't a rat," said Fallon.

"I've had it. I don't know why on earth we couldn't spend the night in a hotel instead of in this hole."

"We're running scared," Fallon explained, as though he were reciting the rules of a game. "Ferguson's been doing it for a few years, so I guess he ought to know how."

"Speaking of whom, where is he?"

"He took some money and went out. He probably needs a drink. I could use one myself."

A rat scurried into the room. It stopped and studied them dispassionately for a moment, then disappeared into a hole in the wall.

"This is it, Peter," she said firmly. "I've run scared for the last night. I don't care whether we find the tea set or not. Tonight I sleep in my own bed." She sat down crosslegged on the rumpled sleeping bag and picked nervously at the lint on her socks.

"You care, Evangeline." He laid his hand on her knee. "You care as much as I do."

"Ferguson told me my father's story, what there is of it. And the reasons for my brother's death are still speculation. We may never know what happened to him. I just want it all to end." She put her hand on his. "I'd like to get to know you under normal circumstances."

"Until we dig up that tea set, nothing in our lives can be normal."

She picked at her socks and stared at the floor. She knew that she would stay. She was too close to turn back. "How do we figure out the missing clue?"

"We start by rereading the ones we have."

"Could we determine the area on Boylston Street that intersects with the old Easterly Channel bed?"

"I suppose, but what if it's a business block? What if the channel intersects at a diagonal? You could have six or seven buildings on Boylston above the channel." Fallon shook his head in frustration. "If the Pratts have all these clues, and they don't have the tea set yet, that last clue is absolutely vital."

"Morning, kids." Ferguson stepped over the tin cans. He felt better after a walk. "I bought us doughnuts and coffee and the Sunday *Globe*." He flung the paper to Fallon. "Your apartment hallway made the front page."

Fallon flipped back the comics and glanced at the story. Then he looked at the picture. It was a mug shot of a man with a gaunt, skeletal face, pockmarks, and a receding hairline.

"Jesus Christ," said Fallon softly. "This is the guy. I knew I recognized him yesterday."

"What guy?" asked Ferguson.

"The guy who shot Kenny Gallagher."

"Are you sure?"

"I'm positive. Could you forget that face?"

Ferguson looked at the picture. "He was an ugly fucker, wasn't he?"

"Why the hell did he kill Kenny Gallagher?"

"Maybe it was another job," said Ferguson. "Didn't they say Gallagher was knocked off for bookin' horses and ballgames?"

Fallon studied the article. He learned that the police wanted to question him, since the murder had taken place in his apartment. However, it reported, Tom Fallon had told the police that Peter had been out of town for several days. Nice work, thought Peter.

"This has to tie in, Jack. It has to."

"I think you should talk to your mother," said Evangeline. "She seemed to know a lot about this Kenny Gallagher. She told me about him the other night. I was looking at a crucifix on the wall in the bedroom. She told me it was Kenny's proudest possession. He had a pair of them. He gave one to her when your brother was sick, and he gave the other to an old priest."

"That's it!" Fallon jumped out of the sleeping bag. "The priest. It's been there all along and I never saw it. The old priest who said the Rosary at Kenny Gallagher's wake. He gave me a ride from the funeral home to Broadway Station."

He had reached the center of the web. He was certain. Two hundred years of striving led, ultimately, through a South Boston bartender to a lonely old parish priest. The astonishment filled him.

"Somehow or other the priest managed to tell me his life story while he drove. He was in love with Kenny's mother, but he never married her."

"You're losing me," said Evangeline.

"The priest said how much he loved Kenny's mother. He called her his 'poor, dear Mary Mannion.'"

Evangeline still didn't get it. Neither did Ferguson.

"Mannion!" screamed Fallon loudly enough to knock plaster off the walls. "Abigail Pratt Bentley's servant—the one she writes about in the diary—his name was Sean Mannion!"

Fallon, Evangeline, and Ferguson arrived at St. Basil's Church just before ten o'clock. The parking lot was jammed for the nine-thirty Mass.

St. Basil's was a purely functional building. No prim, austere New England steeple. No soaring Gothic extravagance. Like the summer cottages in its parish, it was a one-story clapboard shell; long and low, painted white with black trim, topped by a small cupola that housed the bell.

Fallon opened the rear door and peered into the church. Father Gerry Hale, looking tiny and frail before a large summer Sunday congregation, was saying Mass. It was the season of Pentecost, and he was wearing green vestments. The sun poured in the east windows, illuminating the dark knots in the pine paneling and the rough beams that supported the structure.

Fallon turned to the others. "The Mass will be over in a while. Let's wait for him in the sacristy."

They walked to the sacristy door at the rear of the building. The temperature was already nearing ninety degrees, and the sun reflected off the side of the white church with a vengeance. Evangeline noticed that the geraniums and pansies along the path were wilting in the heat.

Fallon opened the sacristy door and stopped. The small eyes were staring at him from behind wire-rimmed glasses. A pistol appeared in the hand.

James Buckley's notes on the Gallagher funeral had included a reference to Father Gerry Hale, an old family friend of the Gallaghers. The Pratts had decided to visit him fifteen minutes before Fallon saw the newspaper.

Fallon slammed the door and pushed Evangeline and Ferguson away. "Into the church."

Evangeline and Ferguson didn't ask questions. They ducked into a side door with Fallon right behind them. There were angry glances and disapproving stares for the latecomers. The consecration was over, and the congregation was saying the Lord's Prayer. Fallon shoved the other two into a pew.

"What's wrong?" whispered Evangeline.

The woman sitting in front of her glared at Evangeline.

Fallon flashed an apologetic smile, and the woman turned around. "Pratt, Soames, and Buckley are in the sacristy."

"How the hell did they figure this out?" whispered Ferguson.

"I don't know, but Soames pulled a gun on me."

"My uncle wouldn't kill an old priest," said Evangeline.

"Maybe not, but that little bastard with the glasses would," said Ferguson.

The woman in front of them looked around again, as did several others.

Fallon picked up a prayer book and pretended to read it. Evangeline gazed up at the altar. She noticed a silver crucifix mounted on the tabernacle. She elbowed Fallon. He was watching the priest open the tabernacle behind the altar and remove the ciborium, which contained the communion wafers.

"We've got to get to him before they do," he said.

From the sacristy, Pratt and Soames were studying the altar. Their attention was focused on the priest's chalice, a beautifully engraved work of silver.

"We've got to get to him first," said Pratt.

Soames looked around the sacristy. His eyes settled on a closet. He opened it. "We will."

Father Hale stepped to the altar rail, and the communicants began to form a line in the center aisle. He held a host in front of the first communicant. "Body of Christ."

"Amen," came the reply. An old woman received Communion, stepped aside, and a child stepped up to the rail.

Father Hale once calculated that, in fifty years of priesthood, he had given the Holy Eucharist almost 400,000 times. He sometimes had difficulty concentrating on the mystical nature of his duty. "Body of Christ."

"Amen."

I wonder if Mrs. Donovan is cooking muffins for breakfast. "Body of Christ."

"Amen."

Why must they stick their tongues out so far? All I need is the tip. "Body of Christ."

"Amen."

I wonder who's pitching for the Sox today. "Body of Christ."

"Amen."

What bridgework. "Body of Christ."

"Amen."

This young man looks familiar. "Body of Christ."

"Your life may be in danger. Don't go into the sacristy after the Mass."

The priest almost dropped the ciborium. His pupils closed down and his eyes fixed on Fallon.

"I was a friend of Kenny Gallagher's," whispered Fallon. "We met at the wake. There are people in the sacristy who may be dangerous."

Father Hale's eyes shifted toward the sacristy door, then back to Fallon.

"Leave by the center aisle. I'll be outside to give you protection."

Fallon didn't open his mouth. He didn't feel quite stainless enough to receive Communion. He turned and went back to his seat.

As the last communicants reached Father Hale, another priest walked onto the altar behind him. Fallon found it strange that a priest would arrive to help dispense the Sacrament when Communion was almost over. Then, he recognized Bennett Soames in cassock, surplice, and stole. Soames knelt and studied the priest's chalice, which was sitting on the altar.

"It's on the chalice," hissed Fallon. "The last set of lines is on the chalice."

"They must have seen the engraving from the sacristy." said Ferguson.

"I think we've lost," whispered Evangeline.

Soames read the line on the chalice and he returned to the sacristy. Father Hale had not even noticed him. He pulled off the vestments he had found in the closet. "I think we have what we want."

"Let's go, then," said Pratt.

Soames hesitated. He did not want to leave. He wanted to end Fallon's interference for good. To do that, he would have to eliminate the girl as well. Pratt would not approve, but Soames no longer cared about Pratt's approval. He stepped to the sacristy door and looked into the church. The Mass was almost over. The priest was cleansing the chalice of any remaining droplets of wine and shooting nervous glances toward Soames.

Fallon, Evangeline, and Ferguson were sitting about halfway down the left side of the crowded church.

"They're going to present a problem later," said Soames.

"We'll deal with it when it happens," said Pratt impatiently. "I don't intend to stay around here."

"Do you see their car in the parking lot, Mr. Buckley?"

"I don't know what they're driving."

"Gentlemen," said Pratt, "I am leaving, and I have the keys."

"Don't be too hasty, Mr. Pratt." Soames peered out at Fallon. "I think we should face our problems when they present themselves."

The priest looked again toward the sacristy. He was polishing the Communion plate. His hands stopped in mid-motion, he pulled himself out of his old man's slouch, and he bellowed with a voice that rumbled from deep inside him, "Leave my church! Get you out of the House of the Lord!"

Pratt headed for his car. Soames decided to deal with Fallon later.

"I haven't yelled like that in years," said Father Hale in the living room of his rectory after Mass. He was still shaking. "It's good to know that you still have the voice of the prophets when you need it."

"You were wonderful," said Evangeline.

The old man beamed.

"May we look at the chalice, Father?" asked Ferguson.

The priest removed the chalice veil and burse. Christ knelt in the garden, carried the Cross, and was crucified in Samuel Blossom's engravings.

"It's beautiful." Evangeline reached out to touch it.

Ferguson grabbed her wrist gently. "Only the priest can touch the chalice. It's consecrated."

"Indeed," said Father Hale. "Consecrated over fifty years ago. Given to me by my poor dear Mary Mannion. It was her ordination gift to me, a family heirloom that she wanted me to have. She had tears in her eyes when she gave it to me. I never knew if she was happy for my happiness, or crying because she knew we could never be together." He paused, then added wistfully, "She was so beautiful."

"Could you read the inscription?" asked Fallon gently.

Father Hale picked up the chalice."It's from Milton. *Paradise Lost.* 'Some natural tears they dropp'd, but wip'd them soon.'"

Fallon repeated the line. It offered them nothing.

"It's not often that you find a chalice, especially one from pre-Vatican II days, engraved with an English phrase from a Puritan poet," said Father Hale. "It's not often you find a chalice with any sort of engraving on it. Usually, chalices are raised when young priests take their vows. I needed special dispensation from Cardinal O'Connell himself before I could use this. However, Mary's grandfather, who had given her the chalice, was an important Boston bricklayer, very influential with the church. He said that he wanted to see his family treasure used in the Sacrifice of the Mass, and so it was done. His name was Joseph Mannion."

"He would have been Sean's son," said Fallon.

"Did he ever say where he got the chalice?" asked Ferguson.

The old priest took a moment to dig back into his memory. "From some Back Bay dowager who had employed his father. It was her token of appreciation for a lifetime of service."

They were certain that this was the final clue.

"What is the context of this line, Father?" asked Evangeline.

"It comes at the very end of *Paradise Lost*. Adam and Eve are being cast from the Garden of Eden because they have sinned. They cry for what they have lost, a perfect world, a world of everlasting happiness. Before sending them out of the Garden, the Archangel Michael has told them of the things that will befall their descendants. They cry for that, too. But he has also given them God's promise— that one of their descendants will be God's Son, and He will bring Redemption. That knowledge, and that alone, gives them the fortitude to go forth."

He lifted the chalice with reverence, awe. As he spoke, he seemed to be reminding himself of the things he had believed for so long. "The contents of the saving cup is the fulfillment of the promise, the Blood of Christ. It gives hope to all men. It offers all men a chance to renew their lives, to wipe away the tears and go on with living."

Fallon was in no mood for a sermon. His mind was racing. He didn't know what they should try next, but he thought they should be on the road. Ferguson was sitting in the corner repeating the line to himself, looking for some significance in it. Evangeline was listening closely to the old priest.

"'Some natural tears they dropp'd, but wip'd them soon,'" said Father Hale again. "Wonderfully epigrammatic."

Evangeline asked the priest if he owned a copy of *Paradise Lost*. She had an idea.

"Certainly, dear." Father Hale went to the bookcase and took down a leatherbound volume of Milton. "Read many times in a long life."

Evangeline opened to Book XII. Fallon saw the purpose in her motion.

She read the line, but her eye did not stop at the semicolon. It traveled across the page to the line number at the outer margin. In most editions, there are guide numbers every five lines for scholarly reference. The quotation on the chalice, the only single-line clue they had encountered, appeared on line 645 of the final book.

Evangeline tried it in her head. 645 Boylston Street. It worked. She knew where the tea set was buried.

Number 645 Boylston Street. The New Old South Church on Copley Square: completed in 1875, built of stone in the Italian Gothic style—campanile, gargoyles, stained-glass windows. Compared with the red-brick simplicity of the Old South Meeting House, the congregation's previous home, the New Old South looked more Catholic than Congregational.

In any other part of the city, its size and beauty would have dominated everything around it. Anchored on the corner of Copley Square, it was like a bishop on a great chessboard. On the space next to it was the granite bulk of the Boston Public Library. Beside that, the Copley Plaza Hotel. And on the far side of the square, the Romanesque Trinity Church.

It was eleven-thirty, and the congregation had gathered at the New Old South.

Peter Fallon drove the rented car slowly past the church. He saw James Buckley and Henry Dill standing in the portico. He swung left onto Dartmouth Street, then left again into the service alley that ran behind the church. Geoffrey Harrison was standing at the rear entrance. Fallon backed quickly out of the alley, then drove around the block and parked on the far side of Copley Square.

He looked at Ferguson, who was sitting in the back seat. "You've spent almost four years of your life searching for that thing. Now that you're about a hundred yards away from it, give or take twenty-seven feet, you got any ideas?"

Ferguson shook his head. "It looks like the Pratts beat us to the church. They may get the bride."

"It's not buried under the church," said Evangeline.

"Isn't that Number 645 Boylston Street?"

"It is, but only about two-thirds of the structure is the church. You enter the church by turning right off the campanile."

"The what?"

"The campanile, the bell tower. If you turn left, you're in a lovely little chapel. Walk through the chapel building, and you enter a library of religious literature which was once part of the pastor's house. There are offices on the floors above the library and function

410

rooms above the chapel. It's all part of the same structure."

"What are you saying?" asked Ferguson.

"That the tea set is buried beneath Number 645B Boylston Street. In her set of clues, Abigail says the tea set is buried ten paces east of the southwest corner of the building. I'd bet she means the whole structure. If we look at the clues again, we may find some sort of reference to a dwelling place or maybe something that pertains to the letter B."

"There might be something we missed," said Ferguson.

"Do you know what's in the basement of 645B?" asked Fallon.

"They have a big seminar room in the basement. I once worked with church members who were visiting the local prisons, and we used to have our meetings there. They lend the room out to civic groups, high schools, different charitable organizations. It's always busy."

"We should find out if it's busy today," said Fallon.

"You think the Pratts are gonna let us dig a hole right next to theirs?" asked Ferguson sarcastically.

"You sound like your losing your nerve, Jack," said Fallon.

Ferguson grabbed Fallon by the collar and almost pulled him into the back seat. "If it wasn't for my nerve, you'd be stone cold dead right now, and you know it."

Evangeline put her hand on Ferguson's. She thought perhaps he needed a drink. She needed one herself. "Nobody's losing his nerve, Jack. We're all getting a little too nervous."

Ferguson released Fallon.

"I meant nothing by it," said Fallon unconvincingly.

Evangeline could tell that he wasn't even thinking about Ferguson. He was staring over at the church.

"Don't ever say it again." Ferguson sounded more offended than angry. "Now, how do you plan to get at that tea set with Pratt men at every entrance?"

"We do it," said Fallon, "without going into the building at all."

CHAPTER XXV

"How thick are the subway walls outside Copley Square Station?"

"You're crazy, Peter." Tom Fallon was seated at his desk in the Fallon and Son shack. Peter, Evangeline, Danny, and Ferguson were crowded into the tiny room with him, and it was stifling.

"That's what you said yesterday morning, but we got the old lady out and the Pratts didn't do a thing about it," answered Peter.

Tom Fallon looked at Ferguson. "What about this guy Rule, the one you're so afraid of?"

"Right now, I don't think we have to worry about him. If he's been watching the Pratts, he's more concerned about them than he is about us. I'm not sayin' he won't come after us, but he can deal with us anytime."

"Well, even if there's nobody shootin' at you, you can't just start diggin' a hole in a subway wall any damn time you please. Trolleys run through Copley Square Station every five minutes."

"Not when I'm waiting for them," cracked Evangeline.

"They shut down at twelve-thirty, Dad," said Peter.

Tom laughed. "If the Pratts have started diggin', they'll have that thing dug up, polished, and sittin' on the mantel by midnight."

"They can't start digging until the church seminar room is empty," said Evangeline. "The room is used by a drug rehabilitation group until eleven o'clock on Sunday nights."

"Which means they'll only have an hour's start," said Danny.

"I don't think you people should be destroying private property," said Tom.

"C'mon, Dad. You said yourself that we need a miracle to stay afloat for the rest of the year. That tea set will pay our bills and pay for any damage we do along the way. The Lord helps those who help themselves, Dad. He's put that tea set down there, and it's up to us to get it."

"What bullshit," said Tom Fallon softly. He glanced at Evangeline.

"We're going to end this thing tonight, Mr. Fallon. Once and for all," she said.

"I'll ask you again, Dad. How thick are the subway walls?" Peter's voice offered no doubt.

"Two feet." Tom Fallon made his decision. He would stay with his boys. "Poured concrete, steel reinforcements."

"How long will it take to cut through it?" asked Peter.

Tom grunted. "With a jackhammer, it'll take you half the night to make a hole big enough to stick your cock in." He looked at Evangeline and apologized.

"I've heard it before."

"If you hit one of the steel reinforcements, you'll have to start again. Beyond that, there's guys diggin' down from above. After you've been cuttin' for a while, the sound of two heavy hammers and a compressor will carry right through the dirt and concrete up into the basement of the church. If they haven't already figured out our plan, that'll give it away for sure."

Peter leaned against a file cabinet, folded his arms, and listened. He always enjoyed hearing his father talk about construction. It was one of the few things they could easily discuss.

"What about the Pratts?" asked Evangeline. "How long will it take them?"

"How many men do they have diggin'?"

"Could be five, could be seven," said Ferguson.

"They'll probably have to dig a hole about five feet square, just to make room for two guys to swing a shovel at once."

414

"But before they start diggin', they'll have to cut through the floor," offered Peter. "They start runnin' a compressor out in the alley, neighbors might get a little suspicious."

"They won't need jackhammers," said Danny. "Most basement floors are only three or four inches thick. They'll cut through in an hour if they have a couple of Hilti hammers."

"What are they?" asked Evangeline.

"They're like a small jackhammer, only you run 'em off a wall outlet. Powerful little buggers."

"Once they're through the floor," said Tom, "they'll probably have about twelve feet more to dig, because the basement and the space beneath it go down about fifteen feet into the landfill. If they have two guys workin' shovels all night, and I mean haulin' ass, they'll be lucky to hit twenty-seven feet before five in the morning. And once they get down seven feet or so into the landfill, they'll have to start shorin' up the sides of the hole. It's a tall order, but they ain't on salary and they ain't workin' for the city, so maybe they can pull it off."

Tom Fallon's mind was spinning now. He was attacking the problem. "You'll have to do some shoring too if you try to tunnel. You'll also have to worry about pilings."

"Pilings?" said Evangeline.

"Damn right. That's not the most stable land in the world, even today. Look what happened when they started building that big skyscraper over there. Buildings all around it started to settle. Back in 1875, it was even less stable. You don't build in fresh landfill and mud unless you sink pilings. Almost every building in the Back Bay sits on pilings. Pilings every four or five feet, granite capstones on top of the pilings, and the foundations poured on top of the capstones. If there's a piling in your way, you'll have to go around it."

"This is sounding more discouraging all the time." Evangeline looked toward Peter.

"You want to solve a problem, honey, you've got to know what it is," said Tom. "And you'd better hope that the old lady was on the money when she said the strongbox was buried right beneath the outer wall. If she's four or five feet off in the wrong direction, a steam shovel dug that thing up sixty-five years ago."

"What do you mean?" asked Ferguson.

"Along Boylston, there's only a few feet of play between the outer walls of the subway and the foundation walls of the buildings above. You've got the foundations going down ten feet. The dome of the tunnel is about four feet beneath the street, and the tunnel floor is about thirty feet underground. If you dropped a line from the outer wall of the foundation, you'd see that you only have about five feet of earth between the foundation and the tunnel wall."

"You sure know your stuff." Jack Ferguson laughed. He had forgotten his anger at Peter. He felt comfortable with all these people. He trusted them.

"Fallon and Son used to do a lot of work in the subways," said Danny.

"If the tea set is right where you think it is," continued Tom, "then you'll have to tunnel in about three feet, which you should be able to do pretty quickly, once you're through the wall. If it's in any farther, you'll be in trouble. Tunneling takes time, and you won't have very much if you're in a race with the Pratts." Fallon paused. "On the other hand, if the old lady was off by a foot or two, the strongbox may be starin' you right in the face when you get through the wall."

"But how the hell do we get through two feet of concrete if a heavy hammer won't do it?" asked Peter.

Tom looked at Danny. "Remember the time we did a job for a guy down near the Blue Hills? We had to move a lot of rock out of the way before we poured the foundation?"

Danny smiled.

Jack Ferguson was right. For the moment, William Rule had stopped thinking about the Fallons and Ferguson. They had lost the race. They might have all the clues, but the Pratts had the strategic advantage.

At four o'clock, Rule's Rolls-Royce Silver Shadow skimmed down Boylston Street, past the New Old South, and parked on the opposite side of Copley Square. Rule got out and sat on a concrete bench. A troupe of Russian folk dancers were performing for a Sunday crowd on the sunken plaza, and the sound of balalaikas reverberated off the surrounding buildings. A little girl just out of the stroller jumped about in imitation of the dancers while her parents shared a joint that smelled sweet and inviting. College kids reclined in the sun and sipped beer. The winos clustered at the southeast corner of the square. A pleasant summer Sunday, despite the heat.

Edward's report had been accurate. There were Pratt men all around the church. Apparently, they had found the tea set.

William Rule gazed at the church and thought about Billy Rulick,

416

the little boy who had refused to give in until he had what he wanted. He thought about Philip and Calvin Pratt, men born into a world where there was no struggle and no hardship. He had frightened the Pratts. He had made them squirm. He had brought them to the brink, and with a little luck, he would push them over.

But William Rule preferred not to rely on luck. He had the proxies he needed to take over chairmanship of Pratt Industries. He had, for years, been trying to tie up loose ends, to track down distant Pratt relations and destroy the handful of missing clues. His first mistake had been in leaving the Korbel woman alone. He had decided that an obscure woman on the West Coast would present no problems. When he learned of Pratt's most recent trip to Los Angeles, he decided, a few hours too late, to eliminate Sally Korbel.

On a tombstone in South Boston, Rule's genealogist—Rule had hired him at an enormous salary to track down all Pratt descendants—read an inscription: "Sean Mannion, December 9, 1806, to October 10, 1863; Beloved Husband of Lillian; Beloved Father of Joseph; Beloved Servant and Friend of Abigail Pratt Bentley." The genealogist had found the inscription most unusual. He had investigated the cause of Mannion's death and traced Mannion's descent. When the Pratts had begun to close on the tea set, Rule had killed Mannion's last descendant. In the long run, a needless death. He wondered briefly if he could have taken control of Pratt Industries without the tea set. Of course not. The tea set had been the key to landing the Hannaford block of stock. A hundred-thousand-dollar forgery for two million dollars' worth. An excellent deal.

Rule had known from the day he first heard Phil Cawley's gravel voice that he would use their own legend, their own greed, to avenge himself on the Pratts. He had engineered everything to that end.

Now, Rule had few options but to wait. If Hannaford's plan succeeded, he might be able to turn back the Pratts, whether they found the tea set or not. And there was always the possibility that the tea set wasn't there, that it had been dug up inadvertently by some construction crew and dumped where no one would ever find it. But Rule was certain of one thing: he could not kill anyone else. He laughed to himself, at himself. He had worked so hard, and now it was out of his control.

Tom and Danny Fallon spent a hot, busy afternoon. They had to prepare for the night's work while the others lay low in Danny's basement. The police were still interested in questioning Peter, and Ferguson figured that, although Soames and his men would be at the church, they might still try to monitor the Fallons. Peter, Evangeline, and Ferguson sat in front of the television set, watched the Red Sox, and waited.

Danny had to place several telephone calls, through a complicated network of cover men, before he found the man he needed. He arranged a deal, then drove to Chelsea and purchased fourteen sticks of dynamite. Danny Fallon had a state dynamiter's license. After tonight, he would probably lose it. He hoped that after tonight he would never need it again.

When he returned, he and his father readied the tools they would need, and they removed three fuses from the electrical box on the pick-up truck. They didn't want tail lights, brake lights, or back-up lights tonight.

At ten-thirty, Bennett Soames was sitting in the basement seminar room of the New Old South Church. The rehabilitation meeting was open to anyone who had a drug problem, and Soames, seated among former heroin users and pill takers, was describing his addiction to amphetamines. Outside, his men waited.

In the house at Commonwealth and Clarendon, Philip Pratt finished a ham and cheese omelette and a cup of coffee. He wasn't hungry. His stomach felt like a clenched fist. He didn't want to go back to the church. He wanted to leave tonight on the *Gay Head IV*. But he had conceived this scheme. He had to see it through. He had a responsibility to himself and his heritage. He had to do what he could to hold on, even if he no longer cared.

Calvin and Isabelle were eating with him in the second-floor living room. Philip was wearing jeans, deck shoes, and a dark jersey.

"We should be getting over there," said Calvin.

"You should be going home," answered Philip. "We have enough men to dig, and if we all end up in jail, we'll need a good lawyer to get us out."

"I've been involved from the beginning," said Calvin.

"There's no need for two Pratts to dirty their hands. Go home and stay by the telephone."

Isabelle went downstairs with Philip. At the door, she touched his cheek. "Good luck."

"In a way, I hope it isn't there," he said.

"It will be. You'll find it. You have to find it."

"I'd rather sail to Hawaii free of responsibilities. Are you still interested in serving before the mast?"

"I won't be here when you come back, Philip. No matter what happens, we can't stay together."

She had been thinking about his offer all day, but she hadn't known what her response would be when she walked him to the door. Now, she faced their reality. "We've given each other strength. Let's leave it at that."

He kissed her on the forehead.

"Be careful, Philip."

He stepped outside. He knew she was right. The clenched fist in his stomach tried to punch its way out of him. He started up Commonwealth Avenue. His pace quickened. His steps became pronounced, angry. He knew that he wouldn't be sailing anywhere with anyone. He had to find the tea set. Pratt Industries was his life.

At eleven-thirty, the drug-rehabilitation seminar ended. On his way out, Bennett Soames slipped into a restroom. He had little problem defusing the alarm system from inside the church, and at midnight, he opened the door. The entrance to 645B Boylston Street was at basement level. A flight of stone steps led up to the street, where Pratt, Harrison, and the others were waiting for him.

By twelve-fifteen, the Hilti electric hammers were cutting into the floor in the seminar room.

On Huntington Avenue, the trolley tracks ran down the middle of the street on a gravel-and-stone roadbed, and automobile traffic traveled on either side. The last inbound trolley stopped in front of the Museum of Fine Arts at twelve-thirty. Huntington Avenue was nearly deserted.

Evangeline Carrington was waiting to board. She was wearing jeans, sneakers, and a sweatshirt. The doors flipped open and she put her foot on the first step. "Is this the Green Line?"

"The trolley's green, ain't it?" said the driver, a heavy Irishman interested only in finishing his run and going home for a beer.

"Forest Hills to Park Street?" she asked.

He nodded. "And I'm goin' to Park."

The pick-up truck shot out from a side street. It pulled onto the vehicle crossing about a block behind the trolley and backed down the tracks, its tires slamming over the railroad ties.

"Can I change at Park Street for Harvard Square?" asked Evangeline.

"Not if you don't get on real quicklike."

Evangeline glanced down the track. The truck was backed up to the rear of the trolley. Peter and Danny were dropping the tailgate. They needed more time.

"Do you make change?" she asked.

"Lady, if you don't have the right change, you can ride for nothin'. Just get on."

She looked down the track again. The railcart rolled off the truck and onto the tracks.

"You don't get on, lady, I'm gonna close the door right on your pretty leg and drag you to Park Street."

As Evangeline stepped onto the trolley, Jack Ferguson came running out of the darkness with a big shopping bag under each arm. "Hey, wait a minute! Wait!"

"Oh, wait," said Evangeline. "There's another man coming."

"I see him." The driver cursed to himself and kept the doors open.

Evangeline knew that although the railcart would ride close to the tracks, the cab of the pick-up was level with the trolley's back window. She looked behind her. The light inside the trolley was bright enough that she couldn't see into the darkness outside.

Ferguson stepped onto the trolley and dropped one of the shopping bags. He stepped off and picked up the packages that had tumbled out. The driver looked at his watch and glared at Ferguson, but Ferguson didn't need to stall any longer. Peter Fallon gave him thumbs up, and Ferguson climbed onto the trolley.

"Be careful," said Tom Fallon to his sons. "I'll be at the ventilator between Prudential and Copley."

The trolley began to move. The railcart coupler engaged. The driver sensed a brief hesitation, but the trolley kicked ahead and the Fallons were on their way.

Tom Fallon pulled his truck off the tracks and watched the trolley rattle past Northeastern University. He was helping them do something dangerous and crazy. But he was helping them. He threw the truck in gear and headed for Boylston Street.

Peter and Danny Fallon held tight to the handles on either side of the railcart, which the Fallons used to transport equipment when they did a masonry job in the subway. Tonight, the Fallons were carrying a gasoline generator, two powerful electric drills for boring holes in concrete, picks and shovels, a set of high-quartz work lights, plywood and planks to support a tunnel, hardhats, fourteen sticks of dynamite, a detonator, and blasting caps. They were also carrying five heavy steel fire doors; Tom Fallon had picked them up on a demolition job and thought they might make good protection against the force of the explosion.

After another stop on Huntington Avenue, the trolley descended into the ground. The breeze turned hot and humid, and the metallic whisk of the trolley across the surface tracks became a deafening roar in the tunnel. Blue fluorescent lights flipped past like pulses from a strobe.

Peter looked at Danny. "Scared?"

Danny nodded and yelled over the roar, "Shitless."

"Wanna turn back?"

"No way."

"Me neither." Peter smiled.

There were four other passengers in the trolley. An old woman sat directly behind the driver and read a tabloid. A teen-age couple clung to each other about halfway down the car. A drunk kept falling asleep and waking up, his head bouncing around as though it were on a spring. All were oblivious to their surroundings.

Evangeline sat in the rear seat. She was excited. She was almost happy. She had never believed she would come this far, but she knew that tonight, it would end. She only hoped that tomorrow, she and Peter would find something more to keep them together.

Jack Ferguson sat a few seats away and stared at his reflection in the window. He barely recognized the face. Years of drinking, searching, and running in fear had made him look old and haggard. But tonight, it would all be worthwhile, and tomorrow, he could begin again.

The trolley stopped at Symphony Station, where the coin booth was not visible from the platform. Peter looked around at the peeling paint on the tunnel walls and realized that he was under the ground of what had once been Gravelly Point. He imagined Horace Taylor Pratt poking his cane into the mud at the edge of the Back Bay. He wondered what Pratt would think if he saw this world today.

The trolley lurched ahead again. Fallon felt a jolt of adrenalin turn his stomach over like an engine. He grabbed the sides of the cart. He felt the strength in his hands and arms. He realized the clarity with which he saw everything around him, even in the half-light of the tunnel. He looked up. Through the back window of the trolley, he saw Evangeline looking down at him. He saw one of her gold earrings catch a reflection. She was beautiful. He waved—a short, confident motion, like a salute.

Philip Pratt had his fingers in his ears. The sound of the electric hammers was deafening. But the fingers didn't help. Every time one of the hammers bit into the floor, the vibration sent shock waves through his feet and up his spinal cord. He wondered why the noise didn't seem to bother Soames, who watched impassively as Buckley and Harrison operated the hammers.

Soames was wondering about other things. He didn't expect any trouble from Rule. He knew that Rule could not afford more overt violence. But he wasn't certain about Fallon and Ferguson. He did not believe that they would give up so easily. For a moment, both electric hammers stopped clattering, and Soames heard the last outbound trolley rumble through the tunnel below. He wondered if they might come in through the subway. They could never cut through two feet of concrete in time.

As the trolley rolled into Prudential Station, beneath the Prudential Center, Peter Fallon looked toward the change booth. At this stop, the booth had a clear view of the tracks. But Fallon wasn't worried. At the moment, he believed he could make himself invisible if he had to. He knew instinctively that they would make it through.

The man in the change booth was counting his money and paying no attention to the platform. Evangeline and Ferguson got off the trolley.

"I thought you wanted Park Street," said the driver.

"I think I'll walk," answered Evangeline.

The doors slammed shut and the trolley pulled away. Evangeline and Ferguson waved as the railcart rattled past. The Fallons looked like a pair of MBTA employees on their way to a repair job in the tunnel. Ferguson looked toward the change booth. The man inside was still preoccupied, and there was no one else on the platform. Ferguson and Evangeline stepped onto the tracks and followed the trolley into the tunnel.

On its last run, the trolley was hitting close to fifty miles an hour. Peter and Danny were both on their knees holding tight to the railcart handles. If not for the ballast of the heavy steel doors, the railcart might have bounced off the tracks.

Peter looked at Danny and hollered, "Now?"

Danny nodded.

Peter let go of the handle and crawled to the front of the railcart. He reached forward and pulled the coupling pin. It came out smoothly, and the cart cut loose.

The driver felt the trolley speed up, although his foot was steady on the accelerator. He reminded himself to make a report.

The cart rolled to a stop, and the trolley spurted on to Copley Station.

"Beautiful," said Danny. "Beautiful."

They jumped off the cart and pushed it to the crossover their father had told them they'd find about halfway down the tunnel. They rolled the cart from the inbound onto the outbound track and sat down to wait. The trolley pulled away from Copley Station, a quarter mile down the tracks, and was swallowed by the concrete tube. Except for the sound of Evangeline and Ferguson running down the tracks to join them, the tunnel was silent.

William Rule sat on his balcony and sipped iced tea. His wife had gone to bed. Edward was reading in his room. Lawrence Hannaford had not yet called. William Rule did not ordinarily mind being alone, but tonight he felt very lonely.

He lifted his toupee and wiped the perspiration from the top of his head. The weatherman had predicted a cold front tonight. Rule hoped it came soon.

By one-thirty, the hole in the church basement was three feet deep. Buckley was watching the door. Harrison was resting. Soames and Dill were digging.

Dill stopped and leaned on his shovel. "I've been digging for an hour. I need a break."

Soames took the shovel and handed it to Pratt. "I think it's time you dirtied your hands for the cause, Mr. Pratt."

Pratt took the shovel willingly, but he sensed an edge of bitterness in Soames' voice. He did not like it.

At two A.M., the clean-up crew finished work in Copley Square Station. Now, the Fallons could start. Danny threw his cigarette onto the tracks. Ferguson pulled a pint bottle of whiskey from his pocket.

"I thought you were on the wagon," said Peter.

"I am. But if I have to be doin' any shootin', I don't want a case of the shakes." He took one gulp, recapped the bottle, and put it back in his pocket. "I had one belt before I got on the trolley, one belt now. When I see that tea set, I'll take one more belt and drop the rest of this booze in a sewer." He knew it wouldn't be that easy, but it sounded good.

He checked the ammunition clip in his pistol. He had eleven bullets left, and the .45 sounded like a cannon when it went off. He didn't want to shoot anyone, just scare the hell out of them. He had already killed one man. That was enough.

They gave the railcart a shove and it began to roll down the gentle grade toward Copley Station. Danny and Jack walked beside the cart so that it wouldn't roll too far too fast.

Peter grabbed Evangeline by the elbow, and she turned to him. "It may get dangerous tonight. Do you want to wait with Dad up in the truck?"

She frowned. "And leave the boys to have all the fun? I'm going to be the first person to look into that box, Peter. I've earned it."

"I can't make you turn back?"

In the quiet moments since they had arrived in the tunnel, his excitement had worn off, and he had been able to think clearly. He knew that in a few moments, the action would consume him. "There may be gunfire."

"You don't need my help anymore, so you want me out of the way?"

"Whether we make it tonight or not, I want you around tomorrow."

"I'll be here if you will." She spoke calmly, rationally.

Twenty minutes later, Soames and Philip Pratt heard the faint rumbling sound of a drill boring into concrete. They stopped digging. They heard it again.

"The Fallons?" asked Pratt.

"Did you ever expect them to give up?"

Pratt shook his head. "Can they get it first?"

"Not if they're trying to jackhammer through two feet of concrete."

The Fallons calculated that, if Abigail Pratt Bentley's directions were precise, they would find the tea set about fifteen feet outside Copley Station, knee-high on the tunnel wall.

Now, Peter and Danny were drilling fourteen holes in a six-foot circle around the spot they had chosen. When they were finished, they would pack the holes with dynamite. Danny was already figuring how to set the charges. In the middle of the circle, he was drilling three holes. He'd wire those to blow first. That way, the top half of the circle would have a place to collapse into when it blew a millisecond later. The charges in the bottom half of the circle would be the most powerful. They would explode a second after the top half fell, and they would move the rubble away from the wall.

About forty feet down the tunnel, Evangeline was fashioning a protective barricade from the steel fire doors. A few feet in front of the area where the Fallons were working, Ferguson was setting up the powerful worklights. He was angling them toward the Copley platform and trying to place them so that they would not be knocked over by the blast. There was little conversation.

Everyone had a task. Everyone worked quickly and methodically.

Evangeline did not think about the danger. Jack tried not to think about the drink he wanted. Peter was not even thinking about the tea set. He thought of nothing but the process. He felt nothing but the drill spinning in his hands.

At three-thirty, William Rule was asleep in a chaise lounge on his balcony. The telephone rang and shook him awake. He spoke briefly, then hung up and called for his butler.

Edward appeared in his shorts. "Yes?"

"Prepare a light breakfast. Mr. Hannaford and I will be eating in an hour."

Edward went off to dress.

Rule looked out toward the airport and realized that he couldn't see it. The temperature had dropped twenty degrees since he'd nodded off, and the fog was rolling in.

The hole in the seminar room floor was over six feet deep, and dirt was heaped in great piles all about. Pratt and Harrison were digging.

"Stop," said Soames. He cocked his head like a robin listening for a worm. "They're not drilling any more."

"Could they have made it through?" asked Pratt.

"Not likely." He wondered if any of them had the training to use explosives. Danny Fallon, the independent contractor. Soames cursed. He should have stopped them when he'd had the chance.

"Do it." Peter's voice trembled with excitement.

Evangeline stuck her fingers in her ears.

Ferguson put his hands on his head.

Danny twisted the crank on the detonator box. An electrical charge streaked down the wires.

Philip Pratt and Geoffrey Harrison were knocked against the side of the hole. Soames staggered. The ground in the hole sank by a foot.

Huge chunks of concrete smashed off Evangeline's barricade and scattered everywhere. The smoke and dust billowed into Copley Station and rolled down the tunnel. For a moment, Peter Fallon was transfixed by the cloud pulsating toward him. Illuminated from behind by the lights in the station, the smoke looked like some giant sea anemone. As it engulfed him, Peter Fallon leaped to his feet.

"Let's go, Danny!" He grabbed a shovel and ran toward the hole.

Soames called for Buckley and Dill.

"My niece is down there," screamed Pratt from the hole.

"Your niece is probably waiting for them in a car someplace down Boylston Street." Soames snapped the Beretta out of his holster.

Ferguson took out his pint and sneaked one more belt of whiskey. Evangeline began to cough. He offered her the bottle. She shook her head. He started to take another drink, then hesitated. It seemed like a good time to stop. He threw the bottle against the wall.

The dynamite had torn a six-foot hole in the side of the subway wall and had bent reinforcing rods like pieces of plastic. The shock snapped the electrical circuit which fed the fluorescent lights, and the tunnel was now in semi-darkness. Except for the emergency lights shining out from Copley Station, the tunnel was in darkness. Water and gas lines running between the street and the tunnel dome had not been damaged. However, groundwater was already seeping through the rubble.

For the Fallons, Evangeline, and Ferguson, the blast had been deafening, and shock waves were rolling all the way back to the tunnel entrance on Huntington Avenue. But Danny believed that the concrete would contain most of the sound twenty-five feet underground. Since Boylston Street was a business section, there were few people on the street or in the buildings above the blast at four in the morning. A security guard in the Public Library might have heard the noise. A sensitive burglar alarm might have been tripped someplace above them, but that was all part of the gamble. The Fallons knew that in most residential areas of the Back Bay, the blast had been nothing more than a faint jolt, not enough to wake a light sleeper.

Peter and Danny attacked the dirt. Evangeline and Ferguson threw the steel doors onto the railcart and pushed it back down to the new hole in the tunnel wall. Ferguson pulled three doors off the cart and set them up so that the Fallons could dig behind them. Then, he set up a pair for himself. Evangeline couldn't start the generator. Danny grabbed the wires from her, and she grabbed his shovel.

Soames, Buckley, and Dill broke into the subway and raced down the stairs through the rising dust.

Ferguson saw them when they reached the platform. "Hit it!"

Danny threw a switch on the generator, and four powerful quartz beams cut through the smoke, momentarily blinding Soames and the others.

"Back off," screamed Ferguson from behind the lights. "Back off and out. We've outsmarted you."

Soames answered by shooting out one of the lights. Dill jumped across the tracks and hid behind a concrete piling.

Ferguson fired wildly down the tunnel. One of his shots caught Henry Dill in the arm. Soames stuck his head around the corner and fired at another light, but the glare was blinding. He missed. Another volley from Ferguson. Buckley leaped across the tracks to Dill and pulled him back behind the cover of the platform. Soames fired into the tunnel again.

Philip Pratt threw down his shovel. He realized that he had surrendered all his authority to Soames. His hands were filthy, his jeans and sneakers black with mud. He had surrendered his dignity as well. He would regain something, even if it meant losing the Golden Eagle.

He jumped out of the hole and told Harrison to follow him.

The steel fire doors had been a good idea. Behind them, Peter, Evangeline, and Danny were pouring themselves into their shovels. But they didn't have to dig far. Just a few feet into the earth, Evangeline hit the strongbox, and her shriek echoed up and down the tunnel.

They'd found it, almost exactly where Abigail had predicted.

Soames fired again, then he looked at Buckley, who was trying to stop the bleeding in Dill's arm. "We're not paying you to cower behind corners. Get over on the other side of the tracks. We'll shoot out the lights and go after them."

"Bullshit." Buckley drew the words out. "I'll trail guys, I'll put the knuckle on guys, I'll dig holes in the mud. But I don't see no future in runnin' down a tunnel into a set of high-beams while some guy is shootin' at me. And I don't like shootin' back too much, either."

Peter and Danny cleared the dirt from the strongbox, then Evangeline grabbed a handle and pulled. The box didn't budge. Peter grabbed the handle with her, and together they tore the Golden Eagle out of the ground. Its weight surprised them, and they dropped it into the rubble at their feet. For a moment, no one dared touch it. All four watched it as though they expected it to open itself, as though it had a life of its own.

"We've done it," said Peter finally.

Soames fired and knocked out another light. Ferguson fired back.

"We've done it," repeated Evangeline, in awe.

Peter grabbed one handle, Evangeline the other, and they started to run.

Soames heard the footsteps in the tunnel. He could not see past the work lights, but he knew where they were going. He turned to Buckley again. "You don't have to do a thing. Just stay here for ten minutes and take pot shots. Both of you. Aim at the ceiling if you want. Just make them think you're chasing them."

Dill took out his pistol. "I'll stay."

"All right," said Buckley. "Ten minutes. Pot shots. Nobody gets hurt."

Soames ran up to the street. Pratt and Harrison were running toward him.

"Get in the car," Soames commanded.

Pratt had no time to protest.

When they were sure that Ferguson and the others were fleeing, Buckley and Dill ran into the tunnel and turned the work lights around. Then, they began to fire randomly down the tube. Every time they fired, they could see the four figures fall to the tracks, get up, and run farther. Ferguson would return the fire, but Buckley and Dill were now safe behind the steel doors.

Geoffrey Harrison spun the Pratt Industries limousine around and careened down Boylston Street. He was going the wrong way on a one-way street, but at four-fifteen, there was no one else around.

"There he is!" Soames pointed to a pick-up parked on the left side of the street, near a subway ventilator grate.

Before Tom Fallon could react, the Cadillac was bumper-to-bumper with his truck and Soames's pistol was aimed at his head.

"Get out," barked Soames.

Tom Fallon climbed out of the truck.

"Against the wall."

Tom Fallon put his hands against a storefront. Soames smashed him across the back of the head, and he collapsed on the sidewalk.

"You didn't have to do that," said Philip Pratt.

"Shut up." Soames turned to Harrison. "Disable it."

Harrison opened the hood of the pickup and pulled out the distributor.

Peter, Evangeline, Danny, and Ferguson reached the ventilator opening with the gunfire echoing down the tunnel after them. The opening was a five-by-ten-foot hole in the sidewalk, covered by an iron grate. A metal ladder led to the surface. Peter looked up into the darkness. "Hey, Dad."

No answer.

"Dad?" Peter looked at the others. "Do we keep running?"

They heard more gunfire traveling down the tube toward them.

"We can run to the next station" said Evangeline.

"This is where the truck is," said Danny. Another volley of gunfire. Danny looked behind him. "The Pratts are down there. We can keep runnin' all night and they're still gonna chase us. Maybe the old man didn't hear us. He's probably asleep."

Peter climbed the ladder, cautiously raised the little door in the grate, and poked his head above the surface. When he saw Soames, he was looking down the barrel of a pistol. Fallon tried to duck down, but Harrison grabbed him by the hair and pulled him up.

Fallon tilted his eyes down the ladder to Evangeline and the others. "Keep running."

"Hand it up," said Soames.

Ferguson had the .45 in his hand. He wanted to get off a shot, but the spaces in the grate were so small that the bullet would probably ricochet.

"Get out of here," said Fallon.

Soames wanted no more hesitation. "Miss Carrington, I killed your brother, and I will kill your lover unless that tea set is in my hands in ten seconds."

Philip Pratt was stunned. So was Evangeline. Jack Ferguson had guessed it was something like this. Evangeline tugged on the strongbox. Ferguson had the other handle. For a moment, he didn't let go. He didn't think that he could.

"I'm waiting," Soames voice rasped out of him. "This young man has caused me no end of difficulty. I will kill him."

Pratt advanced on Soames. "You killed my nephew?"

Harrison leveled a pistol at Pratt. "Stay there."

Evangeline and Ferguson reluctantly handed the strongbox to Fallon, and he climbed out of the hole. Harrison grabbed one handle and told Pratt to take the other. They put the strongbox into the back seat, and Harrison forced Pratt into the car.

"Miss Carrington," said Soames, "please join us."

"Stay where you are," said Fallon.

"I'll count five, then I'll kill him, Miss Carrington. You're doing very well. Don't make a mistake now."

Evangeline climbed up to the sidewalk. Soames forced Fallon back down the ladder and slammed the grate.

"Follow at the girl's peril." Soames pushed Evangeline into the back seat of the limousine and locked the door.

As Philip Pratt had a moment earlier, she noticed that the lock knobs in the back seat had been removed.

The limousine turned around and headed back down Boylston Street. Fallon, Danny, and Ferguson were up on the sidewalk a second later. The sky was brightening, but a thick fog had rolled across the city. They could barely see the campanile of the New Old South, just a few hundred yards down the street.

Danny ran to his father's side. Tom Fallon was unconscious, but he seemed to be breathing.

"It looks to me like the little bastard's screwing his boss," said Ferguson. "If you want to screw a Pratt, who's the best person to go to?"

"Rule?" offered Peter.

"That's right, but we better be careful, because that little bastard'll kill her."

Peter looked at his father. "Is he all right?"

"I don't know," said Danny.

"It's a bump on the head. He'll wake up," said Ferguson.

"I'm stickin' around to make sure he does," said Danny.

"In the meantime, the tea set is gettin' away from us," said Ferguson.

"So get goin'," yelled Danny. "When the old man wakes up, we'll follow you. And be careful."

Peter and Ferguson headed down Boylston.

"Did you kill my nephew?" demanded Philip Pratt.

Soames smiled. "I had to say something to get the tea set out of that hole."

"You haven't answered the question," snapped Evangeline.

Soames ignored her. He looked at Pratt. "I think we should open the box."

"My niece wants to know what happened to her brother," said Pratt.

"Mr. Pratt, I have been dedicated to finding this tea set. All my actions have been dedicated to it and our mutual interest." He smiled. He knew he might still need Pratt's help.

Pratt wanted to accept Soames's response as a denial.

"Let's open the box," repeated Soames.

For a moment, Pratt contemplated the box. Then, he pulled off the padlocks, two of which had already been snapped. The outer steel box was rusted shut, and he needed a screwdriver from the glove compartment to pry it open. After that came an oak liner, rotted into wet powder.

Evangeline forgot Soames. She held her breath and watched her uncle enter the family tabernacle. She hoped that the water hadn't seeped through to the tea set.

But there was another oaken box; it was about an inch thick and in better condition. Philip Pratt opened it and revealed a Revere masterpiece: a copper liner for the strongbox. At the time that he had made the tea set, Revere had been experimenting with rolled copper. Lid and bottom fit so perfectly that the liner seemed watertight.

Philip Pratt's mouth went dry. His palms were sweating. He broke open the liner. First came the red velvet, then, silver.

Silver. Gleaming, luminous, incandescent.

Evangeline did not see the blackened, tarnished metal she had expected. She saw silver, silver glowing in the predawn light.

Philip Pratt was dazzled.

For a moment, no one spoke.

Then, Soames reached into the box and picked up the sugar urn. "After all these years. Exquisite."

"It's almost too beautiful," said Pratt. "Too beautiful to keep hidden."

Soames eyes shifted from the small golden eagle on the urn to Philip Pratt. "I'm afraid that is impossible. We are going to deal right now." Soames slammed the Plexiglas divider between front and back seat and locked it.

The limousine turned off Storrow Drive and headed for the waterfront.

Philip Pratt realized that he was being betrayed. He was losing everything—his company, his stature, his self-respect. He wished he had never heard of the Golden Eagle.

He turned to Evangeline. "I'm sorry, Vange. About Christopher, about everything."

She didn't look at him. Her eyes were fixed on the silver. On the tiny golden bird. On the object which had dominated and destroyed so many lives.

The limousine turned onto Lewis Wharf.

"You know exactly what to do," said Soames.

Harrison nodded and took out his pistol.

Soames climbed out of the car and looked up at Rule's balcony. He had to act quickly. He could see Edward peering down at him. He straightened his sportcoat and put the sugar urn into his pocket. He was nervous, but he had rehearsed this moment a hundred times. After this morning, he would never arrange a schedule, take a phone call, or swallow an insult from Philip Pratt again.

When Edward answered the door, Soames had a pistol pointed at his belly. "Let's have your pistol."

Edward turned over a .22 revolver, and they both went upstairs. Soames was surprised to see Rule and Hannaford having breakfast. It was not yet five o'clock.

"Morning, Soames," said Rule. "Coming rather heavily armed to breakfast, aren't we? I suppose you're mad because you weren't invited."

Soames didn't like Rule's joviality. He backed onto the balcony so that Harrison could see him. He waved, then stepped back into the room. "If I am not out with an answer in two minutes, Mr. Harrison will leave with Pratt and the tea set."

"You have the tea set?" asked Rule.

"Produce three million in cash and securities by nine A.M., and it's yours. Otherwise, it goes to Pratt, and you two gentlemen are revealed for the frauds that you are."

"Do you have evidence of the tea set?" Hannaford was interested in seeing it, at least once.

Soames took the sugar urn from his pocket and put it on the table. "There are thirty-one pieces. Each engraved with a small golden eagle. Do we have a deal?"

Rule could see the perspiration on Soames's forehead. He was glad Soames was nervous. The scheme might work on a nervous man. He looked at Hannaford. "I suggest we call the police. It seems that we have an art thief on our hands." He began to laugh.

"What are you talking about?" said Soames.

"Show him, Larry."

Hannaford reached into the duffle bag beside him and pulled out a lump of silver about the size of a softball. He dropped it on the table. "It's still warm."

"It seems," said Rule, "that thieves broke into the Museum of Fine Arts and stole the Golden Eagle Tea Set. You say you have it in your possession. That's what you call your grand theft."

"I don't believe you." The fury was building in Soames. He was smarter than Pratt. He was smarter than Rule. He was smarter than all of them. He couldn't be bluffed.

"It's true," said Rule. "Listen to the morning news."

Soames leaned across the table. "You listen to me. There is a hole in the subway six feet wide. There is another hole in the basement of the New Old South Church. When we tell the story of this tea set, people will believe us, because no one would make the mess we've made unless there was a reason to make it."

Rule knew that Soames was right, but Rule was gambling. He laughed. "Try and prove it, little man, now that there's no more fake. You can talk all you want to, but there's only one tea set. That's all there's ever been. All that wasted effort." Rule began to laugh, taking in great gulps of air and pouring out derision.

Hannaford began to laugh with him. "Face it, Bennett. You've been outmaneuvered."

Outmaneuvered. He had played it all so well. He had planned everything so carefully. And now, they were laughing at him.

The fury exploded out of Bennett Soames. He raised his pistol and shot Lawrence Hannaford in the chest. He turned the gun onto Rule. Edward streaked across the room and caught Soames with a shoulder in the belly. Together they smashed over the balcony railing and down three stories to the paved wharf.

For a moment, William Rule couldn't move. He looked at Hannaford's body, at the smashed balcony railing, and then, for the first time in his life, he panicked. He heard the engine kick over on the wharf below. They were leaving with the tea set. He had to stop them. He had to destroy the tea set before it destroyed him.

He pulled a .45 from his desk and ran to the balcony. Through the fog, he could see the limousine starting to back off the wharf. He fired five shots. One missed. One hit the radiator, another the hood. Two smashed through the windshield on the driver's side. The car accelerated suddenly, swung in a half circle, and slammed into one of the pilings on the wharf.

Philip and Evangeline were trapped. They couldn't get out of the car, nor could they get into the front seat to get Harrison's keys. Harrison was slumped over the wheel.

Rule reached the limousine as Fallon and Ferguson arrived at Lewis Wharf in a hot-wired car. He took Harrison's keys and opened the back door. He grabbed Evangeline by the arm and pulled her out of the car.

"No!" Philip Pratt tried to grab Rule, and Rule shot him in the chest.

Peter and Jack jumped out of the car. Rule turned and fired at them, then he put the gun to Evangeline's head. She struggled, but his arms were powerful and he held her tight.

"Don't wrestle with me, you little bitch, or I'll shoot you, too. Now pull that fuckin' trunk out of the car." He released her, and she did as she was told. Ferguson started to advance.

Rule fired at him. "Stay where you are, Jack."

Rule and Evangeline backed down the ramp onto the floating dock. Each held a strongbox handle. Evangeline wanted to drop her handle and run, but William Rule was a madman. She knew he would shoot her. They flung the strongbox onto the *Peter*, which was moored at the dock.

"Goddammit," said Ferguson. "He's not gonna dump that tea set."

Fallon grabbed him. "If we let him go, he'll toss her overboard. She can swim back."

In the distance, a police siren was wailing.

"He'll dump the tea set." Ferguson strode down the wharf and fired his pistol into the air. "Hey, you son of a bitch! Take a shot at me. I'm the one who's been on your tail. Shoot me!"

Rule aimed the pistol at Ferguson, and Evangeline jumped into the water. Rule fired. A crimson stain spread on Ferguson's shoulder, but he kept coming. Rule jumped onto the *Peter* and started the engines. He shot again at Ferguson, who was now halfway down the ramp, but he was out of ammunition. He tossed the gun aside and leaned on the throttle. The powerful twin screws drove the boat from the dock. Ferguson leaped and caught the stern.

Fallon could have made it easily if he'd jumped for the *Peter*, but Evangeline had hit the water in panic, and, as the *Peter* pulled away, she was sucked down into its wake. For a terrifying moment, Fallon thought she had gone into the propellers.

He dove and was beside her in an instant. She had taken a mouthful of the harbor and was struggling, fighting, instead of treading water. He wrapped an arm around her. He told her to relax. His presence settled her. After a moment, she didn't need to hold onto him, and they swam together back to the dock.

Peter hauled himself out of the water, then helped her. "Are you all right?"

"I will be," she said weakly.

He looked toward the *Peter*, barely visible in the fog. He could make out the figure of Jack Ferguson clinging to the stern. He jumped into a small Boston whaler moored next to Rule's space. He pulled the ignition wires out of the control panel, touched them in the correct sequence, and the engine kicked over.

"We can't even see them, Peter," said Evangeline.

"We'll follow their wake."

The *Peter* was already skimming past the waterfront restaurants and heading toward the outer harbor. William Rule had navigated this route so many times in his good life that the fog was no more an impediment than a slight easterly chop.

Ferguson managed to get a leg out of the water and haul himself onto the deck. Rule looked over his shoulder, but he couldn't let go of the wheel. He was going too fast.

Ferguson leveled the gun at him. "Turn this thing around."

Rule laughed.

"I said turn it around."

The panic was gone. William Rule realized that it was over, no matter what happened to the tea set. He was finished. If he couldn't convince the world that his tea set had been authentic, he would not give the Pratts the chance to prove that it had been false. "You'll have to shoot me, Jack."

Through a break in the fog, Fallon and Evangeline glimpsed the *Peter*. Fallon corrected his course and fed the outboard more gas.

"I *will* shoot you if you don't turn this thing around," said Ferguson.

"No you won't." Rule looked over his shoulder. "And you know why? Because you're too decent. You're a sucker."

Ferguson stepped across the deck. Rule pulled a fillet knife from the knapsack beside him. "Don't try to wrestle the wheel away from me, Jack. I'll cut you open like fuckin' codfish. You want to stop me, shoot me in the back of the head. Because it's all over for me, Jack. The tea set's ruined me. If you can get it ashore, you've got a whole new life to enjoy. So take a tip from a guy who should know. When you get the chance, kill your enemy. Don't try to nickel-and-dime him to death. Don't mess up his apartment and try to scare him when he figures out you've killed a Carrington. Don't try to get him drunk and hope he drinks himself to death. Put a new set of nostrils in the back of his head and kiss him goodbye."

Ferguson raised the gun.

Rule looked around. "No balls, Jack. You have no balls. I've got 'em to rent. That's why I've lived the way I have, and you've ended up in the gutter."

The *Peter* streaked out past Castle Island and Thompson's Island, past the unmarked grave of a long-decayed cargo sloop called the

Reckless, and out toward the open sea.

The outboard couldn't keep up, and soon Fallon was circling in the fog, cutting his engines periodically to listen for the cabin cruiser. But the heavy moisture in the air captured sounds, and the *Peter* was already too far away.

William Rule had decided that he wasn't going back. His loaded flare gun was on the bulkhead. A quick shot into the gas tank would take him, Ferguson, and the tea set to the bottom. His troubles would be over, and trouble was all he could see ahead of him.

Ferguson held the pistol so that it was close to Rule's ear. "For the last time."

Rule laughed. "You can't shoot a man in the back of the head, Jack. You just can't."

Jack Ferguson knew that Rule was right. William Rule had tried to destroy his life. Jack Ferguson had lived for the moment when he would avenge himself. The moment had arrived, and he couldn't do it. He looked at the strongbox. It was finally within his grasp. If he pulled the trigger, the tea set would be his, and the murderer would be punished. In the pit of his stomach, Ferguson had known all along that Rule had killed Jeffrey Carrington.

He raised the gun. He aimed. He told himself that Rule was no different than the assassin who had done Rule's killing. His hand squeezed the gun, but he couldn't pull the trigger. He was too decent to shoot a man in cold blood. He lowered the pistol. He wished he had the stomach to kill Billy Rulick.

After twenty minutes at high speeds, the Boston whaler ran out of gas. Fallon and Evangeline were left adrift in the fog with no oar and no means of signaling. The air was thick and gray and quiet. They could see nothing but each other and a small carpet of water around them.

"Dammit!" Fallon slammed his hands against the wheel.

"You'd never catch them in this boat."

"We have to keep trying." He wouldn't admit that it was over.

He stood up and tried to listen for the engines, although he had no way of following. He cocked his head one way, then another, but he heard nothing. For almost five minutes, he gazed silently into the fog. He had never felt more helpless in his life.

Evangeline shivered and drew her arms around herself. They were both soaked from their plunge into the harbor, and the air temperature was only about sixty degrees. Cold water was dripping from Fallon's hair and running down his neck. He tried to ignore it.

He slipped down into the bow of the boat and pulled his knees up against his chest. His cotton shirt was plastered to his skin. Depression was closing in around him like the fog. "I didn't even get to see it."

She left her seat and joined him in the bow. "Maybe you're lucky. I saw it. It was beautiful, but all I could think of was the pain it caused." She shivered again. "It wasn't worth it."

Then they heard the explosion. It seemed to vibrate through the fog and water, and the small boat began to roll on the swell. According to the compass, the sound came from the east, the direction the *Peter* had taken. They both knew what it was. They moved closer to each other.

"Poor Jack," said Evangeline softly. Her body shuddered with the cold.

"It's gone," said Peter. "It's gone to the bottom."

"For good."

He gazed to the east. The fog was moving up the scale from dark gray toward white. The sun had risen. "Maybe not."

"Forget about it, Peter." She had dug it up. She had seen it. Wherever it was now, it couldn't hurt her. She didn't want it to hurt them. "Forget about it."

"I can't forget about it. You can't ever forget about it." Fallon was getting colder.

"No matter how hard you look, you'll never find it. You'll just destroy yourself. For what?"

He realized he didn't know.

He shivered.

She said his name. He put his arm around her, and the two bodies shivered together. He wished they had a blanket.

437